Witch Hunt

A DCI Liam Doyle Thriller Book 2

BD Spargo

Published by

Howfen Press

WITCH HUNT

Published Worldwide by Howfen Press. This edition published in 2025

Copyright © 2025 by BD Spargo

The rights of BD Spargo to be identified as the author of this work has been asserted in accordance with the Copyright, Design and Patents Act 1988

All rights reserved. No part of this book may be reproduced in any form or by any electronic or mechanical means, including information storage and retrieval systems, without the written permission from the author, except for the use of brief quotations in a book review.

The story, all names, characters, and incidents portrayed in this production are fictitious. No identification with actual persons (living or deceased), places, buildings, and products is intended or should be inferred.

NO AI TRAINING: Without in any way limiting the author's exclusive rights under copyright any use of this publication to "train" generative artificial intelligence (AI) technologies to generate text is expressly prohibited. The author reserves all rights to license uses of this work for generative AI training and development of machine learning language models.

For permission requests, contact Howfen Press: https://www.howfenpress.co.uk/contact

ISBN: 978-1-7385516-1-3

For my Mum - Val

Prologue

Friday 28 July

Will Perkins stood shirtless on the wall of the old toll bridge. If he fell, it wouldn't kill him, PC Paige Anderton reasoned, but the poor bugger might break his legs. The traffic had been stopped from crossing in both directions and her colleague, Police Community Support Officer Josh 'Nat' Lofthouse, was dealing with crowd control. Anderton took her hat off as she approached Will, hoping he would recognise her. He was, after all, what the police referred to as a 'frequent flyer'. He wasn't a criminal, but his regular psychotic episodes meant he had racked up more police miles than almost anyone else in Barrowford.

A gust of wind blew strands of blonde hair into Anderton's face, and Will threw his arms out wide to keep his balance. Ominous dark clouds were rolling in from the north. Anderton hoped she could coax Will down before the heavens opened, drenching them and making the ground – and the wall – slippery.

'Constable, thank you for coming,' Will shouted at Anderton. 'That woman over there is a witch – she has bewitched my father. You must take her to the magistrate.'

Will was pointing at another frequent flyer – Mia Wright, the proud recipient of an ASBO for aggressive begging.

Anderton was glad Nat was there. Mia's dog scared the shit out of her. 'Your dad had a stroke, Will, remember?' she said, turning back to the man on the bridge. 'He's being looked after in the hospital.'

'It was her. She put a curse on him because he wouldn't give her money. That dog is the devil. You must stop them.'

He was right about the dog, Anderton thought. Though Nat had a way of taming it. He'd taken the beast home on several occasions and looked after it while its owner slept off whatever substances were in her system in a police cell.

'He's fucking cuckoo. You should arrest him and stick him in the funny farm.'

'Thank you, Mia,' Anderton said, glaring at her. 'Let us deal with this, please.' As she turned back to Perkins, the dog barked, making her jump. She was relieved it didn't have the same effect on Will. 'Come down off there, Will, and we can have a chat.'

A horn blasted. Anderton turned to see the driver of a pickup waving his arms. 'Get him out of here – some of us have got work to do.' The passenger of the pickup got out and took a few steps towards them. He was about the same size as Nat and dressed in oil-stained orange overalls. Anderton hoped he wasn't about to try to physically remove Will from the bridge.

'Thank you, sir. Please show some patience and let us deal with this.' The unmistakable reek of skunk filled her nostrils. Anderton didn't have to turn around to know Mia had lit up a joint, taking the opportunity to smoke it right in front of them, knowing they had bigger things to deal with.

'That woman is a witch. She should hang for her crimes!' Will shouted.

'Come on, Will, come down off there.' If she could get Will safely down from the wall, she could do a Section 136 and take him for psychiatric assessment. She wasn't afraid for her own safety. Will had never been violent towards her – or towards anyone else, as far as she knew.

Anderton looked at her watch. Just past ten thirty. If they were lucky, he might be assessed before her shift finished at six. Either way, it looked like her afternoon would be taken up waiting with Will. They couldn't just leave him at the hospital; he'd get up and walk out the door at the first opportunity. If he got injured it would be on her head. Still, there were plenty worse people to be stuck waiting with. Will was a clever guy and knew a lot about local history, but when he was this mad, the past and the present seemed to get jumbled up in his head.

Anderton looked around. Traffic was building up in both directions. A mother was taking her children across the road from the car park to the heritage centre. Anderton could tell the woman was trying to prevent the kids from seeing too much of what was happening. Others had no such worries. Several people, including the man driving the pickup, were filming on their phones. No doubt it would be all over social media in the next half hour.

Will's community psychiatric nurse had told her that, when possible, it was best to try and keep things real, not to pander to his psychosis, but she'd also said that arguing with him wouldn't work either. It would be like telling someone the grass was blue and the sky was green. *Fuck it.* The most important thing was to get Will to safety.

'Will, why don't you pop down from there? I'll take you to see the magistrate and you can tell him what's happened.' She held out her hand to Will.

'Roger Nowell, at Read Hall?'
'That's right, Will. Come on, come down now.'
Will took her offered hand and stepped down onto the road.

Chapter 1

Three months later – Day 1: Sunday 29 October

Mia thought she could hear a knocking – or was that the music? She didn't remember hearing it on the track before. But then she'd probably never had it turned up so loud. The dog was barking at the door. Definitely someone knocking then. She threw the damp cloth in the sink, wiped her hands on a dirty tea towel and turned down the volume. Whoever it was, they were being persistent. No doubt some do-gooder complaining about the noise.

'Alright, I'm coming,' she shouted. 'Shut up, Fury.' She pulled his collar, yanking him out of the way so she could open the door. 'Oh, it's you. What do you want?'

'I want to talk.'

Fury had stopped barking and was wagging his tail as the man stroked his head.

'You're not pissed off with me any more, then? Or did you think you could come round here at half past one in the morning, make up and get a fuck?'

'No, not that. You weren't asleep anyway. Besides, the clocks go back tonight so it's not half past one. What were you up to, having a smoke?'

'Cleaning.'

'Cleaning? You?'

'Yes, me. What do you want?'

'I said. To talk.'

'You better come in then.' Mia stood back from the door to let the man into her bedsit. 'You better not start shouting again, or you can fuck off.'

'Not here. Come with me for a drive.'

'Why? It's late.'

'It's not raining. We can sit out, look at the stars. Like we did before. That first time.'

'Alright, but not for too long. I'll grab my coat and Fury's lead.'

'Leave the dog. Let's just go.'

'Bollocks,' Doyle muttered as he ended the call. 'Harry, you need to get your things together. I'm going to have to take you back to your mum's, I've got to go into work.'

'No, Dad. No. I want to stay with you.'

'You can't stay with me, Harry. I've got to go to work. You knew I was on call this weekend.'

'No. I'm staying here.' Harry started removing his clothes – a favourite tactic to avoid leaving the house or going anywhere he didn't want to. Soon he was down to his underpants. The cuts on his knees were well scabbed over, but the bruises on his shins looked worse than the previous night, when Doyle had photographed them. He felt terrible that Harry was being bullied, and he felt even worse because he didn't know what he could do to make it stop. He didn't have the time now to think about that; he would have to speak to his ex-wife Fiona later.

'Come on, Harry, I'll see you again on Thursday. I've got to go to work. It's an emergency – someone needs my help.'

'I need you.' Harry stamped his feet.

'Get dressed.' Doyle looked at his phone screen: 10.32. He found Detective Constable Derrick 'Birdseye' Nelson's number and called it.

'Boss?'

'Where are you?'

'Just on my way to church. I've got you on speaker.'

'We've had a call-out – body of a young woman, somewhere near Pendle. I'm going to need you in, I'm afraid.'

'OK, boss. I'll be able to drop Gill off in about five minutes. If you text me the address, I'll be on my way. You'll be able to get someone to give you a lift back, won't you, love?'

'No need, Derrick, I'll pick you up at the church. It's the one at Belmont you go to, isn't it?'

'St Peter's, yes. I'll wait for you in the car park of the Black Dog.'

'Great – sorry to be taking him away, Gill.' Doyle knew Birdseye would be trying not to let his wife see his delight at getting to miss the Sunday morning service. 'Can you call Geoff and put him on standby and get Gadget to meet us there?'

'Will do. What about the sarge?'

'Leave her be for now; we'll give her a call if we need her. I'll be with you as quick as I can.' Doyle ended the call and turned his attention back to Harry. 'Come on, son, get dressed. Please.'

'No. I'm not going to. You can't make me.' Harry stamped his feet again.

Doyle took a deep breath. He needed to stay calm. He wasn't known for his patience, but with Harry he'd needed to find a level of serenity he didn't know he had – perhaps middle age had mellowed him. His son wasn't misbehaving because he was naughty or a stubborn child who always had to get his own way. The reality was, he needed certainty in his life to feel safe. He couldn't cope with changes to plans or routines. Doyle was the on-call Senior Investigating Officer for the Major Investigation Team one week in every six, and he hadn't needed to go out on either of the last two occasions. That meant when he'd told Harry he was on call this weekend, it hadn't registered with the boy. He looked at the time again. He would give it ten minutes, trying everything he could from coercion to bribery. If that didn't work, he would have to carry the boy out to the car, stick him in the back and strap him in, then drive him to his grandparents' house. He couldn't wait any longer. At least the child locks would prevent Harry from jumping out of the car while they were moving.

Chapter 2

The whole circus was already in town when Doyle pulled up behind a squad car in the village of Barley. Even the private ambulance was already there, waiting to take the unfortunate victim to the morgue when the pathologist had finished at the crime scene. It hadn't taken Doyle long to get there. He'd managed to placate Harry with the promise of Lego and then been on his way. Doyle had never been to this bit of Lancashire before; since his move up from London in June, work hadn't caused him to venture further east than Blackburn, though his role in the MIT meant he could be called in to investigate cases right across the county.

Having wrestled his giant frame into a forensic suit, gloves and overshoes and given his name for the log, Doyle made his way up the footpath to the inner crime scene. The infamous Pendle Hill loomed over the village with its distinctive flat top nestling just below the grey cloud line. The early morning rain had stopped, which was a relief, though even the air felt damp and the thick grass either side of the path was still sodden. Doyle hoped the heavy morning shower hadn't washed away much evidence.

Rounding a corner, Doyle saw the familiar sight of a white forensic tent under a beech tree, a fast-flowing brook down a bank to the right. Sheep bleated in the fields beyond. It was a pity they wouldn't be able to provide witness statements, he thought. Inside the tent, Dr Gupta, in a white forensic suit, crouched by the body.

'Morning, Vedhika.'

'Morning, Liam,' she said, rising and turning to face him. 'You got the call in the end, I see.'

'It looks like I was the last to know. What have we got?' Doyle asked, looking at the victim for the first time. He'd been told on the phone that she was in her early twenties, so he wasn't surprised that she looked so young. Her face was pale, and a cut on her neck ran under her chin almost from ear to ear.

'I don't think you will need me to tell you that she died from an incised wound to the neck. In short, her throat was cut. From the blood distribution down the front of her coat, it looks like she was held in a vertical position from behind when she died. The left carotid artery is severed. With this amount of blood loss, it wouldn't have taken long for her to die.'

'Well, that's something, I suppose.'

'Indeed. I need you to see this.' Dr Gupta bent down over the body and pulled up the victim's blood-soaked coat and hoody to reveal that her lower abdomen had also been sliced open.

'Jesus, was that done before or after she—'

'It looks like it was done after she died, but I will confirm at the post-mortem. I'm not sure yet and I don't want to delve too deep now, out here, but some tissue or organs may have been removed.'

'You mean from inside?'

'Yes, I think so, from what I can see.'

'Bloody hell... Any idea when?'

'Not long ago, from the body temperature and lividity. Sometime between midnight and 4 a.m. Remember, that is a five-hour window because of the clocks changing.'

'Anything else you can tell me now?'

'Not a lot at this stage, I'm afraid. Jen Knight is around somewhere outside. She's taken lots of photos of the victim as she was when she was found, and she will be able to fill you in on some other aspects.' Dr Gupta followed Doyle out of the forensic tent. 'Anna not with you today?'

'I thought we'd be OK without her this morning. I don't want to overwork her. She's still recovering.' In truth, Doyle's first thought had been to call his detective sergeant, Anna Morgan, when he heard about the circumstances he'd changed his mind.

'I understand, though you might want to talk to her about that. It's important to make sure she doesn't feel shut out.'

'You're probably right, but this...' Doyle waved his arm around at the surroundings. 'Another dead young woman out in the countryside. I didn't want to ... you know ... trigger any more trauma.'

'I can understand that.'

'Hi, Liam, glad to see you made it eventually,' a white-suited figure said, walking over. He recognised the voice under the hood and mask as belonging to Jen Knight, the crime scene manager.

'Yes, sorry. I think I must have got the call after everyone else,' Doyle replied.

'You did.' Knight lowered her voice. 'The local CID who attended first didn't call for the MIT – they called their own DCI, who came out and decided it was their case.'

'What? But why? That goes against procedure. This has all the hallmarks of a premeditated murder.'

'According to that DCI, this is a local dispute, and they know the victim and who's responsible. They've gone to make an arrest.'

'What? Have they got concrete evidence to back that up?'

'I couldn't tell you; we haven't found anything yet that could identify the killer. I wasn't happy and I knew it wasn't right, so I phoned HQ myself and asked them to send the on-call SIO.'

'Thanks, Jen, appreciated.'

'I think you might be in for a bit of a struggle with that DCI. I don't think he'll be keen to hand the case over.'

'Thanks for the heads-up. Vedhika filled me in on the injuries. What else can you tell me?'

'Right, well, her top half was covered by a rug when she was found. Look,' Knight said, showing Doyle a picture on her camera screen.

'Do you think the people who found her put that over her?' Doyle had been to murder scenes before where members of the public had covered up the victim to preserve their dignity in death, much to the annoyance of the forensic investigators.

'Apparently not. But if anyone finding a body decided to cover it up with a rug, wouldn't they cover the whole body, not just the upper part?'

'Good point.'

'We can say from the amount of blood on the ground by the body that this is where she was killed. But take a look at this.' Knight led Doyle down a slight incline to the other side of the beech tree. Carved into the trunk was a circle with a five-pointed star inside it.

'Is that a what's-his-name?'

'A pentacle or pentagram, I think they're called,' Knight said. 'I don't know a lot about them, but I think they're some kind of witch or Wiccan symbol.'

'That's interesting.'

'Of course, we can't say for sure that it was carved by the killer, but see here? There are spots of blood. We'll test it, but I think it's odds on it will be the victim's. I'll let you know if we find anything else.'

'Thanks,' Doyle said, taking a picture of the symbol with his phone. The SOCOs would take detailed pics of the whole crime scene, but it would be useful to have his own photo before he received those.

Doyle met Birdseye back at the car. His colleague was nearing retirement age and had got his nickname because of his white beard, which made him look like the man who appeared on the box of a popular brand of fish fingers.

'You got anything useful?' he asked the DC.

'Just a bit.'

'Good, get in. You can tell me in the car'. Doyle was tempted to add 'and away from prying ears.'

'The victim's name is Mia Wright and she's well known to local police – drug using, antisocial behaviour, begging, and suspected of a bit of low-level dealing.'

'How old was she?'

'Twenty-two. No known next of kin. Came through the care system. Now, this bit you're not going to like.'

'Go on.'

'Well, local CID already have someone in the frame and have gone to make an arrest. It seems like they have taken on the investigation.'

'Have they bollocks. Who's their suspect? Did you manage to find out?'

'They had all buggered off, but a PC told me it was another person known to them: William Perkins. He has schizophrenia, apparently, and had been sectioned in the summer. He'd been accusing the victim of being a witch and saying she should be hanged. He got out of hospital three weeks ago.'

'I can see why he's an obvious suspect, but have they got any actual evidence against him?'

'Not as far as I could tell but, like I said, the CID boys had already gone when we got here. But the PC who told me this...' Birdseye checked his notebook. 'PC Paige Anderton, she knows both the victim and suspect. She did the Section 136 on him in the summer. She seemed doubtful. Said he was mad but she'd never known him to be violent.'

'I guess we'll see who's right. Do you know where they have taken their suspect?'

'Yes, Burnley. Nelson police station is nearer, but it doesn't have any cells.'

'Good, let's go and piss on their parade then. Did you get hold of Gadget?'

'Yes. He was at the gym, but he's ready to come in.'

'Get him to meet us there. Anything else?'

'I spoke to the couple that found the body. It was just after eight-thirty. They were going hiking. It's a popular route. They aren't local but have been here before. I've got all the details.'

'Did they mention a rug at all?'

'Yes, they said it was covering her face and chest when they found her. They didn't remove it. They assumed she must have been dead because of all the blood. They thought someone else might have covered her with it and gone to get help.'

'Sounds possible,' Doyle said.

'I thought so too, but this is the thing, boss – I checked with Control and no one else had called it in.'

Chapter 3

Doyle could hear the noise from the custody suite at Burnley police station before he and Birdseye walked through the door. He was surprised that there were only four people responsible for the racket: two men with Lancashire Police lanyards dressed in plain clothes that marked them out as police officers almost as much as a uniform would. A short, rotund woman with a thick Lancashire accent and what looked like an NHS lanyard around her neck, and a custody sergeant behind the desk who was trying to restore order. The only person who noticed Doyle and Birdseye enter was a handcuffed prisoner sitting on a bench. He looked up at the detectives and rolled his eyes.

'He's not killed anyone. He wouldn't hurt a fly,' the woman bellowed.

'Course he has, he's fucking mental and thinks she's a witch,' one of the plain-clothes officers shouted back, tapping his head as if to emphasise the point.

'You got any evidence of that?' the woman shouted.

'Please, please can you all—' the custody sergeant shouted in vain.

'He was stood on the bridge in Barrowford threatening to hang her – what more do you want?' the other officer shouted.

'He wasn't threatening to hang her, he was saying she should be hanged. There is a difference,' the woman shouted back.

'SILENCE!' Doyle's shout echoed off the walls and had the desired effect. 'I'm Detective Chief Inspector Doyle from the Major Investigation Team, and unless anyone here outranks me, you will all remain silent until I tell you to speak.'

'Can I just ...' the woman said.

'Shush.' Doyle held a finger to his lips. 'Now, Sergeant, please tell me who all these people are and what they are doing here.'

'These two' – the sergeant indicated the two detectives – 'are from Pendle CID. They have a suspect in the cells and want to interview him on suspicion of murder. That lady is his community nurse and is here as his appropriate adult.'

'Thank you,' Doyle said. 'And has the suspect's solicitor arrived?'

'He says he don't want one,' one of the CID men said.

'First...' Doyle turned to face the man. 'I didn't tell you to speak. Second, it doesn't matter that he said he didn't want one; if he is deemed vulnerable enough to need an appropriate adult, with an offence as serious as this, we should get him one. And third, you won't be interviewing him. This is our case now. So, you can fill in DC Nelson here on everything you've got, and we'll take it from here.'

'But sir, our DCI has told us it's our case, and we're to deal with it.'

'And I'm telling you it's not. If your DCI has a problem with that, tell him to come and see me.'

'But...'

'But nothing. The clock's ticking. Go and update my DC on what's been going on. Right, and what's your name?' Doyle said, turning to the woman.

'Dianne Berry, community psychiatric nurse. I'm from the Assertive Outreach Team,' she said, holding up her ID for Doyle to inspect.

'I can see you take the assertive part seriously. And William Perkins is your patient? Have you known him long?'

'Just coming up for ten year now. I see him at least once a week unless I'm on leave.'

'Good. I'm sure one of these custody officers will be able to find us an interview room, along with some tea or coffee, and you can tell me all about him.' Doyle looked at the two civilian officers who had drifted back into the custody suite after the commotion had calmed down. 'Oh, and Sergeant, that man on the bench has been waiting patiently to check in – perhaps you could give him one of your best rooms.'

'Shoplifting again, is it, Robbie?' the sergeant said to the handcuffed man. 'You might as well get a job for the council, the amount of community service you do.'

'Tea or coffee?' one of the custody officers asked Doyle and Berry.

'I'll have what he's having,' Berry said.

'Coffee, white, two sugars,' Doyle said.

'No problem. I'll take you through to interview room two,' the custody officer said.

'Any chance we could go into the car park?' Berry asked. 'I'm dying for a smoke.'

'Want one?'

Doyle looked at the proffered cigarette packet. He always wanted one but had resisted for over ten years now. 'I've given up.'

'Good for you. I need to, really.' Berry shielded herself under her coat to light up. The custody officer appeared in the yard with two coffees in cardboard cups and handed one each to Doyle and Berry.

'Thanks,' said Doyle.

'No problem. I've unlocked IR two for you when you're ready. It's just down that corridor, second door on the left.'

'Right, swap,' said Berry, holding out her coffee cup.

'What?'

'Come on.'

Doyle did as instructed. 'Why?'

'Well, you're the boss. They won't have spat in yours.'

'I'm not the boss here, and I reckon there's an even-money chance they have.'

'Why do I get the feeling I know you from somewhere?' Berry said, exhaling smoke.

'I've got one of those faces. People always say that.'

'Jesus, how can you drink it that sweet?'

'Got to take whatever energy you can get in this job... You sounded convinced that Will Perkins couldn't be responsible for Mia Wright's murder. How can you be so certain?'

Berry took another long drag. 'You can never be one hundred per cent certain in my job, of course you can't. I work with damaged people who often have chaotic lifestyles. But it doesn't make sense to me.'

'What do you mean?'

'Well, the incident that seems to have made everyone in there think that Will killed Mia happened back in July. Don't get me wrong, he was completely psychotic at the time. His dad had had a stroke and all the going back and forward to hospital put

Will out of routine. He'd stopped taking his meds. But we could see the deterioration and had been trying to get a Mental Health Act assessment. But you know how it is: start of the school holidays, half the staff are off and the other half are running round like blue-arsed flies trying to cover everyone else. Before anything could be put in place, he was standing on that bridge with his top off accusing Mia Wright of being a witch.'

Doyle knew exactly how it was. There would be similar stories up and down the country: stretched mental health services struggling to cope, leading to crisis situations requiring emergency responses. The whole system was broken. 'When did you last see him?'

'Friday afternoon, after lunch.'

'And how was he then?'

'He were fine – on good form, actually. He'd done all his shopping and was going to visit his dad later. He's in a care home now since the stroke.'

'What about his mental state? Were there any signs of psychosis?'

Berry took another long drag on her cigarette. 'The thing is with Will, he's always got some residual psychosis. He's never really free of it. He's on as much anti-psychotic as he will tolerate, but he still hears voices. They're intrusive, but he's able to function and stay mostly in reality. When he's acutely unwell, his whole affect changes; he looks different.'

'In what way?'

'When you have worked with someone for so long, you get to know them – their facial expressions, their mannerisms. When Will is floridly psychotic, these change. He's always looking around, holds himself more upright, can't stay still for long. And when you speak to him, he will be delusional, start going on about bloody witches and paranoid thoughts about people putting curses on him.'

'And you saw none of these signs on Friday?'

'No, not at all. We went for a brew in a coffee shop and had a long chat. When he's unwell his thoughts skip about and he finds it hard to follow a conversation. There was none of that.'

'And you don't think there could have been a deterioration in his mental state since Friday?'

'There could've been some deterioration, but not to the extent that he would have gone from presenting as well on Friday to murdering Mia Wright last night.' Berry stubbed out her cigarette and stuffed the butt into the metal ashtray on the wall.

'You sound like you knew the victim too?'

'I do – sorry, did, but not well. She had her own mental health issues. She's never been on my caseload. But I have seen her a few times over the years when I've been covering for colleagues off sick or on leave.'

'Did she have schizophrenia too?'

'No, she had emotionally unstable personality disorder – EUPD. What used to be called borderline personality disorder. Poor girl had an awful childhood, never really stood a chance.'

Doyle nodded; he had come across people with that diagnosis before. 'How well would Will have known her?'

'They were never mates – or enemies, even. But they had both been in mental health services for years and it's a small community round here, so their paths would have crossed on many occasions. And Mia could be very in your face at times. I reckon everyone round here will have come across her at some point. Can we go back inside? It's freezing out here.'

Chapter 4

Detective Sergeant Anna Morgan was sitting on a bar stool in her kitchen, browsing the internet, searching for inspiration. For what, she wasn't sure. It was as though she had lost all motivation to do anything. In the past, a Sunday off work would have meant a long bike ride across the local moors, chasing personal bests up difficult climbs. That seemed like a different life now. That world had come to an abrupt halt back in June when she had spent a week in intensive care after being attacked by a serial killer her team had been pursuing. All things considered, she had recovered well from her physical injuries and the medics had cleared her to return to work and get back to her regular exercise routine. But a mental block was holding her back. At thirty-three she knew she was still young enough that if she got back on the bike both metaphorically and literally, her fitness would return. On the other hand, if she didn't... She'd worked hard to maintain her physique – was she really going to let that go and become a couch potato? It wasn't just her fitness that was on the wane, her hair was a mess too. A patch at the back had been shaved at the hospital to treat her head wound, and since her hair was short already, there wasn't enough to hide the bald spot. Since then, she had let it grow and it was now in a limbo stage between being short and bob length. She looked like she had 1990s-style curtains.

The phone in her hand started ringing, breaking her train of thought. The caller ID read 'The BFG – DCI Doyle'. Bizarrely she realised she wanted to be called in to work – anything to take her out of the doldrums and break the monotony.

'Anna, you OK to talk?'

'Sure, what have we got?'

'A young woman's been found dead this morning in Barley.'

'Want to give me the location? I'll meet you there.'

'We're all finished at the scene now. The SOCOs will still be there. You could meet us at Burnley nick if you're sure you're alright to come in on a Sunday?'

'Course I am. It's my job. Why wouldn't I be?' Morgan was getting tired of everyone checking that she was OK. It was like they were all expecting her to break down at any moment.

'It's just that you've not long been back. I don't want to overload you – phased return and all that.'

'I'm fine, boss. I've been signed off as fit to work, and I just want to get back into it. Sounds like you've been there a while – why am I only getting the call now?'

'We didn't get it until late. The local CID seemed to think that they should be dealing with it, and I thought you would be out on your bike.'

'I do take my phone with me.' Morgan knew she wasn't doing a good job of hiding the irritation in her voice. 'And I'm not riding my bike every waking hour.' *Or any waking hour, these days.*

'Sorry, I just thought...'

'It's alright. I'll be at Burnley police station in about half an hour.' As Morgan ended the call, Sam came in through the back door, the cleats on his cycling shoes clicking on the tiled kitchen floor.

'You should've come with me. It's not bad out there – a bit windy, but the rain held off,' Sam said, taking off his helmet and gloves.

'I didn't fancy it today. OK?'

'OK, sorry.'

'I've had a call. I've got to go in to work.'

'I thought they weren't meant to be overworking you. You need time to properly recover.'

'It's my job, Sam. You know how hard I've worked to get to where I am, and what I've put up with. I'm not about to start being flaky now. I'm recovered from my injuries. I need to get stuck back into it.'

'I'm sorry, I don't want to—'

'I need to get ready and go.'

'When will you be back?'

'I don't know. I'll call you.'

The terraced house in Barrowford that Doyle had sent Detective Constable Zach 'Gadget' Washington to was tiny, especially considering the number of police officers that appeared to be inside rifling through its contents.

'Who the fuck are you?' a big bald-headed man with a thick Burnley accent asked Gadget as he stepped across the threshold.

'DC Washington, MIT. Who the fuck are you?'

Doyle's words to the young detective before he left had been, 'Remember, you're in charge. Stamp your authority on the situation and don't take any shit from them.'

Now he was here, it seemed that would be easier said than done, especially since he had neither the boss's rank or size. He was only twenty-five – at least twenty years younger than the man in front of him.

'I'm DS Felton, and I suggest you don't make a habit of swearing at more senior officers, son.'

'We're taking over the case now. My DCI has told me to come down here and see what evidence you've found.'

'That figures – now we've done all the work and nicked the person responsible, you lot turn up to take all the glory.'

'Have you found any evidence here?' Gadget felt outranked and outnumbered and decided it was probably best to stick to safe ground around the case.

'Plenty. Want to take a look?' The burly DS set off up a narrow staircase.

Gadget contemplated putting on the forensic overshoes that were in his pocket before following, but it didn't look like any of the other detectives in the house had bothered. If this turned out to be a crime scene, it would already be significantly contaminated. He did pull on a pair of nitrile gloves, keen to make sure that at least his fingerprints would not be found at the suspect's house.

Upstairs there was a bathroom to the back and a bedroom to the front. The bed hadn't been made and there were a few items of clothes on the floor, but the room wasn't unduly untidy. What struck Gadget straight away was the writing all over the walls. An attempt had been made to paint some of it out, but the black ink still grinned out from behind the white emulsion.

'See what I mean? The bloke's nucking futs. And look at that.' Felton pointed to the wall. The writing there read *Alizon Device = Mia Wright = witch + black dog = Fury = devil*. Below that was written *Dad = John Law = cursed by Alizon Device = Mia Wright*. The next line read *Me = Abraham Law: must tell constable + magistrate = hanging witches*. A list had been scrawled out below that;

Constable Henry Hargreaves = ? ? ?
Magistrate Roger Nowell = ? ? ?
Old Demdike = ? ? ?
Chattox = ?? Dianne Berry ??

The list went on. None of it made any sense to Gadget, and he had to agree with Felton that the person who wrote it was clearly mad.

'He's named the victim as a witch and said she should be killed.'

Gadget took out his phone and started photographing the walls. 'Have you found anything to link him to the crime scene? The knife used, or any bloodied clothes, anything like that?'

'It's not what we've found that's telling, it's what we haven't found. There's a knife missing from the block in the kitchen.'

The phone in Gadget's hand started ringing, and he answered it on speaker.

'Gadget, are you in there yet?' Doyle's voice boomed out.

'Yes, boss.'

'Good, and are those pricks from CID playing ball?'

Gadget swallowed, regretting his decision to take the call on loudspeaker. 'Yes, boss, pretty much.'

'Got anything?'

'There's writing all over the bedroom walls. The guy's not right in the head.'

'Well, we already knew that. You don't spend weeks on a psychiatric ward just because you're feeling a little bit funny.'

'I was taking pics of it, boss. The victim is mentioned with reference to being a witch and hanging.'

'Are there any symbols or pictures on the walls?'

'It doesn't look like it, boss, no.'

'Gadget, is there any evidence other than circumstantial linking him to the actual crime?'

'There's a knife missing from the block in the kitchen.'

'OK, we'll get forensics to take a look at that, check if the type of knife missing could be the one that was used. Is there anything else?'

Gadget looked across at the DS.

'There are loads of notebooks with writing in them. There might be more evidence in there of what he was planning to do,' Felton said.

'Gadget, have you got me on speakerphone?'

'Yes, boss.'

'Good. Right, I need you to look in the bathroom cupboard. There should be a blister pack made up by the pharmacy for each day's medication. I need that putting in an evidence bag and bringing down here. Also, we're going to need the contents of all the bins and any tablets found on the floor or anywhere else. We need to establish whether Will Perkins was taking his medication.'

'On it, boss.'

'Oh, and Gadget, try not to let any of those pricks contaminate the scene too much. We might need the SOCOs to go over it for any trace of the victim.'

Chapter 5

It hadn't taken Morgan long to find out the address of their victim. With the number of times she'd been arrested, there was a lot of information about Mia Wright on the Police National Computer. There hadn't been any keys found on her body, which meant it was possible that whoever killed her had taken them. This made it a priority to enter her home. Morgan had decided she'd only make a token effort to track down the landlord before she used the 'big red key' to force the front door. As it happened, the first person she spoke to was the Barrowford Neighbourhood Policing PC, Paige Anderton. Not only had Anderton known who the landlord was likely to be, but she had also been able to warn her that Mia had a bloody big dog that wasn't fond of strangers. Thankfully Anderton had a solution for that problem too, in the substantial shape of her PCSO Josh 'Nat' Lofthouse, who knew the dog and would be able to handle it.

Barrowford was about three miles south-east of Barley, the tiny village where Mia's body had been found. Although it was charming, with its heritage centre, tea rooms and park along the river bank, it had its share of low-level crime and antisocial behaviour. Like many villages in England, it had expanded out around its edges and was now really a town in all but name.

Standing at the top of the steps that led down to the basement flat of a Victorian terrace, Morgan heard the dog barking – and saw the door moving as the animal jumped at it from the other side.

'It's OK, Fury, its only me. I've got some treats for you.' Lofthouse's reassurances didn't stop the barking, but the pitch changed to become less aggressive. This was enough for the PCSO, who put the key in and opened the door. In a flash the beast was out and past him, hurtling up the stairs, forcing Morgan to jump back, expecting an imminent attack. But the dog bounded straight past her and into the road, where it emptied its bowels.

Morgan's heart raced; she hoped her fear didn't show on her face. She wasn't normally this jumpy, or at least she didn't used to be. But since returning to work after her ordeal in the summer, this was the first real threat she had come up against. She knew she needed to give herself more leeway. This nervousness would pass – at least, she hoped it would.

'Do you want to go in first, Sarge?' Anderton said.

'Sure,' Morgan said, pulling on gloves and overshoes.

'I can't see anyone in there,' Lofthouse shouted up the stairs. 'Unless someone is hiding in the bathroom. Flat's not much bigger than a shoebox.'

Once in the bedsit and with the dog safely on a lead outside, Morgan felt her heart rate returning to normal. She needed to focus now, concentrate on what she was seeing. The flat was damp; you could smell it even over the odour of dog. Black mould grew around the kitchen window and on the ceiling. There were no overflowing ashtrays, torn Rizla packets or other drug paraphernalia that Morgan had been expecting from reading Mia's entries on the PNC. There was a mop and bucket filled with water in the kitchen and a bottle of cleaning spray and a cloth on the draining board. It looked like Mia had been cleaning, and had been distracted by something – or someone. This idea was reinforced when Morgan entered the tiny bathroom, which also had a significant damp and mould problem. The pedal bin had been emptied and a new bag put in, but the lid hadn't been replaced and the old bag remained untied on the bathroom floor.

Taking care in case of a stray hypodermic, Morgan had a quick check in the bathroom rubbish. She found what looked like a cannabis grinder. When she pulled it out, the whiff of skunk left Morgan in no doubt. Odd that Mia was throwing it away. She delved deeper and came across a pregnancy test. There was one dark red line on the test strip, and a faint pink line. Whoever took the test was pregnant, though from the pale test line, Morgan thought the pregnancy was in the early stages. Mia Wright would seem the most likely candidate. *Interesting*, Morgan thought, then silently berated herself. It wasn't interesting that the victim might have been pregnant; it made the whole situation even more tragic. DNA from the test and the post-mortem would be able to confirm either way. Back in the main room, she noticed the dog bowls next to the kitchen. Beside them was a bag for life that looked as if it had traces of blood inside. Morgan decided against looking further, opting to get the SOCOs to conduct a full forensic examination of the flat. She did spot a mobile phone box on top of a kitchen unit. Standing on tiptoe, she was able to reach it. Inside she found paperwork with the phone number. Predictably, it was pay-as-you-go. Morgan doubted that anyone would have extended Mia Wright credit for a contract phone. If Mia's mobile didn't turn up, having the number was the next best thing.

Chapter 6

With the duty solicitor finally at Burnley police station, Doyle was ready to interview Will Perkins, with Dianne Berry acting as appropriate adult. The mental health nurse had given Doyle a useful background on Perkins' condition and once he had got past his initial impression of the nurse as belligerent, it became clear that she would be a great advocate for her patient. Doyle would have to ensure that she didn't go too far in interview. If she tried to answer for Perkins or lead him in any way in his responses, then he would have to stop the questioning and arrange for someone else to sit in, meaning more time lost. It pissed him off that the local CID had brought Perkins in so quickly. He could see why he was an obvious suspect, but he would have preferred to do more digging first. Perkins had now been in a cell for over five hours. Although getting an extension on the custody clock of a murder suspect wasn't difficult, it wouldn't look great if someone with schizophrenia was left in a cell for several days if it turned out they were innocent.

With everyone ready to go, he was about to ask the now more relaxed custody sergeant to bring Perkins out when another man bowled into the custody suite, looking like he owned the place.

'Are you Doyle?' the man barked. He wore a suit and tie that matched neither his grey hair or red face.

'Yes. DCI Doyle. And you are?' Doyle didn't offer his hand.

'I'm DCI Butcher, Pendle CID. That's my suspect you're about to interview.'

'Oh, I'm sorry. I was under the impression he had been arrested on suspicion of the murder of Mia Wright.'

'Right.'

'Well, don't worry. That's our case now, so we'll take it from here.'

'I'm not worried,' Butcher snarled. 'But we made the arrest before you lot had even bothered to show up, so we're keeping hold of this one. It's clear-cut. A local killing between known associates. We don't need you, so you can go now.'

'You need to mug up on your procedure. This case warrants an MIT investigation, which also calls into question why we weren't brought in sooner. Now you've got a choice: you can either fuck off out of my way or I will call the assistant chief constable and tell her you're interfering in our investigation.'

'You think you're so fucking important, don't you? You come up here, getting in the papers and on the telly, thinking us lot don't know how to do our jobs. I've been policing this area for over twenty-five years! I don't need you coming in for a case of one fucked-up lunatic murdering a junkie.'

'I knew it.' Berry got up from the bench and shouted, pointing at Doyle. 'I knew I recognised you from somewhere. You were all over the press after that young teacher got killed. Now can you two hurry up and finish your willy-waving contest so we can get on? I've come here on my day off, and I don't get overtime like you do.'

Doyle decided not to point out that officers ranked inspector and above didn't get paid overtime. 'Right, well, it seems we are in a stalemate here.' Doyle turned to the custody sergeant. 'Can you call HQ and get them to get ACC Reid to call? It looks like we are going to have to bother her on a Sunday to give out orders.'

'Fine, you do it then, but I'm not happy and I'll be talking to my chief super in the morning.' Butcher turned and stormed out.

'Cor, he's a mardy bastard, isn't he,' Berry said before the door shut behind him.

Will Perkins was tall and wiry, and his foot tapped away under the interview room table. Whether this was a side effect of his medication or due to nerves brought on by his current predicament, Doyle wasn't sure. He was grateful that Dianne Berry was there – she might be able to help the man relax and hopefully answer the questions they put to him.

'Do you know why you're here, Will?' Doyle asked after Birdseye had been through all the legal bits for the recording.

'I know what I've been arrested for, but I didn't do it.'

Doyle was surprised at how well-spoken the young man was. He only had a trace of the local accent that was much stronger in pretty much everyone else around these parts.

'Can I ask you where you were last night, between ten in the evening and eight o'clock this morning?'

'At home. I went to bed just after ten and then slept through until about nine thirty.'

'Was anyone at home with you? Can anyone vouch for this?' Doyle asked.

'No. Sorry, I live alone.'

'And you definitely didn't leave home at all during that time?'

'No, the next time I left home was when those policemen came and arrested me.'

Although Perkins didn't have anyone to confirm his alibi, the fact that he had stated he'd not left home could still be useful. If just one witness or bit of CCTV footage or video doorbell spotted him out after that time, it would put him firmly in the frame. 'Do you know why people might think that you killed Mia Wright?' Doyle asked.

'Because of what happened in the summer. But I was unwell when I said those things. I'm much better now.'

'You accused Mia of being a witch and bewitching your father. Do you remember that?'

'Kind of, but when I think back to times when I was very unwell, it's hard to make sense of it all. It's like trying to remember a dream – it all comes in fragments.'

'Do you know what made you think Mia was a witch?'

'Yes, I was completely mad. My dad had had a stroke about three weeks before. I'd got in a mess with my medication. I was at the hospital the first night and completely forgot to take it. Then the second night I was there again, and I did remember but it's so strong, it knocks me out within an hour of taking it. They were doing tests and he needed me there.'

'What happened after the first two nights? Did you take your medication then?'

'Well, no, and I know this is my fault. But if you miss a couple of days, you can't start up again. You have to be reti-ti – what's that word?' Will turned to Berry.

'Titrated.'

'Titrated, that's it. And they have to do that in hospital to monitor you. My dad was in hospital and I didn't want him to be left on his own. I'm all he's got. I thought that I could just not take it for a few days and keep quiet about it, and when my dad was settled I'd 'fess up and go into hospital then and be put back on my meds.'

'Sorry, Will,' Doyle said, turning to look at Berry and the duty solicitor. 'Am I OK to check a couple of things about the medication?'

The solicitor gave a nod.

'Is Will's understanding correct, that he would have to go into hospital to be put back on the meds if he had missed them for a few days?'

'He's not wrong,' Berry said. 'And partly I blame myself for this. I've drummed this into him for years. Clozapine's a strong drug and Will's on a truckload of the stuff. It can have some dangerous side effects where it knocks out the white blood cells. It needs careful monitoring and regular blood tests.'

'Oh, what do the blood tests show?'

'Just that – your white blood cell count. If this is too low, you have to stop taking the medication as your body wouldn't be able to fight off an infection. We also test patients' levels every so often to make sure the dose is effective and check if patients have been taking it.'

'Would we be able to do that now – test to confirm that Will has been taking it?'

Berry looked towards the solicitor.

'I've got no objections,' he said. 'Providing Will hasn't.'

'It's fine by me,' Will said. 'I'm used to having my blood taken. One more time won't hurt.'

'Thanks,' Doyle said, turning back to Will. 'It didn't quite work out as you thought it would?'

'No. It took longer for Dad to settle, and a couple of days off the meds became a week. I started to unravel. I was getting paranoid but trying to hold it together. My dad said he'd been coming out of one of the shops in town before he had the stroke, and Mia had been badgering him for money as she often does.

Dad normally gives her some change if he's got it. But he didn't that day and she was pestering him, then he fell down with a stroke.'

'And that made you think Mia had bewitched your dad?'

'Well, yes, because it's almost exactly what happened before.'

'What? When before?' Doyle was confused. How psychotic was Perkins?

'In 1612, with Alizon Device and John Law.'

'He means the events leading up to the Pendle witch trials, boss,' Birdseye said. 'Alizon Device was one of the people publicly hanged in Lancaster for being a witch. She was convicted at the Assizes for bewitching a pedlar called John Law.'

'Yes, yes, exactly that. He knows what I'm talking about.' Will pointed at Birdseye.

Doyle couldn't tell if Will's excitement was because he was still quite mad or because he had found someone who knew about this piece of history. 'Do you still believe this now? That Mia bewitched your father?'

'No,' Will said. 'I know he had a stroke, but I wasn't well at that time and my mind was jumbling all kinds of things up and making connections where there weren't any. I started to believe that Dianne might be a witch called Chattox, as she kept asking me if I'd taken my medication and was talking about doing blood tests. I thought she was trying to poison me.'

'Chattox was another one of the witches that was found guilty, boss,' Birdseye added.

'That's charming, that is, Will,' Berry said. 'All the things I've done for you, and you think I'm some old witch.'

Doyle saw Perkins give his nurse a half smile that didn't quite reach his eyes.

'Will, officers searched your home earlier and they saw lots of writing on your bedroom walls.'

'I know. I tried to paint over it, but it still showed through. I'm going to get some more paint when my PIP money comes through next week and go over it again.'

'When did you write all that on the walls?'

'It was the time just before I went into hospital. I was trying to make sense of everything in my mind and thought it would help to write it out.'

'Did anyone see this at the time?'

'I did,' Berry said. 'And another of my colleagues did too. We went to Will's house after he had been sectioned in July, to pick up some things to take to him in hospital.'

'Thanks,' Doyle said. The fact that the graffiti had been written before Will's last hospital admission meant it might be less relevant now. 'The officers who searched your house found that a knife was missing from the knife block in the kitchen. What can you tell me about that?'

'That's been gone for ages. I keep meaning to replace it.'

Doyle had been watching Perkins carefully as he answered. He didn't appear to have been unnerved by the question. 'What happened to the knife? They're not the kind of things that usually get lost.'

'I didn't lose it. I threw it out. I'd lost the key to the garden shed and I tried to use it to prise the hasp off, and it was bent so much it was useless.'

'What kind of knife was it?' Doyle asked.

'It was the bread knife.'

Doyle hadn't heard back from forensics yet, but if it was a bread knife that was missing from the set, that wouldn't be the murder weapon. 'Can I ask, Will, when you are in an acute stage of psychosis, do you often have a fascination with witches? Or are there different subjects at different times?'

'Even before I was mad, I was fascinated by witches and our local history here. It always interested me growing up. I studied history at university and did my dissertation on the Lancashire witch trials. That's when things started to go wrong for me.'

'I'm sorry, Will, do you mind me asking, wrong in what way?'

'I was at Durham. In my second year, my mum had a massive heart attack. She was dead before I could get home. I was down and lonely, smoking a lot of weed. I was getting paranoid and I didn't know what was up. I started to believe that everyone was out to get me, and it was my duty – placed on me by God – to uncover the truth about the witches. I held it all together, more or less, until I handed in my dissertation in my final year.'

Chapter 7

'Anna, how lovely to see you – and perfect timing,' Dr Gupta said as Morgan entered the mortuary. If the pathologist was surprised to see Morgan rather than Doyle, she didn't show it, which made Morgan feel a little more at ease. She was still pissed off and confused with Doyle's behaviour towards her. She felt he was shutting her out, not calling her in until last, and then he had sent her to do one of the grimmest parts of the job. A task he wouldn't normally delegate.

Morgan nodded a greeting to Jen Knight and the guy from the coroner's office, whose name she couldn't remember. Joe and Matt, the mortuary technicians, were laying out tools on stainless steel trolleys.

'If everyone is ready, we will make a start,' Dr Gupta said.

Morgan took in the form of Mia Wright, laid out on the slab, still covered by a white sheet. Dr Gupta folded it back to reveal her head and shoulders and the deep crimson slash across her throat. Morgan felt a fluttering in her stomach, an uncomfortable nervous sensation, but that was ridiculous; she'd attended countless post-mortems in the past and had never had a problem with them. Well, not 'never' exactly; there had been one on a badly decomposing corpse that had made her feel decidedly sick, but it had had the same effect on pretty much everyone in the room. The industrial extraction unit in the mortuary hadn't been enough to remove the foul stench that day.

'The cause of death appears to be exsanguination caused by the cut to the throat. The left carotid artery is severed, along with internal jugular on that side.' Gupta said. She wasn't just speaking for those present. She was recording all her findings, and she would use this recording to compile her report, on which she might later be cross-examined in the witness box. 'There is some damage to the trachea and larynx, but she would have died from blood loss rather than asphyxiation due to her airway being blocked.'

Morgan felt her heart rate rising and sweat forming on her forehead at the mention of asphyxiation. Instinctively her hand went to her throat, double-checking what she already knew – that it was fine, there was nothing there. The memories of her own near-death by strangulation were hazy, but she could feel the cable tie being tightened around her neck and the sheer panic as her airway was cut off. She wanted to turn and run, get out of the room, feel cold, fresh air flooding into her lungs. *Come on, pull yourself together, you can do this.*

'The cut is deeper on the left, and then tails off on the right-hand side.'

Concentrate on Vedhika and what she is saying.

'The edges of the incision are straight. This suggests her chin was raised, stretching the skin taut. The cut was made with a sharp knife.' Dr Gupta looked up, catching Morgan's eye. She gave an almost imperceptible nod in the detective's direction. Much of the pathologist's face was covered by a mask, but there was an awareness in her eyes when she looked at Morgan, as though she knew the struggle that was going on inside her.

'I venture that Mia's killer stood behind her and pulled her chin up with their left hand and cut her throat with their right. As well as being right-handed, I suggest that the culprit was taller than the victim, as the cut comes down from the left and back up on the right. With someone the same height or shorter, I would expect a diagonal cut down from left to right.'

A strange thought occurred to Morgan. For the first time, she felt that she had something in common with the victim in a post-mortem: she was almost seeing and feeling things from her point of view rather than trying to visualise events as an observer. She wondered whether Mia had been aware of what was coming and had time to contemplate her fate, as she herself had done.

'Before making my own incisions on Mia, I need to examine the other one made by her attacker.' Dr Gupta folded the sheet down further to expose more of the dead woman's torso. Morgan was grateful that Doyle had given her a full rundown of the injuries before sending her to the morgue. Even knowing what she was going to see, it was still shocking. The wound across the lower abdomen was wide and deep, slicing through skin, fat and muscle. The tissue had shrunk back on either side of the cut, leaving an open cavity that looked as if it was grinning back at her. Morgan wasn't squeamish – far from it. For many years she had wanted to study medicine and be a surgeon, an ambition that went off course when her father died shortly before she took her A levels. Her grades suffered; although they were still pretty decent, she hadn't got the straight As she needed for a place at medical school. She could have retaken them, but instead Anna Morgan chose to take this as a sign that her destiny lay in another direction and found a place through clearing at Lancaster University studying criminology and psychology.

'Thankfully,' Gupta said, getting in close to examine the cut, 'she was already dead when this was made. There would be a lot more blood if it happened prior to the fatal wound to the throat. She had a C-section at least two years ago, by the look of the scar. I haven't seen her full medical records yet, but they will confirm when she gave birth. It looks like whoever did this tried to follow the line of the original cut, but veered off a bit.'

'We searched her flat earlier and found a positive pregnancy test in the bathroom bin,' Morgan said.

'That's interesting,' Gupta said. The pathologist used a giant set of stainless steel forceps to open up the incision further and look inside. She put her hands in the cavity and delicately manoeuvred tissue and organs, closely examining what was there. After several minutes, Gupta stood back up. 'Her uterus is missing. It's been cut out.'

Morgan gasped, whatever she had been expecting it wasn't that. 'Was this done surgically, for some medical reason?'

'No, this was done post-mortem – and not by a surgeon. The bladder is still there but has been hacked, presumably to get it out of the way. Whoever did this did it in a hurry and with a sharp knife, not a scalpel. My guess is they had an idea what they were looking for and how to find it. There's a lot of damage to the surrounding tissue, but it doesn't look like anything else has been removed.'

'Someone trying to remove all trace of the pregnancy?' Morgan said.

'Could well be, but they won't have been successful. Although the bladder has been damaged, I only need a few drops of urine, which I may be able to get from either of the ureters or the urethra to test. Failing that, a blood test will confirm.'

'Presumably you won't be able to tell who the father is without the uterus, and therefore the foetus?'

'That's true, Anna. It looks like you have hit on a possible motive.'

Chapter 8

Doyle was on the phone as he walked into the office on the upper floor of Nelson police station, which was being set up for them to use as an incident room for the duration of the investigation. 'Sorry, Bea, there's no chance of me getting back at a reasonable time this evening. But hopefully by Wednesday things will be up and running here and we will be able to get together as normal.'

'Aren't you forgetting something?' There was a teasing note in her voice.

'Am I?'

'We cancelled this Wednesday as you've got too much to sort out. Unless, of course, you want me to pop over on Thursday so you can introduce me to your visitor?'

'Christ, no. You'll run for the hills, never to be seen again.'

After ending the call, he walked over to his second-in-command, Detective Inspector Geoff 'the Pearl' Hales. The nickname had come about because Hales' head seemed to be sitting right on top of his shoulders, giving him the appearance of being neckless. His pewter hair and weathered face hinted at him having a few more miles on the clock than someone who'd recently turned fifty. The Pearl was busy trying to set up a large screen on a stand next to a giant map and pinboard that were permanent features of the room.

'You should let Gadget do that,' Doyle said.

'He's busy fetching stuff up from the car park,' Hales said. 'Have you spoken to Anna recently?'

'Not since the PM.'

'That slash wound across the victim's abdomen? Apparently, she'd had her uterus cut out.'

'Jesus,' Doyle said.

'We see some sick things in this job, but that's got to be up there with the worst.'

'You're not wrong, Geoff.'

'Despite this, Dr Gupta was able to confirm that Mia Wright was pregnant. It looks like the test Anna found at the flat was hers.' Hales looked around. The room was empty, but he still lowered his voice. 'Look, Liam, I know it's your call to make, but do you not think it was a bit insensitive to send Anna to the PM after what happened to her? I know you were tied up interviewing, but I would've happily gone. This lot could have waited for a bit.'

'It's a fair point, and that was my first thought too. When I spoke to her earlier, she seemed pissed off that she was the last on the team to be called in. I thought perhaps treating her as normal, throwing her straight back in at the deep end, might show that I've still got confidence in her. You know what she's like. She's not going to want to be mollycoddled.'

'I get that, and I do know what she's like – she's probably not going to say when something is a bit difficult for her, won't want to show any weakness and all that. I think we need to keep a careful eye on her.'

'Where d'you want me to put these, boss?' Gadget asked, entering the room carrying two boxes of files.

'Stick them on that table,' Hales replied. 'Is there much more to come?'

'A bit, but Birdseye should be able to manage it. There was a PC and PCSO in the car park, and he was roping them into helping. Do you think we're going to need all this lot? By the looks of things, we'll probably be loading it all back up tomorrow. Seems a pretty open-and-shut case.'

'We still don't have any actual evidence against our main suspect though, do we?' Doyle said.

'No, but you should have seen his room, boss. The guy's crackers and he had it in for the victim. You've said before you don't believe in coincidences,' Gadget said.

'That's not a coincidence. It might give a possible motive, but we don't know yet if anyone else had a grudge against her or another reason to want her dead.'

'Those CID guys all seem pretty certain it's him.'

'I have my doubts.' A woman came in to the room, carrying two boxes. 'And I reckon I've had more dealings with Will Perkins and Mia Wright than any of them.' She was followed in by a PCSO who was almost as big as Doyle.

'Why's that?' Doyle asked, turning to face the woman as she put the boxes down on the table. She was around thirty and wearing a uniform, complete with tactical vest.

'Sorry, sir, I wasn't meaning to be critical of CID. PC Paige Anderton,' she said.

'No, it's OK. I want to know your thoughts.'

'Well, firstly, and I don't want to speak ill of the dead, but Mia Wright rubbed quite a few people up the wrong way.'

'Oh, how?'

'Well, lots of ways. She could be a pest. All the local shopkeepers were wary of her as she had been caught shoplifting so many times. She also used to beg outside shops with that bloody great dog of hers. They could be quite intimidating, and when she'd had a few she'd often be insulting to people. We never actually nicked her for dealing, but there was always a suspicion she did a bit of low-level stuff. Bit of weed here and there, nothing serious.'

'And what about Will Perkins? What have your encounters with him been like?' Doyle asked.

'I probably shouldn't say this, but I've got quite a soft spot for Will. Deep down he's a lovely guy, quite a gentleman. It's just when he's not well he can be quite vocal, but I've never known him to be violent. I don't think he's got a criminal record. All our dealings with him have been mental-health-related, when he needs sectioning, mostly for his own safety. I just can't see him killing anyone – but then you never really know, do you?'

'That's an interesting insight. Do you know if there was any kind of relationship between Will and Mia?' Doyle asked. 'Other than him shouting at her and accusing her of being a witch?'

'Not that I'm aware of, but that doesn't mean there wasn't. They would've known each other for years, and they both had mental health issues.'

'And what about Mia? Do you know if she was in a relationship with anyone else?'

'Not that I was aware of... I don't mean this to sound bad, but it wouldn't surprise me if Mia might have done the odd sexual favour for money or weed or something.'

'You think she might have been on the game?' Hales asked.

'No, not that exactly. I don't think so. But it's not inconceivable that she might have used sex to get what she wanted. She was pretty messed up.'

'You don't have any clue who might have been the father to her child?' Doyle asked.

'Mia was pregnant? I wasn't aware of that. Presumably they will be able to get the father's DNA from the post-mortem?'

'This doesn't go any further,' Doyle said. 'But her uterus had been cut out by her killer. So I doubt they will.'

'Fucking hell,' Gadget said.

'Jesus,' Anderton said.

'You've got to think, boss,' Gadget said, 'that's the kind of thing a madman would do.'

'Do you think it's worth interviewing him again now?' Hales asked. 'Try and dig a bit further on what kind of relationship he had with Mia? If there was anything sexual between them, that would help build a case.'

Doyle checked his watch. It was after half past eight in the evening. 'Perkins would have been given his night-time meds by the time we get over there, and apparently they're quite sedating. I'm not sure how much sense we would get out of him, and anything he did say might prove to be inadmissible.'

'Oi, you lazy bugger,' Birdseye said, entering the room and looking straight at Gadget. 'I thought you were coming back down to help me. I've struggled up the stairs with these boxes on my own.'

'You should be thanking me,' Gadget said. 'Exercise is good for old people. I saw something about it on *The One Show* last week. At your age, you need to keep your muscles working or you'll lose them and never get them back.'

'I'll keep my arm muscles working by giving you a clip round your ear,' Birdseye said.

'I'd thought you would be less miserable now,' Gadget said. 'You know, being in the town that was named after you.'

'Actually,' Birdseye said, 'the town of Nelson wasn't named after me, and it wasn't named after Admiral Lord Nelson either. It was named after a pub.'

'Are you serious, Derrick?' Hales asked.

'That's got to be bollocks,' Doyle said.

'No, it's true, boss,' Birdseye said. 'It was originally called Marsden, but when they brought the railway here there was already a station called Marsden across the border in Yorkshire. So they called the station Nelson Inn Station after the pub, and the name kind of stuck.'

'I've heard something about that too,' the large PCSO that Doyle hadn't yet been introduced to said.

'It's a good job they didn't have that tradition in south London,' Doyle said. 'As I would have been living close to a place called the Pyrotechnics Arms.'

'You say that, boss,' Birdseye said. 'But you weren't far from the Elephant and Castle, and that was named after an inn too.'

'Every day's a school day with you, Derrick,' Doyle said. 'I'm just waiting for the day that you tell me something useful.'

Chapter 9

Day 2: Monday 30 October

'Right, let's go over what we've got and decide where we go from here.' Doyle addressed the small team assembled in the incident room. 'Mia Wright was found dead yesterday in Barley at the foot of Pendle Hill. Anna, would you like to bring everyone up to speed on the post-mortem findings?'

Morgan opened her notebook. 'Time of death was early Sunday morning, between midnight and 4 a.m. She died from blood loss after having her throat cut. Her attacker held her from behind, and from the direction of the cut Dr Gupta said it's likely that they are right-handed and taller than Mia.'

'How tall was Mia?' Birdseye asked.

'One hundred and sixty-five centimetres, or five foot five in old money,' Morgan said.

'Will Perkins would fit, then,' Gadget said.

'So would over half the men in the country, by that criteria,' Hales said.

'Dr Gupta was able to confirm that Mia was pregnant,' Morgan went on. 'Shortly after she died, someone, almost certainly her killer, sliced open her abdomen and removed her uterus.'

'That's awful,' Shaima Asif, the team's civilian intelligence analyst, said, her hand going to her mouth. Doyle realised that, unlike the detectives on the team, Asif would be hearing this information for the first time, since she hadn't been called in to work the day before. He should have warned her before the briefing. Asif, a young woman herself, had two small children, and even the older, more experienced Hales and Birdseye had been shocked by this level of brutality.

'Whoever did this must have some kind of medical knowledge. I mean, I wouldn't have a clue where a uterus is or what it looked like,' Gadget said.

'That's a good point,' Doyle said. 'Did Dr Gupta have any thoughts about this?'

'She said the cut was made with a sharp knife, but not a scalpel. They'd tried to follow the scar line from a previous C-section but had veered off course. This wasn't done by a surgeon. But assuming it was deliberately removed because she was pregnant, the person would have needed some knowledge of what to look for. Though there is a lot of detailed anatomy information easily available online.'

'OK, all pretty horrific, I think you all agree,' Doyle said, getting up and moving to the large pinboard mounted on the wall. 'Local CID saw fit to arrest a suspect before we were even brought in. This is Will Perkins, who Gadget mentioned.' He pointed to a 10 × 8 photo. 'He's got paranoid schizophrenia. In the summer, when he was unwell, he had some quite delusional thoughts about Mia Wright being a witch and putting a curse on his father.'

'I went to his house, and it was proper creepy. He had written all this mashed-up nonsense on the walls about witches,' Gadget said.

'And yet despite this, we haven't found any actual evidence linking him to the killing,' Doyle said. 'In my experience, people who commit these kinds of offences because of psychotic delusions aren't very good at covering their tracks. We didn't find the knife or bloodied clothes or anything else at his house.'

'There was a knife missing from the knife block in the kitchen,' Gadget said.

'Yes, but when we checked that, it confirmed what Perkins told us in interview – that the knife missing was a bread knife. Not the type of knife used to kill and mutilate our victim.'

'But he's still got to be our prime suspect,' Hales said. 'With what we have circumstantially.'

'Maybe, but let's keep an open mind,' Doyle said. 'Anna, you and Gadget get over to Barrowford. Ask around, see what you can dig up about both of them, in particular the victim. We need to know as a priority who got Mia pregnant.'

'Yes, boss,' Gadget said.

'Birdseye, me and you will go to Burnley and interview Perkins again. Probe a bit more about his relationship with the victim. Geoff, you can coordinate things from here with Shaima. Both of their medical records would be a good starting point, and then on to phones, banks etc. We've only got this morning before Perkins' custody clock runs out. Getting an extension shouldn't be a problem, but I'd prefer not to.'

'You're not thinking of releasing him, are you, boss?' Gadget asked.

'Depends on what we can dig up this morning. But keeping someone with such a serious mental illness in the cells for a long time isn't great.'

'Did you sleep alright, Will?' Doyle asked when they were in the interview room with Birdseye, Dianne Berry and Perkins' solicitor, and they had got the legal formalities out of the way.

'Yes, thank you,' Perkins replied. 'About an hour after I've had my medication, I'm pretty much out for the count.'

'I'd like to ask you about Mia Wright and your relationship with her. How long have you known her?

'I'm not sure – a few years. I've seen her around a bit. She has appointments at the same clinic that I do. She's nice most of the time, but sometimes she can be quite rude, especially if she wants something, like money or cigarettes, and you don't give it to her.'

'Would you say you were friends with her, Will? Did you ever do things together or hang out together?'

'No, not really friends. We chatted sometimes, but that was it. Often in waiting rooms.'

'Did you ever have a romantic or sexual relationship with her?' Doyle asked.

Perkins looked away from everyone, which wasn't easy with four other people in a confined interview room. Doyle couldn't tell whether Perkins' discomfort was because he was constructing a lie or he was shy about being asked such a question.

'No, no, not at all.'

'Have you ever been to her home?' Doyle asked.

'No, never. I don't know where she lives. I mean, I guess it must be local, somewhere in Barrowford, because I see her around a lot, but I don't know where.'

'Do you drive, Will, or have access to a car?'

'No, I had my driving licence rescinded because of my illness and all the meds I'm on.'

'Does your dad have a car?'

'Yes, but he won't be able to drive that now either.' Perkins turned to Berry, his face creased in a frown. 'I hadn't thought of that. We won't be able to go out on our day trips together any more when he gets better.'

'You don't need to worry about that now. Let's see how your dad gets on and take it from there,' Berry said. 'Remember what your father's doctor said. Don't try to get ahead of yourself, take it one step at a time.'

'Do you know where your dad's car is now?' Doyle asked.

'Yes, it's on his drive. It's been sat there since he had his stroke.'

'Do you know where the keys are?'

'They will be in his house in a drawer in the kitchen, where he keeps all his spare keys,' Will replied.

'And do you have keys to his house?'

'Yes, I've been going round there and watering his plants since he went into hospital. He's in a care home now. But hopefully he will be able to come home sometime soon.'

Doyle saw the look on Dianne Berry's face. She obviously didn't think Will's dad would be returning home any time soon.

'I've just remembered it's Monday. I'm meant to be seeing my dad this afternoon. If I don't go, he will wonder where I am. Am I going to be able to leave soon?'

'I'll be honest with you, Will,' Doyle said. 'We need to check out everything you have told us. We can't check your alibi directly, as you told us you were at home alone at the time in question. But we'll check the blood test that was taken yesterday evening to find out the level of medication in your system. I understand it will be able to show if you took your medication on Saturday evening. That will help to corroborate your alibi.

We will also need to check your dad's house and car, as you have access to these. But if we don't find any evidence of your involvement, we will release you, possibly on police bail, while we investigate further.'

'What if I did do it?'

Everyone in the room stopped dead at this remark.

'What do you mean, Will? Is there something you want to tell us?' Doyle asked. 'If you are responsible for the death of Mia Wright, I suggest you tell us now. If you want to take a break and consult with your solicitor, that's fine.'

'No, I don't mean that. I mean ... I don't mean that I did it. At least, I can't remember anything about it. But what if I did?'

'Sorry, I'm not following,' Doyle said. 'What do you mean?'

'What if I did it and I was so off my head that I've blanked it out and I can't remember it?'

'But Will,' Berry said, 'you're not off your head. You're sitting here having a coherent conversation with us all. I've seen you several times when you have been acutely unwell, and you're not like that now.'

'I still hear voices, though.'

'Yes, Will, and you probably always will, to some degree. But the important thing is when you are like this, you recognise them as just that – symptoms of your illness. When you're unwell you give them more importance, you start thinking they are real and God talking to you and all that nonsense. Last time you thought your television was personally sending you messages. Trust me, if you were unwell, I would know.'

'But they didn't notice when I was at university. It was over a term I wasn't right, and nobody said anything. It was only when the lecturer read my dissertation that he picked it up. And these were smart people.'

'Bloody cheek, saying I'm not smart,' Berry said. 'But seriously, they undoubtedly were all clever, but they were academics used to wacky students and far-out ideas. I've been a mental health nurse for nearly thirty years and I've worked with you for about ten of those. Trust me, I know when you are properly mad, and you're not like that now.'

'Look, Will,' Doyle said. 'You be honest with me, and I'll be honest with you. I intend to find out who is responsible for Mia Wright's death and why it happened. I'm going to do that by finding evidence that will prove beyond a reasonable doubt who killed her. This will ultimately either rule you in or rule you out, and one way or another you will know for certain. You spoke about how you were when you first became unwell at university. Perhaps you could give me the name of the lecturer who read your dissertation, and I could chat to him about how you were back then?'

'His name's Prof. Owen, but I think he has retired now.'

Chapter 10

After speaking to Doyle on the phone, Morgan had sent Gadget to meet the SOCOs at the house belonging to Will's father, Reg Perkins. This meant she was left on her own to walk around Barrowford to see what she could find out about Mia Wright. Any hopes Morgan had about her enquiries being discreet were dashed when she saw a *Lancashire Chronicle* sandwich board outside a local shop. The headline emblazoned on it read *Woman Found Murdered on Pendle Hill*.

The shop was the type that appeared to sell almost anything, with narrow aisles bursting at the seams with products.

'Can I help you, madam?' the shopkeeper asked.

Morgan fished in her pocket for her warrant card. 'DS Morgan. Would you mind if I asked you a few questions about someone you have probably seen around the local area?'

'Mia, you mean?'

'Yes, how did you know?'

The shopkeeper tapped the front of a newspaper on the counter. The *Lancashire Chronicle*, it seemed, had not only got hold of the story but had also managed to get a picture of Mia Wright, had stuck it on the front page and named the victim.

'Did she come in here often or hang around outside much?'

'Strictly speaking, she was banned.' The man's accent was a strange mixture of Lancashire and somewhere further afield – Pakistan, Morgan guessed. 'She used to loiter around outside with that big dog of hers, frightening the customers. I caught her round the back a few times too by the bins.'

'Any idea what she was doing there?'

'I didn't look too closely, to be honest. As long as she wasn't trying to break in or vandalising anything, I didn't want to get involved. But I think she was either taking drugs or buying or selling them.'

'Buying or selling? So you saw her with other people?'

'A few times, yes.'

'Did you recognise any of them? Are they customers?'

'There's one guy that I saw her with a few times. Everyone around here calls him Turkish.'

'You don't happen to have a real name for him, do you, or know where he might live?'

'No, sorry.'

'Do you know when he was last in here? Would he be on your CCTV?'

'I can't remember the last time he was in – it could be a week, maybe.'

'Any idea what day, what kind of time?'

'No, sorry. He will be on the CCTV. It's kept for twenty-eight days, but I really couldn't say when.'

'Is there anything else you could tell me about him? What does he look like?'

The shopkeeper took a moment to consider this. 'There is one thing: he is often wearing orange overalls when he comes in. I can't think of the company name, but on the back it says "Farm Machinery Maintenance".'

'Thank you, that's useful. If it's OK with you, I will send a colleague to take a copy of all your CCTV in case we need it later.'

'No problem, Officer. I hope you catch whoever did this. Mia caused me a fair bit of trouble over the years, but what's happened to her is terrible.'

'That's an amazing view you have here, Professor,' Doyle said, looking out through a big picture window at the moors, which were splashed with the oranges and reds of autumn. It had been a scenic drive, across the border as Birdseye called it, from Lancashire to West Yorkshire. They were in the village of Haworth, in what the older detective had told him was Brontë country.

'Please call me Richard,' the academic said. 'We bought this place when we retired six years ago. Had dreams of growing old disgracefully in beautiful surroundings. Sadly, that all rather went to pot. Gareth was diagnosed with lung cancer just after we got here and died eighteen months later.'

'I'm sorry,' Doyle said.

'Thanks. That's life, I'm afraid. At least I've got this tartan carpet to remember him by.'

Doyle looked down. The floor covering was certainly out of keeping with the more subtle decor of the rest of the room. 'He was Scottish then?'

'Yes, and the carpet was his idea of a joke. Thought it would amuse visitors.'

'My dad was Scottish. I didn't get to know him that well, but I can't imagine my mum would've let him get away with something like that.'

Professor Owen smiled. 'Doyle's an Irish name, though, so I imagine you must have some ancestors in the Emerald Isle?'

'My dad's dad came over from Ireland as a boy and then married my grandma, a Protestant girl from Edinburgh. Caused quite a stir, apparently.'

'I'm sure. It's only relatively recently that people have been able to escape their tribal roots. Still, you didn't come here for one of my history lectures. You wanted to discuss one of my former students?'

'That's right. Will Perkins. You said on the phone you remembered him?'

The professor sighed. 'I can't say I can recall many of the students I have taught over the years, there have been so many, but Will is someone I'll never forget.'

'Oh, and why's that?' Doyle asked.

'A couple of reasons. He was incredibly gifted and had a real passion for the subject, especially the Pendle witches and the local history where he grew up. And then it all went so spectacularly wrong for him.'

'Can you remember when you first noticed him starting to unravel?'

'I think he would have been in his first or second year when his mother died.' Owen cocked his head to one side and caressed his chin. 'I checked in with him a few times to see how he was coping, signposted him to the university counselling service. He seemed to be doing OK, but you never really know. He was a young man away from home.'

'What about his mental state? When were you first concerned about that?' Doyle asked.

The professor took a sip of tea, considering his response. 'I guess, looking back, I had been worried for quite some time. But not that he was going mad; more that he might be severely depressed. He had become withdrawn and didn't want to talk. But he always attended lectures and handed in work on time.'

'Did he have any close relationships with any other students? Any girlfriends or boyfriends, best friends, that kind of thing?' Doyle asked.

'That was another of my concerns that he might be depressed. He got on with everyone but didn't seem that close to anyone.'

'And when did you first notice that he had become mad, for want of a better word?'

'Well, it was quite strange. It wasn't until I read his dissertation. Looking back with hindsight, there were some pretty obvious clues, I guess.'

'Like what?'

Owen half smiled. 'Well, one time I bumped into him in a corridor, and I asked him how things were going. He kept looking around, as though he was checking if anyone was watching him.'

'Didn't that set alarm bells ringing?' Doyle asked.

Owen shrugged. 'Perhaps it should have, but at the time I thought he might have been stoned or taken some magic mushrooms or something. That would have been a more usual explanation among the student population.'

'Was there anything else?'

'One time after a lecture I asked him how he was getting on with his dissertation, and he was a bit strange. He told me it was going brilliantly and said that it was going to change everyone's thinking on the subject. This was quite a claim, and very grandiose for an undergraduate paper.' The professor paused; his brow furrowed. 'But again, I wondered if he might have taken something.'

Doyle could see how on a university campus, Owen might have been more likely to believe that this was due to illicit substances rather than mental illness 'Did you enquire further about this at the time?'

'Not really, but later I sat down with him and talked through what he was working on. As I recall, it was quite intense, and he talked almost non-stop about what he was putting together, which was an appraisal of the evidence gathered against the Pendle witches and how we might interpret it in the modern world.' Owen looked down into his tea cup. 'But we never got as far as discussing the conclusion, which I guess I thought at the time would be pretty obvious.'

'You said it was quite intense. Did you have concerns about his mental state then?'

'To be honest, I wondered whether he might be somewhere on the autistic spectrum. We were a bit more aware of that by then, and it wasn't uncommon among academics.'

Doyle thought about his son, Harry. There were times when it seemed as though he lived in a different world and had lost touch with reality. But Doyle had come to learn that the truth was that Harry interpreted the real world in a different way to other people. 'And what was it about his dissertation that made you realise he had become psychotic?'

'It's strange, really. A conventional modern opinion would be that people tried and hanged for witchcraft were innocent and were victims of a society that was obsessed, almost to paranoia, with Satan and witchcraft. It was a particular interest of King James I, who wrote a book about it that endorsed witch-hunting.'

Doyle noticed Owen's voice rise as he talked about the history, he was clearly passionate about his subject.

'Throw in a good dose of prejudice against Catholics too – this was less than seven years after Guy Fawkes had attempted to blow up the houses of Parliament. And if you add that Lancashire was seen then as an inhospitable wilderness, it's no real surprise that these people were singled out.'

Doyle thought that many people back in London probably still thought of Lancashire as an inhospitable wilderness – and he would have been one of them before he'd moved up here.

'At worst' – the professor went on – 'some of those hanged had portrayed themselves as spiritual healers as a way of making a living – charlatans, even. Some of them may have come to believe they were themselves witches.'

'And Will Perkins didn't conclude that they were innocent?' Doyle asked.

'No, quite the opposite.' Owen smiled and half shook his head. 'I will never forget reading it. He concluded that they were guilty and had been rightly hanged for their crimes. Not only that, but he stated that witchcraft was rife in society today, and we needed to take drastic action to rid ourselves of this evil.'

'What did you think when you read that?'

'At first, I couldn't believe it. Obviously, I didn't believe it; I couldn't believe that this was his real dissertation. I thought perhaps it was a joke and he would have the real one that he would hand in later.'

'What did you do?' Doyle asked.

'I invited him to come in for an informal viva. To interrogate him on his work.'

'And did he?'

'Yes' – the professor paused and took a sip of tea – 'and that was when I realised he was quite mad. He robustly defended his position and insisted that all echelons of society had been infiltrated by witches doing the devil's work. He felt his thesis proved that, and had sent copies to the Queen and the Archbishop of Canterbury.'

'Wow,' Doyle said. 'What did you do?'

'At first, I tried to argue with him, on an academic level – demonstrate to him how he was drawing incorrect conclusions that he couldn't back up.'

'I imagine that didn't go down well,' Doyle said.

'No, quite, but I was very concerned hearing all this. He had clearly lost the plot.'

'How did you conclude the meeting?'

'I played along with it. I told Will that he should remain in my study in case witches were after him while I told the principal what he had uncovered.' Owen's voice was now flat. 'I left the room and phoned a colleague who taught the medical ethics course. She's a psychiatrist and was on campus at the time. She came to see him straight away.'

'What was her take on it?'

'She chatted with him for about twenty minutes and concluded he needed an urgent mental health assessment, and we managed to convince him to attend A&E. He was admitted to a psychiatric ward.'

'Did you ever see him after that?'

'Only once. I visited him in hospital when he was ready to be discharged. He was going to live at home with his father. I told him that if he wanted to repeat the year and then graduate, I would support him.' The professor gazed out of the window at the moors. 'It was such a shame, as he was in line to get a first.'

'I take it he didn't repeat the year?' Doyle said.

'No, it was very sad. When I saw him, he seemed embarrassed about what had happened. He didn't appear to be mad any more – well, not to me anyway. But it was as if he was completely washed out; all of his spark and passion had gone. He was like a shell of a man. I suppose he was on quite a concoction of medication by then. I knew he would never finish his degree. It was all so tragic and such a waste of a brilliant young mind.' The professor drained his tea cup. 'You know, some historians think that one of the people hanged at Lancaster, James Device, might have had schizophrenia.'

'Oh, why is that?' Doyle asked.

'Some of the things he said at the trial could be interpreted in a modern world as being psychotic.'

'But you're not convinced?'

'The truth is, we don't know and we never will. Almost everyone back then believed in God, but they also believed in witchcraft and the power of the devil. Where you and I might listen to accounts like these now with incredulity, people then were primed to believe them.'

Doyle nodded. 'I can see how that makes sense.'

'Then, of course, the only actual written evidence from the time comes from an account written by a man called Thomas Potts. He was very much on the side of the Establishment, and it is quite possible that he embellished parts of his work. Plus, the investigation process wouldn't have been conducted as you would do now; they weren't bound by the Police and Criminal Evidence Act back then, so we have no way of knowing how statements were taken. What we do know is that in August 1612 ten people were hanged on the moors above Lancaster, having been found guilty of various crimes relating to witchcraft.'

Doyle considered the professor's words, it was hard to think how anyone now could think of the Pendle witch trials as anything other than a massive miscarriage of justice.

'I have some pictures, Professor, that I would be grateful if you could look at and perhaps shed some light on. Do you know what any of this means?' Doyle showed the professor a photo on his phone of the graffiti on Perkins' bedroom wall.

The professor put on a pair of glasses and studied the photos as Doyle scrolled through them. 'Alizon Device was one of the Pendle witches. The chain of events that led to the trial at Lancaster started when she was accused of bewitching a peddler called John Law. She had a black dog with her at the time which was said to be a familiar – a kind of spirit representing the devil. John Law was struck down lame on one side of his body.' Owen paused and wiped his glasses on his sweater. 'Of course, modern wisdom would suggest he had a stroke. I've never heard of Mia Wright or Fury, though.'

'Mia Wright was a young woman. She was found murdered at the foot of Pendle Hill yesterday. Fury is her dog.'

'Oh, I see.' The professor looked Doyle in the eye. 'And I'm guessing you are here because you think Will Perkins might be involved?' His voice had taken on a sharper tone.

'The graffiti was in his house and he has admitted writing it. Will's dad recently had a stroke after an altercation with Mia Wright.'

'Oh,' the professor said.

'What do you make of this?' Doyle asked, scrolling to the picture he had taken of the symbol carved into the tree at the crime scene.

'It's a pentacle,' the professor said. 'A Wiccan symbol of faith, often misunderstood to represent good versus evil.'

'It's a symbol relating to witchcraft, then?'

'Not exactly. It's a symbol associated with the modern Wiccan movement, but it has no relation to the accused witches of Pendle and would not have been known at that time. It's far more modern.'

'From what you know of Will Perkins – and I appreciate it has been a long time since you taught him – do you think this might be a type of symbol he might use? Do you think Will may have carved this into the tree?'

'Funnily enough, I think that it is decidedly unlikely,' the professor said.

'Why's that?'

'Will knew a great deal about the history of the Pendle witches, and he grew up in the area. There are a lot of people in these parts obsessed with witches and witchcraft. Apart from anything else, there is quite a tourism industry built on the back of it. But Will' – Owen tapped the table as if to emphasise his next point – 'Will, found a lot of this extremely irritating as they weren't interested in what happened back in 1612, but in the modern fantasy of witches with pointy hats riding around on broomsticks. More Hogwarts than Pendle. Certainly, when he was at university he would have seen this symbol as something from the modern era.'

Chapter 11

The short drive back from Haworth to Nelson was a pleasant one, despite the intermittent drizzle. It was a beautiful part of the world – Doyle could see why Professor Owen had chosen to retire there. When he was less than half a mile from Nelson police station, Doyle's phone rang and Dr Gupta's voice came through the car's speakers.

'Liam, have you got a moment? I've got back some interesting results from Mia's swabs.'

'Sure, what have you got?'

'She's positive for gonorrhoea.'

'The STI? I didn't know that was still around.'

'It is, and it's more common than you might think. Easily treated with antibiotics.'

'But presumably she got it from somewhere, and that person will also be positive for the condition?'

'It might not be the same person as the one who got her pregnant. The person who infected her may no longer have it, if they've been treated,' Gupta said.

'But it will be on their medical records, if they have been treated?'

'Not necessarily, I'm afraid. Sexual health clinics allow patients to be treated anonymously for most things. It's to encourage people to get treatment without creating barriers.'

'Alright, so is it possible the other person might not know they've got it?'

'Very possible, yes. Of course, even if a suspect did have the infection, it wouldn't prove that they either gave it to, or contracted it from, our victim.'

'No, but it's useful nonetheless. It might show us if we are looking in the right direction. Thanks for flagging it up.'

'No problem, I thought it would be of use to you. Have you had any more luck with finding a next of kin? Informally, several people have confirmed the victim is Mia Wright, but we will need to formally identify her soon. We can confirm with DNA when that comes back, assuming you have hers on your records.'

'No one so far, I'm afraid, though I've been out of the incident room for a few hours, so they may have found someone by now. If not, there's a community PC who knew Mia who I'm sure would do it if required. It's quite sad that someone her age has no one that close to her in the world.'

'Indeed. Do keep me posted if you find someone to ID her, won't you?'

'Will do.' Doyle ended the call and decided on a quick detour before going back to the police station. Still not completely familiar with the area, he found a new destination and put it in the satnav.

The medical centre that housed the community mental health team for the area was in Clitheroe, a picturesque old town on the other side of Pendle Hill to Nelson and Barrowford. Having never visited the town before, Doyle didn't know what parking would be like, so he decided to jump in the first available space he passed near the town centre and continued the last few hundred yards on foot. He passed a Booths supermarket with a metal statue of what looked like a big black dog outside the entrance. It was the day before Halloween, so at first glance it didn't seem particularly odd to see so many shops with witch-themed decorations on display, until he realised that many of these displays appeared to be permanent, with several having witches on broomsticks depicted on their signage. It reminded Doyle a bit of a trip he had made to Loch Ness with Fiona before Harry was born. Many of the shops in the towns around the loch had displayed images of the legendary Loch Ness monster and sold all manner of souvenirs around this theme. That hadn't felt odd to Doyle; Nessy was a mythical creature. Having spent an hour with Professor Owen, he now appreciated that the Pendle witches were victims of a miscarriage of justice. It felt callous that they were depicted here wearing pointy hats and riding broomsticks, hundreds of years after they had died. History, it seemed, had morphed into mythical legend. Doyle thought back to his days in the Met. There had been several cases of child abuse linked to beliefs in witchcraft and that children had become possessed. A few children had been tortured and killed because of these beliefs, and the problem had become so serious that the Met had set up a specialist team called Project Violet to deal with these cases.

'What's happening with Will?' Dianne Berry asked Doyle as soon as the detective walked into her office. There was a brusqueness to her tone, and Doyle couldn't blame her. She'd spent a good part of her day off at Burnley police station and had been back there again that morning. Still, he was pleased to find her writing up notes rather than with a patient or out on a visit.

'We've been granted a twelve-hour extension on his custody clock, so we've got until nine thirty this evening. But I don't want him kept in the cells for a prolonged period any more than you do,' Doyle replied.

'What's happening now? What's the next step?'

They were fair questions, considering Will's vulnerability.

'I've just been to see Prof Owen, who knew him when he was at uni, to get a bit of background. We have a team going over his dad's house and car. We are wrapping up every line of enquiry as quickly as we can, and when we have done that, we will either have evidence to charge him or we will release him. Which is why I'm here now. I need your help with something.'

'What?'

'Has Will been diagnosed with, or treated for, gonorrhoea recently, as far as you know?'

'What, Will? Not as far as I'm aware.'

'Could you have a look at his records, in case he saw a GP or got treatment elsewhere?'

'You know, there is a procedure for this. I can't just jump into his medical records and give you the information.'

'Sure, and we've made a formal request for all his records, but it will take longer to get that then go through it all. The quicker we know, the quicker we can potentially start ruling him in or out.'

'I'm guessing the reason you are asking is because Mia Wright had it?'

Doyle shrugged. 'I obviously can't confirm that.'

'Look, for what it's worth, I don't need to look at his notes. If Will had tested positive for gonorrhoea via the GP, I would know about it. We would need to consider monitoring his blood more frequently in case his white cells were down. Of course, he could have gone to a GUM clinic anonymously. But I know Will, and first, I'm pretty sure he wasn't having a sexual relationship with anyone and second, if he was worried about anything medical he would have told me. I've had enough conversations with him about unpleasant side effects of his medication over the years – some of them meds can bung you up like you wouldn't believe. If he had a gammy nadger I'm sure he would've mentioned it.'

'Thanks,' Doyle said. He was pretty certain that the words 'gammy nadger' wouldn't appear on Perkins' medical records – or anyone's, for that matter.

'If you want something a bit more definitive, then you could get his blood tested. That doctor of yours took blood from him yesterday to check his clozapine level. If he's got any sense, he would have taken a few vials. They might not be able to test for the disease itself, but it could indicate if he has an untreated infection.'

'Fingers crossed, then. I'll get on to it straight away.'

'Look, do me a favour, will you? As soon as you decide what you are doing, particularly if you're releasing him, let me know straight away. My phone will always be on. I don't want him going through all this and then being turfed out on the street on his own. I'll come and pick him up, check on his mental state and take him home.'

'Will do.'

'Gadget just called, boss,' Shaima Asif said as Doyle entered the incident room in Nelson. 'He'll be coming back soon. He said there was nothing at Reg Perkins' house that looked like it could be related to the victim or what happened to her. Forensics have taken a few samples of various bits, but aren't hopeful about any of it. The car's not been moved off the drive for a while either. There was a build-up of dirt around the wheels and the battery was flat.'

'Thanks, Shaima,' Doyle said, then raised his voice to speak to everyone in the room. 'Has anyone turned up any actual evidence linking Will Perkins to the victim – other than he called her a witch a few months ago?'

'Not so far,' Hales said. 'I contacted the lab. They are going to test his blood for signs of any infection or traces of the antibiotics used to treat it.'

'Thanks, Geoff,' Doyle said.

There was a knock on the door and PC Anderton entered, followed by Lofthouse. 'We are free now, if there is anything you want us to do,' Anderton said.

'There is something you might be able to help me with,' Morgan said. 'I've been asking around Barrowford about Mia, and a couple of people have mentioned someone who goes by the name of Turkish as being an associate of hers. Do you know who that might be or what their real name is?'

'I've heard the name before, but I don't know who he is,' Anderton said. 'Do you know, Nat?'

'No – like you, I've heard the name, but can't put a face to it,' Lofthouse said.

'A shopkeeper said he had seen him with Mia a few times round the back of the shops – sounds like more than a casual encounter. He thought she might have been either buying or selling drugs,' Morgan said. 'He said he often wore orange overalls with "Farm Machinery Maintenance" on the back or something similar.'

'There's a machinery maintenance company between Roughlee and Newchurch, about a mile from Barrowford. He might work for them,' Anderton said. 'I can't remember what they're called, but they're not a big operation. Can you remember, Nat?'

'I think it might be MM Engineering or something like that,' Lofthouse said.

'Oh, there is one other thing,' Doyle said, looking at Anderton. 'And I'm sorry to ask. We haven't found a next of kin to formally identify Mia. How would you feel about—'

'I'll do it.'

Chapter 12

The company was in fact called NN Agricultural Engineering. The premises consisted of a large yard littered with pieces of rusting farm equipment, most of which Doyle did not recognise. There were two barns which, judging by the noise coming from them, were serving as workshops, and a separate portacabin that looked like it was the office. Doyle pulled up next to a white Range Rover Evoque that looked decidedly out of place, parked between a pickup truck and a white panel van.

The woman who sat behind the desk in the office looked even more out of place than the luxury SUV in the yard. Late thirties, maybe early forties, Doyle guessed; her liberal use of Botox and fillers made it hard to tell.

'We're from the police,' Doyle said, while trying to compose his next words. It felt a bit racist to ask for someone by a nickname he'd presumably got because of his nationality. 'We're looking for a man known as Turkish. Does he work here?'

'Why, what's he done?' the woman replied, inadvertently answering Doyle's question. If she'd been surprised to see the police asking after her colleague, it didn't show on her face, but then Doyle wondered if anything could.

'Is he here or not?' Morgan asked. Doyle could detect a note of irritation in her voice.

'Far as I know, he's in the workshop, but he might've gone out on a job.'

'It's the police,' Doyle announced at a volume he hoped could be heard above the whine of pneumatic tools. 'We're looking for someone known as Turkish.'

The noise stopped and all three people who had been working next to a giant wheel on some kind of trailer came over to the barn doors. The oldest of the group, who Doyle guessed was in charge, wiped his hands on his orange overalls but didn't offer a hand to be shaken. Two younger men stood behind him, looking more like doormen than mechanics. One was almost as tall as Doyle and probably a bit wider. Despite his big, bushy beard, he didn't look like he was long out of his teens.

'Turkish will be in next-door barn,' the older man said. His accent sounded eastern European.

'Thanks,' Doyle said. The men didn't return to their work. Instead, they stood in the entrance watching as he and Morgan walked to the next barn. Looking over his shoulder, he noticed that the older man had taken the opportunity to have an impromptu cigarette break and the younger two were puffing on vapes, no doubt all keen to see what might unfold.

In the second barn, there was a small room to the left of the large doors. This was empty. Doyle heard a man talking at the other end of the workshop, but couldn't see where the voice was coming from. Perhaps there was someone on the other side of the tractor that was parked there. As they got closer it became clear that the tractor was above an inspection pit and the voice was coming up from the pit. Peering down, Doyle saw a man with his back to them talking on a phone.

'Police,' Morgan said. 'Are you Turkish?'

The man ended the call and turned to face them. He didn't look Turkish, Doyle thought; he had ginger hair and an orange tan that definitely wasn't natural.

'What can I do for you officers?' When he opened his mouth to speak, Doyle saw his full set of gleaming white, perfectly straight teeth.

Doyle realised he wasn't known as Turkish because of his nationality but because of the origin of his dentistry. 'We'd like to ask you a few questions about Mia Wright.'

'Who?'

'Mia Wright, the young woman often seen outside the shops in Barrowford with a big black dog,' Morgan said.

'Oh her. That Mia.'

'Know a lot of women called Mia, do you?' Morgan asked.

'No, it's just... I don't know her that well. Why are you asking me about her?'

'What's your name?' Doyle asked.

'Terry.'

'Terry what?'

'Terry Handcock. What's all this about? I've not done owt wrong.'

'Like my colleague said, we want to ask you some questions about Mia Wright. We can either do this here or we can take you back to the police station and do it there.'

'Alright.' Turkish looked around, past the detectives. 'Like I said, I didn't know her that well.'

'Didn't?' Morgan said.

'What?'

'You said you *didn't* know her that well.'

'So?'

'Wouldn't it be more normal to say you *don't* know her that well?'

Turkish wiped his brow on the back of his overall sleeve. 'Look, can we go outside?'

Doyle wondered if the man would do a runner. He wasn't sure that he would catch him if he did, but he was confident that Morgan would. Turkish led the detectives to the furthest corner of the yard, well out of earshot of the men who were still puffing away by the other barn.

'Look, I saw on the front page of the paper this morning that she'd been killed.' The man appeared more relaxed now he was at less risk of being overheard.

'What was the nature of your relationship with Mia Wright?' Morgan asked.

'We didn't have a relationship. Like I said, I hardly knew the girl.'

'People have seen you with her,' Doyle said.

'I used to chat to her sometimes, give her some change or some cigarettes. She was always hanging around outside the shops in town.'

'What did you do with her round the back of the shops?' Morgan asked.

'What?'

'You were seen, round the back of some shops with her,' Doyle said. 'And we've got you on CCTV.' That last part wasn't necessarily true, as they hadn't gone through it all yet.

'Like I said, just giving her some fags or money, that kind of thing.'

'Round the back of the shops?' Morgan asked. 'Bit strange, that.'

'Were you buying drugs from her?' Doyle said. 'A bit of weed, maybe?'

'No, nothing like that.'

'You sure?' Morgan said. 'I mean, if you were, we couldn't care less about that. We just need to know more about Mia and what she got up to.'

'Were you shagging her?' Doyle asked, his voice raised a bit.

'No. Jesus, keep your voice down.'

'What, then? Were you selling her drugs?' Doyle asked.

'No. Look, OK. Sometimes I would go with her to have the odd joint, nothing more than that.'

'When did you last do that?' Morgan said.

'It must have been last week sometime. I'm not sure.'

'What did you chat about when you were having a smoke?' Doyle asked.

'Nothing much – this and that.'

'And what did you do Saturday night between 10 p.m. and six o'clock Sunday morning?' Morgan asked.

'You don't think I did her in, do you?'

'We don't know yet, but it would help if you answered the question,' Doyle said.

'I was in all night, watching TV and then in bed.'

'Is there anyone who can verify that?' Morgan asked.

'My wife was with me.' Turkish wiped his brow again. 'Look, do you have to ask her?'

'Is there a problem with that?' Doyle said.

'She'll want to know why you're asking. She doesn't know I smoke weed sometimes, or that I know Mia.'

'We'll see,' said Doyle.

'I don't know why you're asking me all these questions anyway. It's obvious who done her in.'

'Is it?' Doyle asked.

'Course it is. That bloody nutter, Will something. He's had it in for her for ages and he's a total fruit loop. Ask anyone about him. It's been all over social media.'

'So we can verify your story, where can we get hold of your wife?' Morgan asked.

Turkish had gone a shade lighter, and sweat dripped from his forehead despite the chill in the air. 'In there,' he said pointing to the office.

'The woman we spoke to in there is your wife?' Doyle asked.

'Yes, but do you have to—'

'Is this your company?' Morgan asked.

'No, we both just work here. It belongs to her brother.'

'Is there anything else you can tell us about Mia Wright? Other people she was friends with, or people she had fallen out with?' Doyle asked.

'No, like I said, I didn't know her that well. But anyone will tell you about that Will – even your lot know all about him and how he had it in for her.'

'He was lying out of his arse,' Morgan said as Doyle drove out of the yard.

'My thoughts too, but his wife's confirmed his alibi.'

'True, but it was a pretty standard answer. *He was at home with me all that time.* She could have been primed to say that.'

'Fair point.'

'It's interesting that he admitted to smoking weed with her, but then that's the least serious thing and he had to come up with a reason for being round the back of the shops with her.'

'He could have been having an affair with her. But seems unlikely anything would have been going on behind the shops,' Doyle said.

'But she was definitely sexually active with at least one person. We know that from the pregnancy and the STI.'

'She was either sexually active with more than one person or the person who was seeing her must have been.'

'Maybe she was a sex worker and Turkish was pimping her?'

Doyle drummed the steering wheel with his fingers. 'That's certainly a possibility. Or maybe the shopkeeper was right, and she was buying or selling drugs. Turkish could be either her customer or her dealer.'

Morgan nodded. 'So where do we go from here?'

'When we get back, we'll dig up all we can on Terry Handcock and see what skeletons we can find in Turkish's closet and take it from there.'

'And what about Will Perkins?'

'We're going to release him on police bail.'

'You don't think that's a risk?'

'We've got nothing on him other than he accused her of being a witch when he was acutely psychotic.'

'I didn't necessarily mean that,' Morgan said. 'But you heard what Turkish said. If he's right and people are saying that Will did it and it's out on social media, couldn't he be at risk?'

'Maybe, but what can we do? We can't keep him in protective custody, and we don't have grounds to detain him any longer. I'll talk to his community nurse, so she's aware of the situation.' Doyle pulled the car up alongside the kerb.

'What are we stopping for?' Morgan asked.

'I saw this sculpture yesterday on the way back from the crime scene. I want to see what it is.' Doyle got out of the car.

On the grass verge stood a metal statue of a woman with her arms manacled together. She wore a dress and shawl in a dark rust colour, and her face and headscarf were picked out in verdigris. Someone had placed a fresh bunch of carnations in her hands, and a carved pumpkin lantern lay at her feet.

'Alice Nutter,' Morgan said, reading from the plaque. 'There was no evidence that she was a witch and she pleaded not guilty to the charge of murder, but was hanged along with nine others at Lancaster in August 1612. She was from here in Roughlee.'

'And now, here we are investigating a murder with allegations of witches. It feels like everything in this part of the world is somehow trapped in what happened in the distant past.'

Chapter 13

Day 3: Tuesday 31 October – Halloween

'So far,' Doyle said, 'we've only got two people linked with our victim. And they are tenuous links at best. As you know, we bailed Will Perkins yesterday evening because of a distinct lack of any evidence that he had anything to do with Mia Wright's murder.' Having let everyone go home at the relatively civilised time of eight o'clock the previous evening, Doyle had the core team gathered in the incident room at Nelson police station by half past seven that morning to take a fresh look at where they were. 'Is there something we are missing with Will? Somewhere else we should be looking, perhaps, or even something we have overlooked?'

'I can't think what,' Hales said. 'But then, it's hard not to consider him the most likely suspect. He has a motive of sorts and paranoid schizophrenia. I still think it's possible he had some kind of psychotic episode and killed her.'

'But the lack of evidence doesn't add up,' Morgan said. 'If he had done it because of his psychotic delusions, is it really possible that he would have covered up any evidence so well that we haven't found it?'

'It's who she was having sex with that's most likely to link it all together,' Birdseye said. 'Both Will and this Turkish fella have denied having a sexual relationship with her, but we know someone did. Either one of them is lying, or there is someone else in her life that we don't yet know about.'

'It's a bit tragic, isn't it?' Gadget said. 'She was only twenty-two, and we haven't been able to find any relative or next of kin even to identify the body, and of the only two people we have found that had anything to do with her, one accused her of being a witch and the other wanted to deny even knowing her.'

'If she was involved in dealing or sex work, it's quite likely that many more people knew her but don't want to come forward to admit that,' Hales said.

'Which reminds me,' said Doyle. 'Has anything come back from the blood tests done on Will?'

Asif looked at her screen. 'There's something here... The test requested for the level of medication is back. It says: *The levels of clozapine found in the blood taken at approximately 20.00 on Sunday 29 October are consistent with William Perkins having taken his prescribed dose of the drug approximately twenty-four hours earlier.* So, it doesn't look like he skipped his meds or took them much later than normal.'

'If the tests for infection and traces of antibiotics come back negative, it really looks like Will is not our guy,' Doyle said.

'There are a few things that don't stack up with Turkish,' Morgan said. 'But not anything that seems to directly link to Mia.'

'What sort of things?' Birdseye asked.

'He and his wife work at the same company, but neither of them owns it,' Morgan said. 'But when we went there yesterday, there was a brand-new Range Rover Evoque parked in the yard. I got the reg, and it's registered to Tracy Handcock, aka Mrs

Turkish, so I looked further and there is also a Ford Ranger pickup truck registered to Terry Handcock. That's nearly eighty grand's worth of cars between them and they're not leased.'

'Plenty of people spend silly money on cars these days, even if they're mortgaged up to the hilt to get them,' Hales said.

'I get that,' said Morgan. 'But it's not just the cars. He looked like he had a whole new set of implanted teeth, and she looked like a living Barbie doll, the amount of work she'd had done.'

Doyle was glad it was Morgan saying it and not him, but he couldn't disagree with her.

'Even if they don't earn lots of money, they could have had an inheritance or a win on the pools or something,' Birdseye said.

'Bloody hell, Derrick,' Hales said. 'The pools? Do they even still exist?'

'Alright, the lottery then, but you know what I mean.'

'The shopkeeper I spoke to, Mr Syed, said that when he saw Mia and Turkish out the back he thought she might have been buying or selling drugs,' Morgan said. 'What if she was buying them and Turkish was her supplier? That might explain how they've got more disposable income than might be expected.'

'That's a good point,' Doyle said. 'But another thing that doesn't add up is that he seemed very concerned about us speaking to his wife. Presumably, if he was dealing she would know about it and where the money was coming from, especially as she works at the same firm.'

'It could be he didn't want you two speaking to her because he was worried she would crack under the pressure and let something slip,' Gadget said.

Doyle nodded. He noticed Asif looking intently at her computer screen. 'You got something, Shaima?'

'One second... We've had some information come in from the phone company. Anna found a box for a pay-as-you-go mobile at Mia's flat. They've sent through all the call data and text log to and from that phone for the last six months. Two numbers flag up several times a day; there's not much other regular activity. Both of these are pay-as-you-go as well. Neither are for the phone used by Will Perkins, though he might have another one we don't know about.'

'Great! Can we get the cell site activity for all three phones? At least that will give us a steer on which areas they have been operating in,' Doyle said.

'I've just sent off the request,' Asif replied.

Both the Range Rover and the pickup belonging to Mr and Mrs Handcock were in the yard alongside a white panel van when Morgan pulled in. Doyle went straight to the barn that Turkish had been working in the day before. Morgan followed a little way behind, taking out her phone. When she saw Turkish, Morgan rang the number Asif had given her.

Turkish reached into a pocket in his overalls and pulled out a phone. 'Yes?'

'I think we need to have another chat, Mr Handcock. Don't you?' She cut the call.

'I've not done owt! This is harassment or something,' Turkish said.

'It's not a good idea to lie to police when they are investigating a murder,' Doyle said.

'I haven't.' The colour drained from Handcock's face.

'That's quite a lot of calls you made to Mia Wright, for someone who only had an occasional joint with her,' Morgan said.

'That don't mean nowt.' Turkish scowled.

'It means you lied to us,' Doyle said. 'And now we're wondering what you've got to hide.'

'We need to interview you under caution at the police station,' Morgan said. 'You can either come with us now voluntarily, or we'll arrest you.'

'Fine, I'll come, but I'm not happy. And I want my solicitor there.'

'No comment,' Turkish said for the umpteenth time.

Morgan tried to keep the irritation from her voice. This was all par for the course, but frustrating nonetheless. 'Yesterday you told DCI Doyle and me that you hardly knew Mia Wright other than to have the odd joint with, yet today we find out that a mobile you were using has over forty calls to and from her number. How do you explain that?'

'No comment.' Turkish massaged the back of his neck with an oil stained hand.

'Were you buying drugs from her?' Morgan asked.

'No comment.'

'Were you selling her drugs?'

Turkish's gaze darted towards his solicitor. 'No comment.'

'You were, weren't you? Morgan said. 'If it's just that, and a small quantity, you're better off telling us now.'

'No comment.'

'Were you in a sexual relationship with Mia Wright?' Morgan asked.

'No comment.'

A bead of sweat was forming on Turkish's forehead, right where his fake tan didn't quite meet his hairline.

'Were you acting as Mia Wright's pimp?' Morgan pressed.

'No comment.'

'You look a little hot, Mr Handcock, is it too warm for you in here?' Morgan asked.

'No comment.'

'I was asking if you are too warm, Terry. It's not going to harm your defence if you answer that.'

'I think we should stop this here,' the solicitor said. 'You obviously don't have any actual evidence against my client or you would have arrested him. His wife has confirmed his alibi. All this wild speculation about what else he might have been up to is pure conjecture.'

Morgan knew she had to concede, but felt frustrated. She and Gadget had wasted over an hour and got precisely bugger all. She'd been through this charade countless times before, but there was something about it today that got to her. Perhaps it was the glib way the man sitting opposite gave 'no comment' answers. From the number of calls between them, he clearly knew Mia better than he was letting on. This was a young woman who had been brutally murdered, and answering 'no comment' felt like he was saying 'Mia didn't matter. I'm just going to sit here and play the game.' She could feel her anger building: she wanted to scream or punch something or someone.

Chapter 14

Doyle looked out of his temporary office window at the street below. The sun was already setting and it felt like they were still only scratching the surface of the investigation, at the end of the third day. He turned back to Morgan, who was sitting opposite alongside Hales. 'If we could get some kind of steer about what Turkish's relationship was with the victim, it might help.'

'I'm sorry, boss, I tried my best. But he wasn't going to budge from "no comment", no matter what or how often I asked,' Morgan said.

'It's OK, I'm not blaming you. He's going to stick to that unless we can get more on him. He knows what we've got so far is enough to arouse suspicion, but not much else.'

There was a knock on the door and Shaima Asif walked in, holding her laptop. 'You're going to want to see this, boss.'

'What have you got?' Doyle asked.

'We requested the call log info from the network for those two burner phones that had been in regular contact with Mia's. The data for the one we now know belongs to Turkish has just come in. Most numbers I haven't been able to identify yet, as they are also unregistered pay-as-you-go. But there was one that is quite interesting. Turkish called it last night and on Sunday morning.'

'Who does it belong to?' Doyle asked.

'Well, that's just it, boss. I don't know exactly who, but it's registered to Lancashire Constabulary.'

'Shit,' Hales said.

'You want me to get on to our comms team and find out who it's assigned to?' Asif asked.

Doyle took a moment to consider this. 'I think it's probably best we don't at this stage. It could be anyone, and we don't want to risk tipping them off just yet. Can you give me the number, Shaima?'

'It's here, boss.' Asif handed him a page with the phone records on. 'It's the one highlighted in orange.'

'Great, thanks. Leave it with me.' Doyle waited until the analyst had left the office, then took out his mobile and keyed in 141 to hide his number before dialling. When he heard the phone ring he put the phone on speaker and placed it on the desk so that Morgan and Hales could hear. The phone kept ringing, unanswered. The ringing stopped, and for a moment Doyle thought the call had been cut off. Then he heard the voicemail message.

It was a vaguely familiar East Lancs accent. 'I'm sorry I can't take your call right now. But if you want to leave a message for DCI Butcher, I'll get back to you when I can.'

Doyle ended the call. There was silence. Hales was the first to break it. 'Isn't that...'

'That prick I had a run-in with on Sunday, Geoff? Yes.'

'Which begs the question, how has Turkish got his number and why has he been calling him over the last few days?' Morgan said.

'It's not just the last few days,' Doyle said, looking at the orange-highlighted entries on the page Asif had given him. 'They have been calling each other pretty regularly going back weeks, and that's just this page.'

'He could have Turkish as a CHIS,' Hales suggested. 'That would fit if he was involved in dealing or other organised crime.'

'It's possible,' Doyle conceded. It wasn't inconceivable that a CID DCI might be running an informant, or Covert Human Intelligence Source, as they were now known. 'Right, this doesn't leave this room. I'm going to speak to Superintendent Croucher and see how he wants to proceed.'

'You don't seriously think that Butcher could be somehow involved?' Morgan asked.

'Stranger things have happened. And he did seem very keen to keep this case under his control,' Doyle said.

Chapter 15

Superintendent Croucher – the man who most of his subordinates referred to as Mr Burns behind his back because he resembled the *Simpsons* cartoon character both in looks and nature – promised Doyle he would find out if DCI Butcher had Turkish as a registered informant. He urged the detective to proceed with caution and to try not to rub anyone up the wrong way. Doyle didn't let slip that after their run-in on Sunday, that ship had probably already sailed. It was quarter past nine when Doyle finished for the day. He was starving, so he decided to pick up a microwave meal from the local Lidl before heading home.

Where Clitheroe had a nice quaint old English town feel about it, Nelson, the place that Doyle now knew was named after a pub, did not. It wasn't the fact it was Halloween that made it feel like a ghost town, but the distinct lack of people in the town centre. He looked up above the mostly boarded-up shop fronts. Some of the buildings displayed ornate clues to a more affluent past, but were now showing signs of decay. He wondered if the much-talked-about levelling-up money supposedly for deprived parts of the country would ever find its way here.

His mobile rang as he walked. He saw the caller ID and hoped it would be Harry, not his ex-wife Fiona.

'Dad, Dad, I've been out trick-or-treating with Grandad. I've got loads of sweets.'

'That's good. Shouldn't you be in bed by now?'

'Mum said I could stay up a little while. You're not mad at me are you, Dad?'

'No, Harry, of course not. Why would I be mad at you?' Doyle had reached the shop, which seemed remarkably busy in contrast to everywhere else.

'Because of Sunday, when you needed to go to work.'

Doyle decided to wait outside while he carried on with the call. 'No, Harry, I'm not mad at you. Have you been worrying about that since then?' Doyle realised that, while he had put the little drama of getting Harry back to his mum out of his mind, the boy had probably spent hours ruminating on it.

'A bit. I thought you might be cross with me. I was worried you wouldn't love me any more.'

'Oh, Harry, I will always love you – even if you are a pain in the arse at times.'

Harry laughed. 'Grandma said that's swearing. Can I stay over an extra night with you on Bonfire Night to watch the fireworks?'

'I thought you didn't like fireworks.'

'I like the colours. I don't like the noise and the loud bangs. But we could watch them through the window and I could wear my headphones.'

'We'll see. I'll have to check with your—' Doyle was jostled by a couple of women wearing witches' costumes.

'Ooh, sorry luv,' one of the women said, and they laughed and staggered over to a group of similarly dressed people standing in the car park.

'What was that?' Harry asked.

'A couple of witches bumped into me.'

'Real ones?' Harry sounded excited.

Doyle wasn't sure how to answer that, but resisted the temptation to tease the boy. Harry could take things quite literally. 'I don't think so, but they look the part.'

'Dad, Mum said I've got to say goodbye and go to bed.'

'Good idea. I'll call you tomorrow evening.'

'I love you, Dad.'

'I love you too, Harry.'

'I love you, Dad.'

'I love you too, Harry.'

Doyle went into the shop and found himself a ready meal, before joining the queue for the checkouts.

'You're not very dressed up for the occasion, are you?' said a witch standing in front of him with a four-pack of fruit cider in her hand.

'What occasion's that, then?' Doyle asked.

'The Halloween Witch Walk. Are you not coming? There's a minibus picking us up in a minute. We're going to go up on Pendle Hill for midnight to celebrate.'

'Sadly, I've got an early start tomorrow.'

'You're no fun. I'm sure there will be space on the minibus. There's even going to be a seance there to communicate with the spirits of the Pendle witches. There's a proper medium doing it.'

'I'm more of a double extra-large man myself,' Doyle said.

'Go on. Live dangerously.'

Doyle had no desire to live dangerously – and even if he had, he didn't think risking a twisted ankle and a few hours' lost sleep while listening to someone pretending to talk to ghosts would be his thing.

As he walked back to the police station to collect his car, Doyle noticed that a light was on in the incident room and the room next door, which he had commandeered as an office. He had been the last to leave and remembered turning the lights off.

He made a mental note to remind the team not to leave anything confidential on their desks and remove anything too sensitive from the incident board last thing at night. The cleaning staff would be DBS checked, but that wouldn't necessarily stop them gossiping about the case. Not that there was much for them to see, anyway.

Doyle was lost in his thoughts as he went through the gate to the car park, and almost bumped into the hulking figure of PCSO Lofthouse. Nat had an equally imposing black dog on a lead.

'I thought you would've been long gone, Nat. Didn't I see you this morning?'

'It's been one of those days. What with it being Halloween, every loon this side of Pendle Hill is out to play today, but I can't complain; I could do with the overtime. I've just been taking this one for a quick walk while I'm on my break.'

The dog sniffed around the bag Doyle held – no doubt catching the scent of the chicken tikka in there. Doyle pulled the bag away and brought his other hand around to give the dog a stroke.

'I wouldn't—'

The dog barked and went for Doyle's arm, its teeth tearing at his jacket as the detective jumped back, pulling his arm away.

Nat struggled to pull the dog away. 'Jesus, I'm sorry, sir,' he said over the noise of the dog's barking. 'Are you alright?'

'Yes, I think so,' Doyle said, inspecting his coat and flexing his wrist. He'd managed to get his hand away just in time to avoid injury, but the cuff of his coat had been torn by the dog's canines.

'This is Mia's dog, Fury. I've been looking after him. He's not good with strangers, but I didn't think he would go for you like that. I'll have to get a muzzle for him.'

'That might be for the best. Anyway, no harm done. I'd better be getting off home. I hope you have a qu—' He stopped himself short before he said the 'quiet' word so many police officers were superstitious about. 'I hope the rest of your shift goes OK.'

Chapter 16

Day 4: Wednesday 1 November

Doyle arrived back at Nelson police station just before seven in the morning. He hadn't felt like getting up when the alarm woke him, but at least travelling at that time meant the roads were quiet. He wanted an early start to go over everything they had before the morning briefing at eight. It still felt like they were scratching around the edge of the investigation. There was no real evidence linking either of the two suspects to Mia's killing. They needed to know more about Mia's life, and her last movements.

Doyle took out the office keys he had been given and went to unlock the desk drawer where he'd stashed his notebook and some paperwork the previous night. He was surprised to find the drawers unlocked. He knew that he had locked them – and checked they were locked by giving the top drawer a pull. This was his routine whenever he left work anywhere. It wasn't just notes about cases that he kept in these drawers; he sometimes had notes relating to staff members, which needed to be kept confidential. He played around with the lock to see if it was faulty, but it appeared to be working, and there were no telltale marks or scratches to suggest it had been tampered with. This left Doyle with only one other explanation: someone else had opened it. Someone who had been able to get access to the keys and walk around the police station. He'd seen the light on the night before and assumed it had been the cleaner, but what if it had been someone else?

He looked through the notebook and paperwork. Nothing was missing. Because this was just a temporary office, he didn't have much in the drawer, and all he did have was related to the case. But whoever it had been, Doyle knew that they would have a pretty good idea about where the investigation had got to if they had looked around the rest of the incident room and at the evidence board. It couldn't be anyone in his team, he was sure of that. There would be no reason for them to snoop around, and he had never had any suspicions about any of them in the past. But he couldn't say the same for the local CID – and in particular DCI Butcher. He'd been overly keen to hang on to the case, and now they had phone calls linking Butcher's mobile to Turkish's mobile, and he was still a significant person of interest. Doyle was getting an uneasy feeling about this. He knew he would have to think carefully about what he did. Croucher should be getting back to him today about whether Butcher had been using Turkish as a registered informant. Doyle knew he should speak to the superintendent about his concerns, but if the experience of the last four months was anything to go by, he thought his boss would minimise the situation and accuse him of being paranoid. He would have to think of another approach. Whoever had been snooping around, Doyle would make sure he caught them.

Carrying seven coffee cups at once proved to be significantly more difficult than carrying the usual six. Morgan had remembered at the last minute that Jen would be attending the morning briefing, and added her flat white to the order. The six cups were placed in one of those caddy things made out of the same material used for hospital bedpans. They rested on her forearm, with the seventh placed on top. Normally Morgan would use her other arm to secure the load, which worked pretty well. The seventh cup had completely changed things, and the whole lot had wobbled about on her way up the stairs. At the landing she had needed to use her chin to keep the cups in place while she opened the door. This obstacle successfully negotiated meant she was on the home run. When she got to the incident room, she could give the door a kick and someone would come and open it for her.

'BOO!'

Seven cups full of burning hot liquid went flying all over Morgan, and all over the carpet tiles.

'You fucking arsehole!' Morgan shouted before she turned to see who had scared her. When she saw him, she rolled her eyes. Detective Sergeant Steve Fucking Felton. That was just typical. Her first big case since returning to work, and she'd ended up working out of the same police station as him. Felton was almost the most obnoxious human being she had ever met, and he'd made her life a misery when she'd got her first detective job.

'Bit jumpy, aren't you, Anna? Worried the bogeyman's going to get you again?'

'I should've known it would be you. Still like sneaking up on women, I see.' Morgan's clothes were soaked, and her heart raced. She desperately wanted to punch the fucker, but the last time she'd done that, she'd been a DC and Felton had been her sergeant at Burnley CID. It had caused no end of problems. She had been well within her rights – a drunken Felton had grabbed her arse on a work night out – but typically her weak, sycophantic colleagues at the time had rallied around their DS and accused her of overreacting.

'What the fuck's going on here?' a familiar cockney voice said from behind her.

'This prick jumped out on me. Made me spill our drinks.'

'Wallet,' Doyle barked at Felton. Morgan was pleased to see the DS take a couple of steps back.

'What?'

'Give me your wallet, dickhead.' Doyle spoke slowly, as though he was speaking to someone who had difficulty understanding English. 'You owe us for the drinks, and you owe Detective Sergeant Morgan for some dry cleaning.'

'It's not my fault she's so jumpy. Should she even be at work if she gets so easily spooked?'

'You fucking—'

Doyle stuck an arm out, cutting Morgan off. 'And that's how you want to play this? Do you think it's OK to jump out on people in corridors? And what about the victim blaming? I guess it's your career to lose. I'll make the relevant complaint.'

Gadget and Birdseye came out of the incident room, having heard the raised voices. Morgan was beginning to want the coffee-soaked floor to swallow her up.

'No... I'm not saying,' Felton stammered.

'Wallet,' Doyle repeated. Morgan was surprised to see the other DS take it out of his trouser pocket. Doyle rifled through it and removed three twenty-pound notes.

'Hang on, that's a bit—'

'Twenty pounds for the coffees and forty for the dry cleaning. Now run along,' Doyle said, tossing the wallet onto the floor back down the corridor.

'We'll get the drinks, boss,' Birdseye said. Doyle handed him a twenty, giving the other forty to Morgan. She wondered whether Felton would realise that everything she was wearing could go in a washing machine. She hoped so, as that would annoy him even more. Thankfully, she always kept a change of clothes in the boot of her car. Of all the liquids she'd been covered with in the line of duty, tea and coffee were about as good as it got.

Chapter 17

It didn't take Doyle long to update the team on the investigation. Not a great deal had changed since they had last spoken, and for the time being he was keeping the connection between DCI Butcher and Turkish on a need-to-know basis. He wasn't minded to tell the team about the night-time snooper in the incident room. It wasn't that he didn't trust any of them, but he wanted their focus to be on finding Mia Wright's killer, not on working out who the spy in the camp was. Besides, tensions with the local CID were already pretty high, and he knew he should make an effort not to ramp them up further.

Doyle was pleased that Jen Knight was able to attend, and hoped she would have some useful forensic evidence to share that might give them a steer for what warranted further investigation.

'The murder site hasn't yielded a lot so far,' Knight said. 'We haven't found the knife or anything we think we will be able to link directly to the killer.'

'What about the rug that she'd been partly covered with?' Birdseye asked. 'Do you think we'll get anything back from that?'

'It's possible,' Knight said. 'There is a lot of blood on it, which appears to be Mia's, but they are going over it at the lab to see if they can find a hair or something else that might have the killer's DNA on it.'

'Are we sure that the rug wasn't used to cover Mia by someone who found the body?' Hales asked.

'The people who reported it said they found her like that,' Birdseye said. 'I can't see why they would lie about it.'

'Also,' Knight said, 'the amount of blood that was on it would suggest it was placed over her shortly after she was killed, before her blood had started to clot.'

'If the killer put it over her, they must have had a reason,' Asif said.

Doyle nodded. 'Anyone got any ideas what the reason could be?'

'Maybe the person who killed her didn't want to see her face when he ... you know, did that stuff down there with the uterus,' Gadget said.

'That's in keeping with the killer being someone who knows her,' Morgan said. 'And trying to remove evidence that links them to Mia's pregnancy, rather than a killer taking a trophy.'

'We found something else at her flat that might relate to that,' Knight said. 'Anna, that plastic bag you found with blood in it next to the dog's bowl. The blood was Mia's, and it looks like there was quite a lot of it in there at one point. It was smeared all around the inside of the bag along with dog saliva.'

'Jesus,' said Birdseye.

'Are you thinking that her...' Doyle said.

'That the bag might have contained her uterus?' Knight said.

'Bloody hell,' said Birdseye.

'We can't tell for sure.' Knight sighed. 'But it seems like the most logical explanation.'

'So, to get this clear,' Doyle said. 'You think the most likely explanation for Mia's blood being in the bag is that the killer, after removing her uterus, went back to her flat and fed it to her dog?'

'That's sick,' Gadget said, in case anyone in the room was in any doubt about that.

Knight nodded. 'We can't be certain, but, as crazy and horrific as it sounds, it seems the most likely explanation.'

'Then that means whoever killed her knew her,' Morgan said. 'And knew her dog. There's no way anyone would get past that beast if it didn't know you.'

'Unless,' said Birdseye, 'the person just opened the door and threw in the bag, or stuffed it through the letterbox.'

'But it was right by the dog's bowl on the other side of the room,' Morgan said. 'As though it had deliberately been put there.'

'What kind of dog is it?' Hales asked.

'A bloody big one,' Morgan said.

'I saw it last night with the PCSO, Nat, who's looking after it,' Doyle said. 'It looks like a Rottweiler crossed with something else.'

'Most likely a bear,' Morgan said.

'OK. Thanks Jen, have you got anything else?' Doyle asked.

'Not at this stage, but we might get more from the lab.'

'I think we need to focus on finding out more about Mia and her final movements,' Doyle said. 'If the killer was the man who got her pregnant, that will be the key to finding him.'

'Her mental health care coordinator, Dr Sutton, is a psychologist. She's been away on annual leave but is due back today. I'm hoping to see her, see if she can fill in some of the blanks about Mia's personal life,' Morgan said. 'She might even be able to shed some light on who got her pregnant.'

'Good,' Doyle said. 'And I want the rest of you to put together a timeline of Mia's last movements. I know we're unlikely to find any CCTV or doorbell footage between her flat in Barrowford and the crime scene in Barley, but it might help if we can piece together her movements in the hours and days leading up to her death. If you're right, Anna, and she did know her killer, then working out who she had contact with over her last week or so could help us find who it is.'

There was a knock at the door, and PC Paige Anderton entered. 'Sorry to interrupt, but I thought you might want to see this, if you hadn't already.' She handed Doyle a copy of that day's *Lancashire Chronicle*. The headline read *Police Bail Main Suspect in Pendle Ripper Case*. Below it was a picture of Will Perkins standing shirtless on the wall of the old toll bridge in Barrowford in the summer, just before he was sectioned.

'Shit,' said Doyle, tossing the paper to DI Hales. 'This could complicate things.'

'It says here that Mia Wright's throat was cut and her body was mutilated after she was killed,' Hales said. 'How would that low-rent hack Jayden Clark know that?'

'Maybe the people who found her body tipped him off,' Gadget said.

'Doubtful,' said Birdseye. 'They were up here on a weekend break from Somerset. I doubt they've even heard of the *Lancashire Chronicle*, let alone know its chief crime reporter.'

'Also,' Morgan said, 'they wouldn't have known her throat was cut unless they had removed the rug.'

Doyle's phone started to ring. He glanced at the number; it wasn't in his contacts. 'DCI Doyle.'

'Sorry to call you directly. It's Dianne Berry, Will Perkins' community nurse. I got your number when you called me on Monday to say he was being released.'

'Are you calling about the article in the *Chronicle*? I can assure you the information didn't come from us.'

'Kind of, but it's not just that. Will's phoned me in a right panic. He said people have been throwing things at his windows and shouting through his letterbox. Someone's sprayed graffiti on the front of his house and the front door has been half kicked in.'

'Shit.' Doyle's mind went to Christopher Jefferies – an innocent man questioned about Jo Yeates' murder in 2010. He had been hounded relentlessly by the tabloid press after his release.

'I'm in Clitheroe now, got another patient in crisis but I'll make sure I see Will when I have dealt with this. I think we're going to have to find him alternative accommodation. Can you send over some officers to get him out of there? I don't fancy facing an angry mob on my own at my age.'

'Will do.'

'And don't send any of the nasty lot that nicked him in the first place.'

A blast of sirens sent the last of the teenage boys scattering from the street. Most had scarpered when Doyle rounded the corner, the blue lights in the car's radiator grill flashing. One particularly truculent youth paused briefly in the road to turn and give the long arm of the law a one-fingered salute before catching up with his mates. A patrol car came down the road from the other direction and pulled up in front of Doyle's unmarked SUV.

'Not Banksy's best work,' Doyle said, nodding towards the graffiti scrawled across the front of Will Perkins' house. Someone had tried to write the word 'murderer' in green paint but hadn't planned it very well, with the letters getting smaller towards the end of the word as the artist ran out of space. The last 'r' was hardly legible, it was so small.

'Did you recognise any of those kids?' Morgan asked Anderton and Lofthouse as they got out of the patrol car.

'One or two,' Anderton said. 'But we will have picked them up on the car's dashcam.'

'They didn't look that old,' Morgan said. 'Shouldn't they be in school?'

'It's half-term,' Doyle said.

'Jesus,' Lofthouse said, examining the front of the house. 'Look at all this lot.' The pavement was littered with broken glass, eggshells and other detritus that had been thrown at the house. The front door had four panels, and the lower two had been kicked through.

'Will, it's Paige, the police officer,' Anderton called through the broken door. 'You're safe now – could you let us in?'

Morgan nudged Doyle and nodded towards the upstairs window, where a figure was peeking round a curtain.

'Will,' Doyle shouted up to the window, 'you're not in any trouble. Dianne Berry called me. We want to make sure you're OK.'

An elderly man came out of the house next door. 'They've been hounding him for hours. I called the police ages ago. Didn't know what it was about until I saw the paper. Did he do it, then? Did he kill that beggar girl?'

'We don't—' Doyle began.

'He's always seemed like such a nice lad – helped me when my gutter got blocked. Got right up there on the ladder and cleared it out. Still, you don't know what's going on in their head, do you, with these schizophrenics? They can just turn, can't they? Like Jekyll and Hyde. In my day they kept them in asylums, not free to roam the streets. They—' The man stopped abruptly and turned away. Will had opened his front door.

He looked far more dishevelled than he had when Doyle had seen him a couple of days ago. His hair was all over the place, he had bags under his eyes, and he wore several layers of clothing and a winter coat. Inside, the house was colder than outside.

'Your heating not working?' Anderton asked.

'The gas has run out, and the leccy. I went to top it up yesterday, but a bunch of kids started shouting at me and chucking stones so I ran back here.'

'We're going to have to move you somewhere where you're a bit safer,' Doyle said. Perkins paced up and down the room, unable to stay still. Harry often did the same when he was feeling stressed or anxious. Doyle sat down and gestured for the others to follow suit.

'I don't want to go back in that cell or prison.'

'It's OK, Will, we're not going to lock you up,' Doyle said.

'Or the hospital. It's too noisy in there. I want some peace and quiet.'

Anderton looked at Will. 'Will, why don't me and Nat help you get some things together and you can come with us? We can go to the canteen at the police station. It'll be quiet there, and warm. We can get you some food and then work out a plan.'

'Could you stay at your dad's house?' Lofthouse asked.

'He's not there; he's in the home after his stroke.'

'But he wouldn't mind you staying there, would he?' Anderton asked.

'I'll have to take my medication with me. Don't let me forget that. I need it or I'll be back in hospital.'

'Right then, you get ready with Paige and Nat and I'll go and see Dianne Berry, ask her where's best for you to stay for a few days. She said she wants to see you a bit later anyway.'

'What about my landlord? He's not going to be happy. Is there much damage to the house?'

'I'll speak to your landlord and explain it's not your fault,' Anderton said.

'I don't think the damage is too bad, Will. If his insurance doesn't cover it, I'll make sure we pay for the repairs,' Doyle said, knowing this wouldn't make him popular with the bean counters.

Chapter 18

'It was quite a shock to return to work and find out about poor Mia.'

'I'm sure it must've been. Had you not seen anything in the news about it before you got here?' Morgan guessed that the psychologist was about her age. If she had made other choices after finishing her degree, she could be in a similar job. She'd considered psychology at the time, and had got the first that would have enabled her to go on to get a doctorate, but she'd been more interested in criminology. She didn't want to passively listen to other people's problems; she wanted to solve them. Despite everything she'd put up with on her rise to detective sergeant in the Major Investigation Team, she hadn't regretted her choice until recently – until she'd thought that her decision would cost her her life.

'Are you sure I can't get you a drink?' Dr Sutton asked.

'I'm fine, thanks. I'm hoping you might be able to tell me a bit more about Mia and her life. I've been trying to find out what I can since Sunday, and to be honest, I still feel like I don't know much about her,' Morgan said.

'I'll tell you all I can. Please take a seat. I've got twenty minutes till my next patient is due.'

Morgan sat on a solid armchair in a room that, from its colour scheme and decor, left her in no doubt that this was an NHS consulting room. She'd been having her own psychology sessions after the trauma she had suffered in the summer, and even the police counselling room had managed to be more relaxing than this was. 'How long have you been working with Mia?'

'Not long, I'm afraid. I've only been here since May, but I've seen her once a fortnight since then. Except, of course, when I've been on leave or she's DNA'd me.'

'DNA'd?' Morgan asked.

'Sorry, clinical jargon. It's what we write in the notes. Stands for Did Not Attend.'

'Did that happen often?'

'Only twice, and both times I think it was because I'd imposed more boundaries in our relationship. She would call me between appointments if she was stressed, wanting to meet up immediately.' The psychologist looked down and smoothed the front of her skirt. 'My caseload doesn't have the flexibility for me to drop what I'm doing and see someone immediately. Unless, of course, it was an emergency – say, if she was suicidal.'

'And she wasn't at those times?'

'No. I always encouraged her to make a note of things that she had found difficult and bring them into the next session so we could work through them.'

'Did she have friends, partners, lovers? Anyone she was close to?' Morgan asked.

'That's the thing with Mia – she sabotaged all her relationships, one way or another.'

'How?'

'Well, if she got close to someone, she would get too close to them very quickly. Would want to monopolise all their time. She'd get jealous or angry if they weren't available for her every minute of the day. So naturally most people ended up cutting contact, and then she would demonise them.'

'Sounds complicated,' Morgan said, though that might explain why no one close to Mia had contacted the police.

'Sadly, it's an almost inevitable consequence of her childhood. She had no one to love her from a very young age. If you've never been loved and you get close to someone later on, you want to cling on to them and never let them go. But when the other person can't cope with this level of attention and leaves you, all the built-up anger from a lifetime of abandonment spills out.'

'Had she had any relationships like this recently? Someone she had been close to and then had a falling-out with?' Morgan asked.

'No,' Dr Sutton paused, as if giving this some thought. 'At least, not that I know of, but there was something.'

'Oh?' Morgan said.

'Last time I saw her, I got the impression that she might have met someone.'

'Did she say who, or tell you anything about them?' Morgan realised her own voice had risen in the hope that she might be given a new lead.

'No – sorry,' Sutton said. 'I asked what had made her so happy that day, and she said she'd tell me next time, she didn't want to jinx things, or words to that effect. Funnily enough, I took that as a positive sign – a sign that she was trying not to rush things... When I got in this morning, I turned my work phone on. It had been off for the last two weeks while I was on leave.' Sutton paused and took a sip from her water bottle. 'There were two messages on it from Mia. The first she left last Wednesday. She sounded upbeat and happy. The happiest I'd ever heard her, in fact... Oh God.' Dr Sutton put her hand to her mouth, and tears welled up in her eyes. 'Sorry, it's all been quite a shock, and I've not had time to process it.'

'I know this can't be easy.' Morgan gave her what she hoped came over as a sympathetic smile.

'When I heard those messages, I didn't know ... I thought she was still alive. I made a note to call her before my first appointment. I came in early to go through my messages and emails – you know, catch up before seeing any patients.'

'Can I listen to the messages?' Morgan asked, passing Dr Sutton a box of tissues from the table.

'Sure,' Sutton said. She wiped her eyes and got up and started fishing in a handbag under a desk. She pulled out an old Nokia of the type Morgan was used to seeing on suspects using pay-as-you-go burner phones.

'No expense spared with the NHS,' Sutton said, keying in some numbers and then placing the phone on the low table between them.

'Henrietta, it's Mia.' Her voice sounded tinny through the phone's speaker. 'I think you are still on holiday. But I can't wait to tell you, I've got some really exciting news I want to tell you when you get back.'

'And then this one was left on Friday,' Sutton said.

'Henrietta, if you're back, please call me as soon as you get this. Everything's gone to shit. I need your help. I'm in trouble, and no one else will understand.'

'She then sent loads of texts asking me to call her. They were getting more and more desperate.'

'Have you any idea what any of these messages were about?' Morgan asked.

'No, but to be honest when I listened to them and before I knew what had happened, they didn't strike me as too odd' Sutton said. 'I wouldn't have been surprised to hear that Mia had found the new love of her life and on Wednesday she wanted to get married and have his babies, and then by Friday she'd fallen out with him and never wanted to see him again.'

'You said have his babies – did you know that Mia was pregnant?'

'No. Wow, no, I didn't. Are you sure?' Sutton caught Morgan's eye.

'There was a positive pregnancy test in her bathroom bin. And the pathologist confirmed it.'

'That could explain the messages.' Sutton dabbed at her eyes again with the tissue. 'She might have been ecstatic on finding out she was pregnant, fantasising about having a child, living the family life she'd never had. Then a few days later, when reality hit, she'd feel overwhelmed by the responsibility.' The psychologist looked up at Morgan. 'You know she had a baby when she was sixteen?'

'I knew she had at some point,' Morgan said. 'The pathologist mentioned a caesarean scar. What happened to the child?'

'From what I've read about it, it sounds pretty awful. Mia was so distressed during labour that she was given a general anaesthetic, and the baby was delivered by C-section. Social services had already decided that the child would be taken into care. I'm not even sure if Mia ever saw the baby.' Sutton reached for another tissue.

'Did she talk to you about it?'

'No, I asked her once when our conversation seemed to be heading in that direction, but she shut it down. I sensed she wasn't ready to open that box of emotions.'

'I can understand that.' Morgan thought of her own therapy. Talking about something involved thinking about it, bringing up all those painful suppressed feelings that had taken so much effort to tamp down.

'Do you think her death could have been caused by an abortion that went wrong?' Sutton asked.

'No, she died from a cut to the throat, and it definitely wasn't self-inflicted.' Morgan wasn't going to tell the psychologist that Mia's uterus had been removed. She was sure that the other woman would treat that information confidentially, but it wasn't in the public domain; it was still on a strictly need-to-know basis and besides that she didn't want to further add to the psychologist's distress. 'Have you any idea at all who the father might have been?'

'No, I'm sorry.' Tears rolled down the psychologist's cheeks.

'Do you think Mia would have been certain?'

'I honestly don't know. There were times that she could be quite reckless and promiscuous, especially if she was using drugs. But not all the time. Though I only know the bits about Mia's life that she chose to tell me and the background I read in her notes.' Sutton shuffled in her seat and sat more upright. 'If she had a romantic attachment, it must've been pretty recent. She had an emotionally unstable personality disorder. She would have needed to tell me at some point, perhaps that's what those messages were about.'

'Can I ask you about a couple of people you may have heard of, and their relationships with Mia?' Morgan said.

'OK, who are you interested in?'

'Let's start with Will Perkins. Do you know him?'

'I don't know him as such,' Sutton said. 'But I know of him. I think pretty much everyone working here does. He and Mia were never close, or friends, as far as I'm aware. Though I assume you have heard about the incident in the summer, when Will accused Mia of being a witch?'

'Yes, that's kind of why I'm asking,' Morgan said. 'How did Mia react to that? What were her thoughts about Will after that?'

'To be honest, other than goading him a bit at the time, I think she handled it pretty well.' Sutton took another sip of water and dabbed her eyes again. 'Mia had spent enough time in psychiatric wards over the years to have come across many people like Will having psychotic episodes. There's sometimes almost a camaraderie between mental health patients, and they are often quite accepting of other people's relapses.'

'There wasn't any ongoing hostility between Will and Mia?' Morgan asked.

'Not from Mia's point of view – at least, not when I last saw her. Is Will a suspect, then?'

'We are exploring all avenues at the moment,' Morgan said. 'Do you think that it's likely Will could have done it?'

'I don't know. Like I said, I only know of Will, but if he was having a psychotic episode and was having more delusions about Mia being a witch, I don't think it is impossible,' Sutton said. 'Especially if he was having command hallucinations – a godly voice in his head telling him to kill her.'

'His community psychiatric nurse doesn't seem to think it's likely.'

'That's Dianne Berry, right?' Sutton raised her eyebrows.

'Yes, why do you ask?'

'Look, I've nothing against Dianne, and if everyone else working in the NHS was as dedicated as her, it would be a lot better.'

'I sense a "but" coming,' Morgan said.

'I don't want this to sound overly critical. I hardly know her, other than we work in the same building. She tends to get patients with schizophrenia, on lots of medication, whereas my caseload is more people with personality disorders.' Sutton lowered her voice. 'Dianne does have quite a reputation for over-advocating for her patients at times. That can be great, of course, since a lot of our service users don't have anyone else to champion their rights and fight their corner. But there have been times when I think that might have clouded her judgement.'

'Thank you, and duly noted,' Morgan said. 'Can I ask you about another of Mia's associates? Someone called Terry Handcock.'

'I don't recall ever hearing that name come up in any of our conversations.'

'You might've heard him referred to as Turkish.'

'Now that rings a bell. Mia's mentioned him a few times.'

'In what capacity? What was the nature of their relationship?'

Sutton looked up, giving her answer some thought before speaking. 'Strangely, she never seemed either overly positive or negative about him, which was unusual for Mia. With most people, either the sun shone out of their proverbial or they were the devil incarnate, and they often moved from being one to the other in Mia's eyes.'

'Why do you think it was different with Turkish?' Morgan asked.

'Well, if I had to guess, and this is pure speculation on my part,' Sutton said. 'Turkish may have provided something that Mia had an ongoing need for.'

'Sex?'

'I don't think so. I mean, there may have been that at times. Mia liked her cannabis, and sometimes something stronger. If, and I'm not saying this was necessarily the case, if Turkish was providing her with that, she wouldn't want to fall out with him. Much like she rants and raves at times with clinicians, but she never burns her bridges.'

'That's interesting,' Morgan said.

Sutton looked at her watch. 'I'm sorry we will have to leave it there for now. I've got a patient in a few minutes and I think I'd better sort my mascara out first.'

Chapter 19

Dianne Berry tapped at her computer keyboard while Doyle sat opposite her. 'Sorry, I've got to get this risk assessment updated. If anything happens to him and I haven't done it, there will be hell to pay.'

'Will is quite safe now. He'll be in the police station canteen, getting warm and getting fed,' Doyle said. 'I don't think he'll come to any harm there.'

'I'm not so sure with some coppers – present company excluded, of course.'

'Of course,' Doyle said, raising an eyebrow. 'You don't have a very high opinion of the police, do you?'

'I've been married to a copper for thirty-two years, so yes and no.'

'Anyone I might know?'

'Doubt it – he was an inspector in Traffic. He's retired now. Spends all day playing about with his motorbikes while muggins here is out working,' Berry said.

'Oh, right. We were wondering whether it might make sense to move Will into his father's house,' Doyle said.

'It might help a bit, but as soon as people realise he's there, don't you think the same thing will happen all over again? Haven't you got a safe house or anywhere you could put him?'

Doyle considered this. 'There might be one somewhere, but I'm not sure I could swing it for this; they're normally for witness protection. Is there anywhere your NHS trust has where you could house him temporarily?'

'Doubt it, we're bursting at the seams, and we couldn't put him back in hospital with his mental state being relatively stable at the moment.'

'Is there a relative he could stay with somewhere else in the country?'

'He's got an aunt down south somewhere – Brighton, I think. But the trouble with that is Will needs regular support from people who know him,' Berry said. 'Put him in a strange environment with different people, he could relapse without anyone knowing or noticing.'

'Could we try him at his dad's for a few days, until this blows over? Today's newspapers being tomorrow's chip paper and all that,' Doyle suggested.

Dianne shook her head. 'It doesn't work like that round here. People like to know what's going on, and a local story as big as this will have everyone talking.'

'Maybe when we find the culprit and charge them, that will take the heat off Will,' Doyle said.

'How close do you think you are to that happening?'

'I'm not sure,' Doyle admitted.

'A little birdie told me you'd been interviewing that Turkish fella,' Berry said.

'Where did you hear that? Not your hus—'

'No, not him. So, it's true then?' she smiled at Doyle.

'I can't say.'

'You don't have to; it's written all over your face. It's not just the police that can be good at reading people's reactions. You have to be in my job too.'

'Who did you hear it from?'

'A patient of mine heard it through someone else,' Berry said. 'I wouldn't mind you locking Turkish up. Nasty piece of work.'

Doyle studied Berry's face. 'You know him, then?'

'Not directly, no. But I know the effect he has on some of my patients. I can't prove it, of course, but I'm pretty sure he sells a lot of them their drugs. Knows when their benefits land in their bank account, and then they get a phone call from Turkish offering them whatever or getting them to pay back what they owe.'

'Did you not think of reporting this to us?' Doyle said. 'Even if you can't prove it, it's useful intel.'

'D'you think I was born yesterday?' Berry threw her hands in the air. 'Of course we've reported it. My boss went and had a conversation with one of the CID bosses. But that was eighteen months ago and nothing's changed.'

'Thanks for letting me know. I'll look into it.'

'You do that. His real name's Terry Handcock, right?' Berry said. 'One minute.' She turned back to her computer monitor and started tapping on the keyboard.

Doyle took out his notebook and made some notes. The possibility that Turkish was a dealer and this intel had already been passed on to the police made him even more suspicious about Terry Handcock's relationship with DCI Butcher.

'Now that is interesting,' Berry said, staring at the computer screen.

'What?' Doyle asked.

Berry went red and looked flustered. 'I'm not sure I should tell you. I shouldn't have done it.'

'What? What shouldn't you tell me?' Doyle asked.

'You've got to promise you found out somewhere else,' Berry said. 'You didn't hear it from me. I could get struck off for this, lose my pension.'

'OK, but I don't underst—'

'You asked me before whether Will could have had gonorrhoea, and whether he had been in a sexual relationship with Mia,' Berry said.

'Yes?'

'With my card and login, I can access anyone's medical records. This is the bit I will get in real trouble for, so please don't tell anyone. I just had a look on Terry Handcock's record.'

'He's not been treated for gonorrhoea, has he?'

'No, but he's unlikely to have gone to his GP if he's been carrying on behind his wife's back,' Berry said. 'He would have gone anonymously to the clap clinic.'

'OK, so what then?' Doyle was confused.

'Well, on his record his wife is listed as his next of kin. So I had a look at Tracy Handcock's records. She visited the GP recently to complain about pain down there and a burning sensation while passing urine. Thought it was cystitis,' Berry said. 'GP tested her and it came back positive for gonorrhoea. She was given a course of antibiotics.'

'When was this?' Doyle asked.

'She got the result last week, on Friday.'

'That's interesting.'

'But you can't use this information, not like that. Please promise me you won't,' Berry pleaded.

Doyle took a moment to think. 'OK. How long a course of antibiotics was she given?'

'A week's course of Azithromycin, so she will still be on them now.'

'Perfect. I think there's a way we can find that out for ourselves without bringing your name into it.'

There was a knock at the door. Dianne Berry quickly closed the window on her computer before shouting, 'Come in.'

Morgan entered.

'Did you get what you needed from the psychologist?' Doyle asked.

'I think so. I'll fill you in on the way back.'

'How come you managed to get a warrant today, but you couldn't get one yesterday?' Hales asked as Doyle pulled up alongside a semi-detached house in Blacko. The village was a mile to the north of Barrowford, and the distinctive flat-topped Pendle Hill could be seen peeking out between the houses to the east.

'A medical professional told us this morning that they suspect Turkish was dealing drugs to their patients. They've reported it before, but it wasn't followed up. That's given us enough grounds to take a look around,' Doyle said.

'You're not seriously expecting us to find anything, are you, boss?' Morgan asked from the back seat.

'Probably not, but it won't do any harm to take a look.'

'Do you think it would be worth going over the business premises at the same time?' Hales asked.

'I do, but we can't do it ourselves with the numbers we've got. Call me cynical, but the fact that Turkish seems to have had Pat Butcher from Pendle CID on speed dial makes me think that CID aren't the best people to help us with this search.'

Morgan tried to suppress a laugh. 'I think his team refer to him as Frank, but I like your name better.'

A wail of sirens sent a tribe of magpies into flight, and Doyle saw the flashing blue lights of an unmarked police car in his rear-view mirror. Gadget was behind the wheel, with Birdseye alongside him. Doyle caught a glimpse of orange overalls in the back seat.

'Jesus, did he really need to arrive like that?' Hales asked.

'I told him to,' Doyle said. 'Should get the curtain-twitchers going. Doesn't do any harm to advertise that there are other people the police are interested in. Might take the heat off Will Perkins a bit.'

'This is harassment,' Turkish shouted towards Doyle before he was even out of the back of Gadget's car. 'I know people – I'm going to make a complaint about you.'

'Is that right?' Doyle said, walking over to meet Turkish on the pavement. 'I take it DC Nelson showed you the warrant?'

'Yes, but—'

'But nothing. That warrant means we have the right to search your home. Now, are you going to give us the keys or do you want me to break the door down?'

'Fine.' Turkish dug a hand into his overalls and handed over his door keys.

Chapter 20

'Anna, we'll take the upstairs while the others do downstairs,' Doyle said. 'Mr Handcock, you can watch whatever part you like.'

'I'll stay here, thanks, but you won't find anything.' Turkish plonked himself down on a cream leather sofa. Morgan wondered if he would normally do that while wearing his grubby work overalls. From the outside, the house looked like a run-of-the-mill 1930s semi, but inside everything looked expensive and overstated, more in keeping with a hotel suite in Dubai than a house in an East Lancashire village.

'What are we looking for?' Morgan asked when they were upstairs and out of anyone else's earshot.

'Apart from all the obvious stuff, medication,' Doyle said. 'You start in the bedroom and I'll do the bathroom then join you.'

The whole of one wall was lined with built-in wardrobes. Inside, designer clothes hung neatly on hangers. There were shelves with Louis Vuitton and Gucci handbags. Morgan was no expert and had never seen the point of splashing out a week's wages on a bag, but these looked like the real deal to her. Either that or very good-quality fakes. She found a jewellery box in a drawer. The pieces inside were all in individual boxes. She opened one that bore the name of a jeweller in Hatton Garden. The stones on the necklace inside glistened when the light hit them. This wasn't anything like the stuff in Claire's Accessories.

'Bingo,' she heard Doyle call out from the bathroom.

'What you got?' Morgan asked, entering the room.

'This.' Doyle held up a box of medication. 'Take a picture of it. Make sure the label's clear.'

Morgan took out her phone and did as instructed, zooming in while Doyle held the box. The medication was called Zithromax, and the printed label stuck on by the pharmacist showed that it had been prescribed to Tracy Handcock on 27 October with the instructions to take one 500mg tablet daily with or just after food.

'I don't get it?' Morgan said, snapping off a pic.

'It's an antibiotic called Azithromycin. Zithromax is the brand name.'

'So?'

'Well, what do you take an antibiotic for?'

'Treating an infection.'

'Right, and I'm willing to bet that the type of infection this was prescribed to treat was a sexually transmitted one. More specifically, gonorrhoea, which she acquired from her loving husband.'

'You knew this was going to be here, didn't you? How?'

'A lucky guess,' Doyle said with a wink.

'Shall I bag it up and take it away as evidence?'

'Better not. There are still some tablets left,' Doyle said.

'Makes sense, we don't want to be responsible for her bits going manky. They might be the only parts of her that aren't made of plastic,' Morgan said. Her phone started to ring, then cut out. 'That was Shaima, but the signal's dropped out. I'll try to call her back from outside.'

'I'm going to head off now, if that's OK?' Hales said, entering Doyle's temporary office in Nelson police station.

'No problem, Geoff. You know I'm not in until about half nine tomorrow, but my phone's always on if you need anything.'

'We've got most of the CCTV from Barrowford and around. We'll focus on trying to piece together Mia's last movements. I'm sure that will tie everyone up for most of the morning.'

'While they are looking through the footage, get them to keep an eye out for Turkish and his wife. I wouldn't mind seeing where they went in the days before her murder.'

'Will do.'

'Oh, and do you know if Shaima's had any cell site info back for Mia's phone and all those linked to it? That should help narrow down where Mia and Turkish have been. And there's still one unknown pay-as-you-go number linked to hers. We need to work out who's been using it. That might be the missing piece of the jigsaw.'

'Bit early for the cell site stuff, but I'll get Shaima to chase it tomorrow.'

'Thanks.'

When Doyle was certain that DI Hales, the last of his team still working, had left, he pulled up a picture on his laptop and printed it out. He'd got the image from the Lancashire Constabulary's website. He walked over to the incident board and pinned the photo next to that of Will Perkins and Terry 'Turkish' Handcock, under the heading 'Suspects/Persons of Interest'.

'I wonder what you'll make of that, Pat?' he said to the image of DCI Butcher.

Chapter 21

Day 5: Thursday 2 November

Doyle paid a fleeting visit to the incident room at a quarter to seven that morning, when he was sure none of his team would be in. He noticed that the waste bin hadn't been emptied, so the cleaners hadn't been round either. He removed the picture of DCI Butcher from the incident board and had breakfast at a local café before heading to Preston, where he now sat in his car outside the railway station waiting for the train from London Euston to roll in. It was ten minutes late.

He had spent many an hour sitting around in cars in his earlier career. It had felt like half of his time in the Met's flying squad had been spent doing just that, but now he was older he found himself getting impatient waiting when he knew there were so many more useful things he could be getting on with. He'd checked his emails several times and responded to a few that needed dealing with, but now there was nothing more he could do but wait.

A flurry of passengers came out of the station's main entrance and hurried up the slip road, opening umbrellas as they went. Last out was who he had been waiting for. He got out of the car to greet her. She hadn't noticed him; she was more preoccupied with getting out of the rain to light a cigarette. He waved when she looked up, and she dragged her wheeled suitcase towards him.

'What time of day do you call that to get up? Quarter to bloody five the taxi picked me up. Still the middle of the night.'

'It's good to see you too, Mum.'

'Come here, give us a hug.'

As he bent down, Doyle got a waft of smoke and a faceful of wild grey hair, which was blowing in the wind. 'You could have come up last night, like I suggested.'

'I couldn't. I told you I had tickets for an Elton John tribute act in Lewisham. Eltham John, they call him. He was pretty good, an' all.'

'Well, that makes sense,' Doyle said, lifting her case into the boot of the car. 'Couldn't have you missing that, just to see your only son and grandson.'

'I'm here, aren't I? Speaking of which, where's Harry?' Janice Doyle squinted through the car windows.

'We've got to go and pick him up from his mum's.'

'Oh great, just what I wanted at this time of day, to see Fiona.'

'It's OK, you're staying in the car.'

'Charming. Well, come on then, let's get going,' she said, pulling on the handle of the front passenger door.

'Finish your fag first. It's a police vehicle; you can't smoke in there.'

Janice stuck her tongue out at her son by way of reply.

'And don't be slagging off Fiona in front of Harry, will you? She's still his mum.'

'I'm not daft. How's it all going – you know, with the autistic stuff? Is he settling in any better at school?'

'He's still struggling. Are you sure you're going to be alright with him for the next couple of days? He can be a bit challenging at times.'

'Don't worry about me. I'll be fine.'

'I wasn't worried about you. I was worried about him.'

'Thanks. I brought you up alright, didn't I?'

'Yes, but I'm not autistic.'

'No, but you were a little shit – and you still are.'

After picking up Harry and dropping his son and mum back at his house, it was half past nine by the time Doyle was back behind his desk. He had to switch his mind back into work mode. They needed to start making headway on the case. But it wasn't easy to park his concerns about his son. Harry got on well with his nan, but Doyle wasn't convinced that she understood his particular needs and sensitivities. Whenever he'd tried to explain, she always brushed it off or minimised the situation. Janice Doyle had never seen Harry in full meltdown mode, and Doyle didn't know how she would cope if she did. She would more than likely think he was just being naughty or attention-seeking, when in reality these episodes were a sign of the boy's distress. They could be triggered by the most innocuous of things; Doyle himself was still trying to learn how Harry experienced the world. He wondered if somewhere there was a parallel universe where ninety per cent of the population were neurodiverse and lived in a world designed for their needs, and everyone who was neurotypical struggled to live in it.

Doyle was brought back to planet Earth as three men appeared in his office. One was his boss, Detective Superintendent

Clifford Croucher, aka Mr Burns. The other man was DCI Alan 'Frank' Butcher, who Doyle had recently christened Pat. The man Doyle didn't recognise was in uniform. The crown and pips on his shoulder told Doyle he was a chief superintendent, and therefore the most senior man in the room.

Mr Burns dragged a fourth chair into the office from the incident room outside, closing the door behind him and no doubt leaving Doyle's team wondering what was happening.

'I'll come straight to the point, Liam,' Croucher said. 'Why have you made DCI Butcher, a serving officer in this force, a person of interest in your investigation? And more to the point, why is the first I hear about it when Chief Superintendent Lennox phones me this morning to ask me about it?'

'What?' Doyle hoped he sounded sufficiently surprised. 'What are you talking about? I haven't. Where are you getting that from?'

Croucher looked at Lennox, who in turn looked at Butcher, who fiddled with his shirt collar, as though it was a little too tight.

'My photo is up on the incident board with suspects and persons of interest,' Butcher said.

'No, it's not,' Doyle replied. 'Or if it is, that's the first I've heard about it. Why not go outside and take a look?'

The three other men did exactly that, while Doyle remained seated behind his desk. He now knew who his office snooper was – or at least, who they were working for. But the question still remained: what did Butcher want to find out? It must be to do with his relationship with Turkish. Whether that had anything to do with Mia's case remained to be seen. But whatever it was, something dodgy was going on, Doyle was sure of that.

'Well, there seems to have been a misunderstanding somewhere,' Lennox said, coming back into the office with Butcher and Mr Burns. 'I guess we'll leave you to it.'

'Hang on a minute,' Doyle said. 'I want to know why Butcher thinks we made him a suspect. That's not just a simple misunderstanding. He must have got the idea from somewhere.'

'Doyle's got a point,' Mr Burns said. 'I think we're owed an explanation. I've come over here from HQ this morning, that's an hour and a half round trip, and I've had to rearrange several meetings because of it.'

'Well?' Lennox said, standing and looking at Butcher, his jaw clenched.

'I ... er ... I thought I saw it on there. I must have been mistaken.'

'When did you think you saw it on there? When were you in the incident room?' Doyle asked.

'I stuck my head in on my way in this morning – just to say hello, you know.'

'And you thought you saw a picture of yourself on the incident board?' Doyle asked.

'Well, yes, but I must have been mistaken.'

'That sounds like paranoia to me,' Doyle said. 'Are you feeling alright? I thought you wanted paranoid loonies locked up. I think a referral to occupational health might be in order if you're that delusional, don't you?'

'That's enough, Doyle,' Mr Burns barked.

'Come on, we're going,' Chief Superintendent Lennox said. 'Sorry to have wasted your time, Clifford.'

When Lennox and Butcher had left the office, Mr Burns sat back down opposite Doyle. 'What's going on, Liam? I'm not buying that simple misunderstanding crap. If there's an issue between you and DCI Butcher, I need to know about it.'

'Have you found out any more about why there have been phone calls back and forth between Terry Handcock and Butcher?'

'Is that what this is about? I asked Gavin Lennox about that when he called me this morning. He told me that Butcher says he's a casual acquaintance of Handcock, nothing more than that.'

'And you believed him?' Doyle asked.

'I believed that Gavin was telling me what he had been told. Whether Butcher had told him the truth is another matter. Handcock certainly isn't a registered CHIS, but we both know that it's not unheard of for officers to have the odd off-the-record informant who gives them titbits of information here and there.'

'Do you think that's what this is? Do you think we should probe a little deeper?'

'No, I'm not sure that it has any relevance to your case. Unless I'm missing something. This Handcock was a casual associate of the victim, and Butcher was a casual acquaintance of his. That's not so unusual, especially in a place like this where everyone knows everyone. And is Handcock really a credible suspect?'

'I'm not sure how credible he is, but he lied about how well he knew the victim, which always makes me suspicious.'

'That makes a very tenuous link between Butcher and the victim. From our point of view, I'm not sure that it matters what Butcher's relationship with Handcock is – unless there's more to link Handcock to the murder.'

'Butcher didn't want to let the case go either. It was obviously our case – a brutal murder with mutilation. Yet he was slow to bring us in.'

'I'm not denying that, Liam, but see it from his point of view. He has a murder on his patch with an obvious suspect. If he could have got the evidence and wrapped it up quickly, it would have looked good for him and his department.'

'True, but despite the lack of evidence and us having been called in – by the SOCOs, not by the local CID, I might add – he was still intent on interviewing Will Perkins instead of us.'

'I know it's not the correct protocol, but he probably thought Perkins would confess in the interview and earn him some brownie points. I wouldn't read anything more into it than that. And how sure are you that this Will Perkins isn't the killer? He has a motive, albeit a deranged one.'

'We can't be sure either way. But there is a distinct lack of evidence pointing to him. No eyewitness seeing him or anyone fitting his description, no forensic evidence linking him to the crime scene or the victim's house.'

'I hope it does turn out to be somebody else, or this department is going to look pretty incompetent having released him when we could have kept him in for longer. And if it was him and he does something else, then we are both for the high jump.'

'With all due respect, sir,' Doyle said, though he felt the level of respect he owed his boss was minimal. 'I'm more concerned about Will Perkins' safety. We could have done without the *Lancashire Chronicle* naming him as a suspect. And how did they know that anyway? And that the victim had been mutilated? That won't have come from my team, but I wouldn't put it past others working in this nick.'

'They could have got it from anywhere. You know what Jayden Clark is like. A rat sniffing around in the gutter.'

Doyle did indeed know what the *Lancashire Chronicle*'s chief crime reporter was like, having been the subject of his headlines in a previous murder investigation. He pondered something. Doyle did not see eye to eye with Mr Burns on most things. The man's pernickety nature irritated him, and since Burns was a stickler for the rules, Doyle was certain that Burns wouldn't approve of Doyle's tactics, but if things changed, it would be much better for Doyle to tell him now.

Fuck it. 'There's something I need to tell you, and I'm pretty sure you're not going to like it.'

'Go on.'

'Well, on Tuesday night I was working here quite late. I was the last to leave the incident room. I locked up and turned the lights off, but before going home I walked up the road to the supermarket. When I came back to the car park, I noticed the incident room lights were on. I figured it must be the cleaners, so I didn't think too much of it. Then when I got in yesterday morning, my desk drawer was unlocked. I know I locked it – I always do. It's a habit I've always had.'

'Now you're sounding paranoid. Either you didn't lock it or the lock's not working right; they're not exactly highly secure.'

'Well, I was sure I had, and that someone had been in there. So last night I pinned this picture up on the incident board.' Doyle took the picture of DCI Butcher out of his desk drawer and put it down between them.

'Bloody hell, so Butcher wasn't lying. He did see it there.'

Doyle could sense his boss's anger, and wondered how long it would be until the vein on his head started pulsing. 'But the thing is, I came in early this morning, before anyone else was here, and took the picture down. No one could have seen it unless they had been sneaking around in here after the incident room was locked up.'

'Just to be clear, Doyle, are you suggesting that DCI Butcher has been snooping around the incident room and your investigation?'

'Yes. Him, or someone on his behalf. Now, when you put it all together, Butcher having multiple phone calls to a suspect, wanting to keep control of the investigation, bringing in a different suspect without any evidence, and details of that suspect being released to the press, I would say there's enough to question Butcher's integrity, wouldn't you?'

Croucher took a moment before responding. 'I don't like your methods. Some might say that's entrapment. You should have flagged this up to me, not gone and set a trap.'

'And what would you have done if I did?'

'Well, it would have been investigated.'

'And where would that have got us? It's not as if Butcher was an intruder in the building; there's no CCTV in the corridor that would have picked him up going in and out. The question is, now you know, what are you going to do about it?'

'I don't know. I need to give it some thought. But if there are any developments, I want you to let me know straight away.'

'OK.'

'And Liam, no more games.'

Less than a minute after Mr Burns had left Doyle's office, Morgan and the Pearl came in.

'Well?' Morgan asked, shutting the door behind her.

'Well, what?' Doyle knew what she was getting at.

'Well, we assume that royal visit wasn't for a cosy chat,' Hales said. 'What's going on, and is there an explanation for all those calls between Butcher and Turkish?'

'Not one that I'm satisfied with,' Doyle said, wondering how much he should share with his detective inspector and sergeant. 'Turkish isn't a registered informant, and I'm still suspicious about their relationship, but there's not much I can do about that now unless anything else comes up. Has anything useful come in this morning?'

Hales shrugged. 'I'm not sure how useful this is, but we've got some cell site data for Mia's phone and the ones linked to it. Mia was out and about in Barrowford Friday evening, but obviously, we can't say exactly where. The data is approximate at the moment, but with a bit of time the techs might be able to narrow it down further. But on Saturday she mostly stayed at home – at least, her phone did, apart from one brief trip to the shops just before midday.'

'That will help a bit. We can search through the CCTV from that time and see if we can find out what she was up to,' Doyle said.

'Shaima and Gadget are on that now,' Hales said.

'Good. And what about the phones linked to hers?'

'The burner that we caught Turkish with is on and off a lot. Seems like he only turns it on to make calls or when he's expecting a call,' Hales said.

'He's definitely dodgy,' Morgan said.

'Couldn't agree more,' Doyle said. 'And what about the phone we don't have an owner for? The one Shaima has listed as Burner One?'

'This is a little more interesting. That is also on and off a lot. The main locations it's switched on are in the vicinity of the workshop Turkish and his wife work at, and in Barrowford, and here in Nelson.'

'Do you think Turkish might have a second burner?' Doyle asked.

'That was my first thought,' Hales said. 'But there are times when both phones are on but in different locations. In fact, on the Friday before Mia was killed, the one belonging to Turkish called her from the north end of Barrowford, then Burner One called her less than five minutes later from Nelson. Can't be the same person making those calls in that time frame.'

'It could be Mrs Turkish,' Morgan suggested.

'Seems unlikely, if Turkish was involved with Mia,' Hales said.

'Maybe, unless she had just found out about that,' Morgan said. 'It was Friday when she got the antibiotics prescribed, and if they're for what we think they're for, if she wasn't having a bit on the side then she would know that Turkish was.'

'The thing is, Anna, there were calls to Mia from that number for a few weeks before that. Some of them were quite long. And Mia had called that number herself and sent lots of texts, though without either phone we can't see what they said,' Hales said.

'It could've been someone else involved with the drug supply,' Doyle said. 'With the intel from the mental health team and their lavish lifestyle, there's plenty to suggest that Mr and Mrs Turkish were doing a lot more than fixing farm machinery. The business belongs to her brother. They could have been using it as a front. He could be involved too. Burner One might be his phone'

'That would make sense,' Hales said. 'I'll get Shaima to dig up as much as she can on their backgrounds.'

'Good. Will's psychiatric nurse told me that Turkish is well known for dealing in the area.'

'How much do you trust her, boss?' Morgan asked.

'I didn't get the impression she was lying to me,' Doyle said. He wondered why Morgan was asking.

'I didn't mean that,' Morgan said. 'It's just that when I met Mia's psychologist, she let slip that Dianne Berry has a reputation for over-advocating for her patients. Dr Sutton didn't think it was impossible that Will Perkins could have killed Mia.'

'That's interesting,' Doyle said. 'But I still think we would have found something linking Will if it was him. But I take your point about Dianne Berry – she's not shy in coming forward, that's for sure. She's married to a former police officer too.'

'That shows a lack of judgement,' Morgan said.

'Not the inspector who worked in Traffic?' Hales asked. 'Mick Berry – Fruity, they used to call him.'

'I just don't think we should rule Perkins out completely at this stage,' Morgan said.

'Point taken,' Doyle said. If it did turn out to be Will Perkins who had killed Mia, he was at best going to look careless for releasing him, and at worst negligent. But Morgan was right: he needed to keep an open mind and not let the implications for his own reputation cloud his judgement. 'We need to keep all lines of investigation open. It might be that Turkish and his wife and brother-in-law are up to their necks in dealing, but that doesn't necessarily mean that they have anything to do with Mia's murder. But we do need to find out who Burner One belongs to. Keep getting updates on where it is when it's switched on.'

'That's another thing,' Hales said. 'That phone's not been back on since early Sunday morning – around the time Mia was killed.'

Chapter 22

Morgan sat at her laptop in the incident room. It bugged her that, five days into the investigation, she still felt like she didn't know much about Mia or her life. It seemed that lots of people knew her or knew of her, but she hadn't come across anyone who had said they were close to her. There had obviously been at least one person who was physically close to her, and if the BFG was right about what Tracy Handcock's antibiotics had been prescribed for, then it was likely that that person was Terry Handcock. Turkish.

That bothered Morgan too – not the infidelity, but the coldness with which Turkish had sat in the interview room answering 'no comment' to every question about the murder of someone that he obviously knew well, and quite possibly well enough to have made pregnant. Going 'no comment' might make sense if he had killed her. It was a common tactic for perpetrators of all crimes: why say anything and risk being caught in a lie when you could remain silent and leave the police to try and prove your involvement by other means? But if Turkish was responsible for Mia's death, why would he have kept the burner phone he had used to call her? Surely that would be one of the first things he'd get rid of, as it was evidence of a direct link between him and the victim. And then there was Burner One, that hadn't been switched back on since Mia was killed. The calls between that and Mia's phone were less frequent than the calls to and from Turkish's burner, but they were longer, some of them over half an hour. They weren't quick calls to arrange to meet. They were conversations, that suggested a level of closeness between the caller and Mia, but who was the caller? Tracy Handcock's brother, or someone else?

Gadget and Birdseye had done a sterling job of rounding up every bit of CCTV in Barrowford, and Shaima Asif had compiled all the bits that captured Mia in one folder in time and date order. The trouble was that pretty much all of this footage was along the main road that ran through the village and by the shops and businesses surrounding it. This meant that all Morgan could learn about Mia was what she did in this area. She didn't go in pubs. Morgan wondered if that was because she wasn't welcome in any of them, or that she preferred to drink outside because it was cheaper. What Morgan had picked up was that Mia hardly ever went anywhere without her dog and, on most occasions, she either had a can of cheap cider in her hand or was smoking a cigarette or joint.

Mia Wright had been in and around the shops in Barrowford for a good proportion of most days. But on the Saturday, Mia's last full day alive, she had only been once, briefly, to the shop, and according to mobile phone data had most likely remained at home for the rest of the day. Morgan wondered what might have caused this change in behaviour. Mia was notorious for begging, and surely a Saturday would be the best opportunity to make a few quid? She wondered if Mia had been scared of someone, and was keeping a low profile. Perhaps she had already been threatened by whoever had killed her, or she was expecting some kind of retribution for something she had done. She opened the file with the footage of Mia from that day. Because Mia had only been out once, there wasn't much on it. Morgan had gone through it before, but that time she had focused on seeing if Mia had interacted with anyone on camera. She hadn't. Looking at the film again, Morgan realised something was missing – her dog. She didn't have it with her on any of the footage that picked her up going towards the shops, or on any of the subsequent footage. Morgan couldn't believe she had only just noticed this, and she wondered what it meant. It pretty much destroyed her theory that Mia was scared of someone – surely, if she was afraid for her safety, she would have kept her giant hound close to her. But maybe not. It was broad daylight in a busy place, and even if she had upset the wrong person or people, she'd have thought she was at low risk with so many people around. Maybe she had left the dog at home to protect her flat? What Mia had bought from the shops on that trip was quite unusual for her too. She had purchased cleaning products and a small amount of food. Significantly, she hadn't bought any alcohol or tobacco. She also wasn't smoking or drinking in any of the footage from that day. Mia had bought the pregnancy test the previous Wednesday. They had confirmed that from a receipt found in her flat. That tallied with her leaving the happy message on Dr Sutton's answerphone. But then in the message she left on Friday, she sounded desperate, as if she had been upset by something. Dr Sutton had told Morgan that Mia's moods fluctuated. No doubt, finding out she was pregnant would have been a lot for Mia to take in, and she may have felt conflicted. Morgan wondered if the message she left on Friday – that everything had gone to shit – wasn't about Mia feeling that she was in danger, but was more to do with the father of her child not wanting to support her. When Morgan had been to Mia's flat, it looked like she had been in the middle of giving it a thorough clean. The fact that Mia hadn't been drinking or smoking on the Saturday made Morgan think that she hadn't been scared for their safety, but she had decided to keep the baby and was trying to do her best for her unborn child.

'How are you, Liam?' Dr Wade asked as Doyle settled himself in the comfy chair opposite her.

'I'm OK, thanks. How are you?'

'Glad to hear it. I'm fine, thank you. This is the penultimate session we have scheduled, and I wanted to ask you how you want to make best use of it.'

Doyle took a drink of water and used the time to think. He had been coming to fortnightly psychology sessions with Dr Wade – a condition of employment laid down by occupational health when he transferred from the Met to the Lancashire Constabulary. To say he hadn't been keen to have the sessions at first would be an understatement. Doyle had seen it as an unnecessary burden when he was already trying to juggle work, parenting and everything else. There were never enough hours in the day. It wasn't just the time that Doyle had objected to; he hadn't wanted to discuss his fatal shooting of a man in London. That had undoubtedly taken a toll on him, his career and his marriage, but Doyle's solution to getting over it was to let it fade into the past, let it become a memory. Wounds healed best when they were left alone, he thought, not when you kept picking off the protective scabs.

If he was honest with himself, though, the sessions with Dr Wade had proved to be useful – far more useful than he was prepared to admit to her, or to the force HR department, in case they insisted on him having more. The week that Doyle had first met Jackie Wade, his first week in the force, he had just been in time to save Anna Morgan from becoming the victim of a sadistic killer. As a result, many of his bi-weekly sessions with the psychologist had been devoted to talking about that and helping him to process that event. He had spent little time talking about the events in London, which suited him just fine.

Doyle never knew what he wanted to talk about. Jackie always ended a session by saying 'Have a think about what you would like to focus on next time', but he never gave it a moment's thought until the reminder went off on his phone, telling him his appointment was due. Then something occurred to Doyle, something that had been bothering him since his conversation with Morgan and Hales earlier that morning. The clinicians involved with Mia Wright and Will Perkins disagreed about whether the latter could be responsible for Mia's murder. When Doyle first met Wade, she had told him that she used to work as a psychologist at Ashworth High Security Hospital.

'There is something that I would value your opinion on, but strictly speaking, it doesn't relate to me.'

'Go on.'

'It's about a case I'm working on. A brutal murder with post-mortem mutilation. We have a possible suspect: a man with paranoid schizophrenia. But we don't have any evidence linking him directly to the killing, and there are conflicting opinions about whether he could have done it.'

'You know I'm not employed by Lancashire Constabulary as a forensic psychologist working on cases. My role here is as a clinical psychologist, purely to support officers who are referred to me.'

'I know that, but you're a forensic psychologist as well and you're sitting right in front of me when I have this problem, and I think you could help.' Doyle smiled, hoping it might help convince Dr Wade.

'OK, Liam, I will help if I can. But in return, I want something back from you. Quid pro quo, if you like.'

'That makes you sound like Hanibal Lecter.'

'He was a psychiatrist; I'm a psychologist.'

'And that's the main difference between the two of you that you want to point out?'

Wade laughed. 'Well, I'm real, not fictitious, and I can honestly say I've never contemplated eating any of my patients.'

'What do I need to give you in return for your help?'

'At our next session, our final one, I want you to tell me what you have been keeping back about the incident in London. I know there is something, and I want you to share it.'

'Deal.' Doyle was committed now. He would either need to come up with a convincing lie or tell her the truth. But that problem was two weeks away.

Dr Wade listened intently as Doyle outlined the details of the case he was working on and all the information he could recall about Will Perkins. She scribbled a few notes on her pad as he spoke. He wasn't worried about confidentiality; she would know that what he told her couldn't leave the room.

'You said Will had his first psychotic episode when he was at university. Do you know much about his childhood? Was he was exposed to any violence or abuse then?'

'As far as I know, it was relatively stable. He was brought up by both parents until his mother died not long before he became unwell. I can look into it further. Do you think it might be significant?'

'When people become psychotic, it means they have lost touch with reality to some degree. They experience a range of symptoms, which can include delusional thoughts and often auditory hallucinations. In Will's case, that's what the voices he hears are. But these symptoms don't come from nowhere; they are created by the person's own brain. What a person is exposed to will influence the symptoms they experience when they are psychotic. You could think of it as a bit like living in a dream. The thoughts are yours, but they are disordered.'

'I can see that,' Doyle said.

'Take yourself, for instance. You told me that you experienced waking flashbacks after you shot Jamal Campbell, and you still have dreams about it now.'

'But I'm not psychotic.' Doyle didn't intend to sound so defensive.

'No, because you recognise those experiences for what they are: your brain replaying traumatic events. You told me that this Will chap was writing a dissertation on the Lancashire witch trials when he became unwell. Something he had been fascinated by and had studied for a long time. It therefore isn't that surprising that a lot of his symptoms are focused around that.'

'That makes sense.'

'But if he hasn't been exposed to violence in the past, it's far less likely that he would become violent when psychotic.'

'When he was experiencing a psychotic episode, would he be like it the whole time, or would it be something he could switch in and out of?'

'There would be times when he'd experience more or less symptoms, and times when it might be more or less obvious, but we're not talking Jekyll and Hyde here. It's not like he could switch between the two states.'

'Do you think it is possible that he could have killed someone in a psychotic state one night and present relatively normally in a police interview the next day?'

'Assuming you spent a fair while interviewing him and he gave full responses to questions, I think it is very unlikely that he would be able to mask the symptoms of psychosis or that they would have vanished if they had been there the night before.'

'Is there no way he could fake it?'

'I've come across people being guarded and trying to hide their symptoms before, but if you talk to them for long enough, they come out. I've also come across people trying to fake being psychotic in order to serve sentences in hospital rather than prison. But that certainly isn't the case here – without Will's psychosis, there doesn't appear to be any motivation for him to have killed this poor young woman.'

Chapter 23

Will had only wanted to get some fresh air. Get out, walk on the moors and get himself together. He'd been like a prisoner cooped up in his dad's house. It was bigger than his own but still, he'd felt trapped. He'd enjoyed walking in the fields with only the sheep for company, then Chattox had started up, telling him that Mia had gone over to the other side and was with her. Then Old Demdike had waded in, telling Will they would be coming for him next. She'd reminded him that he knew a secret about Mia: he knew about her baby. The magistrate hadn't asked him about that. It was all too much. His peaceful walk had been spoilt by these old witches getting into his head. He'd gone back to his dad's house, but when he was back in Barrowford some youths on bikes had spotted him. They'd started shouting at him, calling him a murderer, and he'd run. He'd run as fast as he could, and he was fast; he'd been a fell runner for years. But they were on bikes. He couldn't shake them off. They'd thrown stuff at him. Something hard had hit him on the back, but he'd got inside and locked the door. Put the chain on. He was hot, the house felt hot. He needed to think. Where could he go to be safe?

Sweat ran down his back, his T-shirt clinging to his skin. He pulled it off over his head and wiped his forehead on it. There was a ringing. Not a bell, and there wasn't someone knocking at the door. The phone.

'Don't answer it,' Chattox shouted. 'It will be them. They're coming for you.'

'Shut up, Chattox. You're not even real.'

Chapter 24

'Daddy!' Harry rushed out of the front door as soon as Doyle pulled up outside his two-bed terraced cottage. By the time he'd reached the pavement, Harry was hugging him tightly. Harry had very little filter on his emotions, which could be difficult when he was distressed or angry, but then there were times like these. when just coming home from work could make his son ecstatically happy.

'Is everything OK? Where's your nan?'

'We've been to see the canal boats and then looked at the horses.'

'Really? Where did you go?' Doyle wondered where his mum would have taken Harry without a car. He'd left money on the table, and cab numbers and the details of some places Harry liked to go to, including the marina in Adlington. But none of them were near any stables.

'The horses were on the telly.'

'Mum?' Doyle called out, entering the house. There was no reply. 'What have you done with her, Harry?' He was only half joking. He walked through the small lounge to the kitchen at the back.

'Nothing, I think she must be in the garden. She likes it out there, even when it's raining.'

I bet she does, Doyle thought, and he knew exactly why.

'Oh, hello love. Had a good day at work?' his mum said, coming through the back door.

'Everything alright?' Doyle asked. 'You two been OK together?' He was quite surprised by how relaxed his mum looked.

'Yeah, course we have, why wouldn't we be? We've had a good day together, ain't we, Harry? Been up to see those narrowboats he likes, and then back here to watch a bit of TV.

'Nan said she is going to give me five pounds out of her winnings,' Harry said.

'Oi, I told you to keep quiet about that. Otherwise your dad will want some.'

'You've been teaching him how to gamble? He's only nine.'

'Leave off, will you? It's only a bit of fun and he's enjoyed it. Besides, it's educational, teaching him all about numbers and that. You should get a dartboard put up in here – that will help him with his taking away.'

'This is a rented house, Mum. I'm not sure the landlord would be too happy with all the pin holes that would end up around the board.' The idea of Harry and his mum being let loose to throw darts around the house was terrifying to Doyle.

Doyle's phone rang. When he saw it was Fiona, he gave it straight to Harry, figuring it would be him she would want to speak to.

'Not been any issues?' Doyle asked his mum in a low voice after Harry had flopped down on the sofa in the lounge, out of earshot.

'No, course not. Like I said, he's been fine. He don't like that school, though. He's been telling me about some boy called Callum. Sounds like a right little bastard. Been pushing him around and calling him all sorts.'

'I know it's hard for him. He's still not settled in,' Doyle said.

'That bloody Fiona should have thought about that before dragging him up here. He ain't got any mates. When you were that age, you were off out with your mates all day. God knows what you were getting up to.'

'Different times and a different child. It's not like Harry had any real friends back in London.'

'He liked the racing, though,' Janice Doyle said. 'Maybe he could end up a gambling genius like that Dustin Hoffman in *Rain Dance*.'

Doyle sighed and looked at his mum. 'It's *Rain Man*, and it's good to see you've not bought into the stereotypes about autism. Harry's nothing like that.'

'Yeah, and you don't look nothing like Tom Cruise either.'

'Tom Cruise played his brother, not his dad... Why are we even having this discussion?'

'I was just trying to be positive...'

'Dad,' Harry called out from the front room. 'Mum wants to talk to you.'

Janice Doyle rolled her eyes as Harry passed the phone back to his dad.

'Hi Liam,' there was a sharp tone to Fiona's voice. 'I just wanted to check with you about next week. You're still OK to meet at the school on Monday afternoon, aren't you?'

'Four o'clock, isn't it?' Doyle checked.

'Good, you haven't forgotten.'

'You don't think they might be able to make it a bit later, do you?' Doyle asked.

'No, Liam, I don't. And there's no way of contacting them before then anyway. This is important – you need to be there.'

Doyle took a deep breath. 'And I will be. It's just later would've been better.'

'Have you seen the state of his legs?' Fiona's question sounded like an accusation to Doyle.

'Yes, I saw them at the weekend.'

'That bloody Callum sent him flying – it was deliberate too.'

'I know,' Doyle said. 'He told me.'

'We're going to have to have a talk soon. Work out what's best for him. It's a struggle getting him to go in at all, you know what he's like when he doesn't want to do something. And I can't blame him; he's having a miserable time,' Fiona now sounded like she might be on the brink of tears. 'How's he been getting on with your mum?'

'OK so far. They've—'

'She's not been smoking around him, and swearing, has she?'

'No, they've—'

'Good. Don't forget Monday, will you? And don't be late.'

'I won't,' Doyle said.

'See you then.'

'Bye.' Doyle went to kill the call and saw that his ex-wife had already ended it.

Chapter 25

Day 6: Friday 3 November

'What was so urgent you had to call me out here in the middle of the night?' Turkish shouted at him.

'We need to talk.' He looked at his watch. 'It's not the middle of the night. It's only half past twelve.'

'I could've been in bed,' Turkish said.

'You weren't, though, were you? If you'd both been asleep, she wouldn't have dropped you off.' *What a fuck-up. She'd seen him.* He opened the heavy barn doors. 'Let's talk in here, out of the rain.'

Turkish followed him inside.

Only the emergency lighting was on, leaving most of the workshop in shadow. Turkish went to the electrical intake, turned off the alarm. He went to turn the main power on.

'Leave that. We can talk in the dark.'

'What do you want to talk about anyway?' Turkish sounded quieter, not so sure of himself.

'I think you know what.' He took a step towards Turkish.

'Do I?' Turkish asked, stepping back into the workshop.

'Mia Wright.'

'Wh-what about her?' Turkish stammered.

'You know what about her. You were ... *with her*.' He spat the last two words out. Even now it was hard to say, hard to think about, what Mia and Turkish had done.

'Oh yeah? Who told you that?'

It was true. If it wasn't, Turkish would have denied it. 'She did, last Saturday.'

'You don't want to believe what Mia says. She was a shit-stirrer – even you can see that.' Turkish backed away further as he spoke.

His hand tightened around the handle of the hammer he had concealed inside his jacket pocket. 'She was pregnant. Did you know that?'

'Was she?' Turkish said. 'Nothing to do with me.'

'Are you sure about that?' The other man struggled to keep his voice calm.

'From what I hear, it could be anyone's, most likely yours.' Turkish's voice trembled.

'The police will find out. They can do tests, DNA and that, work out who the father is.'

'Whether it's mine or yours, they won't find out. I took care of that.'

'What? Wait, how did you—' Turkish's eye's widened. 'It was you. You did it.' Turkish looked like he wanted to run, but there was nowhere to go. He backed up further; he was near the top of the ramp that led down to the pit.

'It was your fault,' the man shouted. 'You. You fucked everything up for me and her.'

'No, it wasn't. I didn't... I couldn't.' Turkish's eyes were darting around, looking for an escape. He made his move then slipped, falling to the ground.

The man was on him in a flash, landing blows and kicks all over Turkish's face and body. Turkish tried to get up, scrambling on his hands and knees, trying to crawl away, but there was no escape.

The man pulled the hammer out of his jacket pocket.

'We won't be questioning him again, then,' Doyle said, staring down at the body in the inspection pit.

'I think we can rule out accidental death,' said Morgan, who was dressed the same as Doyle, in white forensic overalls complete with gloves and overshoes.

'Agreed. I've never met anyone who smashed their own teeth out. Especially when they'd paid so much for them.'

'You think we'll be able to charge the killer with criminal damage as well as murder, boss?'

'You're becoming as inappropriate as me.' Doyle squatted down to get a better look. Turkish was lying on his back in the oil-soaked workshop pit, a good five feet away. His face was a mess. Whoever had knocked out his dental implants hadn't been too careful about it. His lower jaw was at an odd angle and inside his half-open mouth was a dark, bloody mess.

'I'm guessing it wasn't the facial injuries that killed him,' Morgan said, crouching down alongside Doyle.

'I wouldn't have thought so.' It was difficult to determine how much blood loss there had been, as the base of the pit was covered in a greasy, oily sludge. Only the blood on Turkish's face and the front of his overalls could be seen.

'Do you want to take a closer look?' Morgan asked, nodding towards the ramp that led down into the pit.

'I'm not sure we'll learn anything new without moving him. Best to let Dr Gupta and Jen's team get in there first, see what they can find.'

Chapter 26

'It was you who found the body, Mr Nuttall, is that correct?' Doyle asked after he had sat down opposite the other man in the office. Morgan had noticed that about the BFG: he was always quick to take a seat or lean against something before asking any questions of a witness. It wasn't that he was being impolite; far from it. When he wanted to get information, Doyle made an effort to try to make himself seem less intimidating. Not that Morgan thought the man sitting opposite them would be intimidated by Doyle. She hadn't seen him standing, but guessed the business owner would be a similar height to her boss. With his big bushy beard, he reminded her of a Viking.

'Yes, I've just told your mate all this, the bald fella with the white beard.' Neil Nuttall's accent was local. If he was shocked to find his brother-in-law and employee dead on his business premises, he wasn't showing it.

'What time was this?' Doyle asked.

'I got here around seven thirty as normal. Opened up office and stuck kettle on. Then I went and opened both the workshops and switched the power on. I guess it were about ten minutes later that I saw him.'

'What do you do when you open up the workshops?'

'Like I said, I just open them up. Turn the power on for the machinery and lights and turn the alarm off.'

'You don't do a walk round, a visual check, make sure everything is alright?' Doyle asked.

'No. Why would I?'

'How tall are you, Mr Nuttall?'

'What?' Nuttall replied, clearly wrong-footed by the question. Morgan didn't know where Doyle was going with this, but he must have some reason for asking.

'I'm six foot six, and when I was in the workshop just now, standing in the entrance next to the alarm panel, I couldn't see into the bottom of the inspection pit. So, I'm wondering how you came to see the body lying there if you didn't look round the workshop?'

Morgan saw Nuttall's face tighten and a couple of frown lines appear on his forehead. 'I must've gone up to the other end to open the fire exit. We bolt it from the inside before we lock up. I must've seen him lying there then.' If he was rattled, Morgan couldn't hear it in his voice.

'And what did you do when you saw him...'

The portacabin door was flung open and Mrs Handcock entered the office, followed swiftly by Birdseye, who gave his colleagues an apologetic shrug.

'He's dead, then?' She seemed to be addressing the question to her brother rather than to Morgan or Doyle.

'Mrs Handcock, how did you find—' Doyle began.

'I called her, right after I called you,' Nuttall said. 'She's my sister. I had to let her know.'

'Please take a seat,' Doyle said. 'I'm very sorry for your —'

'I don't need to sit down.' Tracy Handcock turned to Doyle. 'You should be out catching who did this to him.'

'And we intend to do just that,' Doyle said. 'But for that to happen, we need to get some details from you and your brother. Please sit down.'

'It was that madman. I saw him when I dropped Terry off here last night.'

'What madman? Who did you see?'

'That one you let go. Will Perkins. I saw him – he was just up the road.'

Oh, shit. This was going to blow up in their faces if they had released Will from custody for one murder and he had gone and killed someone else. There was going to be serious fallout, and Morgan couldn't see how her boss could escape carrying the can.

'Are you certain that's who you saw? Will Perkins?' Doyle asked.

'Yes, one hundred per cent. He was here last night. I knew him anyway, but his face has been all over the papers in the last few days, and on social media.'

'Why were you dropping your husband off last night?' Morgan asked.

'He got a call, quite late, said he had to go in to work. An urgent job.'

'Could he have driven himself?' Morgan asked.

'He'd had a couple of drinks. Wasn't pissed, like, but would have been over the limit, so I said I'd take him.'

'What was the job?' Doyle asked, turning back to Nuttall. 'And why was it so urgent?'

'Nowt to do with me,' Nuttall replied.

'Sorry, what?' Morgan said. 'This is your business, isn't it?'

'It is, but that's just for farm machinery. Terry's a mechanic. I let him use the workshop for a few of his private jobs. Fixing people's cars, that sort of thing, providing it doesn't get in the way and he does it on his own time.'

'What time did he get this call?' Doyle asked, turning back to Tracy Handcock.

'It were quite late; I was in bed. Maybe twelve, something like that.'

'And who was the call from?' Doyle pressed.

'I don't know. He were downstairs. I didn't hear it.'

'And he didn't say anything when you drove him in? You've no idea why it was so urgent? And was it normal for him to work on a car after he had had a few drinks?' Doyle asked.

'If he'd got a call from someone who'd broken down, then he might have suggested the breakdown service drop the car off here to save towing it over later. In which case, he would have had to come out to open the gates to get the car in. He wouldn't have worked on it last night.' Nuttall's suggestion seemed plausible to Morgan, but she couldn't help feeling that he had jumped in with an explanation when his sister didn't have one.

'You're wasting time here.' Mrs Handcock's voice was raised. 'I told you who I saw. You should go and arrest him.'

'And that's exactly what we are going to do,' Doyle said. 'Detective Constable Nelson here will stay with you until we have a family liaison officer to support you. And we will need to take formal statements from both of you later on.'

Chapter 27

Doyle sat in the front passenger seat as Morgan flung the Peugeot hatchback around the country lanes at breathtaking speed. His left hand gripped the handle above the door and his right hand clutched his phone to his ear. He used his legs to brace himself as the car rapidly decelerated before powering round a corner.

'Geoff,' he said in a raised voice that he hoped would be audible above the sirens. 'Looks like it's Will Perkins. The wife's positively ID'd him. We're on our way to his dad's house now.' Doyle thought he heard Hales ask if they needed backup, but he wasn't sure over the noise. 'Gadget's on the radio now, sorting that out.' He turned to Gadget in the back, who gave him a thumbs up. 'I'll call you back with an update – hopefully when we've arrested him.'

This was an unmitigated fucking disaster. What made it worse was that it was entirely his fault. Even though they hadn't had any evidence to charge Will Perkins, he could have got a further custody extension. Kept him locked up while they looked harder to find evidence. If he'd done that, Terry Handcock might still be alive. He'd let himself be swayed by Dianne Berry's opinion that Perkins wasn't capable of murder. It wasn't her fault: she'd worked with Perkins for years, it was natural that she would be too close to him to be objective. But he was the senior detective. At the very least, he should have got an independent psychiatric assessment. But things still didn't all fit for Doyle. He had been sure that if Perkins had been guilty, they would have found some evidence somewhere. But could that be his own stubbornness, not wanting to accept he was wrong? Perhaps he was looking for reasons that it wasn't Perkins after the local CID had been so quick to make the arrest. In most investigations, the simplest theory was usually the right one. Occam's razor, it was straight out of the SIO's handbook. Perkins had been sectioned after having delusions about Mia Wright being a witch and saying she should be killed. Now an eyewitness had placed him at the scene of a second murder – was there really a more plausible explanation? Bad as this was, and it was very bad indeed, somehow he had to shake off those thoughts and concentrate on one thing: arresting Will Perkins before anyone else got hurt or ended up dead.

'Clear left,' Doyle said as they approached a junction, and Morgan turned right without stopping. She killed the sirens, and Doyle realised they were getting close to Will's father's house, where he had been staying since his own place had been vandalised.

'How long till backup gets here?' Doyle turned to Gadget.

'There's a patrol car coming from Nelson. But the nearest Operational Support Unit is the other side of Burnley dealing with an incident. Not sure how long they'll be.'

'Shit, pull in here,' Doyle said.

'Are we going to wait for the OSU then, boss?' Gadget asked.

'We should do,' Morgan said.

'Get back on the radio, tell the patrol car to meet us here,' Doyle said. 'We can't wait too long. We need to bring him in, and if he's not there then we need people out looking for him.

God knows what he could get up to if we don't pick him up soon.'

Morgan went to the boot of the Peugeot and pulled out stab vests for her and her colleagues. 'If we aren't going to wait for the cavalry, we should at least put these on.'

Doyle thought he could detect a note of reticence in her voice. The last physical altercation Morgan had got into at work had nearly cost her her life. He shouldn't be putting her through this, but what choice did he have? Perkins had to be detained, and soon. Doyle wriggled into the protective vest, grateful that he had put his kit bag in Morgan's car earlier, so he didn't have to squeeze himself into a vest smaller than his own XXXL or go without.

'They said they'll put a call out for available units to come to assist, but they can't promise anything soon,' Gadget said.

A marked patrol car pulled up and PC Anderton and PCSO Lofthouse got out. 'Is it true that Will Perkins killed Turkish?' Anderton asked.

'An eyewitness put him at the scene just before it happened,' Doyle said. 'We can't wait for backup, I'm afraid. When we get there, Paige, you follow me into the house through the front. Gadget, you and Nat go straight round the back in case he does a runner that way. Anna, you wait outside, ready to either follow us in or dart around the back as needed.' Doyle had expected a protest from Morgan at not going in first with him, but she just nodded at his instruction.

'Right, let's go.' Doyle leapt out of the front passenger seat the second Morgan brought the car to a standstill. He flicked out the extendable baton as he ran up the front drive. The DCI decided not to ring the bell and instead used one of his size twelve boots, with a lot of weight behind it, to gain entry through the front door.

'Will, are you in here?' Anderton shouted from behind.

In the hallway, an old phone lay smashed on the floor, its cable ripped out of the wall socket. Has there been some kind of struggle in here? Doyle wondered, checking the front room.

'Will, it's the police. It's PC Paige. If you're upstairs, you need to make your way down slowly, with your hands where we can see them.'

The front room was clear, as was the kitchen. If Will was in the house, he must be upstairs.

'Any sign of movement up there?' asked Doyle, coming back into the hall.

'Nothing,' Anderton replied.

'We better take a look, then.'

'Want me to go first, guv?' Anderton asked.

Considering the circumstances, it was a brave offer, but there was no way Doyle was going to let the PC go ahead of him. This mess was of his making, and the least he could do now was lead from the front. 'Call the others in, and then follow me up.'

The boxroom at the front was clear, he could see that from the doorway. Entering the main bedroom, he saw that the double bed was made and didn't look like it had been slept in. He checked underneath, and then in the wardrobes. Out in the hall, Gadget and Anderton were coming out of the bathroom and back bedroom respectively.

'Nothing?' Doyle asked

They shook their heads. Gadget nodded up towards a loft hatch above them on the landing. Reaching up to open the hatch wasn't a problem for Doyle, but squeezing his frame through the aperture might be more tricky. He was grateful to see a loft ladder as Anderton's torch lit up the opening. He pulled it down, and she passed him the torch as he climbed up. As lofts went, this one was about the tidiest he had ever seen. There were about half a dozen cardboard boxes, but none big enough to contain a person. Other than that, the roof space was bare.

Chapter 28

Morgan was relieved that Doyle hadn't asked her to follow him into the house. In the past, she hadn't felt much fear in these situations. There had been some, a healthy amount maybe, but then there had been a rush of adrenaline that would carry her through, along with the knowledge that even the most obnoxious of colleagues would have your back when push came to shove. Now, standing outside after the others had rushed in, she didn't know how she felt. Would it always be like this for her now? Scared of confrontation, nervous about taking on a murder suspect? If so, what did that mean for her job – and career? Had Doyle noticed the fear in her? Was that why he had told her to wait outside? Maybe he didn't think she was up to the job.

An unmarked police car came down the road towards her, the blue lights in the grill flashing. She was relieved that backup was here. If Perkins was in there and managed to get past the others, she wouldn't have to tackle him on her own or, worse still, freeze and watch him get away. Her fleeting moment of relief was erased when she recognised one of the two officers getting out of the car.

'Well, well, well,' DS Felton said. 'Looks like you lot need our help after all. Your guvnor's going to be in a world of trouble, from what I hear. Releasing a killer to go and kill again. Need us in there, do they?' he asked, pointing towards the broken front door. 'You hanging around out here because you're too spooked to go in?'

Morgan realised she no longer felt frightened. Instead, she was bloody furious. It took every ounce of restraint she had not to reach into the pouch on her vest for the Pava spray and empty the can in the prick's face. She'd missed her moment; Felton was making his way up the drive with his DC in tow, just as Doyle was coming out.

'Probably shouldn't have let the madman go, sir,' Felton said to the BFG. Unpleasant as the man was, he wasn't wrong. Morgan knew her boss was going to be pulled apart over his decision-making, and she wasn't sure his career would survive it.

'Not in there, I take it?' Morgan asked Doyle.

'Afraid not.'

'Do you think he could have returned to his own home?'

'It's possible. But I'm not sure he could've got in. The landlord has boarded it up while the front door and other damage are being repaired. But I know someone who might know where he is.'

'Chief Inspector, very nice to—'

'Do you know where Will is?'

'And good morning to you too.' Dianne Berry's sarcastic tones poured from the phone's speaker into Doyle's ear.

'I haven't got time for this. I need to get hold of Will urgently.' Doyle snapped.

'Why? What's happened?' Berry sounded concerned now.

'There's been another murder, and an eyewitness has put Will Perkins at the scene.'

'Jesus. Are you sure? I knew there was something wrong with him yesterday, but I never—'

'Do you know where he is now?' Doyle almost shouted into the phone.

'Yes,' Berry said. 'He's in hospital. I went with him myself. He was clearly distressed and more psychotic than normal. Hearing lots of voices telling him all sorts. But I never thought anything had happened.'

'Which hospital?'

'It's a private one over Darwen way. The Jubilee Clinic, it's called. All the local NHS psych units were full,' Berry said. 'By the time I'd found him a bed and got him over there, I didn't finish work till nearly nine last night.'

'Last night? Doyle wanted to check he'd heard correctly. 'You took him there last night?'

'Yes. I went to see him late afternoon as he sounded a right mess on the phone,' Berry said. 'He thought I was one of those Pendle witches and said that someone working for the devil had been calling him.'

'Is this Jubilee Clinic a secure hospital?' Doyle asked.

'Not secure as such,' Berry said. 'You couldn't put people there who had been given a hospital order by a judge. But he was on a locked ward, where you keep people who have been sectioned.'

'Has Will been sectioned then?'

'No, he was there voluntarily. I'm not sure he would have met the threshold for being sectioned. But there had been a definite deterioration in his mental state, and what with all that had been going on I thought best to get him there before he had a full-blown relapse.'

Doyle was confused, something wasn't adding up. 'He's been in a locked ward since before nine o'clock last night. There's no way he could've got out?'

'Oh, Jesus,' Berry said.

'What?'

'It's not exactly unheard of for patients to abscond from a locked ward. It only takes one person to be careless going in or out,' Berry said. 'Plus, because he was there voluntarily, if he decided to leave they couldn't legally stop him. Though if that had happened, I should've known about it as soon as I got to work this morning. Unless...'

'Unless what?'

'If he had absconded and returned the same night, I probably wouldn't have found out about it until his ward round on Monday. They would have assumed that because he was back safe and well it was no longer an urgent matter by the time I got to work this morning.'

'Has that ever happened before? People going and coming back?' Doyle asked.

'Not Will, but other people. I had one patient who went to watch the cup final in a pub, then returned once it was finished.'

Chapter 29

The only obstacle to getting onto the grounds of the Jubilee Clinic was an automatic barrier to the car park. That would not stop a patient from leaving once they were outside the hospital building, Doyle reasoned, though he did notice what looked like quite extensive perimeter CCTV coverage. When they entered the hospital, automatic doors prevented the detectives from progressing further than the lobby. Doyle held up his warrant card so the woman sitting in the screened-off reception area could see it.

'DCI Doyle. We need to speak to whoever is in charge of the ward William Perkins is on.'

'Just one moment, please.' Her voice came back through an intercom speaker and Doyle watched her look through a folder on the desk. 'Found him. He's on Peel ward. I'll see if someone there can come down.'

'Thanks. It's urgent.'

The receptionist picked up a phone and had a brief conversation before her voice came back through the intercom. 'Someone is coming straight down. Would you all like to come through and sign in?' She opened the automatic doors, admitting the detectives to an 'airlock', and passed a signing-in book through the hatch. Doyle was familiar with this kind of security system, in which the internal and external doors could not be open at the same time, designed to stop patients doing a runner. Though it wouldn't be foolproof and was only as reliable as the person operating the doors. Added to that, there would be fire exits and staff entrances. It certainly wasn't impossible that Will Perkins could have got out.

'Are you the detectives that are here about Will? I'm Clarence, the nurse in charge of Peel ward today.' She had a Jamaican accent that reminded Doyle of his former home in south London.

Doyle shook Clarence's offered hand and introduced Morgan, Gadget and himself.

'Follow me,' the nurse said, holding her ID badge against a reader to open the internal door. 'We'll find somewhere private, and you can tell me what I can do for you.'

Clarence was no spring chicken, Doyle thought, and despite having a considerable limp, she set off along the corridor at a pace. She showed them into a side room.

'We understand that Will Perkins was admitted here yesterday, is that correct?' Doyle asked.

'Yes, though it was quite late when he came in. I didn't see him until after I started my shift this morning.'

'You've seen him here today?'

'Yes, I saw him not ten minutes ago on the ward. I've known Will for a long time. I worked in the NHS before; this is my retirement job. He's a nice man, and very clever when his head's not full of all that witches business.'

'Do you know if he left the hospital last night for any reason?'

'No, we wouldn't have given a patient leave when he had only just got here.'

'I understand that Will hadn't been sectioned. Wouldn't that mean he was free to leave if he wished?'

Clarence sucked in a breath, and it struck Doyle that she was thinking about a measured response to his question. 'Legally we couldn't stop Will from walking out of here if he decided to. But if he wanted to leave, it doesn't mean he would just pop off unchallenged. We would ask him why he wanted to go, and if we felt this was a risk we would do an urgent mental health assessment, and he would be sectioned and detained if necessary.'

'You mentioned risk,' Morgan said. 'Do you see Will as a risky kind of patient?'

'Everyone can be risky when they have lost touch with what is real and what is not. If Will walked out of here at night, I would be worried that he would go out walking on the moors looking for witches. He could fall and do himself a mischief or get hypothermia or something.'

'Is it possible that he could have got out and nobody noticed?' Doyle asked.

'I hope not. It wouldn't say much for the staff on shift if he had. Let me check his notes from last night and see what they've written.' Clarence logged on to the computer on the desk, and Doyle took the opportunity to look across at Morgan. He wished he knew what she was thinking. If the nurse hadn't been in the room, he would have asked her. Something didn't feel right to him; it felt like stretching credibility to think that Perkins could have slipped out of the ward unnoticed, travelled what must be nearly twenty miles, violently murdered Turkish and then returned as if nothing had happened. Or perhaps that was wishful thinking: he was looking for reasons why Perkins was innocent, not wanting to accept that he'd released a dangerous suspect to kill again.

'Here we go,' Clarence said, reading from the screen. 'In the evening, Will was pacing up and down the ward. He appeared anxious, and at times was overheard talking as if responding to auditory hallucinations. He was given his medication at 21.30, which he took without complaint, then retired to his room shortly afterwards. He was checked at 04.30, when he was sleeping in bed, and he has remained in his room throughout the rest of the shift.'

'Would he have been locked in his room?' Gadget asked.

'No, dear, this is a hospital, not a prison.'

'So, according to those notes, the staff didn't see him between shortly after 9.30 p.m. and 4.30 a.m.?' Morgan asked.

Doyle knew what she was getting at: according to those timings, no one had seen Will on the ward at the time when Turkish was murdered, or for a good while after that.

'That's correct, but the staff were doing their jobs. He didn't need more regular obs than that. It would be usual for someone like Will to go to sleep shortly after he had taken his evening medication.'

'It's tablets he takes, is that correct?' Doyle asked.

'Yes, but I—'

'Is it possible that he didn't swallow them? That he spat them out?'

'I guess so, yes. But why would he? He's here voluntarily.'

'Are the doors to the ward kept locked at all times?'

'Yes, they lock automatically as soon as they close. You need a pass to get in or out.'

'Do you know if there was much coming and going on the ward after Will was seen at 9.30 last night?'

'There was an incident with two other patients around 10 p.m. The ward staff had to use their alarms to get backup from other staff. Both patients had to be restrained, and one was given a sedative.'

'So, Will could have left the ward as people were coming onto it?' Morgan asked.

'I guess, in theory. What is all this about?'

'There was a serious incident last night,' Doyle said. 'An eyewitness recognised Will near the scene.'

'Oh.'

Morgan's phone started ringing, and she stepped out into the corridor to take the call.

'Is there much CCTV on the ward?' Gadget asked.

'Not on the ward itself, but there is around the grounds and some other parts of the hospital. Our security will be able to show you that.'

'We are going to need to speak to Will too,' Doyle said. 'Normally we would want to take him in and talk to him at the station. But given his current mental state, I think we might be better doing that here.'

'We can find you a suitable room for that. But I will have to let the consultant know. She may want to sit in.'

Morgan came back into the room. 'Dr Gupta wants to start proceedings soon,' she said.

Doyle knew she had deliberately not said 'post-mortem' in front of the nurse. 'Are you OK to do that?'

'Sure, boss. Geoff said Birdseye is on his way here. The FLO has turned up and is with Mrs Handcock. And I think I just spotted Dianne Berry in reception.'

Chapter 30

'I'm not supposed to be here, mister – can you get me out? Are you a solicitor?' A man in green and white striped pyjamas approached Doyle as soon as they entered the ward.

'He's not here to see you, Dominic. Your advocate will be coming this afternoon,' Clarence said, then turned back to Doyle and Birdseye as she unlocked a door. 'If you wait in here, I'll fetch Will and Dr Morten.'

The two detectives had only just sat down when Dianne Berry bowled through the door. 'Oh, Jesus. Who is it you think Will's killed?'

Doyle thought about keeping that information confidential, but it wouldn't remain that way for long. It was bound to come out who the victim was when he questioned Will. 'It's Terry Handcock.'

'Turkish?'

Doyle nodded.

'Oh God, if he has done it the enquiry will make mincemeat of me. They'll have my bloody pension. I should have seen this coming.'

'Tell me about it,' Doyle said. 'I had him in custody and let him go.'

There was a knock on the door, and then it was opened by a woman about Doyle's age who was dressed in a trouser suit and looked far smarter than anyone the detective had seen around the hospital. 'I'm Dr Ellie Morten, the consultant psychiatrist on Peel ward. Clarence has explained the situation to me, and someone will be bringing Will Perkins along in a minute. Though I'm not sure how much benefit you will get from interviewing him.'

Doyle had just finished introducing himself and DC Nelson when the door to the room was flung open. Will Perkins walked in, wearing green and white striped pyjamas. The bottoms stopped several inches short of his ankles and the top was fully unbuttoned. On his feet, he wore trainers with the laces removed.

'Will, this is—' Dr Morten started.

'Gentlemen, thank you for coming. I remember you – you're the magistrate and the constable. I take it you are here about the witches?'

'Nearly. I'm Detective Chief Inspector Doyle. We met recently.' The DCI had planned on cautioning Perkins, but judging from his current mental state, Doyle didn't think he would necessarily understand the caution. Either way, it was unlikely that anything Will said now could be used evidentially. If they were going to charge him with the murder of Terry Handcock, they would need hard evidence.

'I remember, but I had it wrong last time.' He sat down on the edge of a padded seat. 'I now realise that Mia Wright wasn't a witch, but the witches got to her. You must stop them. They've killed her, and they will kill again.' Will's speech was fast with hardly a pause for breath.

'Can you tell me what you did last night, Will?' Doyle asked.

'Yes, of course, I stayed here waiting for you. But I could hear them. And I heard the screaming.'

'Who was screaming, Will? Who could you hear?'

'The nutters, the nutters were screaming. I heard them from my chamber.'

'Do you know where you are, Will?' Dianne Berry asked.

Will angled his head slightly and stared at his community nurse. 'Of course – we came here yesterday. You came with me.'

'Where are we, Will?' Doyle asked.

'At Read Hall. You need to do something about this. You're the magistrate.' Will stopped talking abruptly and looked away from the other people in the room. 'You tell them.' He paused for a moment. 'No, I can't, you need to tell the magistrate that.'

'Who are you talking to, Will?' Berry asked.

'It's her, Old Demdike. She says it's all down to the nutters.' Will leaned towards Doyle and spoke in a stage whisper. 'I don't think you should believe her. She's a witch too.'

'Do you mean Alice Nutter, Will?' Birdseye asked.

'Yes.' Will clicked his fingers and rose from his seat. 'He's got it.' He pointed at Birdseye. 'He knows. It's her family – they are the witches.'

'Alice Nutter – the one who there's a statue of in that little village?' Doyle asked.

'That's right. Roughlee, the village is,' Birdseye said. 'She was another one of the Pendle witches. She was hanged at Lancaster Castle.'

'I've told them,' Will shouted out, turning away from everyone in the room.

'I think perhaps we should end this here,' Doyle said.

'I agree,' Dr Morten said.

'Will, is it alright if my colleague and I have a look in your room before we go?'

The security guard had been helpful and had shown Gadget the CCTV system. There were eight external cameras covering the perimeter and four inside the building, two each at the main and staff entrances. Although this was quite a modest security system, even looking through all the footage at twelve times the actual speed would take five hours. Speeding this up to thirty times the speed would mean that a person going past a camera could easily be missed. Added to that, the lighting in some places outside wasn't good and on two cameras the image was completely washed out every time a car went past. It would all have to be gone through in detail later, but for now, Gadget had to narrow down the search in order to look quickly.

He reckoned that he only needed one image of Will Perkins outside the hospital ward for them to have enough evidence to request the CPS to authorise him being charged with Terry Handcock's murder. That, with a statement from Tracy Handcock that she had seen him close to the scene, should be enough for now.

'I can't see it myself,' the security guard said from behind Gadget. 'I mean, I'm not going to pretend to you that a patient has never got out of here without being noticed. This place isn't Fort Knox. But getting back in again without being seen would take some doing.'

'You must have fire exits,' Gadget said. 'You don't think he could have ducked out through one of them and stuck something between the door and the frame to keep it from closing properly?'

'If one of those doors is opened, an alarm goes off in here, so loud it would wake the bloody dead. Even if the security guard was asleep, he would soon as heck wake up.'

'You think the security guard might have been asleep?'

'I've been doing this job for over thirty years, lad, and if you think those guys sitting here in the dead of night don't catch forty winks sometimes, you're deluded.'

The door to the security room beeped behind Gadget. He paused the footage he was looking at before turning around and seeing Doyle and Birdseye enter the room, Dianne Berry behind them.

'How's it going?' Doyle asked.

'Slowly,' Gadget replied. 'I've started on the bit before the incident, and then I'm going to work backwards from when he was next seen on the ward. Hopefully, I'll pick him up either leaving or coming back in without going through the whole lot. It'll take at least five hours if I have to go through it all. Even then, I'm not sure it will be conclusive; there are gaps between the cameras which he could have slipped through.'

'I've got good news for you, then,' Doyle said.

Gadget hoped that meant he was going to send the footage to Force HQ for someone else to trawl through. 'What's that, boss?'

'It'll only take two and a half hours with two of you. Birdseye can stay and give you a hand. He's got his car, so he can give you both a lift back when you're done.'

'How are you going to get back?' Gadget asked. 'The sarge has gone in her car to the morgue.'

'I'll give you a lift, boss,' Birdseye said. 'Then come back and help young Gadget.'

Gadget glared at his older colleague. He knew that, with Birdseye driving, it would be over an hour before he returned.

'I don't mind driving you back,' Dianne Berry said. 'Are you going to Nelson police station? I've got a patient near there I need to see.'

'What's happening with Perkins?' Gadget asked. 'Are we arresting him?'

'We will do as soon as you find some corroborating evidence on that CCTV,' Doyle said. 'But I don't want to keep him in a cell longer than necessary, the state he's in.'

'He's definitely lost the plot,' Birdseye added.

'What if he gets out again, boss?' Gadget said. 'That really won't look good.'

'You're not kidding,' Doyle agreed. 'I've got a couple of uniforms on their way here. One will be outside each entrance to the ward. If he tries to leave, they will arrest him.'

Chapter 31

'Are you serious?' Doyle asked when Berry pressed her key fob and the lights blinked on a Fiat 500. 'How am I going to get in that?'

'It's not my fault you're so chuffing big. You can always walk if you prefer.'

Doyle did manage to squeeze his huge frame into the tiny car, but even with the seat right back, his knees were up against the glove box and his head touched the roof. Berry crunched the gears and over-revved the engine as she pulled out of the car park, and Doyle wondered if the car was struggling to get going with his extra weight on board.

'You don't mind if I smoke, d'you?' she asked, steering the car with her knees while fishing in the handbag on her lap for her cigarettes and lighter.

'It's your car,' Doyle replied, though he sensed the question was rhetorical; Berry was already lighting up. 'Will seemed very different today from when I last saw him. What do you think's caused that?'

'I'm not sure, but probably all the stress of what's happened recently, being arrested then all the abuse he got, and having to move out of his home. He's never too far from full-on psychosis at the best of times. It wouldn't take much to tip him over the edge.'

'Do you think he might have stopped taking his medication again?'

'Bloody hell, I hope not. I'm in enough shit as it is. If he's stopped taking his meds, then no doubt some pompous prick who's never set foot in the same room as a patient will say in the enquiry that I should've been round there every night supervising him taking them.'

'This might sound like a funny question.'

'Go on?'

'You don't think he could be putting it on, do you?'

Berry turned to face Doyle, taking her eyes off the road for a concerning length of time. 'You saw what he was like in there. If he was faking it, that was one hell of a performance. Gary Oldman would have been proud of that, and there's no way that Leonardo DiCapachino or whatever his name is could have pulled it off.'

Doyle smiled. He pretty much agreed with her.

'Besides, I've seen him like that before when he's had relapses, and he had no reason to fake it then.'

Doyle's phone rang. He looked at the screen and knew he had to take the call. 'Is everything alright?'

'He's gone radio rental,' a familiar London accent said in his ear.

'What's happened, Mum?'

'He's pacing round the house, shaking his hands non-stop.'

'He's stimming. He does that when he's stressed.'

'It's not normal.'

'It's normal for Harry when he gets stressed or has a sensory overload. Any idea what brought it on?'

'Nothing. One minute we were chatting about school, getting on really well. I was asking him about making friends and that, and he started freaking out. I asked him what's wrong, but he won't tell me. Just keeps saying "I'm not going". Whatever that means.'

'Ask him if he'll talk to me on the phone.'

'Harry, it's your dad – he wants to speak to you.'

The phone went quiet for a moment.

'I'm not going.'

'Harry, it's Dad. What's the matter?'

'I'm not going. You can't make me.'

'Where don't you want to go, Harry? Has your nan suggested you go somewhere with her?'

'School.'

'What, your nan wants to take you to school?'

'No, next week. I'm not going, you can't make me.'

'What's up, Harry? What's brought this on?'

'It's Callum Cameron. He's not nice to me.'

'I know that, but you don't need to worry about that now. It's still half-term. Try to enjoy your time off with your nan.'

'I don't want to go back. I'm not going back.'

'It's OK. Me and your mum have got a meeting with the headteacher on Monday. We'll sort it out, I promise.'

'Promise?'

'Yes, promise. Are you going to be OK?'

'Yes. Can I go now?'

'Yes.'

'I love you, Dad.'

'I love you too, Harry.'

'I love you, Dad.'

'I love you too, Harry.'

Janice came back on the phone. 'You think he will calm down now?'

'Give him a bit of time. He'll settle. Look, Mum, I've got to go, call me back if anything else comes up.'

'OK. See ya, boy.'

Doyle ended the call and slipped the phone back in his pocket.

'Your son?' Berry asked.

'Yes, he's struggling a bit.'

'Autism?'

'Yes.'

'Aw, bless him. How old is he?'

'Nine, he's in Year 5 now. His mum wants him to go to a special school.'

'And you don't?'

'I'm not sure. It doesn't feel right. He's nine years old and we're writing him off already.'

'Have you been to any special schools and had a look round to see what they can offer?'

'No,' Doyle said, wondering why he hadn't thought of that already.

'Tell me to mind my own, if you like.'

'No, it's OK. I never get to talk about this with anyone who understands, other than my ex-wife.'

'Maybe go and take a look; there's no harm in looking. And if he did go to a special school, you wouldn't be writing him off.'

Doyle braced himself as Berry braked a bit too late at an amber light.

'Think of it like this. The world has been designed by people and for people who are neurotypical. It works well for the likes of you and me, generally. But if you're autistic, you're constantly trying to fit in somewhere that's not quite right. Have you ever seen a left-handed person use a pair of scissors?'

'What?'

'My husband's left-handed, and watching him trying to wrap a birthday present is painful. He can cut the paper, but it's all awkward and uncomfortable because scissors are designed for right-handed people.'

'Makes sense, I suppose.'

'A couple of years back, I got so fed up of seeing him all cack-handed, I got him a left-handed pair. And now I don't get a birthday present that looks like my two-year-old granddaughter has wrapped it.'

'At least he remembers your birthday.'

Berry sniggered. 'Well, there is that, I suppose. But the point is, if you put your lad in an environment designed for his needs, rather than writing him off you might help him flourish and reach his full potential.'

It sounded obvious when Dianne Berry said it. Doyle felt foolish for not realising this before. However much he told himself to try to look at things from Harry's point of view, he kept seeing things from his own perspective. He wanted to help his son adapt to the real world, but never considered how part of that world could adapt to Harry.

Berry stopped at yet another red light, this time more gently. 'Have a look around and see what's out there that might be good for him.'

'I will. Thanks.'

The car behind beeped, as the light had turned green.

'Piss off,' the nurse shouted before setting off again. 'You don't think your witness could be mistaken about seeing Will, do you? I mean, it's a bit of a stretch to think he got out at night and killed Turkish and then got back in again, and no one knew anything about it on the ward. No dirty or bloodstained clothes or even muddy footprints on the hospital floor.'

'We'll have to see, but our crime scene investigators will do a thorough search of his room on the ward. If there's anything there, even just a drop of blood on his clothing, they'll find it.' Doyle was starting to wonder about something else. In any murder, the people closest to the victim were always suspects until it had been proven otherwise. It was Tracy Handcock who had positively identified Perkins close to the scene, and she might have her own motive for murdering her husband and Mia Wright. Perkins might have seemed like the perfect person to frame for both. She wouldn't have known he was in a hospital twenty miles away. But Doyle didn't think she was capable of carrying out either murder. At least, not alone.

It had only been five days since Morgan had last stood in the mortuary alongside Jen Knight and the man from the coroner's office. Once again, the three of them watched as Dr Gupta and her technicians laid out surgical tools on stainless steel trollies ready for another post-mortem. What struck Morgan first, when Dr Gupta rolled back the sheet covering Turkish's naked corpse, was the extensive bruising all over his body. It was obvious that Terry Handcock had been on the wrong end of a good kicking.

'I understand that this poor gentleman is linked to Mia Wright in some way?' Gupta said.

'He certainly knew her,' Morgan replied. 'Though he played down that connection. We had him as a possible suspect, and I guess he still is, depending on whether you think the same killer killed both of them.'

'I didn't at first; it's a different MO. Poor Mr Handcock here has been subjected to a violent, sustained attack. I'm pretty sure the CT results will confirm that he died from blunt force trauma to the back of his skull. Probably caused by the same weapon used to smash out his dental implants.'

'I sense a "but" coming.'

'Yeah, something I noticed when I examined him at the scene. If you're not too squeamish, step a little closer to the table and I'll show you.'

Morgan wasn't squeamish, though the fact the pathologist had seen fit to warn her of what was to come made her pulse rise slightly.

Dr Gupta moved Handcock's jaw to open his mouth further. 'I can feel that the lower mandible is fractured in several places. This appears to have been done ante mortem,' Gupta said. Morgan knew this was as much for the benefit of the audio recording as it was for those present in the room. She stepped forward and looked into the now wide-open mouth. It wasn't just his dental implants that were missing. His tongue had been removed.

'Jesus,' Morgan said, taking a step back involuntarily from the mortician's slab. 'Mia's uterus and now his tongue. That can't be a coincidence. The two have to be the same person, don't they?'

'I don't come across many victims where an organ has been removed. In fact, over the whole of my career, I could count them all on my fingers. This week there have been two. So no, I don't believe that's a coincidence. And there is one more thing that makes me certain of that.'

'What's that?' Morgan asked.

'A lot about these killings is different. This attack is very violent – you can see that from the bruising all over his body, all done while he was still alive.'

'The killer would likely have been angry when he did this?' Morgan asked.

'That's not my department, but it seems a sensible working hypothesis. Mia had her throat cut and her uterus removed after she died. Whoever removed this poor chap's tongue did it after he died. But they also displayed a certain level of skill with the knife in doing so.'

'How?'

'The tongue is attached to the lower jaw just below the tip at the front and all the way back by what is known as the lingual frenulum. Your killer has delicately cut this tissue from the front to the back, post-mortem. That's pretty much how I would have done it. For work reasons, of course.'

'Do you think it might be someone with anatomical knowledge? A doctor or surgeon, perhaps?'

'Anatomical knowledge, yes, some, but everyone knows where the tongue is, if not the uterus. But they certainly displayed some skill with a knife in both cases. It's easy to get in a rage and stab someone to death, but making incisions and removing organs takes care. But I don't think this was a surgeon. The knife used was something like a paring knife, as used by chefs and butchers, and no doubt in many kitchens up and down the country. But it was very sharp, which means it was either new or someone had been looking after it and knew how to hone it.'

'Does that not seem a little odd?' Jen Knight asked. 'I mean, it's not my department, obviously, but is it strange for such a violent assault to be followed by a careful, almost surgical, procedure?'

'I was thinking the same thing,' Morgan said. She was starting to wonder whether two killers could be involved. Or, if it was Will Perkins who did it, whether he could have been in different mental states when he killed Turkish and when he removed the tongue. She knew that schizophrenia didn't involve different personalities, like a lot of people mistakenly thought, but maybe if he was hearing different voices telling him to do different things in different ways, it might explain the contradiction in the attacks.

Dr Gupta was now busy with her technicians, pointing out bits of the body that she wanted to be photographed before making the Y incision and starting on the internal examination of Terry Handcock. Seeing Turkish here, laid out in death, made Morgan feel a little guilty. To say she hadn't warmed to him when she first met him and then on the day she'd interviewed him would have been an understatement. But at the time, she had suspected he might have been responsible for Mia Wright's murder – something that now looked decidedly unlikely. Morgan didn't have the same emotional attachment to Turkish as she had experienced to Mia at her post-mortem. But she had some sympathy for him now. Whatever he had been holding back from the investigation, he must have had a reason. Maybe the two victims had been more than sexual partners. Maybe they had been in love, and both had paid a terrible price for that.

'The crime scene is interesting,' Knight said, breaking into the detective's thoughts.

'Oh? What have you found?' Morgan asked.

'Quite a bit so far. We've still got a team there. We're going over everything, including the yard and other outbuildings.'

'Anything stand out that might lead us straight to the person responsible?'

'Sorry, nothing as good as that. But I think we will be able to give you a few more pieces of the jigsaw to put together.'

'Good. The boss is holding a briefing at 8.30 tomorrow. Do you think you will be able to make it?'

'On a Saturday?'

'Afraid so.'

'I'll be there.'

Chapter 32

Day 7: Saturday 4 November

'Sorry to drag you all here on a Saturday, but needs must,' Doyle said to the assembled team in the incident room. No one had complained; they all knew the score. Even so, he had decided not to start proceedings until a leisurely eight-thirty that morning, giving his team an extra half hour in bed. Doyle himself had forgone the extra sleep – not because he didn't need it, but because the sofa bed he was sleeping on while his mum was staying had all the comfort of an iron maiden.

'Anna, do you want to fill everyone in on the highlights from the PM before we get the full report back?'

'Sure, boss. The big news is that, although the methods of murder were different – Turkish was kicked, beaten and killed by a blow to the head with something hard – there is a strong link to suggest the culprit is the same person. Turkish had his tongue cut out after death, and Dr Gupta thinks this was probably done by the same person that removed Mia's uterus. She can't be certain, of course, but I don't see we have any reason to doubt that theory.'

'Unless the killer knew about Mia and cut the tongue out to make it look like the same person had done it,' Birdseye suggested.

'But how would they have known about Mia's womb being removed?' Hales asked. 'The report in the paper only mentioned that the body had been mutilated and her throat cut, not that anything had been removed.'

'Plus, Dr Gupta said it was someone skilled with a knife that did it in both cases,' Morgan said.

A thought occurred to Doyle: that anyone who had been in the incident room and seen the photographs and read the reports about the first murder would have known that Mia Wright's body had not only been mutilated but that a piece of it had been taken. He would keep that thought to himself, for now. 'Jen, I understand your team had a busy day at the crime scene yesterday. Can you let us know how you got on?'

'We're not finished there yet,' Knight said. 'We've widened the scene to include the two workshops, the office and yard. There's a lot to go through, and that's without considering the surrounding land. We can be pretty certain that Mr Handcock was killed in the workshop, where he was found. There are a couple of patches of blood splatter around the top of the ramp going down into the inspection pit, and a few on the ramp itself. We expect they will be confirmed as the victim's blood, but it seems unlikely that these were from the blow that killed him. We think that happened in the inspection pit itself.'

'Do you think he ran in there to get away from his attacker, or was he pushed in?' Gadget asked.

'We can't be certain either way,' Knight replied.

'If he was pushed in there, could that have caused the fatal wound to the back of his head?' Asif asked.

'The shape of the indentation in the skull is not consistent with landing on a hard flat surface. And we think we've found the murder weapon. A lump hammer with blood on it was found in the field behind the workshop. It looks like it was thrown there. Again, we need to confirm that the blood on it is Mr Handcock's, but it seems pretty likely at this stage.'

'Agreed,' said Doyle. 'I don't suppose you found any—'

'Prints on the hammer?' Knight finished Doyle's question. 'Sadly not. Whoever used it wore gloves and possibly wiped it down afterwards. The inspection pit itself has proved to be quite a challenge, as there was sludge about an inch deep in the bottom. A mixture of engine oil, diesel, grease and God knows what else, alongside a good amount of the victim's blood. We have bagged it all up and will see if the lab can get anything further out of it, but I wouldn't get your hopes up. We did find the victim's tongue among the grime, so it wasn't taken as a trophy.'

'Or fed to a dog,' Gadget added.

'We also found a digital scale in the little room off the workshop. This isn't that unusual in workshops; sometimes parts and bits and pieces need weighing. But what was unusual was how clean it looked for the environment it was in. We took some swabs and found traces of cocaine, cannabis and heroin on the scales.'

'There's definitely been dealing going on there, then,' Morgan said.

'That sounds like a fair assumption,' Doyle agreed.

'That's not all,' Knight said. 'There was a drum full of used engine oil. Again, not that unusual in that kind of workshop. After an oil change, the dirty oil has to be stored somewhere before it's disposed of. This was so thick and black that you couldn't see through it. One of our guys fished around in there and found a plastic airtight container inside a dry bag. In the container was about sixty grams of what looks like cocaine, forty grams of heroin, and approximately two hundred grams of skunk.'

'I think we can say where Mr and Mrs Turkish were getting their money from then,' Hales said.

'It looks that way. Though others had access to the workshop too,' Doyle said. 'Anything else, Jen?'

'That's all for now, though I did wonder whether it might be worth getting the drugs dogs down there to go over the rest of the site to see if they can find anything we've missed.'

'Great. Thanks, Jen,' Doyle said. 'Right, Gadget and Birdseye, do you two want to let the others know what you found, or didn't find, from the hospital CCTV?'

Gadget sighed. 'Well, while the SOCOs were uncovering all sorts at the crime scene, me and the old fella spent the best part of three hours watching CCTV and turning up precisely bugger all.'

'You sure you weren't just stretching the job out, sitting in a nice warm office watching TV?' Hales said, smiling at the young detective.

'Trust me, I would rather have been doing anything else. There is nothing more boring than staring at a screen for hours where literally nothing is happening.'

'Bet you enjoyed it though, Birdseye,' Morgan said. 'You like watching cricket, so it must have been just as exciting.'

'That's because you don't understand the intricacies of test match cricket. For those of us with more sophisticated minds than yourself, it's a fascinating game,' Birdseye said, adding a 'Sarge' at the end.

'Is this a case where the absence of evidence may be evidence in itself?' Asif asked.

'Go on,' Doyle said, wanting the analyst to explain her thoughts to the team. He had been thinking the same.

'Well, I know the cameras covering the hospital grounds don't cover everything. Gadget spent ten minutes moaning to me about that before this meeting,' Asif said.

'It's true,' Gadget said. 'What's the point of having a perimeter CCTV system if there are gaps in it where people can pass through undetected?'

'But you would have to know where those gaps were to get out and back without being detected, unless you were extraordinarily lucky,' Asif said. 'Added to that, not one staff member saw Perkins anywhere that he shouldn't have been, or noticed he was gone, or saw that a door was left open or anything else.'

'You've got a point, Shaima,' Morgan said. 'Something I was wondering about was how he would have got from the hospital to the workshop and back again. It's too far to walk in the time. I know he hadn't actually been sectioned, so might he have had access to any money or a phone while he was on the ward?'

'The SOCOs who looked over his room while we were at the hospital checked,' Birdseye said. 'He wasn't allowed any of that. It was all locked away, just like when we have people in custody. He didn't even have his shoelaces, for obvious reasons.'

'So, the only reason we suspect Perkins at this point is because Tracy Handcock claims to have seen him near where she dropped her husband off, and we've got nothing else to corroborate this?' Hales said.

'Pretty much,' Doyle agreed. 'That, and the fact Perkins had a possible motive for killing Mia Wright – his delusions about her bewitching his dad.'

'But if Turkish had a relationship with Mia Wright and contracted gonorrhoea and passed it on to his wife, then Mrs Turkish would have quite a strong motive for killing both of them, wouldn't she?' Asif said.

'I agree,' said Morgan. 'About the motive, I mean, but she couldn't have done it. You've all seen her: she's always immaculately turned out, without even a line on her face. There is no way she'd batter her husband to death in that inspection pit.'

'How tall is she?' Knight asked.

'I've only seen her standing once and that was in heels, but I reckon she's a good bit shorter than me. Maybe five foot three,' Morgan said

'It seems doubtful, then, that she could have killed Mia,' Knight said. 'Dr Gupta thought her killer would have been taller.'

'She could have had an accomplice,' Birdseye said.

'Her brother would be the obvious candidate,' Hales said. 'Shouldn't we bring them both in?'

'Let's start with Tracy Handcock, and see if she sticks to her account of seeing Perkins when we put some pressure on her. Anna and I can pick her up. We'll take her to Burnley nick and interview her there under caution,' Doyle said. 'Geoff, you and Shaima can chase up anything that is still outstanding, and get more background on Tracy and her brother. Gadget, you get yourself down to NN Agricultural Engineering, I want all the paperwork from the office bagged up and taken to HQ. We will get some analysts to go through it on Monday, see what it throws up. The business might be a front for the dealing, and if it is we need to know ASAP.'

'Liam, I know they have been a pain in the arse, but is it not worth bringing in the local CID lads to handle the dealing side and let us focus on the murders?' Hales asked.

'Perhaps,' Doyle said. 'Though at the moment it looks like the two could be linked, and I would rather we had a look at the whole picture before deciding what we can pass on to them.' What Doyle didn't say was that he was becoming increasingly concerned that DCI Butcher might be involved. It was one thing when he was only a 'casual acquaintance' with a possible suspect in Mia's murder, but now Doyle knew he'd had contact with the second victim. This, combined with Butcher's snooping around the incident room, set alarm bells ringing for Doyle. He would have to speak to Mr Burns before deciding how to pursue that line of enquiry.

Chapter 33

'What's this all about? And why've I been dragged all the way over here to answer more questions? I told you yesterday all I know.'

'We needed to get your statement recorded officially, Mrs Handcock,' Doyle said.

'Well, why did you need to read me my rights?'

'It's a caution, makes everything a bit more formal. That can help later in court.' Doyle hoped his words would help Tracy Handcock to relax. It wasn't that he was concerned about her welfare, but if her guard was down, she might slip up and reveal something she hadn't intended. Then they could apply the pressure.

'It feels like I'm being treated like a criminal. I'm the victim here.'

Doyle resisted the urge to point out to Mrs Turkish that it was in fact her husband who was the victim, and they were unlikely to get a statement from him. 'If you like, you can have a solicitor present. They will be able to give you any legal advice you might need.'

'Why would I need legal advice? I haven't done anything wrong.' Tracy folded her arms across her chest.

'Shall we get started then?' Morgan said.

'If you like.'

'Right,' said Doyle. 'Let's go back to when Terry received the phone call. Where were you at the time?'

'I were in bed upstairs.' Tracy sat back in her chair.

'And your husband?' Doyle asked.

'He were downstairs.'

'Did you hear him on the phone?'

'No, but he came up after that and woke me.' Mrs Turkish unfolded her arms and took a sip of water from the plastic cup on the table.

'You were asleep when he got the call?' Doyle asked.

'I don't know – kind of dozing, I guess. I never really sleep properly before he's come to bed. The light was still on.' Tracy splayed out her hands with their immaculately painted nails on the table and looked down at them.

'What time was it when he came upstairs and woke you?' Doyle probed.

'I don't know. Twelve, maybe a bit later.' Mrs Turkish lifted her left hand and examined the nail on the little finger.

'And why did he wake you up?'

'He'd had a few drinks and would've been over the limit. Needed me to drive him to work for a job.'

'How far away is your house from your work?' Morgan asked.

'What?' Tracy looked up at Morgan. 'You know how far it is. You were there the other day going through all our stuff. If you'd been doing your job properly, that Will Perkins would've been locked up and Terry would still be here.' Whether Tracy was unnerved by the question or the change of questioner, Doyle couldn't tell.

'I reckon it's about a mile, mile and a half maybe,' Morgan went on. 'I wonder why Mr Handcock felt the need to wake you up to drive him to work. It wouldn't have taken much longer to walk, by the time you had got up, got dressed and driven him.'

'It were raining, and he knew I wouldn't mind.' Tracy's voice had risen in volume.

'What time was it when you left home with your husband, Mrs Handcock?' Doyle asked, his own voice still soft – he could play good cop when he had to.

'It was just past half twelve,' Handcock looked back at Doyle. 'I know that because the clock's on the dashboard.'

'Before you got to the workshops, did you pass any cars coming in the other direction?' Morgan asked.

'What?' Handcock blinked several times.

'It's a straightforward question. Did you pass any cars coming the other way?' Morgan said.

'No, I don't think so.'

'It's a narrow lane,' Morgan went on. 'You would know whether you passed another car or not. You would've had to pull in and find a place you could pass.'

'I didn't, then.' Handcock spat back.

'And what about on the way back? Did you pass anyone then? Morgan asked.

'No.'

'And you told us yesterday that you saw someone close to the entrance to the workshops. Is that correct?' Doyle asked.

'Yes,' Handcock looked back at Doyle. 'Will Perkins. Exactly like I told you before.'

'And where exactly was Will Perkins when you saw him? Was he right outside the gates?' Doyle asked.

'No,' Tracy looked away again. 'He were a bit up the road, on the bend before the gates.'

'Was he walking along the road?'

'Yes.'

'In which direction?' Doyle pressed.

'Towards the entrance to the yard.'

'In the same direction that you were heading?' Morgan asked.

'Yes.' Handcock said.

'So, you only saw him from behind?'

'He turned round when he heard the car. I saw his face then, it was definitely him.' Tracy's volume had started to rise again.

'What was he wearing?' Doyle asked.

'Jeans, I think.' Handcock looked back at Doyle, but didn't meet his eye.

'Did he have a coat on?'

'Yes.'

'You said it was raining, did he have the hood up?' Morgan asked.

'What is it with all these questions?' Handcock turned on Morgan. 'I've told you. I saw Will Perkins. I recognised him straight away.'

'Relax, Mrs Handcock,' Doyle said. 'If Will Perkins gets charged with your husband's murder, these are exactly the sort of questions his barrister will ask you in court. It's good to get your answers straight now while it's still fresh in your mind.'

'You said you recognised him straight away. Was that before he turned around?' Morgan asked.

'Yes,' Tracy said slumping down in her chair. 'I think so. He's quite distinctive. All tall and gangly.'

'Still, it's quite something to recognise someone so quickly in the dark, walking away from you and wearing a coat,' Morgan said.

'Did you know Will well?' Doyle asked.

'Not know him, as such. But I know who he is – everyone around here knows who he is. And you should've had him locked up for that other girl's murder. Then Terry would still be alive.' Her voice rose again in frustration.

'You said you recognised Will, but can you remember the last time you saw him? Can you be certain it was him?' Doyle asked.

'Yes, yes I can. And I saw him earlier that day, now I come to think about it. He was hanging around up the lane from the workshop when I left work.' Tracy Handcock almost shouted her answer.

'Will Perkins was?' Doyle asked, keeping his voice soft. 'You're quite certain?'

'Yes,' she almost pleaded. 'Around the same place. I got a good look at his face – he was wearing the same clothes.'

'This would have been Thursday afternoon?' Doyle said.

'Yes,' Tracy said, raising both arms in frustration.

'Can you remember what time?'

'It was about ten past five.'

'And you are certain of that?' Doyle said.

'Yes!' Handcock shouted.

Gotcha, Doyle thought. 'Right. I've got no further questions at this stage.'

'Good. Finally. Can I go now?'

'I'm afraid not, Mrs Handcock,' Doyle said.

'What? Why?'

'Tracy Handcock, I'm arresting you on suspicion of perverting the course of justice,' Doyle said. The Botox did not stop Mrs Handcock's jaw from dropping.

'How did it go?' Hales asked as Doyle and Morgan walked back into the incident room in Nelson police station.

'We've arrested her,' Doyle said.

'Bloody hell,' Hales said, sitting up and almost spilling coffee down his shirt. 'That escalated quickly. But surely there's no way she could have killed Turkish – at least, not on her own?'

'Sorry, Geoff, I should have been clearer,' Doyle said. 'We've arrested her for perverting the course of justice. It may end up as conspiracy. She lied about seeing Perkins.'

'What? Are we one hundred per cent certain he hadn't got out of hospital now?'

'No, but it's looking unlikely. But Mrs Turkish doubled down, claims to have seen Perkins at ten past five on Thursday afternoon. And that was when Dianne Berry and a colleague of hers were sitting with Will Perkins in his dad's house waiting for an ambulance to take him to hospital. And I'm pretty confident that they will both give statements to confirm this.'

'Has everyone else gone?' Morgan asked.

'Yes, I sent them home,' Hales said. 'We've requested all the info we need from phone companies, banks, etc., and we're still waiting for some forensic bits to come in. Gadget has been going around the lanes in the area, trying to get CCTV footage from near the time Turkish was killed. There isn't much. He's found a few video doorbells that might have something, but I'm not hopeful.'

'That's great, Geoff,' Doyle said. 'And there's something I want to chat to both of you about, but it mustn't go any further at this stage.'

'That sounds ominous,' Morgan said.

'As you know, there were several calls between DCI Butcher's phone and Terry Handcock's. Up until this point, there was only so far I could push this. Handcock was only a person of interest in Mia's murder, so Pat Butcher was effectively one step removed from that.'

'Pat Butcher!' Hales laughed. 'That's one of the best nicknames yet. And believe me, I know a thing about nicknames.'

'Do you think he could be involved?' Morgan asked.

'Honestly, I don't know, but so far he's been evasive about his relationship with Turkish, but we can't have that now. Not now that Turkish has been murdered.'

'You know, if Turkish had been dealing, which let's face it someone connected to the workshops has, maybe Butcher had been taking a backhander to turn a blind eye,' Hales said.

'Makes sense,' Doyle agreed.

'You don't think he could be a suspect in both murders?' Morgan asked.

'I think at this stage he has to be,' Doyle said. 'I haven't told you this, but Butcher has been sneaking around the incident room after it's been locked up for the night.'

'How do you know that, boss?' Morgan asked.

'The how is not important; I'll explain another time. But it's the why that's bothering me now, even more than before,' Doyle said. 'When I found this out, it was before Turkish was murdered. And I thought Butcher was checking up on how we were getting on with Mia's case and to what extent his mate, informant or whatever the hell Turkish was to him was in the frame.'

'Bloody hell, this is sounding a bit serious. And he's a DCI as well,' Hales said.

'Exactly, Geoff, and that was before Turkish turned up murdered. We now have to seriously consider Butcher as a suspect.'

'And it was him who had Perkins arrested in the first place,' Morgan said. 'Keen to get it all wrapped up before we got involved.'

'Maybe he could be in it with Mrs Handcock,' Hales suggested.

'It's a possibility,' Doyle agreed. 'There has to be a reason why she lied to us about seeing Will. And looks like she has a motive. Presumably, we will find out from pathology soon whether Turkish had gonorrhoea. And I'm willing to bet a lot of money that the antibiotics we found prescribed to Mrs Handcock were treatment for gonorrhoea too.'

Morgan frowned. 'How come you're so sure of this? And how come you knew exactly what to look for when we searched their house?'

Doyle tapped the side of his nose and winked. 'Some things you're best off not knowing. But now we have arrested her in relation to all this, we have reasonable grounds to make a formal request to check with her doctor.'

'There's still something missing, though,' Morgan said. 'Even if Turkish was having an affair with Mia and his wife found out, that might give her a motive for murder, but we know she can't have done them alone, don't we? It's just not credible – in either case.'

'Maybe Butcher did it for her,' Hales suggested.

'But why? What would be his motive for doing that?' Morgan asked.

'I don't know,' Hales said.

'We still need to look at her brother more closely,' Doyle said. 'He could have acted on his sister's behalf.'

'True,' Hales said. 'Should we bring him in now? We've already got a reason to arrest him – the drugs found in his business. Maybe he will give something away.'

'My hunch is if we do, he will deny knowledge of the drugs and try to blame Turkish for them being there,' Doyle said. 'Even though it's his business, others had access, so it will be hard to pin the drugs on him. Mrs Hancock is going to be spending a night in the cells. Let's interview her tomorrow and see if she's willing to start telling the truth when a bit of reality has hit home. We'll take things from there.'

'Do you want me and Birdseye to do that? I let him go before lunch and he was happy to come in on Sunday.'

'I bet he was,' Morgan said. 'Poor Gill must think most murders get solved on a Sunday, Birdseye needs to work on the sabbath so often.'

Doyle laughed. 'Are you sure you don't mind, Geoff? I could do with putting together all we have on Butcher and running it by Croucher. I'm going to let him decide how to proceed.'

Chapter 34

Day 8: Sunday 5 November – Bonfire Night

Detective Inspector Geoff Hales stared at the woman opposite him, while Birdseye started the recording and read her the caution. Morgan had warned him that it would be hard to read anything from her expression. She had been right. It wasn't that Tracy Handcock was unattractive, though a night in the cells didn't leave anyone looking their best. It was that she almost didn't look real. Her cosmetic enhancements had left her looking like a living doll. Hales found himself wondering what he would look like if he had a team of plastic surgeons do their worst on him. He reckoned they would be able to deal with most of the lines on his face, and maybe even do something with his red drinker's nose. But he doubted they could do anything about his lack of a neck, which had earned him his nickname, the Pearl. His appearance was caused by Klippel–Feil syndrome, a condition that meant two vertebrae in his neck were fused together. It hadn't held him back much, and he'd considered it an advantage when he was younger and playing rugby league. It helped that there had been a kid in his school class who had the opposite problem, which had earned him the nickname ET.

'I don't understand why I'm here,' Tracy Handcock said, snapping Hales from his thoughts. Her solicitor sat next to her, staring at her laptop screen, apparently not paying much attention. Hales had explained to her brief in the disclosure meeting before the interview that there were certain aspects of Mrs Handcock's statement the previous day that he knew to be factually incorrect, but he wasn't prepared to give either of them any further information at that stage.

'You are here because you lied to our colleagues yesterday,' Hales said.

'No, I never. What am I supposed to have said that wasn't true?'

'You should know that, as you must know which bits of your account you made up,' Hales replied. 'If you can't work out what that is, then it makes us think that very little of what you told us is true.'

'No, I told you everything just as it happened. You should be out there looking for Terry's killer, not sitting in here harassing me. This is a breach of my human rights or something.' Handcock looked over to her solicitor, who returned a noncommittal look.

'From where I'm sitting, it's not *what* you lied about that matters,' Hales said. 'I'm far more interested in the why. I mean, we're investigating your husband's murder, trying to catch whoever killed him. I would've thought you would be doing everything you could to help us.'

'It's obvious who's done it, and you should've locked him up by now.'

'But instead you have been lying to us. Why? What have you got to hide?'

'I haven't got anything to hide. And what am I supposed to be lying about?'

'You know that very well, Tracy. And I'm pretty sure we have enough now for the CPS to authorise a charge of perverting the course of justice.'

Handcock glanced at her solicitor, who didn't meet her eye.

'I'm wondering whether you are behind the murders of your husband and Mia Wright.' Hales watched her eyes widen. 'Or are you covering for someone else?'

'No! Why would I?' Her gaze darted sideways and up. That was it, Hales thought. Her face might not crack an expression, but she couldn't keep her emotions from her eyes. She had looked shifty when he'd asked if she was covering for anyone.

'Mrs Handcock,' Birdseye jumped in. 'If for some reason you are covering for someone else, you need to tell us. If you say who you are trying to protect, then it might not be in the public interest to charge you.'

'Alternatively,' Hales said, 'if you don't tell us, then we are going to have to start looking at the possibility that you are involved in both of these murders.'

'But. I—'

Now she did look rattled, Hales thought. 'When we searched your house on Wednesday, one of our officers found a packet of Zithromax,' Hales said, consulting his notes. 'They are antibiotics. The label on the box said they were prescribed for you.'

'So?' Handcock said. The words implied indifference, but she had gone red and a film of sweat glistened on her forehead.

'I'd like to know what they were prescribed for.'

'Is this really necessary?' the solicitor asked. 'My client's medical records remain confidential unless they are significant to the case.'

'We think they are, and to both murders,' Hales said.

The solicitor looked puzzled.

'If you'd like to take a break and consult with your client, I'm sure she might be able to fill you in on why that might be the case.'

Tracy Handcock shifted uncomfortably in her seat. Hales doubted that was due to the symptoms of her infection.

'Look,' Birdseye said, 'in a case this serious, we will be able to get access to your medical records one way or another, even if we have to get a warrant.'

'Can they do that?' Handcock asked her solicitor.

'If they can demonstrate that it might be important to the case, then yes, I'm afraid so,' the solicitor said. 'It might help if we take a break and you disclose what the complaint is, and I will be able to advise you.'

'It's the clap. Bloody gonorrhoea,' Handcock blurted out. This silenced everyone in the room for a second.

'I know this must be pretty difficult for you, Mrs Handcock,' Birdseye said, 'but do you know who you contracted it from?'

'It was him.'

'Who?' Hales asked.

'Terry, who else? I've not been near anyone else, so it must've been him.'

'Were you aware that he was having a sexual relationship with someone else?' Birdseye asked.

'No, I bloody weren't.'

'Did you ever suspect him of being unfaithful?' Hales asked.

'I suspected him of all sorts over the years. But not specifically then, no.'

'How did you find out?' Birdseye asked.

'Oh God.' Tracy Handcock put her head in her hands. 'I went to the doctor because ... well, because things didn't feel right.'

Hales thought about asking her to be more specific, then decided against it, and was relieved that Birdseye didn't either.

'I thought it would be just some women's problem or other, not an STI. She asked lots of questions about ... you know, then did some tests. I was shocked when I got the results back.'

'I bet,' Hales said. He was starting to feel some sympathy for her. 'Did you confront your husband about it?'

'No, not then.'

'Later on?' Hales asked.

'No. I was going to, but never found the right time and then – well, you know.'

Hales let the silence rest in the room for a bit before he broke it. 'Tracy, were you involved in the murder of your husband?'

'No,' she replied, a note of incredulity in her voice.

'Do you know who killed him?'

'No.' Her reply sounded less assured, and Hales noted her gaze dart towards her solicitor. He was sure she was covering for someone, but who – and why? And there was the first inconsistency. Previously she had been adamant that Will Perkins had killed her husband.

Doyle glanced at Harry in his rear-view mirror. He was unusually quiet and sat stock still, staring out of the side window. The detective knew that a lot must be running through his son's brain right now. Doyle's mum, on the other hand, would not shut up as he drove her to the station. She seemed determined to give him a full appraisal of Lancashire, despite the fact she'd only seen a bit of it, and 'northerners', despite the fact she'd only met a few.

'I'm not saying there's anything wrong with 'em. But you've got to admit they're a bit weird.'

'Are they?'

'Well, they're all a bit too cheery. Smiling and saying hello when you've never even met 'em before.'

Doyle laughed. 'And that's a bad thing?'

'No, I'm not saying that, it's just a bit weird. If I started saying hello to everyone walking up Lewisham High Street, people would think I'd gone nuts.'

'And they wouldn't be far wrong.'

'Oi, cheeky sod.'

'I don't want you to go, Nan,' Harry said from the back as Doyle turned into the road by Preston station.

'Don't worry, Harry, I'll be back soon enough. We've had a good time, ain't we?'

'Yes.'

'And you've learned a bit being with me, ain't ya?'

'Nan showed me what a Yankee is, and how to put one on.'

'You took him into the bookies? He's only nine.'

'Oh, they didn't mind, we were in and out. Besides, he's been helping me with that internet. You can do it all on your phone now.'

As Doyle pulled up at the drop-off point, Harry began to sob.

'Oh good, I've got time for a fag,' Janice Doyle said, getting out of the car.

Doyle got out and let Harry out of the back. The boy immediately ran over to his grandma and grabbed both her legs tightly while Doyle got her case out of the boot.

'Please don't go. I don't want you to go,' Harry wailed.

'It's OK, Harry. Maybe your nan could come and stay at Christmas,' Doyle said.

'Can she, Dad?' The tone of Harry's voice changed in an instant from despair to excitement.

'If she promises to behave herself.'

'Bloody cheek. 'Ere, Harry, maybe next time I come up your dad'll introduce me to his new girlfriend.'

'How did you—'

'I got it out of him. I knew you would never have said.'

'Harry. I told you not to say anything to her.'

'She asked me, Dad. I couldn't lie.'

Doyle ruffled his son's hair. He was right: he really couldn't lie. Telling a lie was wrong, and Harry could never bring himself to do it. If every suspect Doyle got in the interview room was like Harry, his life would be a lot easier.

'He tells me she's a Mickey Mouser.'

Harry looked confused. 'What's a Mickey Mouser?'

'A scouser – someone from Liverpool. It's rhyming slang,' Janice Doyle said.

'It's rhyming bollocks. Right, Harry, say goodbye to your nan. She's got a train to catch and we've got to get on. I've got a surprise for you.'

'Yes!' Harry said, his arms pumping out sideways, all thoughts of his grandma leaving temporarily banished. 'What is it?'

Chapter 35

'You alright there, Harry?' Bea said, getting into the front of Doyle's car. She somehow managed to maintain a hint of glamour even in a winter coat and woolly hat. Doyle didn't lean over and kiss her, not wanting to be so intimate in front of his son.

'My dad won't tell me what the surprise is. Do you know?'

'No, he wouldn't tell me either, He just said to wear warm clothes and bring a flask of mulled wine.'

Doyle was regretting saying to Harry he had a surprise for him. It was getting built up way too much and he was worried it would end in disappointment. He was also worried that Bea would be pissed off with him. They had got into the habit of spending Sunday evenings together after Harry had gone back to his mum. Last week Doyle had had to cancel because of work, and he had decided against their usual midweek meet-up as he'd had too much to do with his mum coming to stay.

'What's mulled wine?'

'It's hot red wine,' Bea said. 'I don't think you'll like it.'

'Yuck.'

There was a rapid burst of explosions and the sky was lit up by multicoloured lights from a firework set off not far away. Harry tensed up and clamped his hands over his ears.

'Here, put these on,' Doyle said, handing his son a pair of purple ear defenders. Doyle drove along dark country lanes, which were periodically lit by starbursts and flashes in various colours.

'Where are we going, Dad?' Harry asked as Doyle rounded a hairpin bend and turned onto a road that went sharply upwards.

'You'll see in a minute,' Doyle replied, unsure if his son could hear him. He pulled the car into a parking area. During the day, it had views across West Lancashire and beyond. Doyle was relieved to see there were no other cars parked. He had wondered if at night the place might be used by those seeking alfresco passion. He'd thought about checking this out with a colleague, but decided not to in case they misunderstood his reason for asking.

'Why are we here?' Harry asked, pulling the ear defenders off one ear so he could hear the answer.

'I thought we could watch the fireworks from here. It is Bonfire Night, after all.'

'No, no. I don't like fireworks,' Harry said. 'I'm not getting out of the car.'

'It's the noise you don't like, Harry. You said the other day you liked looking at them. From up here you will hardly be able to hear them, but you'll see all the bright colours.'

Harry shook his head, but it wasn't a complete rejection; Doyle could see a sliver of curiosity on his son's face. He got out of the car, leaving the door open, and wandered over to Bea, who was sitting on a bench watching the display.

'This is amazing,' she said. Her warm breath was visible in the cold air. 'What a great idea to come up here. It's like we've got our own private display.'

Doyle didn't think it would be a good idea to remind her that he had discovered this place on his second day in the Lancashire force last summer. That day, he hadn't been there to admire the view, beautiful as it had been, but to investigate the murder of a young woman whose lifeless corpse had been thrown over the cliff in front of them. The case had proved to be quite an introduction to his new job.

'Here,' Bea said, handing him a plastic mug and linking her arm through his. 'Do you think he will get out of the car?'

Doyle turned and looked back towards his son. Since the door was open, the light was on in the car, and he could see Harry leaning forward in the back seat to get a better view of the display.

'Come on, Harry,' he called, waving to the boy. 'You can hardly hear them from up here.'

Bea got up and went back to the car. Doyle watched as she coaxed his son out. They had only met a few times, but she was good with him and there was no doubt that Harry liked her, but that just made things even more complicated, in Doyle's eyes. His relationship with Bea, if you could even call it that at this stage, was still new. If things didn't pan out, he didn't want that to be another cause of distress for his son. But thanks to his work, sometimes it felt impossible to find enough time to spend with either of them.

'Do you want to put your hat on, Harry?' Bea asked as they reached the bench. 'You don't want to catch a cold.'

Harry looked at the offered beanie, confused.

'Here,' Doyle said lifting the ear defenders from his son's ears. 'I think you can take these off. It's really not that noisy up here.'

Harry looked reluctant. 'Can I still hold them just in case?'

'Of course,' Doyle said, removing them and handing them to his son as Bea slipped the hat on the boy's head.

'Hey, Harry, do you want a drink?' Bea asked, waving a flask at him.

'I don't want any of that hot wine.'

'I thought you wouldn't like that, so I've got some hot chocolate for you.'

Harry's eyes lit up.

'And I've even bought some squirty cream and marshmallows to go on top,' Bea said, holding up a hand for Harry to high-five.

Several bursts of light lit the sky all at once. Harry watched, mesmerised. Doyle looked from his son to Bea, who looked equally transfixed. She had one hand on Harry's shoulder. When Doyle had been growing up, Bonfire Night had been a bigger occasion than Halloween. Kids would make models representing Guy Fawkes out of old clothes and newspapers and hang around outside shops asking strangers to give them a penny for the guy. Then, come Bonfire Night, the effigies – of a man from four hundred years ago – would be burned on a big bonfire. Doyle had never really thought about how strange it was that things from the distant past were still marked in the present.

Bursts of colour filled the sky, and Harry and Bea cheered.

'Hey, Harry, what do you think about fireworks now?'

'I love fireworks!'

Chapter 36

Day 9: Monday 6 November

Detective Superintendent Croucher was a pernickety man who, in Doyle's view, was too keen on policy and procedure and making sure everything was done according to the rules rather than getting results. This trait usually infuriated Doyle, but today he had to concede he quite liked it. Having discussed the issue extensively with his boss at the weekend, he now found himself sitting in a large interview room at Force HQ in Hutton. With him and Mr Burns sat Detective Inspector Lisa Cavanaugh from the anti-corruption unit of Lancashire Constabulary's Professional Standards department. Her presence in the room would, no doubt, be making the man sitting opposite, next to his federation rep, feel concerned. Doyle had been the subject of an investigation in the past, and he knew it was a special kind of copper who made a career out of investigating their colleagues. They tended to take their jobs very seriously.

Croucher had started proceedings by informing DCI Butcher, who had been summoned to HQ on arriving at work that morning, that the interview was being conducted with the agreement of Assistant Chief Constable Reid and Butcher's direct boss, Chief Superintendent Lennox. The interview was also to be recorded and, as had been explained to Butcher when he arrived, it would be conducted under caution. Croucher had confirmed that Butcher hadn't changed his mind about not wanting a solicitor before starting. Doyle could understand why his fellow DCI didn't want legal representation; he didn't think he would in his shoes either. Asking for a brief in this situation, when you should be familiar enough with the process not to need one, made it look as if you had something to hide.

'We have the call records for your police mobile phone and a mobile phone found in the possession of Terrance Handcock,' Croucher began as soon as the caution was out of the way. 'As you are aware, Mr Handcock was found dead at his place of work on Friday 3rd November, and we are treating his death as murder. There are many calls between these phones going back to January last year. Can you explain your relationship to Mr Handcock?'

'He was an acquaintance, that's all. There was no relationship between us.'

'You hadn't been using him as an unregistered informant, then?' Croucher asked. 'You never paid him for any information?'

'No, and I told the chief super that when he asked me last week.'

'Did he ever pay *you* for anything?' DI Cavanaugh asked. She had a Glaswegian accent.

Doyle watched Butcher carefully, like a poker player studying an opponent for a tell. He moved slightly in his seat, as though the question had made him physically uncomfortable. 'No. Of course not.'

'What were all the calls about, if you were only acquaintances?' Croucher asked.

'He would sometimes let me know if he'd heard anything about any crimes in the area. Turk— Mr Handcock knew a lot of people, and drank in a few of the local pubs. He would hear about things and would sometimes pass them on.'

'So he was an informant?' Cavanaugh said.

'No, just a concerned citizen passing on information when he had it. No money ever changed hands.'

Doyle had to stifle a laugh. Turkish, a concerned citizen? 'He must have been very conscientious to have called you over sixty times in the last nine months.'

'Like I said, he heard a lot of things and passed them on. It's good community policing, building up contacts in the local area. Not that you'd know much about that, only popping up when there has been a murder, with no idea of how the land lies locally.'

'No doubt there will be a record of all these crimes that Mr Handcock's intel helped you clear up,' Cavanaugh said. 'What about the calls you made to him? What were they about?'

'Well, I was probably calling him back when I hadn't been able to take his call.'

'No,' Cavanaugh said. 'That can't be true. There were some when the previous calls had lasted some time and others when he hadn't called you for a while.'

'Maybe I was calling him to ask if he had any information about anything we were investigating.'

'Maybe?' Cavanaugh said. 'Does that mean you aren't sure? It wasn't that long ago – surely you can remember?'

'OK, then yes, I was calling him to see if he had any information about things we were investigating at the time.'

'He called you at 9.30 a.m. on Sunday 29th October,' Doyle said. 'What was the reason for this call?'

Butcher took a deep breath. 'He called me to tell me he had information about who had killed Mia Wright.'

'And you're only just mentioning this now?'

'No! When he called me, I was on my way to work. I had just been informed about the murder. He told me, off the record, that he had been told that Will Perkins had done it. This seemed plausible, because there had been a previous incident between Perkins and the victim. So we arrested Perkins. Then your lot came bounding in and took the investigation off us.'

'Off the record?' Cavanaugh said. 'Is it normal in a murder investigation to get information off the record? Why not ask him to give a statement?'

'He didn't want to do that. He was just passing on what he had heard.'

'Did you ask who he had heard it from?' Doyle asked.

'Yes, but he wouldn't say.'

'And this was only forty-five minutes after Mia's body had been discovered? Had he known this before she was found?' Doyle asked.

'I don't think so.'

'You didn't ask him?'

'Not that I recall. The priority had been arresting the suspect.'

'I assume you made a record of this call, and it was logged on Holmes 2 as an entry for the case?' Cavanaugh said.

'I might have overlooked that. But it doesn't fundamentally change anything, as we had Perkins in custody when the case was taken over by the MIT. It's not as if this tip off could be used in evidence without a formal statement.'

'If you had entered it, or even told us about this, we could have used the information when we had Handcock in for questioning,' Doyle said. 'Or was protecting the source of your information more important to you than the enquiry?'

'No. Honestly, it never crossed my mind.'

'Not even when we brought Handcock in to interview? You knew we'd done that, didn't you?' Doyle said. 'You didn't think that was significant? If Handcock had killed Mia Wright, he might have wanted you to think it was Perkins who had done it. If we had known that he'd contacted you, we could have asked him about that when we questioned him.'

'Well, considering he gave a no-comment interview, it wouldn't have made a blind bit of difference,' Butcher said. 'Besides which, this is all a bit rich, isn't it?' He looked over to Croucher. 'Him.' Butcher pointed at Doyle, his voice rising. 'Asking me about all this when the massive elephant in the room is that he let Perkins go, and then he went out and killed Handcock.'

'DCI Butcher,' Burns said, his voice matching the volume of the other man's. 'This interview is about you and what you did. The decisions made by officers on my team are my concern, not yours.'

This exchange had told Doyle something. Butcher didn't know about the developments over the weekend. He still believed that Perkins was in the frame for both murders, so he probably hadn't heard that Tracy Handcock had been arrested.

'How did you know that Mr Handcock gave a no-comment interview?' Cavanaugh asked. Doyle was beginning to like her.

'What?'

'It's a straightforward question,' Cavanaugh said. 'You were no longer involved in the investigation when Handcock was questioned. How did you know he gave a no-comment interview?'

'Someone must have told me.'

'Who told you? Was it Mr Handcock? Did you have any further contact with him since then? There is nothing in the phone records.'

'No, it wasn't him. I overheard someone talking about it. They must have heard it from someone else.'

'Have you been into the incident room at Nelson police station since my team commandeered it?' Croucher asked.

'You know I have. We were in there together on Thursday.'

'And that's the only time?'

'I might have popped my head in once or twice to say hello.'

'Just so we are clear, you haven't been there at any other times? Not at night, when the room was unoccupied?'

'No.'

'What if I was to tell you that we had evidence that you had been in there?' Croucher asked.

'What evidence?'

'Well, you told us, in a roundabout way.' Croucher said.

Butcher slumped back in the chair, his head bowed. It had clearly dawned on him. Up until this point, he had probably assumed that Doyle had stuck the picture of him on the incident board so the MIT team could have a laugh at his expense, and swiftly removed it when the top brass had turned up.

'You could only have seen your mug shot on the board if you'd gone in after Liam had locked up for the night. He was first in the next day and removed it.'

'Isn't that entrapment?' Butcher glared at Doyle.

'DCI Doyle had reason to believe that someone had been in the incident room the night before, unauthorised. We needed to establish who. It might be unorthodox, but it was effective,' Croucher said. 'Now, we're wondering why you were so keen to know how the investigation was going. On Thursday, we thought it might be because Handcock was a person of interest, and also connected to you. With Handcock then being murdered, we are asking ourselves whether you played a role in either or both killings.'

Butcher began to say something, then stopped. Doyle seized the moment. In a measured voice, he asked, 'Did you kill Mia Wright and Terry Handcock?'

'No. If that's what you're all thinking, then I'm not prepared to go any further without a brief.'

'OK,' said Croucher. 'We'll stop here while you arrange for a solicitor to be present. But I need to state quite clearly now, on the record, that you are suspended from duty until further notice. You will need to surrender your warrant card and work mobile phone and laptop. We will also be seizing your personal mobile phone. While on suspension, you will not be able to enter any police premises without invitation or contact any police officers or staff on this force, either directly or through anyone else. Is that clear?'

'Yes.' Butcher had gone pale. He slumped in his seat, looking like a broken man.

'One more thing,' Croucher said. 'When you come back here with a solicitor, don't think that sitting there responding "no comment" will save you. If you are involved in these murders, or in anything else, we will find out. Not answering our questions won't save your career – or pension.'

Chapter 37

'Got something!' Gadget shouted out across the incident room. Morgan and Hales scurried over to his desk. 'This is taken from a video doorbell on the gate of a house just up the road from the workshop. Now watch this.' Gadget fiddled with the mouse and got the image on the screen to move. 'Going by the time she gave us, this has to be Tracy Handcock's car driving down the lane to drop Turkish off. I know the image isn't very clear, but from the shape of the car, I'd say it looks like a Range Rover Evoque, and it's white or a similar light colour.'

'OK,' Morgan said, though she wasn't convinced that the image would be able to be improved enough to say with certainty that this was Tracy Handcock's car.

'I've checked back and forward either side and no other cars come through, so assuming she didn't make the whole thing up about dropping her husband off, it has to be her.'

'Seems reasonable,' Hales agreed.

'And this is her coming back up the road less than two minutes later. Again, no other similar vehicles came that way.' Gadget rolled the footage on. 'And look at this – less than twenty seconds later, this panel van passes the camera going back down the lane towards the workshop. She said she didn't pass any vehicles in either direction, which wouldn't have been surprising

– it's a quiet lane and it was late at night. But she must have passed that van, and the lane is so narrow that she must have had to find a passing place and go by slowly. She should remember that.'

'It gives her more questions to answer. I'll give Liam a call and see how he wants to play this before we bail her. We might be able to get another extension granted,' Hales said.

'What is the BFG doing over at HQ?' Gadget asked. 'Bit unusual for him to be out all day in the middle of a double murder case.'

Morgan looked at Hales. Doyle had briefed them on the phone earlier, but they had been under strict instructions not to tell anyone else about the situation with DCI Butcher.

'I'm sure he will fill us all in when he can,' Hales said. 'In the meantime, we've got plenty to be getting on with.'

'That's what I mean,' Gadget went on. 'There's tons to do and only the five of us here doing it. Shouldn't those up-them-selves CID lot next door be looking at the drugs angle? Shaima and Birdseye have been on that all day, and it might not even be linked to both the murders.'

The young detective had a point, Morgan thought. They could do with another team investigating that, but that team couldn't be the one whose boss might be involved in the case. 'Sometimes, Gadget, it's best to trust the boss and see what he comes back with.' She felt bad for fobbing him off with a cryptic answer, but she wanted to close this conversation down before others joined in. She really couldn't tell him the truth, and Morgan knew that lying was not one of her strong points.

After DCI Butcher decided that he did want a solicitor present, they agreed that his interview would be adjourned until the next day to enable him to get suitable representation. Not wanting to waste time driving back and forth across the county, Doyle stayed at his office in Hutton to work there. He'd received regular updates from the Pearl about the progress – or lack of progress – of both murder investigations. The investigation was throwing up lots more questions, but so far they didn't have answers. Doyle had been so wrapped up in considering what information they had and what they needed to get that he was startled when the alarm on his phone went off. Cursing himself for forgetting at the same time as congratulating himself for setting a reminder, he managed to arrive at Harry's school in Darwen without needing to resort to improper use of the blues and twos.

Harry had been happy to remain in reception with headphones on, watching something on his iPad about canal boats, which had become his latest obsession, while the adults went into another room to talk. Harry's class teacher, Mrs Kennett was there, along with the school's Special Educational Needs teacher, Miss Duffy. They were told that the headteacher would be joining them later to discuss Harry and the bullying he had been subjected to. Doyle mostly listened while his ex-wife Fiona, a primary school teacher herself, asked lots of questions about Harry's educational progress. The grim reality was that he wasn't making any. For a long time, Doyle had clung to the hope that at some point everything would click with Harry and his educational and developmental delays would turn out to be just that. Delays.

His autism diagnosis when he was seven had come as no surprise, as Harry had shown significant signs of the condition long before starting school. It had taken that long to get a formal assessment as the waiting lists were long, and the Covid lockdowns hadn't helped. When he was finally diagnosed, Doyle was on suspension from work while an investigation took place into whether he had acted lawfully in shooting dead Jamal Campbell. His marriage to Fiona was also well and truly on the rocks; to some extent, they had both seen the formal identification of Harry's difficulties as a possible lifeline to haul their relationship and family onto more solid ground. It hadn't worked, partly because having a label of autism or autistic spectrum disorder didn't come with any magic solutions to help Harry adapt to the world he lived in. But the main reason Doyle's marriage had failed had nothing to do with his son. It was down to Doyle and his inability to juggle a relationship and parenthood with his demanding, all-absorbing job. Harry could have been an academic high-flyer and a sporting champion and Doyle and Fiona would still have found themselves arguing over access arrangements and who Harry spent Christmas Day with.

'We need to consider that, as well as the autism and learning difficulties, Harry may have a mild learning disability,' Miss Duffy said.

'Sorry, what?' Doyle asked. 'What's the difference?'

'Something like dyslexia is a learning difficulty – an obstacle that makes it harder to learn, but that doesn't affect a child's intellectual potential. A learning disability does impact on a child's intellectual ability and potential to learn.'

'It's difficult to know the full picture with Harry,' Mrs Kennett said. 'As we've said before, he is significantly below the level we would expect for a child of his age. That may be because he's finding it hard to learn in the classroom environment – a busy room with thirty nine-year-olds and just me and one teaching assistant would be a challenge for anyone on the autistic spectrum. Or there may be more to it. It's hard to know.'

'Is there any way this can be assessed? So we know what is best for Harry?' Doyle asked.

'We have sent off the application for Harry's EHC plan. If the local authority agrees to it, we will have more money to support Harry in school,' the Miss Duffy said.

'If? You mean there's a chance it might get turned down?' Doyle had assumed that the council would agree to the Education, Health and Care plan.

'There's always a chance with these things,' Miss Duffy said. 'But we have put together a strong application and I am reasonably confident.'

'Let's assume that the application is successful,' Fiona said. 'What would you propose putting in place?'

'We would put in an additional classroom assistant with experience in working with children like Harry. To be with him throughout lessons to help him to better access the curriculum and hopefully begin to catch up.'

Doyle looked across at his ex-wife. Although he also wanted the best for Harry, this was something she knew much more about.

'That sounds sensible,' Fiona said. 'At least we might get more of a picture of how, and why, he is struggling.'

'I understand there was another matter you wanted to discuss,' Mrs Kennett said. 'The head should be joining us at any moment.'

'Yes. The bullying...' Fiona began.

Then a younger man in a suit knocked and entered the room. Doyle had never seen him before, and Mr Chapman wasn't what Doyle had expected. He wondered if a sign of getting old was when head teachers started to look young.

'Sorry for the delay,' Chapman said before shaking Doyle and Fiona's hands and introducing himself.

'It's OK,' Mrs Kennett said. 'We were just coming to the bit we need you for.'

'Right. The bullying allegations?'

'They're not allegations,' Fiona said. 'Callum Cameron and his hangers-on have been picking on Harry something rotten. He's terrified of them and every day it's a battle to get him to go to school.'

Doyle knew that the anger in Fiona's voice was an attempt to stop her from succumbing to tears.

'OK,' Chapman said, holding up his hands. 'I didn't mean to minimise this. We take bullying very seriously at St Christopher's. And I know this is not the first time we have had this conversation about Harry and this particular pupil.'

Doyle took his phone out and opened up the photos. 'These are pictures that I took of Harry last week when he showed me his injuries. He told me they were caused by Callum Cameron on Friday 27th October at lunchtime in the school playground. This is backed up by a note that he was sent home with, saying that the school nurse had cleaned and dressed his cuts in the medical room.' Doyle knew he was sounding like a police officer, but that was his intention. 'So, I know you are aware of it, and I want to know what you have done about it.'

'Well, we acted straight away. That day we called Callum's mother into school and we have excluded Callum for three days this week. He will not be back in school until Thursday,' Chapman said.

'Did you report it to the police or raise it as a safeguarding issue with the local authority?' Doyle asked. He had no expectation that this would happen, and he knew that schools couldn't rush to the police every time one child hit another, but he wanted to make a point.

'Well, no. But we wouldn't normally do that in this situation.'

'Why not? In any other walk of life, if someone attacks someone else and causes them physical harm it's assault at the very least.'

'I understand that,' Chapman said. 'But we are dealing with children here. If we can educate them not to behave in this manner, then that is a better course of action in the long term.'

'I'm not sure I like the idea of my son being a tool in teaching Callum Cameron not to be a violent little shit. Can I ask how his mum reacted when you spoke to her?'

'Can I be honest with you both?' Chapman asked.

'Please,' Doyle said.

'Callum has two older brothers who have been through this school. I have called his mother in countless times to speak to her about her sons' behaviour, and it hasn't made a blind bit of difference. To be fair to her, she never shouts and swears and says I'm picking on her little darlings, like some parents do. She sits and listens and says she will tell them off, but nothing ever changes. I don't think she has a clue what to do to stop them misbehaving.'

'Are you saying there is nothing more you can do?' Fiona asked, her voice breaking slightly.

'I'm not saying that, but we are limited. We can stop Callum from taking part in some of the fun stuff we do here, such as school trips and playing in the football team. We can make it clear to him that he will be excluded from all of these until his behaviour improves.'

'Do you think that will work?' Doyle asked.

'To a degree, perhaps. But there is something else we can consider.'

'What's that?' Fiona asked.

'I don't want to sound like I'm victim blaming or saying that what has happened to Harry is acceptable, because it's not.'

Fiona looked like she was going to protest. Doyle put his hand on her arm, wanting to let Chapman finish.

'But we can look at how we can best protect Harry from being exposed to this type of bullying. It is a sad fact of life that children can be horrible to each other. And it's often the ones who are seen as different who are the targets. Before I came in, I understand you were discussing what additional support could be put in place to help Harry with his learning. I know we were going to look at one-to-one support in the classroom. Perhaps we should look at extending that, to make sure there is an adult allocated to Harry at all times, so he's not as vulnerable to being bullied.'

Doyle considered this. A year or two ago, he would have thought it a backward step. The real world was full of horrible people and the best way to survive was to become streetwise as a kid. But Harry might never develop the social skills that would help him survive in the playground. Doyle thought back to his school days. Harry would have been eaten alive in the playgrounds of Peckham.

'That's great in theory,' Fiona said. 'But the extra support won't be put in place until the EHC plan is approved, and that could take months.'

'Leave it with me for a week or so,' Chapman said. 'We might be able to put something in place sooner than that. Harry is a lovely boy, and none of us want to see him miserable.'

During the meeting, Doyle had felt his work phone vibrate several times in his pocket. He stopped to check his messages while Harry and Fiona walked on ahead across the school playground towards the gates. It was gone five and he hoped he wouldn't need to go back into work; he could really do with an evening off. Mr Burns had sent him a long and convoluted text which said that Doyle did not need to be at DCI Butcher's second interview the next morning. He could go back to Nelson to continue to run the murder investigation. This suited Doyle fine. His gut told him it was unlikely that Butcher was directly involved in either murder, though clearly he was up to no good. If Doyle was a gambler, he'd have bet that bribery would be involved. He got the impression that DI Cavanaugh would be tenacious in getting to the bottom of whatever was going on. By the time he had replied to his boss, Harry and Fiona were on the street, walking towards Fiona's car.

Then a football hit Harry on the back. It had been kicked by one of a group of four boys walking up the road on the other side. Fiona shouted at them and the boys ran off around the corner. Doyle jogged over to check on his son. 'You OK?'

Harry nodded. His body had stiffened and he was rooted to the spot.

'Little so and sos,' Fiona said. 'I'd like to wring their bloody necks.'

Doyle crouched down so he was at eye level with his son. 'Is one of those boys Callum?'

Harry nodded.

'The one in the yellow coat?'

Harry nodded again.

Doyle wasn't surprised. It was always easy to spot the ringleader in a group of kids. 'You're OK now,' Doyle said, pulling his son in for a hug. He felt Harry relax in the safety of his dad's arms.

'That exclusion from school's not done any good,' Fiona said. 'Little git. Imagine doing that right in front of me.'

'Can't you arrest him, Dad? And put him in jail?'

Doyle smiled at his son, glad that he had relaxed enough to talk. 'I wish I could, Harry, but don't worry. I'm going to sort this out. Stop him bullying you.'

'We'd better get going, Harry,' Fiona said. 'Get you your tea. Thanks for making it, Liam. It was good that you were there.'

'No problem.'

'I love you, Dad.

'I love you too, Harry.'

'I love you, Dad.'

'I love you too, Harry.'

'Come on, then,' Fiona said. 'Let's get you home.'

Chapter 38

Doyle screeched the Skoda to a stop, killing the siren but leaving the blue strobes on.

'Police,' he said, getting out of the car and brandishing his warrant card towards the four boys. 'Stay where you are.'

'What? We've not done owt,' the boy in the yellow coat said, showing more bravado than the other children.

'We'll see about that,' Doyle said. 'Are you Callum Cameron?'

That took the wind out of the boy's sails, and he stepped back onto the pavement away from Doyle.

'What if I am?'

His words might have sounded tough if they hadn't been mumbled.

'Right, the rest of you get lost. Me and Callum are going to have a little chat.'

The other boys didn't need telling twice. They set off down the road, abandoning their mate.

Doyle crouched so that he was eye level with the boy and spoke softly. 'Do you know what a hate crime is, Callum?'

The boy got out a mumbled 'no'.

'It's a crime that is motivated by hostility towards anyone with a protected characteristic. I don't expect you to know what that means. How old are you?'

'Nine.'

'Right, well, listen very carefully. A crime is when you do something that's against the law. Such as hurting another child. Understand?'

'Yes, but I—'

'What makes that a hate crime is that the child you hurt has a disability. And you were bullying him and hurting him because of his disability. And disability is one of the protected characteristics that I just mentioned.'

'I never.'

'Unfortunately for you, Callum, I've got evidence and photos of the boy's injuries. If you keep saying you didn't do it, I'll arrest you and take you to the police station, call your mum and a social worker and interview you there. Is that what you want?'

'No, please. I didn't mean—'

'So, you do know what I'm talking about?'

'Yes.'

'What?'

'Harry Doyle, but I never meant to hurt him, it was just a bit of fun.'

Doyle took out his phone and pulled up the photos of Harry's injuries. 'See these bruises here. Do they look like fun to you?'

'No.'

'If someone battered you so you had bruises like that, would you like it?'

'No. Please, I'm sorry.'

'Now, Callum, you just told me that you're nine. Do you know what that means?'

'No.'

'That means you are under the age of criminal responsibility in this country. I don't expect you to understand that either, but it means if you break the law, it is your mum who will get punished. Hate crimes are something we take really seriously, so at the very least your mum could get a big fine. Big enough that she won't have any money left for Christmas presents for you and your brothers.'

'No! They'll kill me.'

'Or worse still, she might get sent to prison, and then where would you and your brothers live?'

The boy gulped, lost for words.

'Now, I'm pretty sure you don't want that, do you?'

The boy shook his head. 'No. Please, I won't do it again.'

'And do you know what happens when you are ten?'

'No.'

'Well, then you are responsible for your actions. And if something like this happens again, it's you who will be taken away from your family and taken to live somewhere where other naughty boys live. Boys who are much bigger and much nastier than you.'

'No, please. I swear, I won't do it again. I promise.'

'Good. I'm going to give you one last chance. If anything like this ever happens again, I am going to make sure the full force of the law comes down on you. And either you or your mum will be punished. Do you understand?'

'Yes,' the boy stammered.

'Good, then we have an agreement. But Callum, I am going to be watching you very closely.'

Chapter 39

Day 10: Tuesday 7 November

Doyle was glad to be back in the incident room at Nelson police station. The nature of the relationship between DCI Butcher and Terry Handcock was an important line of enquiry, but it wasn't the only avenue that needed investigating. Spending the previous day away from his team had been frustrating. Although he had been kept up to speed on his team's progress, it wasn't the same as being there. Ideally, first thing in the morning he would've had a full team briefing and a rundown on where they were, but Doyle couldn't do that. He had been expressly forbidden from discussing the situation regarding Butcher with anyone other than Hales and Morgan. Doyle had tried to argue with Croucher that his team couldn't possibly be expected to investigate a murder when they had not been given all the information, but Mr Burns had been unbending. As a result, it was just Hales and Morgan who joined Doyle in his office first thing.

'Inspector Cavanaugh will be interviewing Butcher again today with Burns, but I don't expect we will get anything useful from that. If he was going to come clean about what was going on with him and Turkish, he would've done it yesterday. He's hardly likely to say any more with his solicitor present,' Doyle said.

'You don't seriously think he could be directly involved in the actual murders, do you?' Hales asked.

'I don't think it's likely. Turkish being killed hasn't worked out well for Pat. If it wasn't for that, I doubt it would've got as far as Professional Standards getting involved,' Doyle said.

'Do you reckon his connection to Handcock is as simple as he described it?' Hales asked. 'Just someone giving him the odd bit of intelligence, and maybe Butcher giving him a drink now and then in return?'

'I might've thought that if we hadn't had our own intel that Turkish was dealing, and then found a load of drugs at his work. Plus, if Butcher was paying him he would have been doing it out of his own pocket, as Turkish wasn't registered.'

'It would make more sense to me the other way round,' Morgan said.

'That's what I'm starting to think, Anna,' Doyle said.

'Turkish could've been paying him to ensure his drug dealing didn't come to the attention of the local CID, or anyone else,' Morgan said. 'It's a bit suspicious that Terry Handcock doesn't even have any markers against his name for dealing, let alone any convictions.'

'Especially when you consider that a manager of the local mental health team passed on intelligence about him dealing to the police,' Doyle said. 'DI Cavanaugh is going to be taking a close look at the work of the local CID. It will be interesting to see what she uncovers.'

'I almost feel sorry for him,' Hales said. 'When those bastards in Professional Standards get their claws into you, they don't let go.'

'Good,' Morgan said. 'The man's an arsehole.'

'Couldn't agree more,' Doyle said. 'But none of this gets us any closer to our killer. Assuming we are correct in thinking that, despite the different MOs, it's the same person, because not many killers remove body parts, then neither of our original suspects looks likely.'

'Agreed,' said Hales. 'Will Perkins would have to be Harry bloody Houdini to have got out of that mental hospital, killed Turkish and got back in undetected.'

'Exactly,' Doyle agreed. 'And Turkish didn't smash his own expensive teeth out before doing himself in. So where does that leave us?'

'Tracy Handcock?' Morgan suggested. 'Except we don't think she is physically capable of either murder.'

'The thing is,' Hales said, 'we know she's lied to us in interview. And when we challenged her about seeing Perkins, she doubled down and said she saw him earlier too. She either has to be directly involved or covering for someone.'

'Her brother would be the obvious candidate,' Morgan said.

'He is,' Doyle agreed. 'And we will need to bring him in at some point. We've got grounds for arrest due to the drugs found at his business, but it might be worth seeing what else we can dig up on him first.'

'You sound a bit reluctant, boss,' Morgan said.

'I'm still not sure it's a strong enough motive,' Doyle said. 'Think about it. His sister has been cheated on by his brother-in-law and employee. He's given his sister an STI and made the other woman pregnant.'

'Seems like a strong reason to be pretty mad to me,' Hales said.

'Bloody mad, yes,' Doyle said. 'But enraged enough to kill Mia and cut out her womb and then kill Turkish and cut out his tongue? If we were just investigating Terry Handcock's murder, and he hadn't had his tongue cut out, I would think this more likely. He got a good kicking for treating his wife badly, and it went way too far.'

'We don't even know if Tracy Handcock and her brother knew Mia was pregnant. Didn't she tell you yesterday that she hadn't had a chance to talk to Turkish about getting the clap, so how would either of them know about the baby?' Morgan said.

'Good point, Anna. But if it's not him, then who is Tracy Handcock protecting, and why?' Hales asked.

'We can't rule him out, that's for sure,' Doyle said. 'But he's got to his forties with only a couple of speeding convictions. If he was that sadistic, I think he would have more of a record.'

'True,' Morgan said. 'But then maybe the local CID were turning a blind eye to whatever he got up to in the past.'

'Maybe, in recent years,' Doyle conceded. 'Something Butcher told us yesterday, and I've no reason to doubt this, was that he went after Perkins because Turkish phoned him and gave him an off-the-record tip-off.'

'You think he was doing the same as his wife?' Hales asked. 'Covering for someone else?'

'That's what I initially thought, but it doesn't make complete sense. If he was covering for someone else, leading the police in the wrong direction, then he couldn't have expected whoever that was to go on and kill him next.'

'Or,' Morgan said, 'he wasn't covering for someone else. He genuinely believed that Perkins was the killer when he called Butcher.'

'Now we're getting somewhere,' Doyle said. 'But if that's the case, why did he think that? And perhaps more to the point, how did he know Mia was dead so soon after her body had been discovered? Sure, anyone going through Barley that morning would have known there was a police incident happening, and news travels fast in these parts, but they wouldn't have known it was a murder – and even if they did, they wouldn't have known it was Mia.'

'Maybe it was Mia herself who had told him?' Hales said. 'I mean, before the event; she might've told him she was worried about Perkins, and then when he found out she was dead he put two and two together and called his tame DCI.'

'That's it!' Doyle said.

'What, that Mia told him?' Morgan asked.

'No, not that, but Geoff just said "when he found out she was dead". Turkish either had to have been there when she was killed, or someone had to have told him about it, possibly knowing Turkish would pass it on to the police. If we find out how Turkish knew about Mia's murder, we will be getting very close to the killer.'

'Turkish said that he was at home with his wife,' Morgan said. 'We didn't give that complete credibility because it's easily faked. But if he was telling the truth and he was at home at the time, then whoever told him about the murder must have either visited him there or phoned him or Tracy Handcock.'

'Right. Let's get Gadget and Birdseye out chatting to their neighbours and checking for doorbell cameras in the vicinity of their house. We can get Shaima to go over phone records for Turkish's phones and his wife's phone as well as their landline, if they have one. Any number that called them on the night of Mia's murder or that morning before nine thirty has to be checked out.'

'There's one thing I'm still not getting,' said Hales. 'Tracy Handcock didn't just lie about seeing Perkins on the night of her husband's murder. She also said that no vehicles passed her on the lane on her way back from dropping Turkish off. If she was telling us she saw Perkins because she believed he was the killer, why not mention the van she passed? She might not have remembered it straight away, but when we asked if she passed anyone, she must have remembered.'

'Yeah,' Morgan said. 'And her headlights would have been shining straight at it when she passed. She might even have known the driver.'

'And that might be your answer, Geoff. Whoever killed Mia and Turkish is known to Tracy Handcock, and is someone she is either very close to or she's too frightened of them to give us their name.'

Chapter 40

'There's definitely something going on,' Gadget said.

'For once you might be right,' Birdseye said.

'Cheeky old git. What do you think it is?' Gadget asked. 'First, the BFG spends the whole day away yesterday. Now they've been in his office for ages.'

'It wasn't just the boss who was away yesterday,' Asif said. 'Paige told me that DCI Butcher had got into work and was called away to HQ with no explanation, and he hasn't been back.'

'You don't think they were being given a bollocking by the brass for the row they had about whose case it was?' Gadget asked.

'That wouldn't take all day, would it?' Birdseye said. 'It's got to be something else.'

'Maybe there's more to these murders than we've realised. Perhaps they're linked to something else,' Gadget said.

'I couldn't find anything on the Connect database or Holmes 2 going back ten years that looked like it might be linked to these killings,' Asif said. 'Although the murders were different. Body parts being removed is quite specific, along with the two victims knowing each other.'

'It might be something completely unrelated to the case,' Birdseye said. 'It could be about resources – or lack of them. We are well understaffed, especially as this is now a double murder. Maybe we're going to join forces with the local CID until we get this wrapped up.'

'You don't think that, do you?' Gadget said. He was starting to regret swearing at DS Felton the first time he met him.

'Stranger things have happened,' Birdseye said.

'I hope not. They seem like a right bunch of pricks.'

'It would make more sense if they got on with investigating the drugs found at the business and let us concentrate on—' Asif stopped as the door to Doyle's office opened.

If Gadget had wanted to maintain the illusion that they hadn't been gossiping while she'd been in the BFG's office, Morgan thought, then he should probably have clicked the mouse so that the laptop he was pretending to stare at didn't have the screensaver showing.

'Birdseye, Gadget. I've got a job for you that needs doing now,' Morgan said.

'What's that, Sarge?' Birdseye asked.

'You need to get down to Mr and Mrs Handcock's house. We need to know whether anyone visited them on the morning when Mia's body was found, or if either of them went out.'

'Sunday 29th October,' Birdseye said, looking in his notebook.

'Speak to neighbours. As it was a Sunday morning, most people should be able to remember what they were doing, especially as it was the morning after the clocks went back. If they did have any visitors, there is a decent chance that people would have been around and seen them,' Morgan said. 'We're specifically interested in the time before 9.30 a.m. If anyone does have a camera doorbell, make sure we get the footage from that.'

'We already checked – there isn't anything close by,' Gadget said. 'Sarge, can I ask you something?'

'Go on.' Morgan had a pretty good idea where this was heading.

'It's just that you and the Pearl have been in with the boss for half the morning. Is there something we should know about?'

'If it was something you should know about, I'd have told you.' It came out a bit shorter than Morgan had intended.

'It's just that if there's something to do with the investigation, we share it as a group,' Gadget persisted.

'It's nothing to do with the investigation.' Morgan hated lying to her team, but she wished Gadget would take the hint and shut up.

'Are we going to be working more closely with CID to get this wrapped up?' Birdseye asked.

'No. Why would you think that?' Morgan asked.

'Well, we're short-handed at the moment, and both DCIs were at HQ yesterday.'

'Why are we so interested in Turkish and his wife on the morning after Mia's murder?' Gadget butted in.

'We just are,' Morgan said, and knew she had sounded like a worn-out parent speaking to a toddler. 'Look, just get yourself down there and start asking questions. I'm sure all will become apparent soon enough.'

'Sarge, can't you give us a hint?' Gadget pleaded.

'If you really want to know what we were chatting about, then why not knock on the boss's door and ask him yourself? I'm sure he will be delighted to hear you questioning how he's running the investigation.'

'Come on,' Birdseye said, getting up and grabbing his coat from the back of his chair. 'Let's go and knock on some other doors.'

'Shaima, can you look into calls to and from both of Turkish's phones that morning? And Tracy Handcock's phone, plus the landline, if they've got one?' Morgan said.

'Will do,' Asif said. 'Is there anything specific I'm looking for?'

'Calls in and out, or texts, and what numbers they are from, and where the calls were made from. Anything you can get about anyone they communicated with that morning.'

'Will do.'

'Thanks. Fancy a brew?'

'Please. Are you OK, Sarge?'

'I'm fine, just got a lot on.'

Chapter 41

Making tea was a good opportunity for Morgan to compose herself. She knew she had been too hard on Gadget. If she had been sitting outside in the incident room not knowing what was being discussed in Doyle's office, she would have been just as keen to find out. Maybe she wasn't cut out for leadership after all. You couldn't be an effective manager if every time someone asked a difficult question you bit their head off. She hadn't always been like that, but these days anything seemed to get under her skin. She knew why; she wasn't stupid. She knew irritability was a symptom of PTSD, along with everything else she was experiencing. It was inevitable after what she had been through. But knowing what the problem was didn't help. What she needed to know was how to make it stop. How to make things get back to normal. Maybe there wasn't a way; maybe this was her new normal, oscillating between being grumpy and apprehensive – frightened, even, if she was being honest. She was seeing a psychologist, she hadn't been given any choice about that, but she spent most sessions trying to avoid confronting her demons.

The kettle clicked, startling her. Her right hand immediately went to her throat, subconsciously checking that the tightness she felt there wasn't real. *Jesus, get a grip. It's just a fucking kettle boiling*. She took some deep breaths and poured water into the cups. She needed to shake herself out of this, compose herself, get back in the incident room and get on with her job. She heard footsteps coming towards the kitchen and hoped it would be someone from her own team. She couldn't keep the disappointment off her face when she saw who it was.

'You can't hide in here all day, pretending to make tea.'

'Fuck off, Felton. I'd have thought you would have plenty to worry about besides me.'

'What's that supposed to mean?'

'Why don't you ask your boss?'

'He's not – wait, you knew he wasn't in, didn't you?'

'Did I?'

'Don't piss about, Anna. Do you know what's going on?'

'Don't you?'

'Come on, if you know what's happening you've got to share. None of us in CID have got a clue. All we know is the DCI got called away yesterday and hasn't been back.'

'Why don't you call and ask him?'

'Tried that. His phone's switched off. Come on, Anna, we're both coppers at the end of the day.'

'No, I'm a copper and you're a prick. Now fuck off and get out of my way before you get two cups of tea chucked in your face.'

Felton didn't need telling twice. Morgan walked past him without looking back. She hoped he hadn't seen her hands shaking. So much for making a cuppa to compose herself.

Chapter 42

The three doors Birdseye had knocked on so far had all gone unanswered, and it didn't look like Gadget was getting on any better on the other side of the road. It wasn't really surprising: it was nearly lunchtime on a Tuesday, and most folk would be at work. The next house looked more promising. There was a Ford Ka on the drive with a National Trust sticker in the windscreen. Birdseye didn't like to stereotype, but he reckoned there was a better than fifty-fifty chance that the person living there was retired. He had a National Trust sticker in his car, and he wasn't far off drawing his pension. At least when he did retire he would be able to get full value for money out of his membership.

A dog barked before he had rung the bell, and the door was answered by a woman carrying a toddler, almost certainly her grandchild.

'DC Nelson,' he said, holding out his warrant card for inspection. 'I wonder if I might ask you some questions? It's about your neighbours from three doors down.'

'Oh yes, I heard what happened to Terry. You don't expect that. Not round here.'

'Do you know Mr and Mrs Hancock well?'

'No, not really. You'd better come in. I don't want to be seen gossiping on the doorstep, and I can put her down.' She gestured for Birdseye to come into the house. 'No need to wipe your feet. I'll be mopping the floor when this one finally has her nap.'

Birdseye walked through to the back as directed, a springer spaniel running around his legs as he went.

'Don't stand on ceremony. D'you want a brew?'

'No thanks, Mrs...' The detective patted the dog and perched on a kitchen chair.

'Myra. Myra Holt.' She placed the infant in a playpen. Birdseye wasn't sure if that was to protect the child from the dog or to protect the dog from being harassed by the toddler. He suspected the latter.

'Have you lived here long, Myra?'

'We moved here in 1982, so you could say so.'

'How long have you known Mr and Mrs Handcock?' Birdseye said, taking out his notebook.

'Since they moved in here. It was before Covid, but not long. Must've been 2019. I know that because they were flaunting the rules in lockdown, always going out, having people round.' Mrs Holt lowered her voice. 'I reported them twice to the local police, but nothing was done about it. It wasn't right. My Clive's got emphysema.'

'Is it fair to say they're not friends of yours, then?'

'Not likely, though we always say hello, keep it civil like.'

'Can I ask you about a couple of Sundays back, the 29th October? Did you see them then? See if they went out, or notice if they had any visitors?

'I can't remember seeing them then, to be honest.'

'It was the Sunday before Halloween. Would you have gone out anywhere, taken the dog out?'

'I would've taken the dog out.' She put her finger to her lips, as if this would help her remember. 'Yes, both their cars were there. I remember because hers was on the drive and his was parked so far up on the kerb that I had to walk out into the road to get past it. Bloody monstrous truck thing. I know you shouldn't talk ill of the dead, but that was him all over. Inconsiderate.'

'Was that just with the parking, or was there other things he did?'

'This man used to come round – hulking great big fella. He's got a white van. Often came late at night and he and Terry would go off together. No consideration for anyone else – they'd slam doors, talk loudly.'

'Was his van there that Sunday morning too?'

'No. No, I would've noticed it. Wait – that Sunday was when that girl was killed in Barley, wasn't it? Are you thinking it was the same person?'

'Honestly,' Birdseye said, despite what he was about to say not being true, 'we're not sure at the moment. It's unusual for anyone to be killed around here, so if two people are murdered close together, we have to consider the possibility that they're related. Tell me a bit more about this man that often came around. You said he was big – do you know anything else about him? Is he a friend or relative of Terry's? A work colleague, perhaps?'

'I'm not sure. I don't think he's a friend as such. He looks quite a bit younger, but it's hard to tell. He's got one of those big bushy beards they all have these days. I'd say he's probably a colleague, but it's often late at night when he comes, and they go off together. Funny time to be out doing work, if you ask me. Now I think about it, he might be a friend. I think he might have even been staying there for a bit a while back, but I don't remember seeing the van then. But I'm not one to pry into other folk's business.'

Chapter 43

Morgan never drank alcohol during the week, and seldom at the weekends these days. She'd shrugged off her wild drinking days shortly after meeting Sam during her second year at university and had enjoyed a healthy lifestyle since then. She didn't miss those times. She had been young and lonely, away from home and grieving for her father. Nights out crawling the bars of Lancaster had been a good distraction from the pain, but she knew they weren't going to take her to where she wanted to be in life. She'd known that then and she knew that now. So why was she standing in her kitchen with a large glass of Pinot Grigio in her hand on a Tuesday night?

She'd stopped off at the late shop on her way home and picked up two bottles of the first white wine she found that was ice cold and ready to drink. Morgan had contemplated getting a packet of menthol cigarettes as well. She wasn't sure if you could still get them; she'd heard somewhere that they might be getting banned. Besides, if Sam saw her smoking she reckoned his head might explode. She'd heard him tinkering in the garage and shouted a hello to him when she got in. She took a large swig of wine and felt it slide down her throat, cool and soothing.

Something smelled good. Next to the hob, she found a moussaka covered in foil. It was one of Sam's specialities. The mince was bulked out with lentils to make it healthier, but despite this it still tasted good. One portion was missing from the dish. Sam planned his nutrition down to the last gram. Morgan plated herself up a similar-sized portion, leaving enough for two further meals. She drained her glass while the food warmed in the microwave and found a rocket salad in the fridge while she was getting a refill.

The food tasted good washed down with the wine. Morgan hadn't realised how hungry she was. She knew she shouldn't really, but fuck it, it had been a bad day. She helped herself to another portion. Putting the solitary remaining helping in the fridge, she retrieved the wine and emptied the rest of the bottle into her glass.

'You found your dinner, then,' Sam said, coming into the kitchen. He stopped and Morgan could sense him staring at her. 'Is that a glass of wine?'

'Yes. Want one?' She knew her nonchalance would wind him up, but right now she didn't care.

'What? No, it's Tuesday. Why would I... Are you alright?'

'Yes. Why wouldn't I be?'

'Well, drinking on a school night, it's not like—'

'I'm a grown-up. I don't go to bloody school, and if I want a glass of wine after a hard day at work, I don't see why I shouldn't. Most people do the same.'

'So that's it?'

'That's what?'

'Work. Your work's stressing you out. I knew you shouldn't be back yet. You need time to recover.'

'Work was stressful before. I don't need time off. It's the nature of the job, that's not going to change.' She took another large mouthful of wine.

'But before, you wouldn't have come home and got stuck into a bottle of wine. You'd have gone for a run or done a session on the turbo trainer, got it out of your system that way.'

'I didn't fancy that tonight. I just wanted to relax with a glass of wine. That's perfectly normal.'

'You know what I think would help? Come out with me this weekend. We'll go for a nice ride, nothing too challenging. Enjoy being out in the countryside. Get back on the bike – literally and figuratively. It's got to help. That's what the pro riders do as soon as they can after a crash.'

'Jesus, Sam. I didn't fall off my bike and get a bit of road rash. Someone tried to kill me. Bloody well nearly did. I'm not sure that getting back on the bike will make that go away.'

'I know – I was involved, remember? Look, I didn't mean... I know it's been tough.'

'But you want to tell me what I should and shouldn't be doing. I shouldn't be back at work, but I should be back riding my bike. I shouldn't be having a drink, because it's Tuesday.'

'I'm going for a shower.'

'Last week you said it was good for me to talk about it, and I should do it more. And now I am, you're fucking off to have a shower.' Deep down she knew she was being unreasonable, but she was fed up with being told what was best for her. As if anyone knew. Morgan got the second bottle of wine out of the fridge and settled down on the sofa, intent on watching whatever meaningless crap she could find on TV. Perhaps she had pushed herself back to work too early, but she didn't think it would've got any easier the longer she was away. It didn't help that she was working in an office next door to Steve Felton and could bump into him at any time. Then there was the fear – not the fear of Felton. She wasn't afraid of him. This was worse, though: it was the fear of physical conflict. It wasn't new; it had always been there. In a way, she had always thought it was healthy. If you weren't a bit frightened going into a potentially dangerous situation, then you might not take sensible precautions. But it felt different now. In her probation years working in emergency response, she'd soon got used to it. Her nerves would jangle as she rushed to an incident, then she'd be in at the deep end with a flood of adrenaline and then afterwards she'd almost be on a high as she chatted about it with her colleagues. Assuming no one had got seriously hurt, that was.

Stop it. Why was she thinking about work? The whole idea of having a few drinks was to try and forget about that and give herself a night off. She topped up her glass. The alcohol was starting to have an effect, she noticed. Her hand was unsteady and she spilled some wine as she poured. When was the last time she had been drunk? It must have been years ago.

'Look, I'm sorry. I didn't...' Sam was standing in the doorway, looking sheepish.

'No. I'm sorry, it's not your fault. It's just...'

Sam took a seat at the opposite end of the sofa, then reached over and took her hand. 'I know your job means a lot to you. And I know how hard you have worked to get where you are. But that doesn't stop me worrying about you.'

'I know, but it's just... Oh, I don't know.' Morgan had lost her train of thought. She was sure she had something meaningful to say, but she couldn't recall what it was.

'Are you OK?'

'Yes,' she said. 'But what are you doing all the way over there?' She pulled him towards her and he didn't resist.

'How much have you had?'

'Enough. Why? Want a glass?'

'No, I'll pass, thanks. One of us has to remain responsible.'

'Why? Who do we have to be responsible for? It's not like we've got a houseful of kiddies upstairs in bed.'

'True. Do you still want that?'

'What?'

'Kids.'

'Yeah, but maybe not a houseful. One or two.'

'Maybe we should start thinking more about that.'

'What is there to think about?'

'Well, when...'

'Oh.' Morgan wasn't quite sure what he meant. 'As in the when when? Like now?'

'Like soon. Or now.'

'Now?'

'Well, not right now, obviously. But soon.'

Morgan knew that now wasn't the best time to be thinking about this. But maybe it did make sense. They could start a new chapter in their lives and look forward, not back. 'Come on, then,' she said, getting up.

'Where?'

'Upstairs. Let's make a baby.'

'But you're on the pill.'

'And you don't enter a triathlon unless you've been training for it. Let's go and practise.'

Chapter 44

Day 11: Wednesday 8 November

'What I am about to tell you does not leave this room.' Detective Superintendent Croucher addressed those assembled in the incident room for the morning briefing. As well as Doyle's team, which had been boosted by PC Anderton and PCSO Lofthouse, now officially seconded to work under him, DI Cavanaugh was there with another team of detectives and analysts. One notable absence from the ensemble was DS Morgan. This concerned Doyle – not because she particularly needed to be there, but because it wasn't like her. Morgan was normally so reliable, and the one time she'd gone missing she'd been in serious danger. He had to remind himself that there could be many reasons she wasn't in the incident room that morning. It was unlikely that she was in danger.

'During the course of this investigation,' Croucher went on, 'it has come to light that DCI Butcher of Pendle CID had been in regular contact with the second victim, Terry Handcock. When questioned about his relationship with Handcock, Butcher was unwilling to provide a satisfactory explanation. He has now been suspended from all duties and is being investigated by DI Cavanaugh here and her team from anti-corruption in the Professional Standards department.'

Cavanaugh held up her hand so everyone could see who she was. Doyle noticed a look pass between Birdseye and Gadget. He knew the two detectives had been speculating, but he doubted that either of them had thought of this scenario.

Mr Burns carried on. 'To be clear, we don't think Butcher is a suspect in either murder at this stage. But we do think he may have been involved in supporting a dealing operation that we think Handcock was involved in. As you are all aware, under normal circumstances CID would investigate localised dealing. However, for obvious reasons, we've decided that's not appropriate in this case, and all of the CID officers on Butcher's team will be operating out of Burnley once they have been interviewed by DI Cavanaugh's team and cleared to continue. We will be running three separate investigations alongside each other. DCI Doyle's team will continue to focus on the two murders. DI Cavanaugh's team will look at Butcher's involvement, as well as digging into the dealing angle after the drug seizure at NN Agricultural Engineering. I will be overseeing all three cases. Is there anything you want to add, Liam?'

'Although there will be three separate investigations, there could be some significant crossover in each. It's important that we all share information as we uncover it.' Doyle looked across at Cavanaugh's team as he spoke. Anti-corruption officers had a reputation for keeping their cards close to their chest, but whatever Butcher had been up to, the most important thing was catching a double murderer. 'Shaima Asif will be coordinating all the mobile phone data, call logs and cell site analysis for all three investigations, assisted by another analyst based at HQ. Any additional information – new phone numbers, that kind of thing – needs to go through her.'

Morgan still couldn't believe it. She'd overslept, and not just by a bit, by an hour and a half. Sam could have woken her, but he hadn't. He was working from home and when she asked him why he'd left her sleeping, he'd said she clearly needed the rest and that she had worked more hours than she should over the last ten days. He still didn't get it; her job wasn't one where you could do your nine to five then sod off, leaving things for the next day. She felt like shit too, but that wasn't Sam's fault. She'd gulped down a pint of water before leaving the house, but that had done little to quell her hangover. Why today of all days? She knew Mr Burns was going to be in the morning briefing and she didn't want to look like a slacker in front of him – or, worse, make him think that she was so affected by what had happened in the summer that she couldn't do her job.

She took a deep breath and walked into the incident room. *Shit, who are all these people? And who is that woman in a suit? She looks like she belongs on The Apprentice.*

'Ah, Anna,' Doyle said without missing a beat. 'Go alright at the dentist?'

'Yes, thanks, boss,' she said, taking the nearest seat, grateful that Doyle had covered her absence.

'I'll fill you in on everything after this meeting,' Doyle said. 'I was just updating our colleagues from Professional Standards on where we have got to with the murder investigation.'

Jesus, Professional Standards as well as Mr Burns. What a morning to be late and hungover.

'And this Will Perkins, you've definitely ruled him out as a suspect now?' Suit Woman asked. She had a Scottish accent and sounded quite abrupt.

'As far as we can,' Doyle said. 'But how far can you go to prove a negative? The only actual information linking him to the case is Terry Handcock telling Pat – er, DCI Butcher, that Will Perkins was the culprit in Mia's murder. Then Tracy Handcock said she saw him near the scene when her husband was killed. But we know she lied in at least part of her statement.'

'I'm satisfied that he's not involved,' Croucher said. 'Which is why I've authorised removing the two officers stationed outside the ward he's on. Resources are down to the bone right now, especially since we've effectively lost a whole CID department.'

'So, as it stands now, the most likely suspect is Neil Nuttall, Mrs Handcock's brother and owner of NN Agricultural Engineering?' Suit Woman asked.

'There is a possibility that the culprit is someone unknown. But yes, the next logical step will be trying to rule Nuttall either in or out,' Doyle said.

'How do you want to play this, Liam?' Croucher asked.

'We need to bring him in. We've still got to interview him about the drugs found on his premises and go through his statement about finding Terry Handcock's body,' Doyle said. 'I think it is unlikely he will be very cooperative. We've had his sister locked up and his business shut down since Friday. Let's ask him to give an interview under caution, but if he refuses we'll arrest him.'

'If that's how you want to play it,' Burns said. 'Is his business still an active crime scene?'

'Until at least the end of today,' Jen Knight said. 'We've got a specialist coming up to do a radio frequency survey to establish the strength of the mobile phone signal from various masts around the area. That will help with the work Shaima's doing in establishing the exact locations where the calls were made from.'

'And Tracy Handcock? Croucher asked.

'We've bailed her for now,' Doyle said. 'We've not charged her with anything yet, but there is enough there for a conspiracy charge. I thought it might be wise to hang on to that for now, in case we want to try and use it as leverage down the line.'

'Right, well, it sounds like we've all got lots to do,' Croucher said. 'I guess we should get cracking.'

Chapter 45

Doyle had barely sat down behind his desk when there was a knock on his door, followed by Morgan entering. Her eyes were bloodshot, and her face was a couple of shades paler than usual.

'I'm so sorry,' Morgan said when the door was closed behind her. She slumped rather than sat in the seat opposite.

'You don't look well. Should you even be here?'

'I'm fine, boss. I overslept. I just need to get a coffee and I'll be good to go.'

'Fair enough. You know, though, it's OK not to be fine. If you need to take some time off, get a bit of rest or relaxation or whatever, it's not a problem.'

'Thanks, but honestly, I'm OK. I picked a hell of a day to be late for the first time in forever, what with Mr Burns and Professional Standards being in the morning briefing.'

Doyle smiled. 'Don't worry about Professional Standards. They've got plenty to do with looking into Pat Butcher and his band of merry twats in CID. And as for Mr Burns, he's too caught up in trying to impress the higher-ups by solving a double murder and uncovering corruption in the force to worry about you.'

'That's good to know.'

'You might say you're alright. If it was the Pearl who'd come in here this morning looking like a badger's arse, clammy and smelling of last night's booze, I wouldn't have batted an eye, because that would be a normal day at the office for Geoff. But it's not like you, and it concerns me for two reasons.'

'I guess you want me to ask what they are?'

'Correct. So at least some of your brain is switched on this morning. Well, first, and rather obviously, how are you coping with being back in the thick of it on another murder investigation? And is there anything else we could or should be doing for you to make things easier? Then there's a much more practical question.'

'What? If I'm fit to do my job?' Morgan's voice rose.

'No, not that. I have no doubts there. I was thinking, have you got the required skills and experience to know how to get through a day's work with a grade four hangover?'

'I'm not—'

Morgan was silenced by another knock on Doyle's office door. It was PC Anderton.

'Sorry to disturb, guv, but I remembered something a little odd from a few months back that might be useful. Could be nothing, though.'

'Take a seat,' Doyle said.

Anderton sat next to Morgan. 'Back in June, me and Nat got a call over the radio to say there was a burglary in progress in Barrowford. This was the middle of the day in broad daylight. We weren't working response, but there were no other units anywhere near. We shot round there, blues and twos on, expecting that whoever had been there would've legged it.'

'But they hadn't?' Morgan asked.

'No. That's the odd thing. Everything looked secure at the front, so we went round the back. There were some French doors, old wooden ones. They'd been jemmied open and a guy was coming out, laptop under one arm and an Xbox under the other. He saw us and, I'm not exaggerating here, made the most half-arsed attempt to get away that I've ever seen.'

'You think he wanted to get caught?' Doyle asked.

'I'm almost certain of it. Nothing in the house had been ransacked, like he'd been looking for hidden valuables. From us getting the call and driving there must have taken at least three minutes, plus the time it took for Control to take the call and dispatch us. He could have been in and out with the computer and console. They were both in the lounge.'

'And what's the connection to our case?' Doyle asked.

'Well, that's the thing. We processed him and then handed it over to CID. It was an open-and-shut case. An easy win for them. But the next day I came into work and found that he'd been released, all charges dropped.'

'You think now with the anti-corruption lot sniffing around Butcher and his team that there might be something more sinister to him being let off?' Doyle asked.

'At the time I wondered if he might be an informant for them. But then a couple of weeks later I saw him in the street in Nelson, begging. He was slumped in a shop doorway, and you could tell by looking at him he'd taken one hell of a kicking. I did wonder whether he had been trying to get himself nicked to avoid being beaten up. He was a known user, heroin and crack – one of our frequent flyers. I don't know. It's probably a long shot, but he might be worth having a chat with, find out if he knows why he got released.'

'It's worth looking into. Do you and Nat want to see if you can find him?' Doyle said.

'We can't now, guv, as we're going with Birdseye and Gadget to pick up Nuttall. We could probably do it after that.'

'If you've got his details and an address, Anna and I will go and see if we can track him down.'

'This is everything that's on the PNC. His name's Dean Millar, everyone calls him Deano.' Anderton said, handing over a few pages of printouts.

'I thought we were meant to be looking for someone,' Morgan said, following Doyle into a quiet café in Nelson.

'We are, or at least we will once you've had your medication.'

'What's my medi—'

'Two full English breakfasts, please,' Doyle said to the woman behind the counter. 'And a couple of strong coffees.'

'Take a seat, love, and I'll bring them over.'

'Can I have mine without the black pudding?' Morgan asked, not sure if she should be addressing the waitress or her boss.

'I'll let that go for now,' Doyle said, trying to squeeze his large frame into a bench seat. It and the table were bolted to the floor. Morgan knew he had chosen that table so their conversation wouldn't be overheard. She hoped he wanted to talk about the case, not about her.

'The fact you didn't complain about the fry-up means you're definitely out of sorts. When was the last time you ate something so unhealthy?'

Morgan smiled. 'It's been a while. Strangely, today it does sound rather appealing.'

'I know you don't want to be having this conversation,' Doyle said. 'I certainly wouldn't in your shoes.'

He wasn't wrong. Morgan had hoped that Paige Anderton's interruption in the office had got her off the hook. She didn't want to talk about things with her boss. What she wanted to do was pretend that everything was alright and muddle through.

But at the same time, she hated herself for thinking like this. It was exactly the type of old-school attitude that she despised in others: pretending you were untouchable and afraid to show any kind of vulnerability or weakness to your colleagues.

'I can't pretend to know how you're feeling or what you've been through. I have no idea. But I do know that you're a good detective, and that won't have changed.' Doyle stopped talking as the waitress came over and placed two mugs of coffee on the table. 'I also know that you've been having regular sessions with a psychologist, so there's no need to go into any of that with me.'

'Thanks.' Morgan knew that, as her line manager, Doyle would have been told that she'd been referred to psychology and got the nod to return to work. Even if he hadn't been informed, everyone knew that you couldn't go through what she had and waltz back into work without approval from the men in white coats – or a woman in a cable-knit cardie, in her case.

'You know what happened to me in London before I came up here, don't you?'

She did. Everyone had known about that before he had even walked through the door at Lancashire MIT. Doyle had been on a joint murder and drug squad investigation. He'd shot a man dead, who was holding a knife to a little girl's throat. It had been all over the press at the time. Many months later, an enquiry had concluded that Doyle had acted lawfully in killing the man.

'Of course. Everyone knows.' But Morgan had never heard her boss mention it before.

'Well, after that incident...' He paused again as the waitress placed two plates of food in front of them. 'I was suspended from work while it was investigated. I was off for five months.'

Morgan didn't like where this was going. She'd already had over three months off, recovering from her physical injuries. She hoped her boss wasn't about to suggest she needed a further period of absence.

'It was the worst thing for me. I went from being busy all day, non-stop, to being stuck at home with literally nothing to do. Harry was at school. Fiona was at work. It was just me on my tod with only my thoughts for company. Replaying what happened over and over in my head.'

Morgan didn't reply at first, as she had a mouthful of food. Maybe her boss did have a better idea about what she was going through than she had thought. She swallowed. The food was about as unhealthy as you could get, but it tasted amazing. 'Did you feel guilty about what happened? For taking another man's life?'

'No, not for one second. He'd already killed someone, and I don't doubt he would have killed the kid. But if others had viewed it differently, I could've been charged with murder.'

That had never occurred to Morgan, who had never been an authorised firearms officer. She knew of course that in the UK any police officer who shot someone was held to account for their actions, but had never thought too much about the impact of that on her boss. 'Is that what was weighing on your mind? That you might end up serving a life sentence?'

'Not really, to be honest. I never thought it was that likely. But there was something.'

'What?' Morgan said, before putting another forkful of food in her mouth.

'There's something about what happened in that underground car park that I've never told anyone.'

Morgan froze, her fork in mid-air.

'What I said in my statement just after the event wasn't entirely true.'

'Are you sure you want to be telling me this, boss?'

Doyle gave a half laugh. 'I think to a certain extent I've already been rumbled. When I started up here, HR insisted that I see a psychologist for a number of sessions to check I was still fit for work.'

'So that's where you go every other Thursday afternoon.'

'Spot on. You should be a detective, Anna.'

'Have you told her that things didn't happen as you said in your statement?'

'Not yet, but she's sussed me. She knows there's something I've been holding back in those sessions. It's the last one next week, provided I tell her what it is.'

'What are you going to do?'

'My first instinct was to lie, make something up that doesn't sound as bad.'

'But you're not going to?'

'No – at least, I don't think so. I've been haunted by this for a long time and I'm starting to think the only way to move on and put it in the past is to face the reality and what really happened.' Doyle wiped a piece of white bread around his plate, mopping up the juices. 'It started as a small white lie on my statement. I wanted to sound like I was in control and acting as per procedures. But you know how it is once you've said something – you can't go back and change your story.'

Morgan did know that. Any judgement call made in the heat of the moment could be picked apart and scrutinised in the cold light of day, by people who encountered nothing more dangerous than a stapler in carrying out their job. 'What was it?'

Doyle opened his mouth, then paused as someone entered the café and made their way to the counter. 'Most of what I told them was true,' he said in a low voice. 'I did what I was meant to. Shouted a warning that I was armed. Told him to let go of the girl. He said he was going to kill her, and I shouted a second warning. Still, he kept the knife to her throat.'

'What was wrong? I'm no expert, but two warnings sounds textbook to me.'

'There was nothing wrong with that, but when I took the shot, I was further away than I said in the statement. I had more chance of missing.'

'You didn't miss, though.'

'No, but I also said the girl was standing on the ground, held against his waist.'

'But she wasn't?'

'No, he was holding her against his chest, her head just below his. Given that, and the distance between us, I should never have taken the shot. The risk of missing him and hitting the girl was far too high.'

'Why did you shoot?'

'You've got to remember, all this happened in a split second, but as I saw it then and still do, I had a choice. Don't shoot, and let him get away and risk him killing the girl, and forever wonder if I could have stopped him, or shoot and end it there, at the risk of me killing the girl.'

'Damned if you do and damned if you don't.'

'Exactly. But if I'd told things exactly as they happened, the enquiry would've crucified me and my judgement. It would've been the end of my career for sure.'

'I don't see a problem. The circumstances weren't ideal, but the outcome was about as good as it could be.'

'You finished?' the waitress asked, scooping up the plates and mugs before Morgan had replied.

Doyle waited for the waitress to leave before saying more. 'The problem isn't the enquiry, or the fact that I lied. It's that my brain couldn't quite shake it off. The conscious part of my mind says it was all OK, no problem, move on. But the subconscious bit, the bit I don't have control of, kept replaying it over and over. Kept exploring the "what ifs". At first, even when I was awake, I'd have flashbacks, total recall, like I was watching a film of the event, exactly as it happened, right up to the point where

I'd fired. Then that agonising moment when I was running towards them, not sure if I'd hit him or the girl. There was so much blood. But in these flashbacks, instead of seeing the hole in his forehead, often it was in hers.'

Morgan didn't know how to respond. She had expected the BFG to ask difficult questions about her and how she was doing. She hadn't expected him to tell her about his experience. 'Do you still get flashbacks now?'

'Not like that. But I still dream about it. Sometimes it's the girl I hit, sometimes it's Jamal Campbell. I guess it all depends on how my subconscious is feeling. But it's lessened over time.'

'You think that's what helped – the passing of time?'

'To an extent. It now feels like something in my past, not my present.'

'Do you think that will be the same for me?' She paused. She was still reluctant to acknowledge that anything was wrong. 'You think I just need time, and things will get back to normal?'

'I think it will help, but I don't think things will ever be the same again. We are all shaped by our experiences. But I think, like me, you're not just troubled by what happened. You're thinking about the "what ifs" too.'

Morgan nodded. As bad as things had been, and as much as she had suffered from her injuries, she was haunted by the fear of what might have happened.

'I wouldn't have been a very good psychologist,' Doyle said. 'All I've done is talk about myself.'

Morgan was relieved; she didn't know what she would have done if he had started to ask her how she was feeling. 'I guess I need to get things in perspective and work out where I go from here.'

'Sounds like a plan, but you don't need to think too far ahead. Your next move is going to the counter because you're buying breakfast. Then we'll go and find this Deano fella and see what he can tell us.'

Chapter 46

Derrick 'Birdseye' Nelson quite liked interviewing suspects and persons of interest, but this morning he wasn't so keen. It wasn't just that the man sitting opposite him, accompanied by his solicitor, was almost as big as the boss and wore a scowl that did nothing to hide his contempt for the process. The person next to him was from Professional Standards – and the anti-corruption department at that. Birdseye had never crossed swords with Professional Standards, but despite that and even though he was fast approaching the end of his career, DI Cavanaugh's presence in the room still filled him with dread. He thought he knew how Gill felt when she talked about having Ofsted inspectors in at her school.

The first part of the interview hadn't elicited anything new; Neil Nuttall had stuck to his account of how he had found his brother-in-law's body, and said he didn't know why Turkish had been there that night, but assumed he had been doing a private job fixing someone's broken-down car.

'And where were you on the night of Thursday 2nd November, Mr Nuttall?' Birdseye asked. 'The night Terry Handcock was murdered.'

'I were at home.'

'All night?'

'Yes.' Nuttall yawned.

'Were you alone? Or could someone confirm that?' Birdseye asked.

'I was on my own. I live alone.'

'And what about the night of Saturday 28th October, the night Mia Wright was killed?'

'As far as I recall, I had a drink in a couple of pubs in Barrowford and then went home for an early night.'

Birdseye didn't believe for a second that Nuttall's recollection of what he'd been doing on the night Mia was murdered was anywhere near as vague as he was making it out to be. Murder wasn't a common event in this part of the country, and a local should have no trouble remembering what they'd been up to on the night in question. 'Were you home alone again that night?'

'I was.'

'And what time was it when you got home?' Birdseye asked.

'I think around half ten. I can't remember.' Nuttall leant back in his chair.

'And no one can vouch for your whereabouts after that time?' Birdseye wondered why he was being so vague about where he was, and the timings. It wasn't as if he was giving a verifiable alibi at the time the two victims were killed. He thought Nuttall just wanted to be difficult.

'No, they can't. But unless you've got some evidence that proves I was someplace else, I suggest we're done here.' Nuttall rose from his seat and picked up his coat.

'Sit down, Mr Nuttall,' DI Cavanaugh said. 'We're not done here.'

'Oh, I think we are,' Nuttall said. 'You've had my sister in here, accusing her of all sorts when she's grieving for her husband. You've had my business closed since Friday morning without even letting me back onto the site. And now you've got me in here, asking questions, as though it was me that killed

Terry and that girl. You know who it was – my sister saw him. You said at the start, I'm not under arrest, so I'm leaving.' He turned to his solicitor. 'Come on. Pack up, we're out of here.'

'I don't think that's—' the solicitor started to say.

'If you don't sit back down, Mr Nuttall,' Cavanaugh said, 'then my colleague here will arrest you.'

Birdseye wanted to protest. Why did he have to make the arrest? But he thought it best not to. Nuttall also seemed less sure of himself. He didn't sit, but stopped in his tracks. 'What are you going to arrest me for?'

'Possession with intent to supply,' Cavanaugh said, her voice deadpan.

'What?' the big man said, collapsing back into the chair.

'Yes, what is this about?' his solicitor asked. 'My client agreed to come here and be interviewed under caution about the two local homicides, and now you're throwing around spurious accusations.'

'When our crime scene investigators went over your business premises, they found a quantity of class A and class B substances in a drum of used engine oil in the workshop where Mr Handcock's body was found.'

'They're nothing to do with me.'

Birdseye had been watching Nuttall's body language. Despite his protestations, he hadn't looked the slightest bit shocked when DI Cavanaugh had put this new development to him.

'Really?' Cavanaugh said. 'That's all you've got to say for yourself? The drugs were found on the premises belonging to your business.'

'Just because they were in my workshop, that don't make them mine.'

'Who else would have put them there?' Cavanaugh asked.

'You're the police, you work it out.'

Cavanaugh raised an eyebrow. 'How many people work for your company?'

'Three – me, my sister and Terry. I guess that means just two now. I'm going to have to get a new mechanic.'

'Three? That doesn't seem like many for a business that size. You've got two big barns you use for workshops and an office. Do you have one each or something?' Cavanaugh said.

'That's right. Tracy does the office stuff – ordering, invoicing, appointments, that type of thing. Terry does – sorry, *did* the engine mechanics and vehicle bits in one workshop, and I do the engineering and metalwork in the other one.'

'Do you ever hire in other labour to help you?' Birdseye asked.

'Occasionally.' Nuttal placed his palms flat on the table in front of him.

'When was the last time?' Birdseye studied his suspects hands, they were huge, with thick sausage-like fingers.

'I couldn't tell you.'

'Recently?' Cavanaugh pressed.

'Not for a while. Probably back in summer, when things were busier.' Nuttall began tapping out a rhythm on the table with his fingers.

'The workshop that you found Mr Handcock in,' Birdseye said. 'Was that the one you work in, or the one Terry worked in?'

'That was his one. I hardly go in there.'

'But then you opened it up that morning when you got to work,' Birdseye persisted. 'Is that usual?'

'Only if Terry wasn't already there. I switch the power on so the compressors start charging. We dump the air out of them at the end of the day so they need to fill up again the next morning.'

'So, you didn't realise at that stage that Terry had been there the night before, working?' Birdseye asked.

'No. Like I said before, I had no idea. And his truck wasn't parked in the yard.' Nuttall stopped the tapping and looked up. 'It must've been one of his private jobs he was there for.'

'What about the drugs, Mr Nuttall?' Cavanaugh pressed. 'Do you think they might have been something to do with Terry Handcock?'

'I don't know. They're nowt to do with me.'

'Did you ever think that your brother-in-law might be dealing on the side?'

'No, never crossed my mind.' Nuttall looked at his watch.

'But you must've known him quite well. He worked for you and was related to you.' Cavanaugh said.

'Only by marriage.'

'Does that mean you didn't get on well with Terry Handcock?' Cavanaugh asked.

Nuttall looked at Cavanaugh. 'No. I never said that; you're twisting my words.'

'No, I'm not. I'm just asking you for clarity. Why did you say "only by marriage"? It sounded like you were distancing yourself from Mr Handcock.'

'No, it's just we weren't, like, best mates or anything. We didn't hang out much together.'

'Have you ever heard of someone called Alan Butcher?' Cavanaugh asked.

'No, should I have done?'

Birdseye thought he saw a flicker of something in Nuttall's face. What could it mean?

'You might know him as DCI Butcher.' Cavanaugh said.

'Never heard of him.'

'He knew Terry,' Cavanaugh said.

'Terry knew a lot of people. Like I said, we didn't hang out together.'

Doyle rang the bell then knocked on the door, the way delivery drivers do who don't want to waste precious seconds waiting. It wasn't that he was pushed for time, but he wanted the person on the other side to think he might be getting a parcel rather than a visit from the police. He was standing with Morgan in the first-floor hallway of a two-storey block of flats in Nelson. He was just about to knock again when the door opened. A man in a dirty grey T-shirt and jogging bottoms that had seen better days stood there. From the lines on his face, he looked like he could easily be in his late fifties, though Doyle knew from the information held on the Police National Computer that Dean Miller was only forty-one.

'DCI Doyle,' he said, holding up his warrant card and sticking his foot in the door before Miller could close it. 'Can we come in, Deano?' Doyle pushed the door, along with the man on the other side, and walked into the apartment. 'Thanks.'

'What, I didn't… Have you got a warrant?'

'Don't need one. You invited us in.' Doyle walked into the lounge, which was thick with tobacco smoke and in the same state of dishevelment as its tenant. He took in the well-worn sofa, checking for hypodermics before taking a seat.

'What's this about? I've not done owt. You can't just come in here—'

'Sit down, Deano, we only want to have a chat,' Doyle said.

The other man's gaze was darting around. Doyle didn't think this was because he was high; more likely he was concerned about what Morgan, who had taken the opportunity to look around the flat, might find.

'She can't be wandering about like that, not without a warrant. I've got rights.'

'We could always arrest you, then we wouldn't need a warrant.'

'What for? I've been clean for months.'

'The burglary in June. You were caught red-handed, and admitted it at the time.'

'I've already been nicked for that. The charges were dropped. You can't nick me again – that's double jeopardy or something.'

'You want to brush up on your criminal law, Deano,' Morgan said, walking into the lounge. 'Double jeopardy only stops you being tried twice for the same offence, not being arrested again, and it's not always applicable any more.'

'It's not fair. You could've had me locked up then and didn't, leaving me to face the music. Now that's all behind me, you want to lock me up.'

'We never said we wanted to lock you up,' Doyle said. 'We just want a bit of information from you. But if you're not going to cooperate, then we might have to take a fresh look at that burglary.'

'Information about what?'

'Mia Wright, for starters,' Doyle said.

'Jesus, you don't want much, do you? It's terrible what happened to her. I mean, she could be a right pain in the arse at times, but I heard she had her throat cut. That's dark.'

'You knew her, then?'

'No.'

'Sounds like you did,' Morgan said.

'No, well, just a bit. Look, I don't want to get involved in any of that.' Deano held his arms out in front of him, his wrists together. 'I haven't got a death wish. If you want to arrest me, take me now, but I'm not crazy. I'm not saying owt about that.'

'Put your hands down, Deano, we're not going to cuff you,' Doyle said. 'If we have to take you down the station, we'll make it look like you're cooperating, put it about that you're helping us with our enquiries. Or we can stay right here and have a quiet chat, just the three of us. No one else needs to know.'

'It's rich you coming here asking me about this, seeing who you can fit up for Mia's murder. Anything to avoid your man and his crew going down.'

Doyle looked across at Morgan, who raised her eyebrows. Deano was certainly holding another piece of the jigsaw, but how could they get it off him? 'Who do you mean by our man and his crew? Are you suggesting that it was a police officer who murdered Mia?'

'No, and you know. You lot have been turning a blind eye for years to what goes on around here.'

'Deano,' Morgan said, 'we're not from round here. We're not the local CID. We're from the force's Major Investigation Team. We work all over Lancashire, mostly investigating murders. We don't know anything about what's been going on here for years. We're here to get to the bottom of two murders.'

'Two murders?' Deano leaned forward, looking interested now. 'Who else has been murdered?'

'Terry Handcock,' Morgan said.

Deano looked back blankly.

'You might know him as Turkish,' Doyle said

'Jesus.' Deano was up on his feet. 'Wow, you're not shitting me? Turkish? As in Turkish Turkish. I don't mean Turkish from Turkey. But Turkish – the one with the teeth.'

'The very same,' Doyle said. He couldn't tell whether Deano's animated reaction was one of shock, joy or upset.

'Jesus, that's heavy. Fuck. He's really dead?'

'Yes. I'm surprised you didn't know.' Doyle had no doubt that Deano had just heard the news about Turkish for the first time. If he was such a good actor that he'd faked the performance, he would probably be snorting coke in Hollywood, not smoking smack in Nelson.

'It's been all over the internet and in all the local papers.'

'You can't get the internet on that,' Deano said, holding up an old Nokia. 'And I don't go out much now. Just to the pharmacy for my Subutex. I keep my head down.'

'How did you know Turkish? Doyle asked.

'Oh, come on,' Deano said, still bobbing up and down on his feet. 'You know, don't you?'

'Know what?' Doyle asked. He had an idea what Deano was alluding to, but he wanted to hear it from the man.

'You don't, do you?'

'Look, Deano.' Doyle softened his voice. 'We aren't interested in a bit of petty dealing or whatever's been going on. But we do need to get to the bottom of these two murders; we can't have someone out there killing people. Anything you say doesn't have to go any further, but we need to know what's been going on.'

'But what about others in the police? If I tell you anything, it will be on the computer system. Other officers will know I've talked and that might get back to...' Deano's voice tailed off.

'Back to who?' Morgan asked.

'I was going to say Turkish, but I guess that can't happen now.'

'Anything you tell us here will be confidential. It won't be put on the system.' This wasn't strictly true. Doyle would share it with his team and put it on Holmes 2, but access to anything to do with the case was now restricted.

'Promise?'

That one-word question made Doyle realise how vulnerable Deano was. It was a question he was used to Harry asking. He sensed that the other man wanted to tell them, but he needed reassurance that everything would be alright if he did. 'Promise.'

Doyle looked up, his eyes meeting Deano's.

Deano flopped down on a bean bag. 'It started back in 2019, I think. It was before Covid, anyway. Mia wasn't much more than a kid then, but she'd been around a while. Foster care spits them out when they turn eighteen, and they soon end up fuck-ups, like the rest of us. But anyway, there was a big crisis and no one could get hold of anything.'

'You mean drugs?' Morgan asked.

'Yeah, but I don't mean just H and crack. Charlie, weed, pills, spice, whatever pulls your chain, there was none of it. Everywhere you went, people were clucking their bollocks off. Word got around there'd been a big bust, your lot had taken down some serious players. People were going all over trying to score, but no one was having any luck. I reckon all the dealers from other places were too worried about getting caught to make the most of the new opportunity.' Deano's hands shook as he rolled a cigarette: whether from excitement or withdrawal, Doyle couldn't tell.

'Most of us old-timers were straight round the rehab services – not 'cause we wanted to quit, but out of desperation.'

'When your dealer lets you down, a doctor's the next best thing?' Doyle asked.

'Something like that. Only what they serve up isn't up to much unless you want to stop, like me now. But back then, I didn't. I wanted to get wasted.' Deano paused, shaking a lighter before igniting his roll-up. 'I was coming out the centre one day and this bloke gets out of a pickup and calls me over. Pats me on the back and shakes my hand like he's known me for years. Only he doesn't just shake my hand – he gives me a wrap.'

'And you didn't know him?' Morgan asked.

'Never seen him before in my life. I couldn't wait to get back and see what he'd given me. I was on methadone then, a maintenance dose, but I was itching for the real thing. I couldn't believe it when I unwrapped it and it was a bit of brown. I was back there the next day with money, ready to score. I got in his pickup, and he said he was called Turkish, but he wasn't going to sell me any more gear. He gave me six wraps, the same size as before, and told me he wanted paying for five the next day. I wasn't sure, like. I couldn't get through that much myself. I couldn't afford it, and it would kill me. But he said that's the deal, take it or leave it. He wasn't into selling single wraps.'

'I don't want to sound rude,' Doyle said, trying to be as tactful as possible. 'But that sounds like a bit of a flawed business model, giving a bag of drugs to a user you've just met and hoping they will pay for them the next day.'

'I might be a fuck-up, but I'm not stupid. I was thinking the same myself. But he gave me a mobile phone, said his number was on there and to call him after five the next day and he'd tell me where to meet him with the money. Then he looked me straight in the eyes and said, "I've done my homework on you, Dean Miller. You live at Flat 46, Admiral Way, your date of birth is 22nd April 1982, you've got previous for possession, burglary and criminal damage, and you've done time in Durham and Strangeways".'

Doyle didn't need to look at the paperwork in his jacket pocket to know that this was exactly the information Anderton had given him earlier, printed out from the Police National Computer. 'And you took that as a threat?'

'Like I said, I'm not stupid. But I did take the gear. And what with the drought, it wasn't difficult to sell. I put an extra little mark-up on it too. Basic economics, isn't it? Demand and supply. I'm pretty sure most people did the same.'

'Most people?' Morgan asked.

'It wasn't just me; he soon got around plenty of others in the area, just enough so that he had everywhere covered. That'll be how Mia got involved, though not with the smack. I think she just liked a bit of weed and charlie now and then. She loved a drink too.'

'Did you get to find out what happened if you didn't pay?' Doyle asked.

'Twice. The first time I got a warning. It was only twenty quid I was short. Used a bit more than I sold that week. He met me with some monster of a guy he called the Flesher. Told me I'd have to pay an extra forty quid next week, and if I didn't this Flesher would be paying me a visit. I didn't need telling twice. The man was the size of a tank. Bigger than you. Only a young guy, but he's not quite right in the head, so I heard.'

'Do you think Mia might've been behind in what she owed?' Morgan asked.

'I don't know, but I heard off one of the people I sold to that when a girl was behind with the money, Turkish would let them off if they paid him back in other ways, if you get my drift. It wouldn't surprise me if he'd had that arrangement with her.'

'And the second time you owed him?' Doyle asked.

'I fucked up big-time, went on a bender. Had just picked up a week's worth, and while I was off my head someone nicked it. I owed nearly five hundred. I'd heard a bit more about this Flesher bloke by then, none of it good. I knew I was bang in trouble.'

'Was that the reason for the burglary in Barrowford?' Morgan asked.

'Yeah. Took your lot long enough to get there. I figured if I got caught, I'd go down for sure with my record and I'd be off the hook at least for a bit. Then those detectives got involved and I were released. No further action.'

'Then you met this Flesher again?' Doyle asked.

Deano sighed. 'Four broken ribs and a ruptured spleen. Was pissing blood for a week.'

'Ouch.' Doyle knew all too well what broken ribs felt like, and that was without the ruptured spleen. 'I think you'd better tell us all you know or have heard about this Flesher.'

'OK, but we better be quick. I need to leave to take my Subutex soon.'

'I'd offer to give you a lift,' Doyle said. 'But I'm not sure it's a very good idea.'

'You're joking. The last thing I need is to be seen in the back of a car with you two.'

Chapter 47

'Gadget, just the person,' Doyle said, striding into the incident room. He gave the younger detective an evidence bag with a cheap mobile phone in it.

'Where did you get that?'

'From a concerned citizen and ex-business associate of Turkish. He couldn't find the charger.'

'No problem, boss. I'll find one that fits it.'

'Good. Get everything you can off it and pass it on to Shaima. The PIN's 1966.'

'The year we won the World Cup,' Birdseye said.

'Was that the year you turned fifty?' Gadget asked.

'You may mock, young one,' Birdseye retorted. 'But with great age comes great wisdom.'

'Shame you're too old to remember any of it,' Gadget said.

'Shaima,' Doyle said, turning to the analyst. 'How are you getting on with all the phones?'

'We're getting somewhere. We've got numbers and call logs for all the main persons of interest. The Handcocks had a landline, so we've got that too.'

'Have you found anything of interest yet?'

'It's early days, boss. We still don't know who Burner One belongs to, and that calls both Mia and Turkish's phones quite frequently. But it's remained off since Mia was killed.'

'Finding who owned that has to be our number-one priority,' Doyle said.

'With the tech guys doing the RF surveys, we should be able to get a more detailed picture of where each phone has been whenever it was switched on. It's going to take a bit of time, though.'

'We need that info as soon as you can,' Doyle said.

'We've found one other number which we're calling Burner Two,' Asif said. 'This was first switched on the morning Mia's body was found, just after 9 a.m. It then immediately called two numbers, one as yet unknown and the other the Handcocks' landline. It mostly stays switched off, but makes more calls over the next few days, significantly, one to Mr and Mrs Handcock's landline on the night Turkish was killed.'

'That's got to be our guy. We need to track down who's been using that phone,' Doyle said.

'Isn't that a bit weird? If the phone does belong to someone involved, why would they call a landline with it, not Turkish's burner?' Gadget asked.

'Reception,' Morgan said. 'When we were searching the Handcocks' house, Shaima tried to call me, but the phone cut out as the reception there was so bad. If the person wanted to contact either of the Handcocks urgently, they would have to use the landline.'

'Of course, because it was a landline, we don't know whether it was Mr or Mrs Turkish who took each call,' Doyle said. 'Gadget will hopefully get some more numbers from the phone I've just given him. I think it's likely that Turkish has changed burner several times over the last few years, so we might be able to get those numbers and cross-reference them.'

'We can do that, but we won't be able to get any cell site data from over a year ago. It's not kept longer than that,' Asif said.

'OK, do what you can. If you come up with anything significant, call me straight away. Birdseye, how did you and Cavanaugh get on with Nuttall?'

'Not great, boss. He wasn't very forthcoming. But he said one thing that didn't ring true,' Birdseye said.

'What was that?'

'Well, I remember that you and the sarge said that when you first went down to the workshops to speak to Turkish, there were other people working there.'

'That's right,' Morgan said. 'There were three people working in the other barn to Turkish.'

'Right,' Birdseye said. 'But he denied having any other employees, and said he hadn't used any hired labour since the summer.'

'He sounds dodgy as fuck to me,' Gadget said.

'Agreed,' Morgan said. 'And do you remember, boss, when you first asked him about finding Turkish, he said he saw him as soon as he got into the workshop, until you pointed out you couldn't see into the bottom of the inspection pit from there.'

Doyle did remember that. He had been sidetracked immediately afterwards by Tracy Handcock coming in and saying she had seen Perkins there the night before. 'Right, that's it. Let's bring him back in. Arrest him on suspicion of murder and do a full search of his house. See if we can find either of those burner phones or anything else that will link him. Cavanagh's team are going through the paperwork from his business anyway. We can ask them to see what they can dig up about other people working there. It's probably unrelated, either a tax dodge or maybe employing people who don't have the right to work, but it needs checking out. Oh, and if anyone hears someone called

Flesher being mentioned, let me know straight away. He's built like a brick shithouse, apparently.'

'Have you looked in the mirror recently, Liam?' Hales said.

Doyle laughed. 'I think having one DCI as a person of interest is enough without making myself another one.'

'Neil Nuttall ticks that box too,' Birdseye said.

This was certainly true, Doyle thought, but the person Deano had described had sounded a lot younger. He wasn't sure even someone high on heroin would think Neil Nuttall could pass for early twenties.

Doyle's phone rang, and the display told him it was Dianne Berry calling. He wondered what the nurse could want. They had pretty much ruled out her patient as a suspect. He ducked into his office while swiping the screen to answer.

'You know I told you that when we sectioned Will, he was hearing voices that he thought were coming from the phone?'

'Good afternoon to you as well, Dianne.'

'Never mind all that. This might be important. I'm trying to help you out here.'

'Go on. I'm listening.'

'Well, I was just talking to that psychologist Henrietta Sutton. She was Mia's care coordinator. She's a bit upset. I mean, we're all used to our patients dying, it's a sad part of the job, but we're not used to them being killed. Anyway, she let slip that your sergeant had told her Mia was pregnant. Is that true?'

Doyle thought about his answer. The information wasn't in the public domain, but would come out in a trial if they ever caught the person. Morgan had needed to tell the psychologist to find out if she knew who the father was. 'Yes, but I don't see—'

'When I was waiting with Will and that social worker for the ambulance to take him to hospital, he was pacing up and down, going on and on. I wasn't focusing too much on what he was saying. I was more interested in trying to keep him calm. I didn't want him walking out of his dad's house and wandering the streets in that state.'

Doyle wanted to ask if she was getting to the point, but she wasn't stopping for breath.

'Anyway, he told me he had been hearing this new voice. I think he thought it was the devil or someone. But he kept saying the voice was accusing him of making Mia pregnant. I didn't think anything of it at the time. I could understand how he would be having auditory hallucinations about Mia Wright after being questioned about her murder, and I didn't know back then that she was pregnant.'

'What do you make of that now?' Doyle asked. He was perplexed himself.

'Honestly, I'm not sure. But it seems a bit odd that he would have that in his head, and it turns out to be true.'

It did to Doyle too, and coincidences in cases bugged him. 'What type of mental state is Will in now?'

'I spoke to his primary nurse on the ward earlier. He's improving. I mean, he's still quite psychotic, but not as agitated as he was when you last saw him.'

'Can we go and see him?'

'What, now? I'm meant to be knocking off in fifteen minutes. I've got that bloody diet club thing. I've got to go and look surprised that I've gained weight again and act like I haven't been stuffing my face with cake and chocolate all week.'

'It could be important. We need to try and get any bit of info we can.'

'You think it might help?'

'I don't know. But you obviously thought it might be significant, or you wouldn't have called me.'

'I'm beginning to regret that now. Alright, I can meet you there in half an hour. But don't keep me waiting.'

'I won't.'

'Good. And bring that Captain Birdseye with you. Will seems to like him.'

'That does sound quite psychotic.'

Chapter 48

'You've got to roll up your sleeves before coming onto the ward,' Clarence said to Doyle and Birdseye as she led them and Dianne Berry along the hospital corridor.

'Why's that?' Doyle asked, not that he had any objection.

'Infection control. Them's the rules.'

'I didn't realise schizophrenia was contagious.'

Clarence laughed. 'You try telling that to the CQC.'

'Don't, Clarence,' Berry said. 'We've got an inspection starting next month. I get about fifteen emails a day about it. All the bosses running around in a flap trying to work out what might bite them on the arse.'

Doyle followed Berry's lead in using the hand sanitiser before Clarence used her swipe card to let them onto the ward.

'You go in there,' Clarence said, opening a side room. 'I'll fetch Will. I've not seen much of him today, so I've no idea how helpful he'll be.'

Doyle sat down on a vinyl-covered sofa close to the door and Birdseye took the space next to him. This was standard practice, to ensure they could make a swift exit should things become volatile. Berry took a seat in the furthest corner, leaving an armchair for Will closest to the door. Doyle didn't think this was negligence on the part of the nurse; after all, she had years of experience working with patients like Perkins. Doyle suspected Berry's choice of seat was to give *Will* a quick exit from the room if he wanted it, and to stop him feeling cornered or penned in.

When Will entered, he looked less dishevelled than he had the previous week. The open-at-the-front pyjamas had been replaced by a T-shirt and jogging bottoms and the lace-less trainers had been substituted for sliders, though even in this less than salubrious environment Doyle still thought that wearing socks with any kind of sandal should be a crime.

'How are you doing, Will?' Berry asked.

'I'm alright.' Perkins sounded hesitant, as if he was asking a question rather than answering one.

'You remember these two, don't you?' Berry said.

'Yes, of course, but I don't—'

'It's OK, Will, you're not in any trouble and we don't think you've done anything,' Doyle said. 'But we think you may know some things that might be useful to us in working out who killed Mia Wright.' Doyle wasn't sure if Perkins had heard about the second murder yet, or if he knew Terry Handcock. 'I know this might be painful, but DC Nelson and I would like to ask you some questions about the day you came in here and the events leading up to it. Is that OK?'

'Yes, but I'm not sure I can... The thing is, Inspector. It is Inspector, isn't it?'

'It's Chief Inspector, but you can call me Liam.'

'The thing is, Chief Inspector, what you have to realise is, that day and the time leading up to it, I wasn't very well. I had all sorts going around in my head. I still do, but I'm starting to realise what is real and what is not. But I don't know about that day. It all feels real, but I know it wasn't.'

'I'd like to ask you some questions about what happened from your point of view, and you can let us work out what bits might be real, if that's OK?'

Will nodded.

'We've got Dianne with us because she has known you for a long time and she might be able to help us unpick it.'

'Alright, if you think it might help, so long as you don't think I'm wasting your time.'

'I think at this stage anything's worth a try. Now, on the day you were taken here, Dianne said that the phone in your dad's house had been smashed. Can you tell us about that?' Doyle didn't want to mention that he had seen this himself when he had kicked down the door when he had gone to arrest Will.

'I'll make sure I replace that. He won't be cross with me, my dad, he'll understand.'

'I'm sure. But what I'd like to know, if you can remember, is what caused you to break the phone.'

'It was the voices.'

'The voices told you to smash the phone?' Doyle had come across people who experienced command hallucinations before: when voices tell people to do things, sometimes with serious consequences.

'No, but one of the voices was coming from the phone. A nasty one. I didn't like it.'

'Have you had that before? A voice coming down the phone?'

Will looked at Doyle, confusion on his face. 'Well, yes, all the time. But normally it's actual people. Mostly her,' he said, nodding towards Berry and smiling. 'Checking up on me.'

'Someone's got to,' Berry said, smiling back.

'But this time the voice wasn't real?' Doyle asked. 'It wasn't Dianne or someone else you knew?'

'That's the thing – at the time, I thought it was real. But they all feel real, all the voices feel real. But now, I know they're not – at least, I know that other people can't hear them.'

'Was it one of your usual voices?' Berry asked, before turning to Doyle. 'Sorry, I know it's you that is meant to be asking the questions.'

'That's OK. What do you mean by usual voices?'

Will looked across at Berry.

'Would you like me to explain?' Berry asked.

'Please.'

'Will has some voices that he hears regularly. They all tend to have names, mostly to do with the witch trials from way back when. There's Chattox and Old Demdike. Then there's the Thomas Potts who wrote about the trial. And what's his name, the Quaker guy?'

'George Fox?' Birdseye said.

'That's him,' Berry said.

'You know your history,' Perkins said to Birdseye with an appreciative smile.

'We've not heard from him for a while,' Berry said. 'Then there's the dog.'

'Dandy,' Perkins said.

'There's a statue of the dog outside Booths in Clitheroe,' Birdseye said. 'Didn't it belong to one of the witches?'

'That's right,' Will said. 'James Device. It was said to be his familiar.'

'You hear a voice belonging to a dog?' Doyle asked.

'I know it sounds quite mad. But I guess that's one of the reasons I'm here.'

Interesting as this was, Doyle didn't want to lose track of the thread he had been pulling on. 'The voice coming from the phone – have you had that before, when you think it might be a hallucination?'

'Honestly, I'm not sure.'

'He's had similar before,' Berry said. 'Voices from the telly and radio.'

'And you knew they weren't real, Will?'

'Not at the time, but Dianne has helped me work things out.'

'It wasn't that difficult. I mean, what are the chances that Old Demdike, a witch from the 1600s, has a job DJing on Heart Radio?' Berry said.

Will laughed, and Doyle could see the camaraderie between nurse and patient. Dianne Berry helped Will Perkins navigate his way through life and a world he was struggling to fit into. It wasn't too dissimilar to Harry's situation, only Harry mostly knew what was real, but not how to process it.

'This voice from the phone, Will, the one you heard that day,' Doyle said. 'What did it say? Tell me from the start.'

Chapter 49

Will wanted to get out. The atmosphere in there was stifling, but he knew he had to stay. He was a hunted man. He needed to stay in the house with the curtains closed. But he wanted to be free, walking in the hills, up on the moors where the air was clean. He needed to work things out in his head. *Murderer*, they'd shouted at him. He'd run non-stop until he was back here. Locked the door, put the chain on. But they knew where he was. They'd come for him eventually.

The house felt hot. Not like the fires of hell, but warmer than he'd like, and his pacing up and down the hall was making him sweat. He needed to think. How could he get out of here? Where could he go to be safe?

'They'll find you,' she said. It was her, Chattox; he recognised the voice. He could hear her, but he couldn't see her. Of course he couldn't see her: she was dead, a ghost, but she was talking to him, and she was right. They would find him. Just like they had found her at Malkin Tower. And he would be put on trial too.

Sweat ran down his back, and his T-shirt clung to his skin. He pulled it off and wiped his forehead with it. There was ringing – not a bell, and there wasn't someone knocking, but it was by the door. The phone.

'Don't answer it,' Chattox shouted. 'It will be them. They're coming for you.'

'Shut up, Chattox. You're not even real.' But was she?

'It'll be a trap.'

She might be right. He picked it up. 'Hello?'

It was still ringing. He pressed the green answer button. 'Hello?'

'Will Perkins?' A man's voice

'Yes, who is this?' Will didn't think he'd heard this voice before.

'You've been bad, Will. You've been very bad.'

'No, no, I've not.' *What is he talking about? What does he know?*

'What about Mia?' the voice boomed.

'That wasn't me. I didn't kill her.' *Did I?*

'No, you didn't kill her, Will. I did. But it's your fault that she's dead.'

'I didn't mean it. I know she's not a witch. I was mistaken. I didn't mean for her to be killed.' *This isn't real. He's not real. He's just another voice. But Mia is really dead, isn't she?*

'You made her pregnant, and that's why she had to die.'

'No, I didn't, that wasn't me.' *I know that wasn't me.*

'Yes, it was, Will. She told me it was you. Now you have to die.'

'No,' Will shouted into the phone.

'Yes. But I'm going to give you a choice. You can do it yourself or I'll come and do it for you. Do you know what they call me?'

'No...'

'The Flesher. Do you know why?'

'No.' Will couldn't remember hearing that name before.

'Because I cut people up. And I'll tear you apart.'

'But I—'

'The choice is yours, Will. You either do it yourself or I'm going to do it.'

'How? What must I do?'

'That's up to you. You must have lots of tablets – take all of them. But make sure you take enough, or I'll be coming to finish the job.'

'B-but I've only got a few days' worth. That won't be enough.'

'Do something else then. Throw yourself off a building, a tower or something.'

'Malkin Tower? That doesn't exist any more.'

'No, not Malkin Tower, any fucking tower. That Rocket Tower or Blackpool Tower or, I don't know, jump in front of a train. But you better do it today or I'm coming for you, Will.'

The voice was shouting, angry. This Flesher was a new voice, but it was scarier than the others.

'But why? Please. I didn't do anything.' Will pleaded.

'Yes, you did, Will. She told me it was you. You made her pregnant.'

'I didn't. But I know who did.' He remembered something he had heard and he was sure that it was real.

'What?'

'Mia was outside the clinic in Clitheroe. She was talking on the phone. She was shouting, telling someone they needed to give her money because they'd made her pregnant. She was swearing, angry.'

'I don't believe you. Who was she angry with?'

'I don't know, but she was saying she wanted money for her baby.'

'You're making it up.' The Flesher shouted.

'No, I'm not.'

'Who was it, then?'

'I don't know, but she said something to him. I can't quite… She called him a Turkish man.'

'If you're lying, I'm going to rip you apart.' The Flesher was screaming.

Will pulled the phone from the wall, ripping the cable from its socket, and flung it away from him. This Flesher was terrifying; it was as if the devil himself had been shouting down the phone.

'Liam, Shaima's found something in the phone records.' Hales had begun speaking the moment Doyle answered the phone. 'You'll never guess whose landline Burner Two rang the day before Turkish was killed.'

'Reg Perkins, Will's dad?'

'How did you—'

'Will Perkins just told us. He received a call the day he went into hospital from someone calling themselves the Flesher, but he wasn't sure if it was real or a voice in his head. How did they get on with Nuttall?'

'He's in a cell in Burnley. The house search is still going on. Do you want to interview him tonight?'

Doyle looked at his watch. 'It's getting on a bit now. Let's let him sweat overnight. Can you set up a full team briefing in the morning? We'll go through it all then and we can work out how we want to play things.'

'Will do.'

Chapter 50

'You're quiet tonight,' Bea said, though it sounded more observational than accusatory. Doyle had thought about cancelling their regular Wednesday evening get-together as he was so busy and thoughts about the case were spinning in his head, but he'd missed the previous week and felt he needed to put some effort into trying to have a life and relationship, if that's what this was.

'You're right,' he said, looking up at her. Bea was plating up an appetising-looking pasta dish as he perched on a stool at her kitchen island. 'I'm sorry, I've got a lot whirring around my brain with the case. But I need to switch off and relax.' Easier said than done, but he knew he had to try.

'I do understand, you know. I find it difficult to put work down when there's a lot on, and what I do is hardly life and death.'

That was true, of course, but since his experience of selling a house in London and moving to Lancashire, Doyle had a new respect for estate agents – at least, the good ones. Bea might not be dealing with life and death, but people had so much tied up in their homes, both financially and emotionally. Moving house was a big deal to most people. He'd heard people screaming down the phone at her when their house sale had fallen through and at other times she had gently consoled others when their dream move and new start had hit the rocks.

'Have you thought any more about what you want to do on Saturday?'

'Saturday?'

'Don't tell me you've forgotten your own birthday?'

'Oh, that. Yes. I'm not sure we'll be able to do too much. I might have to do some work from home and I'll have Harry. It won't be worth the stress to try and get him to come out somewhere to eat.'

'You could invite people round for drinks late afternoon, evening.'

'I could do, I guess... I don't know. It's late notice.'

'Even the great detective is allowed a few hours off to celebrate his birthday.' Bea winked and placed down two bowls of pasta. She came round to the other side of the island, stood behind him and draped her arms over his shoulders. 'You could always invite people here if you wanted a bit more space than at yours. I won't be back from work until about half four, but you're welcome to start earlier.'

'Thanks, but I don't know that many people up here. My place will be fine.'

'Good, so that's settled then. Drinks at yours, Saturday evening.' She kissed him and took a seat on the stool beside him.

'I'm still not sure about Harry. He won't know anyone, and he might find it overwhelming.'

'Speak to him before, let him know he can go up to his room if he's finding it difficult. I don't mind sitting with him up there if he gets a bit stressed out. He'll be OK.'

'I guess so,' Doyle said, unable to think of a reasonable excuse to get out of it.

'Don't forget to invite people, will you? You could send a message now in the group chat to your workmates.'

'They're not my mates. I'm their boss.'

'That's good, then. They'll all behave themselves. Will you invite your boss – what's his name? The one with the vein on his head?'

'Mr Burns. Not a chance. I don't even like seeing him at work, let alone in my actual house.'

Chapter 51

Day 12: Thursday 9 November

'DI Cavanaugh, would you mind bringing everyone up to speed with your side of the investigation?' Mr Burns said.

Doyle wasn't too pleased to have his boss at the morning briefing, taking control, but they had separate, but linked, investigations, and he didn't want to take responsibility for all of them.

Cavanaugh came to the front of the incident room. Doyle wouldn't have been surprised if she had pulled up a PowerPoint presentation on the big screen, but she didn't. 'As you know, my team and I have been investigating the link between DCI Butcher and Terry Handcock, and the suspected drug supply by Mr Handcock and possibly others.'

Doyle noticed the lack of background noise in the incident room. It wasn't that the officers present were hanging on to the Professional Standards detective's every word, but the presence of her and the superintendent in the briefing had put everyone on their best behaviour. The sooner the two of them fucked off and they could get back to normal, the better.

'The information provided by Dean Miller, alongside his phone records, has been illuminating. Miller mentioned a shortage in drug supply in 2019. He wasn't exactly sure of the date, but by checking the records on the phone he handed in, we can see that this would have been June 2019. Interestingly, this was just after DCI Butcher and his team arrested several key players in a local drug supply chain. The phone that Miller claims was supplied to him by Mr Handcock had a number listed as "Turkish" in the contacts list. This was for another unregistered phone that has been out of use for over a year.'

'Will we be able to get the location data for that phone and confirm that it belonged to Turkish and where it's been?' Gadget asked, his hand up as though he was in class.

'Sadly not. Cell site data isn't kept that long, and I doubt we will even be able to get the call and SMS log at this stage. But Shaima has uncovered something interesting. Perhaps it would be easier if you explained?' Cavanaugh said, looking towards the analyst.

'OK,' Asif said, not coming to the front of the room but popping her head up above her computer so all could see her. 'Although we don't have those records, because DCI Butcher is a serving officer on this force, it was no problem getting his phone records. And there are numerous calls between his mobile and the number listed in Deano's phone as "Turkish", right up until that phone stops being used.'

'Bloody idiot,' Hales said. Doyle was pleased that someone had finally broken the formal atmosphere in the room. 'I'm sure everyone here hates a bent copper. But to be stupid enough to use your police issue mobile beggars belief.'

'Oh, you'd be surprised,' Cavanaugh said. 'As you can imagine, I've come across many corrupt officers, and it's not unusual for them to use their work phones. I think they assume they can pass it off as getting intel, as Butcher tried to do when we interviewed him.'

Mr Burns' phone rang and he stepped out of the incident room to take the call. Some of the tension in the air lifted.

'I've had a couple of officers from my team going over the accounts of NN Agricultural Engineering and the finances of Mr and Mrs Handcock. They have uncovered a couple of what you might call peculiarities.'

'It was tax evasion that got Al Capone,' Hales said.

'And he had gonorrhoea,' Birdseye added.

'Jesus.' Doyle stared at the older detective. 'You don't half know some useless information.'

'It's not tax evasion we're looking at here,' Cavanaugh said, deadpan. 'Quite the opposite, in fact.'

'What, they've been paying too much tax?' Hales asked.

'In a way, yes. Neil Nuttall and Mr and Mrs Handcock have all been paid considerable salaries by Nuttall's business. All three of them well in excess of a hundred grand.'

'I'm in the wrong job,' Hales said.

'You and me both,' Cavanaugh said. 'But this doesn't quite stack up.'

'The business wasn't doing enough trade to sustain those wages?' Doyle asked. This information was new to him.

'Not quite,' Cavanaugh said. 'They were getting the work in, and it was all legitimate as far as we can tell. But there was a distinct lack of money going out of the company to other employees or hired labour. One of my team was able to get through to someone at HMRC who knows about these kinds of businesses. For the turnover their business has, he would expect them to have at least eight full-time employees on the books and to be bringing in extra casual labour at busy times. NN Agricultural Engineering has just these three employees.'

'But we know that's not true,' Morgan said. 'There were other people working there when we first met Turkish.'

Doyle took a moment to consider this new information. 'What do you think is going on? Are they paying the hired labour in the workshops cash made from selling drugs?'

'I think so,' Cavanaugh said. 'That would mean the money they paid themselves as salaries would appear to be legitimate. Money laundering, in other words.'

'Clever,' Hales said.

'Does that mean we think that Neil Nuttall and Tracy Handcock were involved in the drug supply too?' Birdseye asked.

'Almost certainly,' Cavanaugh said. 'But proving that might be a different matter.'

'Have you found out anything else?' Doyle asked.

'A couple of other bits,' Cavanaugh said. 'When Dean Miller was arrested for burglary, the info was passed on to CID. DCI Butcher got a call on his mobile from Handcock's burner that evening. It was after this that Butcher authorised Miller's release, with no further action.'

'Jesus,' Anderton said from the back of the room. She had been silent until this point. 'I saw Deano shortly after that. He was in a right state after his kicking, and now we find out it was one of our own – and a DCI, no less – who released him to get beaten up.'

'To be fair to DCI Butcher,' Cavanaugh said, 'we don't know that he released him knowing he would get a kicking. But it does look likely that he let him out at Handcock's request.'

'Hard to prove that,' Hales said.

'On its own, yes,' Cavanaugh said. 'But we have something else. Clinicians from the local community mental health team passed on intel about a person known as Turkish supplying drugs to a number of their patients. We followed the paper trail of the report, and it went all the way up to DCI Butcher – where nothing was done about it.'

'That makes me sick. He wants locking up,' Anderton said.

'Rest assured, if we get enough evidence to bring criminal charges against Butcher we will,' Cavanaugh said. 'But at the very least, with what we've got so far, his career as a police officer is over. And we're looking at other members of that team who may also have been involved.'

Doyle looked across at Morgan, who smiled back and raised her eyebrows. He knew how much she despised DS Felton. No doubt she'd be hoping he was in for a roughing up from Professional Standards.

'Right then. Moving on to our murder investigation,' Doyle said. Mr Burns had still not returned, and Doyle was hoping that now he had all the information from Cavanaugh's side, she would be happy to depart and leave them to it. But when she'd finished her briefing, she'd taken out her notebook and sat at the front, looking like the class swot waiting for the teacher to speak. It wasn't that he objected to her personally – or professionally, but they were getting to the stage where they needed to start looking at possible hypotheses to prioritise lines of enquiry. Doyle was quite capable of putting forward his theories, and he had one that had been developing in his mind since last night. But he needed his team to play devil's advocate, to spot the flaws he hadn't, and come up with their own ideas.

'A new name, or at least a nickname, came into the frame yesterday from two separate sources,' Doyle said. 'Deano said the person Turkish had been using as his enforcer was known as the Flesher, and Will Perkins told us one of the voices he heard the day he got taken into hospital called himself the Flesher.'

'I know you don't like coincidences, boss,' Gadget said. 'But surely we can't read too much into one of Perkins' hallucinations.'

'The thing is, I don't think this was an auditory hallucination. I think he thought it was because he was having other hallucinations at the time. Will was staying at his dad's house, and there was a call to the landline from the number that Shaima has listed as Burner Two. This call lasted several minutes. It's the same number that called the Handcocks' landline on the morning after Mia was killed, and again on the night Terry Handcock was killed. I think we can start looking at the theory that whoever is using this phone is our killer, and the person known as the Flesher. The problem is, we don't know who that is. As you know, we arrested Neil Nuttall yesterday evening. It may well be him, but so far, the search of his property hasn't come up with anything, including either of the unknown burner phones.'

'Have you had any thoughts about motivation, Liam?' Hales asked.

'This is what I have been mulling over half the night, and I have a possible theory. I know this won't hold much value in court as witness testimony – I mean, Perkins doesn't even know what's real and not. But he said the voice that was talking to him down the phone, the one that called himself the Flesher, had accused him of getting Mia pregnant. It sounded pretty horrible. He was trying to get Perkins to take his own life. Perkins said he had heard Mia talking on the phone outside the clinic in Clitheroe to someone, telling them she wanted money for her baby. Will told this voice on the phone that she'd called the person she was talking to a Turkish man.'

'Something is fitting together, but it's difficult to see what,' Hales said. 'And as you said yourself, what Will has told us from an evidential perspective won't hold much weight.'

'But we do know there was a call made to Will's dad's landline, so that's something,' Birdseye said.

'I've had an idea,' Shaima Asif said.

'Go on,' the DCI encouraged.

'If we know the time of Will's last few appointments at the medical centre, we can cross-reference with Mia's phone records and calls to Turkish's phone. We can also check the rough location of both phones. If she was speaking to Turkish at the time, and from there, it would add weight to Will's account.'

'Brilliant,' said Doyle. 'Get straight onto that after the briefing.'

'Sorry, Liam,' Hales said. 'I interrupted you when you were going through a theory.'

'What I was thinking was that this Flesher' – Doyle hated using that nickname, but it was all they had for now – 'was angry at Perkins because he thought he had got Mia pregnant. Then Will told him about the call he overheard, and the Flesher got angry with Turkish instead for the same reason. Remember, this happened only hours before Turkish was killed. We know there are many calls from Burner One back and forth to Mia's phone and also to Turkish's burner. Burner One was last used the night Mia died, and has not been back on since. I think it's probable that this phone belonged to the Flesher, and he switched to using Burner Two after he killed Mia.'

'That sounds reasonable,' Hales said.

'Could it be that the Flesher was in a relationship with Mia?' Doyle went on. 'She got pregnant and he either realised or she told him that the baby might not be his. He got enraged and killed Mia. Then, thinking Perkins was the father, he tried to frame him for the murder?'

'That would fit, boss,' Asif said. 'There was a call to the Handcocks' landline from Burner Two the morning Mia's body was found. Turkish then called DCI Butcher.'

'Exactly,' Doyle said. 'And according to Butcher, Turkish told him it was Perkins who had killed Mia.'

'I was told by Mia's psychologist that she tended to sabotage her emotional relationships,' Morgan said. 'If she was in a relationship with this Flesher, it's quite possible she told him one day they were having a baby and was over the moon about it and then a few days later she told him it wasn't his.'

'But if that was the case,' Birdseye said, 'why tell him that poor Will Perkins was the father and bring him into it?'

'Money.' Cavanaugh spoke for the first time since the briefing had moved away from her case. 'From the bits of the conversation it appears Perkins overheard, it sounds like she was after money from Handcock. If she outed him as the father, she would lose any blackmail potential she had over him. Sure, she might get child support payments if it turned out the baby was his, but he would no doubt then want a paternity test and she might not be sure who the father was.'

'Whereas by saying Perkins was the father, she could keep tapping Turkish up for money, with the threat of it all coming out hanging over his head,' Morgan said.

'That all makes sense so far,' Hales said. 'But what doesn't make sense is why Tracy Handcock was so keen to falsely accuse Perkins of being there, putting him back in the frame? Surely, however pissed off she was with her husband for giving her the clap and everything else, she would want his and Mia's killer caught.'

'She must know who this Flesher guy is and that he'd just killed two people,' Gadget said. 'She was probably too scared of him to give us his name.'

'But that wouldn't explain why she gave us Perkins' name instead,' Hales said. 'She could've just told us she hadn't seen anyone when she dropped her husband off.'

'Or it could be that this Flesher is also close to her,' Morgan suggested. 'And blaming someone we already had as a possible suspect was an easy way to stop them being caught. She couldn't have known that Perkins would have a perfect alibi by going into hospital that day.'

'Her brother would fit the bill,' Hales said. 'We previously thought Neil Nuttall might not be our man, because it was a stretch to think he committed both murders just because Turkish was cheating on his sister with Mia. But if Nuttall was in a relationship with Mia himself, that would give a much more plausible motive.'

'That's a good point,' Doyle said. 'Geoff, why don't you and Gadget get down to Burnley now and interview Nuttall? I don't think he will tell us much unless we can put some actual evidence in front of him. But it's worth a try.'

'I agree,' said Cavanaugh.

'If it is him,' Doyle said, 'the key will be linking him directly to Mia. Or linking him to Burner One or Burner Two. But I think we should keep an open mind that it might be someone else. Remember, Deano described a much younger man.'

'Just a thought, boss,' Birdseye said. 'I was thinking about this last night after we spoke to Will. Sometimes, way back, people who worked in abattoirs were known as fleshers. That might be where he got the name from.'

'Or it could be just a nickname used to make him sound intimidating to those who don't pay what they owe,' Gadget said.

'I think Birdseye might have a point,' Morgan said. 'Whoever killed Mia and Turkish had decent anatomical knowledge and were skilled at using a knife.'

'Good thought, Birdseye,' Doyle said. 'Straight after this briefing, start looking into this. Check Nuttall's background, see if he was employed in the past at an abattoir or similar. If that doesn't throw anything up, get onto all the abattoirs in the area. Start with the closest and move out. I want to know of any employees they have that fit the description. There aren't that many people about my size. Check previous employees too, especially any who were sacked or who displayed any worrying tendencies.'

Chapter 52

That morning's briefing had thrown up a few additional lines of enquiry, and the rest of the team had been busy all day following these up. Neil Nuttall still appeared to be the most likely suspect. But it still didn't feel quite right to Doyle. Could Deano really have thought Nuttall was only in his twenties? If Doyle was right and the killings had been motivated by jealousy and revenge, then it was unlikely that anyone else was at risk if they did have the wrong man in the cells, which was at least a little reassuring.

A knock on his office door broke Doyle's train of thought.

Morgan entered the room. 'Sorry to interrupt. I thought you'd want to know, Will Perkins had an appointment at the clinic in Clitheroe on Thursday 26th October at 11.30 to have a blood test done for his medication. At around the same time, the receptionist remembers Mia turning up and making a fuss about seeing her psychologist, who was away on holiday. She was quite agitated apparently, and security had to be called to get her to leave.'

'Well, that makes what Perkins told us about overhearing her conversation sound plausible. Can we get hold of the CCTV from the clinic to back this up?'

'We're on it. But, better than that, Shaima has checked the phone records and cell site data, and there was a call from Mia's mobile to Turkish's burner at 11.18 that morning lasting nine minutes, from the vicinity of the clinic.'

'So, Perkins probably heard her on the phone on his way in?'

'It would appear so. And from what the receptionist said Mia was shouting when she came in, if she was like that on the phone to Turkish, it's not surprising that Will overheard her.'

There was another knock on the office door. Hales came in, limping and wincing as he did when his gout was playing up.

'How did you get on with Nuttall?' Doyle asked.

'He's a tough nut to crack. Went "no comment" all the way. He didn't seem rattled by being arrested on suspicion of murder. I can't see that we'll get anywhere further unless we can put some indisputable evidence in front of him.'

'Can't say I'm surprised, Geoff.'

'But we might be getting some better news,' Hales said, sitting down. 'We've had more detailed cell site data in for all the mobile phones, from the radio thingy surveys they were doing. Shaima's plotting it on the map now, so hopefully we will get a much better idea of where they have been at different times.'

'Let's hope it comes up with something useful,' Doyle said. 'Oh, and while you're both here, I've remembered something. It's my birthday on Saturday and...'

'Have you only just remembered because you're getting old, boss?' Morgan said.

'What I was going to say was...'

'I hope you're not expecting me to make you a cake,' Hales said. 'I mean, I've watched *Bake Off* a few times but I'm no Paul Hollywood.'

'You're alright, Geoff, I'll let you off. I know it's short notice, but I'm having a few people round for drinks – an afternoon/evening type thing, if you're free. I would go out somewhere, but I'll have Harry with me and he's not good in unfamiliar noisy places.'

'I'm free. Who else are you inviting?' Hales asked.

'Well, the rest of the team and Jen and Dr Gupta, and my er ... estate agent.' Doyle still wasn't sure what Bea was to him, but he realised of all the things he could have called her, what had come out of his mouth was probably the worst.

'Your estate agent?' Morgan asked. 'Do you move house that often?'

Doyle looked across at Hales, hoping he might chip in something useful, but he just smiled back, obviously enjoying his colleague's discomfort.

'No, you know who I mean,' Doyle said. 'Bea helped us out before when...'

'I do know, but a little tip from another woman: you might want to find a different way to introduce her to people.'

'Fair point. So, are you going to come? You can bring Sam – the more the merrier.'

'Yes, we'll come,' Morgan said. For some reason, Doyle felt relieved. He knew Morgan had avoided any out-of-work functions for a long time. Perhaps readily agreeing to spend some free time with her colleagues was a good sign.

'You're not thinking of inviting Mr Burns, are you?' Hales asked, a note of concern in his voice.

'Oh, Christ, no,' Doyle said. 'I can barely stand to be around the bastard at work.'

'And what about what's-her-name, DI Taggart from Professional Standards,' Morgan said. 'You're not inviting her, are you?'

'No,' Doyle said. 'That's why I'm telling you in here.' Though he did feel a bit guilty as he sensed DI Cavanaugh was a good copper, albeit one in a pinstriped suit. But no one in their right mind would invite Professional Standards into their home.

Chapter 53

'Boss,' Asif said, striding into Doyle's office holding her laptop. 'The detailed cell site data has shown something interesting.' She put the computer on the edge of the DCI's desk so that he and the two other detectives in the room could come around to see the screen, which showed a map of the area with different coloured dots on it.

'The dark blue dots are for Burner One and the green ones are for Burner Two. I've plotted all the other relevant phones on the map too, but I've stripped those out for now to make it easier to see these two. Both these phones spend more time off than on, which is unusual these days. I mean, who turns their phone off?'

Doyle nodded. An unregistered phone that was only used sporadically could be an indicator of criminal activity.

'This cluster of blue dots here' – Asif zoomed the map in – 'are in the vicinity of Mia's flat. You can see that Burner One was here quite a lot prior to Mia being killed.'

The analyst clicked the trackpad on one of the dots, which brought up a box showing the date and time. 'Incidentally, whenever this phone was there, Mia's phone was too.'

'That would make sense,' Morgan said. 'If whoever had this phone was in a relationship with Mia.'

'Exactly,' Asif said. 'What's also interesting is the times it was there – they were mostly at night. There are a few times when it's switched off from there late at night and is switched on again there first thing in the morning, as if the person had spent the night at Mia's flat.'

'This fits with your theory, Liam.'

'Still a lot of "ifs" in there,' Doyle said. 'But we are getting closer.'

'What I think we can say is that this phone almost certainly belonged to Mia's killer.'

'We can?' Doyle asked.

'I think so,' Asif said. 'You know how you always say you don't believe in coincidences?'

'I'm not sure I always say that. but go on.'

'You do,' Morgan chipped in.

'This phone was briefly in the vicinity of Mia's flat at 12.31 the night she was killed. It then travelled to Barley at the same time as Mia's phone. The tech people couldn't be too specific about where it was in Barley. Because the village sits right under Pendle Hill, a larger area than usual gets the same mast readings. But the time it was there fits with the time Mia was killed and the time her phone was turned off for the last time. This phone then returns briefly to the vicinity of Mia's flat at 01.58.'

'And its owner feeds Mia's uterus to the dog,' Morgan said.

'I still can't believe that,' said Hales. 'But it's hard to think of another explanation for that carrier bag being there with her blood in it.'

'It's then on the move again in a vehicle along Gisburn Road out of Barrowford. On Scotland Road, Burner One is switched off for the last time.'

'That's near the junction for the M65. He could have gone anywhere from there,' Hales said.

'He could have,' Asif said. 'But take a look at this.' She zoomed out on the map and then back in again on a cluster of blue and green dots in an area of Nelson. 'Both Burner One and Burner Two are frequently switched off and on in this area. Often last thing at night and first thing in the morning.'

'You think this is where the killer lives?' Morgan asked.

'It looks that way,' Asif said. 'And look, if I add the red dots back in for Mia's phone, you can see that she has been there quite a few times too, and often spent the night.'

'Is that where Nuttall lives?' Doyle asked.

'No, sorry,' Asif said. 'He lives the other side of Nelson, towards Colne.'

'Presumably we can narrow this down to just a dozen or so addresses?' Doyle asked.

'Not quite, I'm afraid. There are rows of old terraced houses there, some divided into flats. These signals could have come from over a hundred properties.'

'And the techs can't narrow that down any further?' Hales asked.

'No, not without going there and setting up antennae from lots of different places and taking readings.'

'Be hard to do that without alerting the suspect we're on to him,' Morgan said.

'I've sent a request for electoral roll details for everyone living there. When they come back, we can check if anyone on there has previous,' Asif said.

'We might not get that lucky,' Morgan said. 'Forensics got several sets of prints from Mia's flat. One set belonged to someone with large hands who could well be our man, but they didn't match any prints we have on file, so he might not have a criminal record.'

'That's perhaps not as unusual as it sounds,' Doyle said. 'All the time Turkish had DCI Butcher on speed dial, there were unlikely to be any charges brought against anyone in his operation.'

'Because of the areas they were used in, it is safe to assume that Burner One and Burner Two belonged to the same person,' Asif said, zooming out again on the screen. 'Burner One is also active several times around the Handcocks' house and at NN Agricultural Engineering. I have found another burner that I think, from the cell site mapping, could be Nuttall's, and Burner Two made a call to it at 6.30 on the morning Turkish's body was found.'

Doyle raised his eyebrows. 'So it looks like Nuttall didn't kill Mia or Turkish, but he knows the person who did, and they called him after they had killed Turkish.'

'Exactly,' Asif said.

'And that might explain why Nuttall's account of finding Turkish's body was inaccurate,' Morgan said. 'If he already knew it was there, he might not have gone all the way into the workshop to take a look.'

'Incidentally,' Asif said, 'that number we think Nuttall has been using also made calls to a known county lines dealing number in Merseyside.'

'That figures,' Doyle said. 'If Nuttall was the boss of the organisation, he would have been communicating with whoever they were being supplied by.'

'With Turkish selling it locally and his wife washing the money through the business,' Morgan said.

'Looks like you've got to the bottom of all parts of the dealing operation, Shaima,' Hales said.

'All except the person we need to get,' Doyle said. 'Their enforcer. It doesn't sound like Nuttall will tell us who he is, however much pressure we put on him.'

'Tracy Handcock must know who this person is,' Asif said. 'Can we bring her back in and get it out of her?'

'I'm not sure we will get much,' Doyle said. 'Whatever reason she has for not telling us, whether she is close to this Flesher character or scared of him or both, we've threatened to charge her with perverting the course of justice and that's not had any effect. We don't have any more leverage to use at this stage. That might change if we get the right person in custody, though. What do you think, Geoff? You interviewed her last.'

'I agree. I don't think she will give us anything else now. We could try doing it the old-fashioned way – put some surveillance in the area where this Flesher lives, pick up anyone who fits the description and check them out.'

Morgan shook her head. 'The trouble with that is we've only got a pretty vague description at this stage, other than he's big, white and probably a young man with a beard that he might well have shaved off since Deano saw him last. We don't know much else. And if we pick up anyone fitting that description in the area, we risk getting the wrong person and letting the Flesher know we're on to him.'

'There is something we could do to stack the odds in our favour, though,' Doyle said.

'What can we help you with, Detective Constable?' the foreman asked Birdseye after he had introduced himself.

'It's a bit of a long shot. We're looking for someone who may have worked in an abattoir over the last few years. Just following up various leads on a case.'

'Is it the one with that girl in Barley and that bloke near Roughlee? I read in the papers something about the bodies being mutilated.'

'I'm afraid I can't say what it's regarding.'

'If it is, and that's why you're looking here, you may well be looking in the wrong place. What we do here is slaughter the animals, but we don't butcher them. That's all done by the butchers, funnily enough.'

'Like I say, it's a long shot, but we have to cover all our bases.'

'I saw a documentary once on that Jack the Ripper. They thought he might have been a butcher, didn't they? Have you got a name or photo of the person you're looking for?'

'I'm afraid not, but we do have a description. He's a very big lad, about six foot six, and well-built. White, dark brown hair, quite young, late teens to mid-twenties.'

'Chunk.'

'I beg your pardon?'

'That sounds like Chunk. A feller we had working here a few year back.'

'What happened to him?' Birdseye asked.

'We had to sack him in the end.'

'Why was that?'

'It wasn't his work; there was nothing wrong with that. He were a grafter, I'll give him that, and strong too. I would have liked to keep him. But we couldn't. We probably kept him far longer than we should have done, if truth be telt.'

'What did he do?' Birdseye tried to keep the impatience from his voice. This could either be a vital lead or a complete red herring.

'He took a bit of a shine to Tina in the office. More than a bit of a shine, in fact. It started quite innocently, I think. They were friendly, would chat and that. I think he asked her out and she knocked him back. She had a boyfriend, see. Works over Barnoldswick way as a forklift truck driver.'

'And he didn't take that well, this Chunk?'

'No, kept pestering her, trying to get her to leave her boyfriend. I think this had been going on for quite some time before we were made aware of it. He'd been following her home from work, watching her, that kind of thing. I think he even threatened her boyfriend. We had no choice. We had to let him go. She would've gone to the police. She were saying he were a proper stalker.'

'How did he take it when you sacked him?'

'Well, it was old muggins here that had to do it, with HR, of course, but they made sure I was in the room. I won't lie. I was worried, like, in case he kicked off. He was huge, and if I'm honest, I'm not sure he were totally right in the head.'

'Did he get violent?'

'No, he sat there and looked like he were going to burst into tears. We had to tell him that if he came back after we let him go or if he harassed Tina any more, we would be reporting him to police.'

'Have you got his real name and address, or even a photo?' Birdseye asked. This sounded promising and would fit with the BFG's theory that the killer was infatuated with Mia if he had a pattern of that type of behaviour.

'We will have. I don't have access to all that stuff, GDPR and all that, but our HR will do. They don't work out of this site, but if you give me your details, I'll get them to contact you.'

Birdseye handed the foreman a card. 'Please can you tell them it's urgent? And can you remember what his real name was?'

'We just called him Chunk. I think he might have been Carl or Kyle, something like that, but I can't remember.'

Chapter 54

It was getting dark by the time Doyle had outlined his plan to the team and everyone was ready to go. Paige Anderton and Nat Lofthouse had dispensed with their uniforms and now wore civvies. One advantage of it being autumn – and quite frankly bloody miserable outside – was that stab vests could be more easily concealed under bulky coats. Since the Flesher was known to use a knife, Doyle had insisted that everyone involved in the operation wear them, and had their extendable batons and pepper spray close at hand. In an ideal world, he would have drafted in more officers and, if not an armed response team, then at least the ball-busting Operational Support Unit, but he didn't know how far DCI Butcher's network of corruption had spread. He couldn't risk the Flesher being tipped off about what they had planned. He was just about to get everyone to move out when his phone rang. Dianne Berry. He thought about not taking the call, but the last time she had rung it had proved crucial to the investigation, so he felt he should answer.

'Will's absconded from the hospital,' she bellowed the moment he accepted the call.

'What?'

'Will. He's done a bunk from the hospital!' Her voice was even louder.

'Yes, I heard you, but how?'

'There was some commotion on the ward with another patient, and he went out through a closing door as more staff were rushing in, and then out a fire exit.'

'Jesus, and nobody noticed or tried to stop him?'

'I don't know, but that's not the point. They found a note in his room. He wrote "Flesher was right – it's me, I'm the witch. It's my fault Mia and the Turk are dead. I must do as he says and save everyone".'

'Shit,' Doyle said. 'You think he means—'

'Yes, I do. That man, the Flesher, told him on the phone to kill himself. What was it he said? Throw yourself off a tower, or something?'

'Fuck. Have you called the police?'

'The hospital has, though I'm not sure how much use they will be. You've got to help me find him. If we can get to him before he does something, I might be able to talk him down.'

'Look, I'm sorry, this is an awkward time. I'm right in the middle of—'

'What's more important than saving someone's life?'

'But can't the police who are dealing with it help you?'

'What bloody use do you think they will be? A couple of wet-behind-the-ears PCs straight out of training school? I know how these things work. My husband was one of you lot, remember.'

She did have a point, Doyle thought. Fewer experienced officers were working in response these days. It was such a thankless task that most moved on to something else as soon as their probation was over.

'This is down to you, you know. If you hadn't questioned him about it all yesterday, bringing it all back up, he would have stayed settled. He was starting to get back on track.'

'Liam,' Hales said. The volume of Dianne's voice meant that he could hear Doyle's conversation. 'Why don't you go find Perkins? I'll take your place on the op.'

'One second, Dianne. But what about your gout, Geoff? You were limping earlier.'

'It's OK. I'll be sitting in a car mostly, and I'm not so crippled I can't manage that.'

Doyle looked at his watch. 'Birdseye should be back from checking out the abattoirs soon. You could send him instead.'

'It's OK, I'll go. I can get him to come and relieve me if needed.'

'If you're sure?'

Hales nodded.

'Right, Dianne, where are you? I'll come and get you and we'll go and track down Will.'

'How many bloody towers are there in Lancashire?' Doyle said, looking at the Google search results on his phone.

'We do like a tower in these parts,' Berry said from the passenger seat.

'It looks like there's one on top of every hill.'

'There's not one on Pendle Hill,' Berry said. 'Which is a shame. If there was, I'd put money on him going there.'

'We need to narrow it down a bit. We need to get into his head. Where would Will go?'

'I've known Will a long time. Take it from me, the last place you want to be is inside his head.'

'There's a Hoghton Tower this side of Preston.'

'It won't be there. That's more of a castle, stately home type place. He mentioned Blackpool Tower, but how he'd get that far with no money on him I don't know. I mean, Will's a good runner, but that would take him all night.'

'I'll put the police there on alert. If anyone fitting Will's description turns up at Blackpool Tower, they can pick him up.'

'It's not a tower as such, but there's the ruins of Clitheroe Castle – you can get right up into the ramparts there. It might not be high enough to kill you if you jumped off, but you'd do yourself a heck of a lot of damage.'

'Clitheroe is still quite a way from the hospital. We need to find the closest ones and work out from there.'

The screen on Doyle's phone flashed up an incoming call with the name Birdseye. He answered it on speaker.

'Ask him,' Berry said. 'He's bound to know.'

'Boss, I think I might be on to something—'

Doyle cut him off. 'I'm afraid that will have to wait, Derrick. I need your help with something urgent. Will's done a bunk from the hospital. It looks like he might have taken what the Flesher told him to heart.'

'Or more likely to his jumbled-up head,' Berry cut in. 'I think he's planning to throw himself off a tower, like he said the Flesher told him to.'

'Trouble is, which one? I never knew there were so many towers in Lancashire,' Doyle said.

'There are a lot,' Birdseye agreed. 'More if you count all the big chimneys that are still standing.'

'Bloody hell, you're no help,' Berry said. 'We were hoping you would narrow it down a bit, not come up with more.'

'Sorry,' Birdseye said. Doyle could tell by his change of tone that he'd grasped the urgency of the situation. 'Right, well, I doubt we have to worry about any of the chimneys; even if he did go to one, he wouldn't be able to get up it unless he'd been an apprentice to Fred Dibnah.'

'So, towers then,' Doyle said, circling his hand in front of the phone's screen in a pointless attempt to encourage the other detective to think faster.

'He mentioned Blackpool Tower,' Birdseye said. 'But that's quite a trek from the hospital.'

'Didn't he mention another one?' Berry said. 'I can't think of it – funny name. Not one I've heard of before.'

'That's right,' Birdseye said. 'The Rocket Tower.'

'Rocket Tower,' Doyle said, already punching it into Google. 'Where is that?'

'I think he means Jubilee Tower in Darwen. The locals call it the Rocket Tower because it looks like a space rocket.'

'Yes,' Doyle said. He knew the tower. He had seen it on top of the hill when he'd picked up Harry at his grandparents'. It was wider at the base and had a dome on top, and battlements surrounded the top deck of the tower. It looked like a cross between a castle tower and a cartoon space rocket.

'That's only about two miles from the hospital,' Berry said. 'He would've gone there.'

Doyle had already started the engine and was pulling out, the blue lights on.

'It was built to celebrate Queen Victoria's jubilee,' Birdseye said.

'Fascinating,' Doyle said. 'How do we get there?'

'It's a bit of a walk,' Birdseye said. 'Not difficult in the day if you know where you're going, but not as easy now it's dark.'

'Will you be able to guide us in when we get closer?' Doyle asked.

'I'll try my best.'

'How far are you from the incident room?'

'I'll be there in five minutes, boss.'

'Good. When you get there, call me back and I'll share our location from my phone with Shaima, and she should be able to plot us on the map as we go.'

'You better hurry,' Berry said. 'Will's a fit lad; it won't take him any time to cover that distance and he knows all the hills round here well.'

Chapter 55

Morgan sat alone in the Peugeot, in the driver's seat. In an ideal world, there would have been two detectives in each car, but resources didn't allow for that, so they had to make do. She could see the unmarked car containing the Pearl at the other end of the street. Periodically she spotted the glow of his cigarette. Strictly speaking, officers weren't meant to smoke on surveillance, but no one was likely to remind Geoff Hales of that, and someone sitting in a car smoking probably looked more natural than someone doing what she was doing, sitting aimlessly and twiddling her thumbs. She could also see the car containing Paige Anderton at the other end of the road that intersected hers. She too had forgone making a flask of coffee before setting off, no doubt for the same reason as Morgan. Nobody would take any notice of a bloke at night peeing up a lamp post; a woman, on the other hand, was bound to draw attention – and, at pub chucking-out time, spectators too. Morgan was all for championing equality, but she didn't know what that would look like in this situation.

She couldn't see Gadget, but knew he would be in the car on the opposite corner to hers. She hoped Gadget would be keeping his eyes peeled, looking out of the window and not glued to his phone. Between the four of them, they should be able to spot if a giant man came or went from any of the houses within the perimeter they had set up. Unless they got lucky with a streetlight it would be hard to tell anyone's ethnicity, let alone their approximate age. That's where Doyle's secret weapon came in, waiting in a van with Nat, ready to help with the identification. Nat was parked between Anderton and Gadget next to a ginnel that dissected the terraced houses, meaning it shouldn't take him long to get to anywhere in the vicinity. Morgan had no idea if the boss's plan would work, but it was a novel idea and worth a try.

Before taking up their positions, the team had tried a more conventional method of policing: driving around and getting all the registrations of the white vans in the location. It was amazing how many there were in such a small area. All the numbers had been called back to Asif and she would check with the DVLA who the registered keepers were; they might get lucky that way too. Although all driving licences now carried a photo, there was nothing on them to indicate the height or weight of the licensee, so they were unlikely to get a definitive identification of their prime suspect.

The waiting around was boring, not to mention cold, and the rain meant Morgan had needed to crank the window down a bit to stop the glass getting steamed up. But that wasn't what was bothering her most. Normally at times such as these, she would be feeling a nervous excitement about what lay ahead, wanting the waiting to be over quickly and to get on with the action of nabbing their suspect. But not this evening. She felt different. She would rather spend all night sitting in the car with nothing happening than confront their killer and arrest him. *Jesus, your bottle really is going. There's five of us and one of him. I know he's big, but our odds are good.*

'Right, Birdseye,' Doyle said. 'I'm on that service road opposite the pub – what now?'

'Go as far as you can up there. Then you'll have to get out and walk. Have you got good footwear? It can get quite slippery and might be boggy in places.'

Doyle had on a decent pair of boots. The terrain in Lancashire could vary considerably, unlike in London, and he had learned in his first few days up here to always be prepared for that.

Doyle pulled up in front of a gate that stopped the 4 × 4 from going any further. 'This is us then. On foot from here.'

'Bloody hell, I'm too long in the tooth for this,' Berry said. 'I should be at home tucked up with a Horlicks watching *Corrie*, not hiking up hills.'

'Are you still here?' Doyle said into his phone, not sure if cutting the car's engine had ended the call.

'We've still got you,' Asif's voice said. 'And I've got your location on the map screen of my iPad.'

Outside, it was blustery. Even with his phone on speaker, Doyle could only just hear it when he held it right next to his ear. He retrieved a torch from the car's boot. The beam was more powerful than the one on the phone, and he suspected the battery would last longer.

'Boss?' Birdseye's voice was almost lost in the wind. 'Follow the footpath you're on.'

Doyle set off, Berry following. Before they had gone far he could hear her panting, struggling to keep up. He slowed. He would be much quicker on his own, but if Will was up there and suicidal, she would be much better equipped to talk him down. That's assuming Will hadn't already jumped... What if they were rushing up here, only to find a mangled body at the foot of the tower? He stopped again and lit the path ahead of Berry so she could catch up with him once more.

'Oh Christ,' she said when she reached him, bending forward and putting her hands on her knees. 'How much further is it?'

Doyle looked up. He couldn't see the tower in the dark and the rain. He shone the torch ahead on the path. It looked steeper and turned right further up; beyond that, he couldn't see.

'Birdseye,' he shouted into the phone. 'How much further is it?'

'He's on another call, boss,' Asif said. 'But you've still got a fair way to go. It gets a bit steeper, but you're on the shortest route to the top.'

'For fuck's sake,' Doyle muttered, hoping it wouldn't be picked up by the phone's speaker. Birdseye had picked a fine time to make another call. He turned and saw Dianne Berry sitting on a rock, puffing on an asthma pump.

'I can't... You go ... on.'

She was right, of course. He couldn't wait for her. She would be no use to Will if she managed to make it to the top and was too out of breath to talk. Besides, time was of the essence.

'OK,' he told her. 'But keep your phone on. I may need you to talk to Will.'

She gave him a weak thumbs up, still too breathless to speak.

'Shaima,' Doyle said when he judged he was out of the nurse's hearing. 'Can you send some help here? Some local uniforms and an ambulance. If we don't need it for Perkins, we might well need it Dianne.'

'Will do, boss.'

'Sarge?' It was Birdseye calling Morgan's mobile. 'I've got something. I think I know who—'

'A white van's just parked up my side of the road,' Gadget's voice came through the radio earpiece. 'Someone's getting out. He's a big lad – looks like he could be our man.'

'I'll have to call you back, Birdseye. Looks like something is happening.' Morgan ended the call before the other detective could respond.

'OK, Nat, you're on.' Hales' voice in her ear. 'Do your stuff. Everyone else, stand by.'

Morgan felt nerves like she'd never felt before on an operation. This could be it. Any second now she might hear the 'go' over the radio. Time seemed to have slowed down. It felt like she'd been holding her hand on the car door handle, waiting to move, for ages. It made it worse that everything was happening on the opposite corner to where she was. Unable to see, she was relying on updates from the radio.

'Nat's set him free.' Gadget's voice. 'Any moment now.'

Doyle was quicker on his own. Birdseye hadn't been wrong; some of the ground was treacherous, and he nearly slipped several times. He had to remind himself that, although he needed to get there quickly, if he twisted an ankle he would end up taking far longer. It was getting steeper too, and despite the blustery wind and lashing rain, he was starting to sweat. He had donned a stab vest in anticipation of being on the operation with the others and was now paying the price for that extra weight, along with the additional flab he carried around his belly. He really needed to get fit. He suddenly remembered the operation. In his rush to find Perkins, he had put it to the back of his mind.

'Shaima. Any news from the others? How are they getting on?'

'Something's happening now, boss. It's just coming over the radio. Not sure if it's our man or not.'

Fuck. I should be there with them. 'Shaima, if it's confirmed, send anyone you can down there as backup.'

'Will do, boss.'

'Bollocks!' Doyle shouted into the air like a sweary primal scream. Too late now. Even if he turned back, it would all be over by the time he got there. He kept going up.

Then he caught a sound that carried on the wind – a splintering crack. He looked up in that direction, the torch beam picking out what might be the tower.

Chapter 56

Hales stepped out of the car. A stabbing pain shot through his right foot – a pain that made putting any weight on that leg feel like torture. Bollocks to it. He had to get round the corner towards Gadget, ready to close the net if this was their man. It wasn't far – twenty-odd feet. If the target took off running, Gadget would catch him, and if he got back in the van and drove, Morgan or Anderton would be able to follow.

'Nat's set him free,' came Gadget's whispered voice in the earpiece. 'Any moment now.'

Hales rounded the corner. A massive hulk of a man in a black jacket was walking towards him, about thirty yards away. Then something else caught his eye: another large black object running up the road behind the man. Even though he knew the dog was muzzled, Fury still looked terrifying going at full pelt. The dog ran straight past the figure. For a split second, Hales thought perhaps this wasn't their suspect; either that, or their plan had failed. Then Fury skidded to a halt and turned back towards the man. The dog didn't growl or bark or jump up aggressively. He stopped and did a kind of side-to-side dance at the person's feet, as if he wanted to play. But Fury wasn't a playful dog, at least not with strangers, which meant he knew this person, had caught their scent on the way past.

This was the man they were looking for.

Hales dipped his head and spoke into the mic on his lapel. 'It's him. All units go.' He looked up at the same time the figure in black did. Their eyes met, and realisation dawned in the other man's eyes.

'He's going to run!' Hales just about got the words out before the figure turned and set off in the opposite direction, pursued by Fury. 'Gadget, he's coming your way. Nat, for fuck's sake, get hold of the dog.'

Doyle was almost running up the last steep section of the path. He slipped several times but was able to right himself with his arms. Sweat poured off him, and he thought about dispensing with the stab vest and the heavy bits of kit in its pockets, but wriggling out of it would take precious time. He pressed on. The tower was now fully in view. He could make out the gallery on top, but couldn't see if there was anyone up there. As he reached the brow of the hill, the landscape plateaued. The tower sat on top of a raised mound, and Doyle scrambled up it to the building.

The broken door banged in the wind. A large rock lay on the ground. Perkins must have used it to break in. Inside, stone stairs wound up into the dark. Doyle started up. Soon he came to a closed wooden door leading out to the lower platform. He kept going up. As he got towards the top, the stone steps were replaced by a tightly wound wrought-iron spiral staircase ascending into the dome. Doyle slowed his pace, conscious of the noise he was making on the metal treads, not wanting to risk startling Will and making him jump. The door at the top was locked, but a window in the dome had been smashed. Safety glass littered the floor, thousands of tiny pieces crunching under Doyle's feet. He could make out the shape of Perkins, standing outside, on the battlements, bare-chested, his arms spread wide, looking like Jesus on the cross. If he'd noticed Doyle's arrival, he didn't show it. He was stock still, staring into the distance, wind and rain lashing his body.

Doyle wriggled out of his stab vest; there was no chance he would get through the window with it on. Out on the walkway the flags were slippery underfoot. The wind howled more powerfully up here. Will almost leaned into it, balanced on top of the wall. It wouldn't take much for him to topple over the edge. The lower level of the tower must be about sixty feet below them, the sticking-out platform giving the building its strange rocket-like appearance. Doyle suspected that if Perkins jumped or fell, the platform was where he would land. It might not kill him instantly, but his injuries would be horrific.

The detective inched towards Perkins, wanting the other man to catch him in his peripheral vision, hoping to avoid surprising him. He contemplated moving quickly and trying to grab him before he knew what was happening, but it would only take a millisecond for Perkins to react and jump.

'Will, it's OK, I'm here to help you.'

'Magistrate, is that you?' Perkins said, still staring out in front of him.

'It's DCI Liam Doyle. We've spoken several times before.'

'I remember DCI Doyle, like Roger Nowell,' Perkins said, almost rhyming the words. 'He was the magistrate in 1612. You're one and the same. Just in a different time. I expect you want me to come with you, don't you?'

'I want you to step down from there so we can talk.'

'To take me to Lancaster to be hanged, you mean.'

'No, Will, you haven't done anything wrong. You're not in any trouble.'

'I now know what you were doing when you interrogated me the other day at Read Hall. You got it out of me. I heard this morning that the Turkish man is dead, another prisoner told me. And it's my fault that Mia died too. I catechised the spirits to do it. The one who's called the Flesher. I told him it was the Turkish man who gave Mia a baby, and both of them have been struck down.'

'The Flesher isn't a spirit, or even a voice in your head. He's a real person, and he killed Mia Wright and Turkish. It's not your fault. Get down, Will. You are innocent, you've not done anything wrong.' Doyle again inched closer to Perkins. He was only feet away now, but still not close enough. He might be able to lunge and wrap his arms around the other man's legs, but if he fell, he doubted he would be able to hold him, let alone pull him back up.

'If I jump into the wind, then God can judge me. If I am innocent, then he will let me fly.'

Jesus, how could he reason with him? Negotiate with a madman? 'Will, I have weighed up the evidence and judged you already. You are innocent. I am certain of that. You don't need any further judgement.'

For the first time since he had arrived at the top of the tower, Perkins turned his head towards Doyle. 'You're telling me the truth, Chief Inspector? You're not here to take me to be hanged in Lancaster?'

'Remember when I first met you, Will, I told you I would find out if you were responsible for Mia's death?'

'I think so. It's all a bit jumbled. Was that at Read Hall where you had me locked up?'

'I've concluded my investigation, Will. You are innocent – you didn't kill Mia or Turkish.' Doyle closed the two steps between him and Perkins, and held out his left hand.

Perkins contemplated Doyle's outstretched hand. He turned, reaching out to take his hand, but his foot slipped on the wet stone and he fell backwards.

Doyle grabbed Perkins, but his naked flesh was wet and his arm slipped through Doyle's fingers until he was holding his wrist as Perkins dangled over the side of the tower. That fragile grip was all that was stopping Will Perkins from plummeting to the platform below.

Chapter 57

Gadget saw the giant figure turn and run towards him, moments before he heard DI Hales' warning in his ear. He needed to stop him, and then the others would get there in no time. Gadget had never been a rugby player; he was more of a football man. But he needed to produce the rugby tackle of his life to bring down this big bastard. His old PE teacher's words came back into his head: *get down low and take him at an angle round the top of the legs*. Between the houses and the parked cars, there was nowhere for the other man to go. Gadget was on his haunches, the man was close. Any second... Then he saw the glint of metal in his hand. *Fuck – a knife*. Gadget lunged, and tried to wrap his arms around the suspect's legs, but the other man came over him like a steamroller, the knife thrusting up and into his side, a fist smashing into his face. The man kept going, flattening Gadget in the process. The world felt like it was spinning. Then the dog was on him, pinning him down, snarling and growling, the muzzle the only thing between Gadget and his face being savaged. He felt someone – Nat? – pulling the dog away. Then the Pearl shouted into his radio. 'Gadget's been stabbed. Ambulance – now!'

'Hang on, Will,' Doyle shouted. His arm felt as if it was being ripped out of its socket, and Perkins was gripping his arm, right on the scar where his forearm had made close acquaintance with an angle grinder in the summer. The combination of the two was excruciating. Perkins flailed around with his other arm and found a hold on the top of the battlement. Doyle leaned over, between the teeth of the battlements, and tried to get a grip on Will further down his body. But there was nothing to grab hold of, since Will was shirtless. All he could feel was cold, slippery skin.

'For fuck's sake,' he shouted into the air.

'Don't let go. Please,' Perkins cried back, seemingly in a moment of lucidity.

Doyle knew he had to try to grab hold of Will's jeans and pull him up. But he couldn't reach far enough down. He was tantalisingly close. If only the hospital hadn't stripped Perkins of his belt; he might have been able to grab on to that. He just needed a bit more.

'Use your feet, Will,' he shouted. 'Push yourself up a bit on the side of the tower.'

Perkins did as commanded, and Doyle pulled him up as far as he could with his left arm. Then his grasping right hand finally felt material. Doyle hooked a finger into a belt loop on Will's jeans then grabbed a fistful of denim. With an almighty roar, Doyle pulled with all his might, then flung himself backwards. Perkins came with him, scraping his body against the battlements as Doyle pulled him to safety.

Doyle was still lying there, panting, with Will on top doing likewise, when a woman and two men appeared in front of him, dressed in red overalls. The mountain rescue team had arrived.

Chapter 58

Morgan leapt from the car and ran towards Gadget's position. She heard the Pearl's voice in her ear. 'Gadget's been stabbed. Ambulance – now.' She picked up her pace, wanting to get to him. Needing to help. Then she saw a giant figure crossing the road ahead of her. *Fuck.* She wanted to keep going and get to Gadget. Get to the safety of her colleagues. *But fuck, I can catch him if I'm brave enough.* She heard other footsteps running along the path, coming the way their suspect had. Paige Anderton was going after the Flesher. If Paige was, that meant Morgan had to too. There was no decision to be made now. She couldn't let Paige confront him on her own.

The suspect ducked up a ginnel ahead. Anderton slowed, talking into her radio, no doubt giving her location. Morgan pressed the panic button on her radio and sprinted past her colleague. She got the baton out of her vest while she ran, holding on to it like a relay runner in the last leg of an Olympic final. The gap was closing, but not fast enough. The Flesher broke out the other end of the alleyway and onto the street. She thought she saw him go left. When Morgan emerged onto the road, she couldn't see him. She looked under the rows of parked cars, and couldn't see any feet. He wasn't hiding behind them. The ginnel on the other side of the road went between two blocks of terraced houses. He must have gone down there.

She couldn't see him in the ginnel. It was dark, its far exit lit by a streetlight. There was no way the Flesher could have got that far. But he could be hiding in the shadows in between. A gate led to the tiny back yard of every house on both sides; he could have gone through any of them. Control should be sending more units – they could do with a dog team and even a helicopter with a thermal imaging camera. He had to be in here somewhere. Morgan walked along; there was no point running now. This had gone from a chase to a game of cat and mouse – except what she hunted wasn't a harmless rodent. It got darker the further she moved from the road, and the comfort of the streetlights. Puddles of light spilled out from some of the windows, too weak to be of use. She pushed against each gate as she went, checking for one that might be unlocked or had no give at all, as if a giant man was leaning against it. Morgan tried to move quietly, listening out for any telltale sound. Heavy breathing, perhaps. She wondered how loud her own breathing was. *Not as loud as your heart racing.* The ground was firm but uneven underfoot; street cleaners didn't go down the ginnels, and as a result years' worth of detritus had collected there, along with weeds and puddles.

About halfway along, Morgan turned around. Where was Paige? She'd expected the PC to be following. She mustn't have seen where Morgan had gone. Morgan should have waited for her to catch up. She carried on. Her airwaves radio would be sending her location to Control, and other officers would be here soon enough. Morgan contemplated speaking into it, to guide Anderton and others in the area down the alley. But it felt perilous to break the silence and give away her own location to the person she was looking for.

Then the silence was broken, but not by her. The unmistakable note of a mobile phone alert. She turned. It wasn't far behind her. In a garden off to her right. She heard a rustling – perhaps someone trying to silence the device.

'Police!' she shouted. 'Come out slowly. We have the area surrounded.' Morgan didn't expect the Flesher to comply, but she hoped she would disturb enough of the neighbours and get them looking out of their back windows. They might point her colleagues to the location.

Another noise, this time the scrape of a bolt being pulled back on one of the gates about twelve feet away. The giant figure emerged into the alley. Morgan raised her baton, extending it in the process. Protruding from the man's right hand she could see the glint of a blade. Without taking her eyes off him, her left hand found the Pava spray in the pocket of her vest. It was too dark for Morgan to see the man's face, but something about the way he stood seemed familiar. He took a step away, then turned to look back down the ginnel in the direction they had both come from. Morgan knew he was weighing up his chances of getting away. But as he did so Paige appeared, silhouetted in the glow of a streetlight at that end of the alley. The Flesher was trapped between them. Morgan felt trapped too. There was no room to step aside and let him pass, even if she wanted to.

It hadn't taken Doyle and Will long to walk down the hill to where Dianne Berry was sitting on a boulder accompanied by a couple of paramedics. A uniformed police constable was standing a little bit further away, talking into his radio. The mountain rescue team had wrapped Perkins up in a foil blanket and helpfully lit the path with their powerful torches for the descent. Berry had a blood pressure cuff on her arm and a pulse oximeter on her left index finger. Doyle would have been a bit more concerned about the nurse if she didn't also have a lit cigarette in her right hand.

'Thank goodness for that,' Berry said. 'You had me worried sick, Will.'

'Sorry,' Perkins said. Doyle wondered what he was making of the situation. He hadn't spoken on the walk back down the hill, and the detective had no idea what was going on in the man's mind and what he was thinking.

'We need to get you back to the hospital, Will,' Berry said. 'These nice paramedics are going to give us a lift there in the ambulance.'

'I'm being taken to the hospital?' Perkins asked. 'Not Lancaster Castle?'

'That's right, Will,' Berry said. 'You're not a witch, you're just unwell. We need to get you better.'

Whatever Perkins was thinking, he appeared to be compliant.

'If everyone's safe now, I need to get off,' the uniformed police officer said. 'Sorry, we're really busy. An officer has been stabbed in Nelson, and half our units have been sent over there to help.'

Chapter 59

'Drop the knife,' Morgan shouted. The Flesher was looking around. He had no intention of obeying; he was still focused on escaping. She stepped back, wanting to be well out of reach of his blade. Beyond him, she saw someone else with Anderton; Morgan couldn't tell who it was. She hoped there were other officers behind her, at the other end of the alley, coming to back her up, but she didn't dare look back. She didn't want to take her eyes off the man in front of her.

Morgan took another step back. The man turned away. She thought he was going to run that way, away from her. For a brief moment, she felt a selfish relief he was going to go towards Anderton and whoever was with her.

He turned again. Now he was coming back. Towards her. He'd clearly decided he had less chance the other way. There was no time for further thought. She swung the baton and sprayed the canister up towards where his face was. She felt a jolt as she connected, and turned for another swing. He was almost past her when she landed a blow on the back of one of his knees. She sensed him falling and stood back out of his way. Her eyes and nose were burning; she must have got some of her own spray. She raised the baton again. He was on all fours. Her arm went to swing, to bring the weapon down on the back of his head, as hard as she could, to take the fucker out. Another arm grabbed hers, stopping her strike as a body squeezed past her. A pinstriped knee went into the Flesher's back, forcing him all the way to the ground. Morgan's arm was released, and Paige Anderton pushed past her and joined DI Cavanaugh on the suspect's back, pulling his arms behind him and cuffing his wrists.

'Are you alright, Sarge?' She turned to see Birdseye who was behind, red in the face and panting. 'You got him.'

She could hear more footsteps, and looked up to see several dark figures moving down the ginnel. The Operational Support Unit, fashionably late to the party.

'Shaima,' Doyle shouted. 'Who is it? Who's been stabbed?'

'It's Gadget, boss,' the analyst's voice came back through the car's speakers. Doyle had sprinted down the track to his car and was hurtling through the back streets of Darwen, hoping to get to Nelson as fast as was humanly possible.

'How bad is it?'

'I don't know. He was wearing a stab vest. He was caught under the upper arm, so hopefully it's not too serious. But he was hit quite hard in the face too. He might have concussion.'

'Thank fuck for that. I don't mean about the concussion, but at least he's not dead or dying. What about everyone else, what's happening?'

'I'm not entirely sure. DI Hales is with Gadget, and I think Nat too. Sounds like Anna and Paige have gone after the suspect.'

'Oh Christ, I hope they're OK.'

'All available units have been sent down there, and Birdseye has gone with DI Cavanaugh from here to help out.'

Chapter 60

Doyle pulled up behind the police van that Morgan was leaning against. 'What's happened? Is everyone OK?'

'Gadget's been hurt, boss,' Birdseye said. 'But he'll be OK.'

'Everyone else?'

'We're all fine,' Morgan said. 'Though my eyes are stinging a bit. I copped some of my own pepper spray. Your plan worked; we got him.'

Anderton and Cavanaugh emerged from the alleyway. The DI looked down at her knee when she was under the glow of a lamp post. 'That bastard's ruined my suit,' she moaned.

'Where is he, then?' Doyle asked.

'He's still up there with the OSU guys,' Anderton said. 'They were searching him before moving. He'll be out soon.'

'Good,' said Doyle. 'Then we can find out who he is.'

'I know who he is,' Birdseye said.

Doyle and the others stared at the older detective with a look of incredulity. 'What? What do you mean, you know who it is?'

'I tried to tell you on the phone earlier, boss. But you had a more pressing matter with Perkins, and then all this went off. The HR person from the abattoir got back to me. His name is Kyle Green. Didn't have a current address for him, though.

I checked. He's not got any previous, which is why his prints aren't on our system anywhere.'

Doyle heard footsteps and looked over to see a group of police officers walking a large man out of the alley. For the first time, he saw the face of their suspect. He was younger than Doyle had imagined. Something about him was familiar, but he couldn't say where from.

'We've seen him before,' Morgan said.

'Have we?' Doyle asked, but he was sure she was right.

'That first time we met Turkish, he was working at the farm machinery workshop. Had a beard then, just as Deano described him. He obviously decided to shave in the last week or so.'

'You're right.' Doyle remembered now. He'd been watching them from the other side of the yard when they had been talking to Turkish. Terry Handcock had wanted them to keep their voices down. When Doyle had found out that his wife also worked at the same place, he had assumed that was why Turkish was so jumpy about being overheard when Mia was mentioned. It had felt a little odd at the time – paranoid, even. But it wasn't just Tracy Handcock that Turkish hadn't wanted to overhear. He had been worried about his paid enforcer, the Flesher – or, as they now knew him, Kyle Green.

Chapter 61

Day 13: Friday 10 November

There was an end-of-term feel in the incident room that morning. News that Gadget wasn't badly hurt and was being discharged from hospital that day came as a relief to everyone. But despite their elevated mood, they still had quite a job to ensure the CPS would have enough evidence to press charges.

'What have we got so far forensically on Green?' Doyle asked, turning to Jen Knight.

'One set of prints we found in Mia's house were his, which is circumstantial and doesn't link to either murder.'

'It gives us something to pick at in interview, though,' Morgan said. 'He can't now credibly deny knowing Mia.'

'It will be a while before we get DNA results to back this up, and we've currently got forensics going over his house and van,' Knight said. 'But again, we're unlikely to find a smoking gun, so to speak. Neither victim was killed there, and if he knew both then that could explain any traces of them we find.'

'We might not have a smoking gun, but we do have a bloodied knife, don't we?' Hales asked.

'Yes, but it's not the knife that was used on Mia or Turkish. And so far the only blood we've found on it is Gadget's.'

'Could we do a photo ID parade and see if Deano could pick him out?' Birdseye said.

'We could,' Doyle said. 'But all Deano would be able to confirm is that Kyle Green was the person nicknamed the Flesher who gave him a kicking when he owed money to Turkish.'

'What about your team, Lisa?' Hales said turning to Cavanaugh. 'Do you think you might be able to put pressure on Butcher to supply more info? I mean, he's really in the shit now, by the look of things, and being cooperative might be in his best interest.'

'It's worth a go,' Cavanaugh said. 'And we will be interviewing him again. This time while under arrest. He's well past saving his job, and is probably looking at doing some time. But the problem is, I don't think he knows anything about the murders other than what Turkish told him after Mia was killed.'

'We need more leverage,' Morgan said. 'We've got a good idea about the motive for killing Mia and Turkish, which fits with what Birdseye dug up about him yesterday. But we need more – something that will get him talking in the interview room. Because as it stands, if he goes no comment, we won't have enough to charge him.'

'At the very least, we will charge him for the assault on Gadget last night, carrying a knife, and anything else we can throw at him,' Doyle said. 'It's not ideal, but it's enough to keep him on remand while we investigate further.'

'I think I might have something,' Asif said. 'While you were all out last night, I made some enquiries after Birdseye had given me his name. I've just got something back which might change things.'

Kyle Green did look young. Sitting as he did now, wrapped in a blanket and clutching a plastic coffee cup, he didn't look as threatening as he had when Morgan had seen him the night before.

'The thing you have to realise, Kyle,' Morgan said, 'is this doesn't just affect you. Tracy Handcock has given us a false statement to protect you. And we can prove it's false. We can charge her with attempting to pervert the course of justice. She'll do some time for that. Is that fair? That she gets locked up for protecting you.'

Green didn't reply, but his shoulders appeared to stiffen under the blanket and Morgan thought she saw a flicker of something in his eyes. 'She took you in, didn't she? Over six months you were living in her house. You've still got her address on your driving licence. Finding that out came as a surprise to us. But then, it still didn't explain everything, like why she would protect you after you killed her husband. So we dug a little deeper.'

'We traced you back,' Birdseye said. 'All the usual stuff – DVLA, electoral roll. We know you moved from North Yorkshire sometime in 2019. Your National Insurance number tells us you were working as a butcher in Ripon before that. We haven't spoken to that employer yet. But we will do.'

'My guess is you were sacked from that job too,' Morgan said. 'For something weird or creepy.' Still Green didn't respond, but Morgan knew he was listening. 'Same sort of reason you were sacked from the job in the abattoir in Barnoldswick.'

'I spoke to them yesterday. They gave me the full story,' Birdseye said.

'But that still didn't explain your connection to the Handcocks and why Tracy would try to protect you. We had to go further back to work that out. Right back to your birth, or more precisely your birth certificate. Your mum, Ann Marie Green, is from Nelson. Only sixteen when she had you, but she named the father on the birth certificate – Neil Nuttall. Tracy Handcock is your aunt, and maybe that's why both she and your dad tried to protect you. Even though you killed Tracy's husband.'

'He was a bastard,' Green blurted out, then looked at the duty solicitor sitting next to him.

'We'll come back to that,' Morgan said. 'But we think we know why you killed Mia Wright and Terry Handcock.' She paused to choose her next words. 'You were infatuated with Mia the same way you were with ... what was her name? The woman from the abattoir?'

Birdseye made a show of looking in his notebook. 'Tina Clayton.'

'But Mia wasn't interested in you, just like Tina wasn't.' Green tensed, his huge hand squeezing the plastic cup. *Good, she was getting to him.* 'Mia had been around the block a few times. She'd even had a baby before. She didn't want a big awkward virgin like you. She wanted a real man, like Turkish.'

Green crushed the plastic cup in his hand, and it imploded with a loud crack. Birdseye and the solicitor moved back, Birdseye's hand hovering over the panic button. Just then, Morgan realised something – or perhaps the absence of something. She wasn't afraid. Despite this beast of a man in front of her getting visibly angry, she felt in control. It probably helped that she was in an interview room at Burnley police station and that the BFG and the Pearl were watching on a screen in the room next door. But that didn't matter. She wasn't afraid.

'It wasn't like that!' Green shouted.

'I think it was. She didn't want you; she wanted your uncle, Terry Handcock. And you couldn't handle that so you killed them both.'

'No, she was my girlfriend.'

'Maybe in your head. But not in real life. You're just a sad, infatuated virgin and that's why you killed them both.'

'No,' Green said, rising up then slumping back down in his seat. 'It wasn't like that.'

'What was it like then, Kyle?' Morgan's voice was soft now as she sensed him breaking. 'Tell me.'

'We were together... We'd been seeing each other for nearly two months. A couple of weeks back she texted me, saying she needed to see me that evening. That she had some big news. I went round hers, and she told me she was pregnant. We were going to have a baby.' Green stopped talking and looked at his solicitor again.

'How did that make you feel, Kyle?' Morgan asked.

'I guess nervous ... excited too. We both were. We started making plans, talking about how it could be, how we could make a family... The next day everything was OK, but she was getting worried by then. The baby she'd had before had been taken off her, and she was shitting it that the same thing would happen again. I tried to calm her down, but she was stressing about it. Worried about money too, how we'd cope. I told her not to worry, I was earning good money.' Green's eyes were tearing up. 'She said she'd been to the health centre to see her psychologist, but she wasn't there.'

Green wiped his eyes with his sleeve. 'The next day I saw her, she was drunk. I was fucked off with her. We had a row, I said she shouldn't be drinking. That she could fuck up our baby by drinking. She got nasty ... she did that a lot when she was pissed.' Green let out a loud sob and put his head in his hands. 'She said the baby probably wasn't even mine... I thought she was joking at first, saying that to wind me up because she was drunk and fucked off with me, then she said I should get myself to the clap clinic, get tested. Said she'd caught gonorrhoea, and I probably had it too. I didn't believe her. I thought she was winding me up.'

Green stopped talking and wiped his face again. Morgan let the silence hang, knowing Green would have to fill it, but leaving him to do it in his own time.

'I did get tested, the same day. One of those walk-in places. They phoned me the next day. I had gonorrhoea, and I knew then she'd been fucking someone else. I was fucking fuming. I rang her straight away. Told her she should get rid of the baby, as she didn't know who the father was. She refused, said she was having the baby anyway and it wasn't up to me. She said she'd already had one baby taken off her and she was having this one and keeping it. I wanted to know who the other man was, screamed at her. But she wouldn't tell me.'

Tears were pouring down Green's face, but he didn't stop to wipe them away. 'I said if she didn't tell me who it was, I'd come round and make her tell me. I didn't want to, but I had to know. She said it was Will Perkins. I didn't know who that was. She told me he was the nutter who'd said she was a witch. I didn't believe it. It didn't make sense. She didn't even like him. But she said they had known each other for years and they went back a long way... It kind of made sense then.'

'I think we should take a break now so I can consult with my client,' the solicitor said, and Morgan felt like kicking him under the table. Green was about to confess.

'No, I don't want a break. It's over.'

'What happened then, Kyle?'

Chapter 62

The music was blaring. He recognised the song but didn't know who it was by. Some pop song, maybe Taylor Swift, not the heavy rock he liked. It meant she must be in, though, or maybe not. He wouldn't put it past Mia to go out leaving the music on loud to piss off her neighbours. Fury barked the second he banged on the door. He liked the dog; it was a bit like him, big and frightening on the outside but with a caring soul. He mustn't get soft. How she'd treated him was out of order. He'd given her his love and in return she'd given him the clap, and a baby that might or might not be his. He knocked again.

'Alright, I'm coming.'

She was in, then. This was it. He would soon be past the point of no return.

'Shut up, Fury.' The door opened. 'Oh, it's you. What do you want?'

'I want to talk.'

'You're not pissed off with me any more, then? Or did you think you could come round here at half past one in the morning, make up and get a fuck?'

What was the matter with her? She'd taken the love he'd given her and thrown it back in his face and now she was acting like they'd just had a little argument. *Stay calm. Stay in control.* 'No, not that. You weren't asleep anyway. Besides, the clocks go back tonight so it's not half past one. What were you up to, having a smoke?' *And no doubt hurting that baby you want to keep so much.*

'Cleaning.'

'Cleaning? You?'

'Yes, me. What did you want?'

'I said. To talk.'

'You better come in, then. You better not start shouting again or you can fuck off.'

'Not here. Come with me for a drive.'

'Why? It's late.'

'It's not raining. We can sit out, look at the stars. Like we did before. That first time.'

'Alright, but not for too long. I'll grab my coat and Fury's lead.'

'Leave the dog. Let's just go.'

Neither spoke as the van picked its way down the dark country lanes.

'Where are we going?' she asked as he pulled up near the entrance to the path.

'For a walk. It's not raining.'

'Up Pendle Hill? At night?'

'Not up it, just along the path for a bit. I bought some drinks.' He showed her the carrier bag with the cans of cider and a rug in it.

'I've stopped drinking and smoking ... because of the baby.'

He hadn't planned on that. He'd hoped she would be pretty pissed by this time of night and not thinking too clearly. He'd brought along a couple of joints loaded with skunk for her to smoke. He pressed the key to lock the van. The chirp sounded noisier than ever and the flashing lights lit up the road. He hoped all the locals were asleep in bed. He didn't want to be seen. He set off along the path, knowing she would follow. It would be a long walk in the dark to get back to Barrowford from Barley, and she wouldn't want to do that on her own.

'This place is creepy. It freaks me out. That hill, it's like you can see it from everywhere around here, looming over you.'

She wasn't wrong. With the moon almost full as it was now, the flat top of Pendle Hill was lit up against the sky.

'You ever think about those witches? What happened here?' she asked.

People were obsessed with the witches. It all happened over four hundred years ago. He shook his head. Mia's interest probably came from talking to that psycho – the one who had thought she was a witch. She'd still fucked him, though, and she'd pay for that. They both would.

He took the rug from the bag and spread it out under a tree. 'Come on, sit down, have a drink.'

'I told you, I'm not drinking. I don't want to fuck things up for the kid.'

It's a bit fucking late for that now, after what you did. 'One drink won't hurt.'

'What did you want to talk about, and why did you drag me out here?'

'I don't... What you did ... with him. Why did you do it?'

'I'm sorry, OK? I don't know what to say.' She turned away from him. Stood staring up at that fucking hill. He stood behind her, draped his left arm over her shoulder. She didn't push it away. She held on to it.

'I do love you,' she said.

He took a deep breath. Filled his lungs. He felt the rise and fall of her chest against his arm. The sheep were silent; there was only the rushing of the stream. His right hand found the knife inside his coat. She felt his movement, went to say something, but his left hand grabbed her chin, pulling it up, silencing the words before they were out of her mouth. He pressed hard as he drew the knife across her neck. Her body convulsed. He held her tightly against him as the blood pumped out of her. When it had stopped, he laid her down on the grass.

The bark of the tree was rougher than he'd expected. He hoped it wouldn't dull the blade of the knife. He thought about not carving the trunk. The idea had only come to him that afternoon, but it was a brilliant one. He'd looked it up online, seen the symbol. That psycho Perkins would be an obvious fit, especially if Turkish gave his pet pig the tip-off. It was only fair that he paid too for what they had done to him.

He didn't want to do the next bit. He was far from squeamish; he'd cut up plenty of dead flesh before, but he'd loved Mia until she'd betrayed him. That was unforgivable. He thought about not doing it. In some ways, that might work better. If the baby was the psycho's, he would be in the frame with DNA. But then if the baby was his, he might end up getting done. They didn't have his DNA on file, but if he ever got nicked for anything they would take it, then he would be linked to Mia by the baby. He'd seen it on some programme on YouTube. Years after the event, people were getting done for murder because of DNA. He had to do it, or he would be forever looking over his shoulder.

Her eyes were open. He didn't want to see her face. He couldn't stand it – it was like she was looking at him, blaming him, when it was all her fault. He draped the rug over her head and shoulders. That was better.

Then he got to work.

Chapter 63

Morgan took a deep breath. She had to compose herself, not become emotional. She'd felt some kind of connection to Mia when she had looked through her flat and then at the mortuary, feeling a tightening in her own throat as Dr Gupta carried out the post-mortem. It had brought back her own ordeal and reminded her how close she had come to being laid out on the pathologist's slab. She'd wondered then what type of sick individual would have mutilated Mia in such a horrific way, and why.

'What did you do afterwards?' Birdseye asked.

'I changed my clothes back at the van – I was muddy and covered in blood. Then I drove to Mia's flat.'

'Why did you go there?' Morgan asked.

'I hadn't planned to. But I remembered she had some photos there of the two of us together. I thought you lot would go through her flat and find them, then come looking for me, so I had to get them back... We never went out anywhere together, and only Turkish knew I was with her. Fury was pleased to see me. I kind of wanted to keep the dog, look after him. I didn't know how long it would be until you worked out who Mia was and went to her flat. I thought I'd better feed him and leave some water. But there wasn't any dog food in the cupboard.'

Morgan braced herself.

'I had that piece of her in a carrier bag. I was going to stuff it into a bin somewhere on the way home, but the dog needed feeding, and it was just flesh, after all. It was natural.'

Morgan couldn't think of anything less natural. She wanted to scream and cry out and shake the man in front of her. It was as if he felt all his actions had been justified because Mia had betrayed him, a damaged young woman who couldn't manage relationships. That had cost her her life.

'What did you do with the knife and clothes?' Birdseye asked.

'They stayed in the back of my van for a few days in a bin bag. That time when you came to the workshop and spoke with Turkish?' Green looked directly at Morgan. 'They were in my van then. I knew I needed to get rid of them, but I didn't know where. Then I saw a big bonfire pile in Barrowford that had been built ready for fireworks night. I stuffed them right in the middle of that. They'll all be ashes now. Well, not the knife, obviously, but I reckoned even if that was found after the fire there wouldn't be any trace of me on it.'

'And you called Terry Handcock later that morning?' Morgan asked.

'I'd been up all night, all kinds of shit going around in my head. It didn't seem real. But I knew it was going to get real. Turkish knew about us, but he also knew that Mia had argued with that psycho – we'd both watched as it happened. I told him I'd heard that Mia had been killed, and said she'd gone to meet Will Perkins that evening. He went mental about it, said it was really bad news and could fuck everything up for all of us.'

'Do you think he believed you when you said Perkins had killed her?' Morgan asked.

'I reckon. He went on about how people like him should be hanged. I didn't even have to ask him to call that copper, he said he was going to, make sure he got locked up. When Perkins was arrested, I thought that would be the end of it. Then you let him go.'

'Why didn't you leave it there?' Morgan asked. 'There was no more Mia and no baby.'

'But he had to pay for his part in it too. I wanted to get to him. I was still raging that he'd ruined everything for me. But I couldn't get close to him. There were too many people around. People giving him grief because they thought he'd killed Mia and then the police and nurses and people looking out for him, even the press. I knew he was staying at his dad's house, everyone knew that, but I couldn't get close without being seen. Then I realised I could call him there.'

'How did you get his number?' Birdseye asked.

'I knew his dad was old. Mia told me about when he'd had a stroke, she'd been there and seen it. Old people still have phones in their houses – landlines, I mean. I got the number from directory enquiries.'

'And what did you hope to achieve by calling him?' Morgan asked.

'I wasn't sure at first. I thought I could fuck him up. Mess with his head. But his head was already messed up. I thought maybe I could get him to admit to killing Mia and get himself done for that. But I wasn't sure that would work. You'd already let him go and I thought you might have some reason that you knew it wasn't him.'

Morgan thought back. If Perkins had come up with a confession at that stage it would probably have been enough to have him charged – maybe not with murder, but with manslaughter on the grounds of diminished responsibility.

'He was proper loopy when I spoke to him, thought I was one of those voices in his head. I thought I could get him to fuck himself up, take an overdose, throw himself off something – you know, like crazy people do when they think they can fly.

I said it was punishment for getting Mia pregnant, and he said that it wasn't him.'

'And you believed him?' Birdseye asked.

'Strange as it might sound, I did. He was messed up in his head and thought I was part of his imagination or something. He had no reason to lie. And when I thought about it, it never really did make sense, the idea that Mia would have fucked him. And then he said something about a Turkish man, and it all clicked into place.'

Green leaned back in his chair. 'I was employed as muscle to make sure people paid up when they owed for the gear. Turkish gave me the name the Flesher. I wanted to be called the Butcher, but he said we already had a Butcher on the firm. I didn't mind that. Roughing up a few junkies wasn't exactly difficult. But I didn't want to hurt any of the girls. I'm not like that. I don't agree with hitting women.'

Morgan wondered if he – who had just confessed to the murder and mutilation of a young woman – could see any irony at all in that statement.

'Turkish said not to worry, he would take care of them and make sure they always paid, and he did. I thought for ages he was just having a quiet word with them, threatening them to make sure they paid up.'

'But he wasn't?' Birdseye asked.

'No, he was making them work it off in kind. I was fuming when I found out. Tracy was my aunt and she'd been good to me, taking me in when I moved over here. I'd had a difficult relationship with my dad, 'cause he hadn't wanted anything to do with me. She helped me sort that out. Got him to give me a job after the abattoir sacked me.'

'Did you tell her what he'd been doing?' Morgan asked.

'No. I wanted to. He said what she didn't know wouldn't hurt her and if I didn't like it this way then I would have to get them to pay up like I did with the lads... When Will mentioned a Turkish man with Mia, it all made sense. She was shit with money, so there was every chance she'd spent what she owed on tick.'

'So you confronted him that night?' Morgan asked.

'He denied it. But if I wasn't sure before, I was then. I could just tell, you know? All my rage came out on him and I'm not sorry.' Green was getting more animated, his voice rising. 'He fucking deserved it. He treated everyone like shit and thought he could talk his way out of anything.'

'Was that why—' Morgan said.

'Why I cut his tongue out? Partly, but also because I'd fucked up.'

'Fucked up how?'

'When I phoned him. I thought Tracy would be in bed. She always went to bed earlier than him, so she wouldn't know it was me who called him or who he was meeting. But when I was driving down to the yard, she was driving back. He'd got her up in the middle of the night and made her give him a lift there. She saw me and waved as we passed each other.'

'And why did that lead to you cutting out Terry Handcock's tongue?' Birdseye asked.

'Well, then I thought it would look like a psycho did it, the same person who killed Mia. You know, taking trophies. I saw something on Netflix about serial killers doing that.'

It was so bizarre, listening to him talking about other people being psychos, at the same time as describing killing two people because he couldn't control his own emotions. Morgan wondered if Green would be classed as insane. 'But you didn't take his tongue. You left it in the inspection pit in the grime.'

'I wasn't thinking clearly. I phoned my dad early that morning. I told him Turkish had been killed. I didn't say I'd done it, just that I'd seen him there and then I'd seen Perkins running away. I said I'd panicked, locked up and left. I told him Tracy had seen me going there. He said he would sort it out. Said he would call her.'

'Sort it out how?' Morgan asked.

'I knew he wouldn't want my name involved. Not because he wanted to protect me. He was more interested in protecting himself.'

'Protecting himself from what?' Birdseye asked.

Green laughed. 'From the dealing. You don't think it was Turkish doing all that, do you? He was the frontman. All talk, supplying all the local fuck-ups to sell to their fuck-up mates. But it was my dad who was pulling the strings. Cleaning up the money through his business. He told Tracy what I had told him and told her to say she had seen Perkins when she dropped Turkish off.'

'Anna, I'm glad I bumped into you,' DI Cavanaugh said. Morgan wasn't entirely sure the feeling was mutual. 'I hear your man has confessed to both murders? That's a good result. Well done.'

'Thanks. He said some things about Butcher and Neil Nuttall which will help with your investigation.'

'I know, I was watching.'

Course you were. It seemed those in Professional Standards had access all areas warrant cards, like a police version of a backstage pass at a festival.

'I need to have a quick word. Come with me.'

Morgan had a horrible feeling she knew what was coming. Cavanaugh had been there the night before, when Green was arrested. She'd rushed up behind Morgan to help. Morgan had her baton raised above her head, ready to lay into Green as if he was a piñata at a children's party. If it hadn't been for Paige Anderton, she would have done it. She didn't think it would be enough for her to lose her job – after all, she hadn't actually done it, and the man had come at her with a knife. But it might be seen as a loss of control, no doubt attributed to what had happened to her in the summer. Enough for her to be taken off front-line duties.

'Where are we going?' Morgan asked as she was led around the corridors of Burnley police station. She had expected to be taken upstairs to see the brass, but they were heading towards a conference room on the ground floor.

'You'll see.'

Inside, reporters were milling around while technicians set up equipment. The stage was being set for a press conference.

'As part of our investigation, we pulled all the phone records for everyone on Butcher's team. DS Felton made a couple of calls to an unregistered mobile at certain key points during your enquiry.'

'Right...?' Morgan said, confused about where this was going.

'I understand there is some history between the two of you.'

I despise the arsehole with every fibre in my body. 'You could say that, yes.'

'I don't know if you know this, but it's not just criminals who use burner phones. Some journalists have them too, so people can give them anonymous tip-offs without the numbers they have called showing up. The gutter press, mostly.' Cavanaugh took her mobile phone out from her suit jacket. 'I got this idea from you, from how you linked Handcock to one of the burner phones.' She made a call and put the phone on speaker.

Across the room, Morgan saw the rat-faced Jayden Clark remove a phone from his pocket.

'Hello?' the voice came from the mobile in Cavanaugh's hand.

'Is that Jayden Clark, the reporter?' Cavanaugh said. 'I think I've got a story for you.'

'Speaking,' Clark said.

Cavanaugh ended the call, and Clark stared at his phone, looking bemused. 'I think that's probably the end of DS Felton's career, don't you?'

Morgan looked at the other woman in astonishment. Just like that, Steve Felton, the bastard who had caused her so much grief in the past and had come back recently like a filthy stench, was gone. Toast. You didn't give key details of a murder investigation to the press and recover from it.

'What are you two up to?' It was Doyle, looking predictably awkward in a suit and tie.

'I'll tell you later,' Morgan said. 'They've roped you into doing the press conference, then?'

'Looks that way. I tried to get out of it, but Burns wasn't having any of it.'

'Burns?' Cavanaugh asked.

'Detective Superintendent Croucher,' Doyle said. 'We call him Burns because ... well, he looks—'

'Like Mr Burns from *The Simpsons*,' Cavanaugh finished. 'He does. I hadn't noticed that until now.'

'Try not to spill water down your shirt this time,' Morgan said.

Chapter 64

Day 14: Saturday 11 November – Remembrance Day

'Do you like the card, Dad? I made it myself.'

'It's wonderful, Harry, thank you.' It *was* wonderful. He couldn't quite tell what the picture on the front was meant to be, and the second 'd' in 'Dad' had been written the wrong way round so it said 'Dab'. But Harry had spelt 'birfday' correctly, in Doyle's view. Being from south London, he'd never understood why the English language needed an 'f', 'th' and 'ph' to make essentially the same sound.

'It's a canal boat going through a lock.'

'I know, I can see. I've got a little something for you too, Harry.'

'What, a present?'

'Yes, but just a little one. Don't get too excited.'

It was too late. Harry jumped up and down, his arms pumping wildly to his sides. 'Yes, yes.' The boy didn't do emotions of any kind by halves. When he was excited, he was ecstatic.

Doyle handed him the small box and his son ripped off the wrapping paper like a predator tearing into its prey. 'It's a thing like you've got,' he said, taking the chain from the box.'

'It's called a dog tag. Look.' He showed Harry the disc. 'That says *Liam Doyle, Dad* and it's got my date of birth underneath it – *11.11.78*. See here.' Doyle pulled out his own chain from around his neck. 'This disc here says *Sgt Aidan Doyle* and it's got his army number. That's my dad, your granddad.'

'He's dead.'

'Yes, Harry, but part of him is always with me, which is why I wear this. The other dog tag is with him. But look – I've put another disc on my chain. Can you read what it says?'

'Harry Doyle.'

'That's right, and it's got your birthday below it. So, I'll wear this round my neck and it will be like a bit of you is always with me, and you wear yours around your neck and it will be like a bit of me is always with you.'

'Will you actually be with me all the time?'

'No, not actually,' Doyle said, not quite sure how he was going to explain this to someone so literal. 'It will be like I will always be with you in spirit, and you will always be with me in spirit.'

'Thanks, I love it,' Harry said, putting it round his neck. 'What are they doing on the TV?'

'It's Remembrance Day. They're having a service to remember all the people who died serving their country.'

'Like your dad?'

'Like my dad.'

'Is that why they have it on your birthday? So you can remember your dad on your birthday?'

Doyle laughed. 'No, that's just a coincidence.' *Maybe that's why I don't believe in coincidences.* 'When I was a boy, your grandma used to take me every year to watch this service. Some years my uncle Kenny, my dad's brother, would be on parade.'

Doyle's phone rang. 'Speak of the devil,' he said, answering and putting it on speaker.

'Happy birthday.'

'Thanks, Mum.'

'He called you a devil, Nan.'

'Did he now? Little git. You tell him to watch it or next time I see him I'll give him a clip round the ear. You got the service on the telly, son.'

'Yes.'

'Remember we used to go every year?'

'How could I forget?'

'I saw you on the TV last night. At least you didn't spill water all down yourself this time. Mind you, you've put on weight.'

'It's the camera, it does that to you.'

'It's all them bloody fry-ups you have. Anyway, shut up now, the two-minute silence is coming up.'

'Is that what you called me for? To tell me to shut up?'

'Shush.'

Harry stood up and copied the soldiers on the TV, standing to attention and saluting. They all remained motionless until the bugler had finished playing the last post.

'Right, I'd better be off, son. Got to get a bet on. I've had a hot tip on the 1.10. Down Memory Lane – seems appropriate today. You should stick a fiver on it too.'

'You're joking! The last tip you gave me romped home last.'

'Yeah, well, that was probably the jockey's fault.'

'It was a greyhound, Mum.'

'Do they have jockeys on greyhounds?' Harry asked.

'No, Harry,' Doyle said.

'Next time you come down we should go to the dogs, Harry. If there are still any tracks left. Anyway, best be off. Enjoy your day.'

'Will it be noisy later?' Harry asked the moment the conversation had ended.

'No, it will be just a few people chatting and a bit of music, but not too loud.'

'Will you sing and play your guitar?'

No chance I'm doing that in front of my colleagues. 'I can't, Harry. You know where I hurt my arm in the summer? I hurt it again at work the other day.'

'Will it get better? Will you be able to play the guitar again and sing with me?'

'Yes, at some point.'

'Promise?'

'Promise.'

Geoff Hales didn't see why he was sitting in an interview room that morning, but he didn't mind. The chance that the soon to be former DCI Butcher would shed any further light on either murder case was slim. Butcher was under arrest for improper exercise of police powers and privileges, and it was likely that the CPS would find a lot more to charge him with by the time they had got the full bundle of evidence. Hales was quite happy to be alongside his colleague from Professional Standards that Saturday morning. Apart from getting the chance to enjoy seeing a bent copper squirm, he was curious about what would make someone with a decent wage and final salary pension risk losing it. Not to mention having to spend a number of years in prison.

'How did you first come into contact with Terry Handcock?' DI Cavanaugh asked.

'He approached me one evening as I was coming out of a pub in Colne. It was early 2019,' Butcher said. 'He knew who I was, said he had information for me, but wouldn't say what at first. I said he should call 111 and report it and stop wasting my time. Then he said it was about someone called Roddy Kerr. Then I was interested.'

'I remember that name,' Hales said. He hadn't remembered, but Cavanaugh had given him a thorough briefing on Butcher's past cases before the interview started. 'Wasn't he a serious player in East Lancs?'

'He was, and we'd been after him for a while and could never make anything stick. You know how it is.'

Hales wasn't surprised that Butcher had decided to dispense with the old favourite 'no-comment' interview. This was about damage limitation now. The other man knew he was going down; he was just hoping a judge would look favourably on him for cooperating now when it came to sentencing.

'And Turkish was able to give you enough to take Kerr down?'

'Not just him, his whole operation too. It was just what I needed at the time.'

'Why did you need it?' Cavanaugh asked.

'I was a DI and there was a DCI's post coming up. I badly needed the extra money that would come with promotion. I'd split up with my wife and she kept the house. I was renting somewhere else. Both my kids were in private schools, the fees were crippling me.'

Hales stared at the other man. He was a DI and divorced, and he'd paid the price for that. His daughters had gone to the local state high school, like most kids did. Butcher wouldn't be getting any sympathy from him. 'But the promotion and extra money wasn't enough?'

'No. I was drowning in debt and running out of credit. And then Turkish was there again, waiting for me outside my rented house one evening. He asked me to come for a drive with him. I genuinely thought he was going to give me some other bit of intel, but when we stopped, he pulled a shopping bag from under the seat and handed it to me. It had ten bundles of twenties in it. He said it was ten grand.'

'And what? You just couldn't resist?' Cavanaugh said.

Butcher looked down at the table, like a naughty kid who had been caught stealing the lunch money. 'I did say no at first. Then he said I didn't have to do anything for it.'

'You seriously expect us to believe he was willing to give you ten grand without you doing anything for it?' Hales asked.

'Well, yes, that was precisely what he wanted me to do at first. Take ten grand and then do nothing, but specifically do nothing when it came to investigating certain crimes in the area.'

'And you didn't think about arresting him there and then?' Cavanaugh asked.

'Of course I did. But it was ten grand, and I was desperate. I think because he saw that I was weighing it up, he knew he had me. He said there would be a further three grand a month on top of that. All I had to do was turn a blind eye and make sure he and his operation didn't attract any police interest.'

'So that was it?' Hales asked. 'Ten grand and a further three a month to change sides and work for the likes of him?' He added a sarcastic 'sir' at the end, hoping it would show his contempt for the man who was, for now, still one rank above him.

'And of course it didn't stop at that, did it?' Cavanaugh said, her voice level. 'They wanted more bang for their buck than you just turning a blind eye.'

Most of the guests were already at Doyle's house when Bea arrived.

'This is Bea,' he said by way of an introduction, mindful of Morgan's advice not to add the prefix 'my estate agent' and deciding he didn't need to qualify their relationship any further. It felt weird to call her his girlfriend at their age. Shortly afterwards Gadget arrived, to cheers and applause from his colleagues. The young detective's face was bruised and puffy around the mouth and nose, and his left arm was in a sling.

'Sit yourself down here, lad,' Birdseye said, getting up from the sofa.

'I must look bad if an old man is offering me a seat,' Gadget said, though his voice had a muffled nasal quality to it due to the swelling.

'What happened to you?' Harry asked.

'I got into a bit of a tussle with a bad guy,' Gadget said. 'Don't you think the bruising makes me look cool, though?'

Harry took a moment to look more closely. 'You look a bit like Voldemort.' This brought laughter from Morgan, Hales and Asif.

The lights went out and Birdseye appeared with a birthday cake, and everyone sang happy birthday to Doyle.

'Can I blow the candles out, Dad?' Harry asked.

'Thank you all,' Doyle said. 'And thanks for coming. Who made the cake?'

'It was Gill,' Birdseye said, nodding towards his wife.

'Well, thank you, Gill, it's very much appreciated.'

'We didn't know how many candles to put on, so we just stuck a few on,' Morgan said.

'It's forty-five,' Doyle said.

'You were six years out with your guess, Anna,' Hales said.

'You thought I was thirty-nine?' Doyle asked Morgan.

'Um, not exactly,' she replied.

After the cake had been served, Doyle stepped outside for some fresh air and to join the Pearl, who was having a smoke. 'Thanks for doing that this morning, Geoff.'

'No problem. We can't have you working on your birthday if it's avoidable.'

'Did Butcher shed any light on Felton and why he was feeding stuff to the press?'

'Same reason, more or less. Money. Though I'm not sure in Felton's case whether it was greed or desperation. Butcher admitted that he knew about it – it had happened on other cases too. But he also knew that Felton had worked out he was on the take as well, so he couldn't really do much to stop it.'

Doyle's mobile pinged with a text. It was from DI Cavanaugh and after he read it, he handed his phone to Hales.

'Sorry, Liam, I've left my glasses inside. What does it say?'

'Good news,' Doyle said. 'From Lisa Cavanaugh. The CPS has authorised charges against Nuttall and Butcher. When her team interviewed Green, he not only confessed to his part in the dealing operation, but he gave them enough to charge his dad with conspiracy to supply, and possibly money laundering. They're still deciding what they can charge Tracy Handcock with.'

Morgan joined them outside the back door, having sensed something was going on. 'I just caught the end of that. Nuttall is being charged?'

'Yep, and not just him. Pat Butcher is going to be charged with several offences related to bribery.'

'The brass aren't going to be happy that one of their DCIs is up to his neck in shit. Not a good look,' Hales said. 'I'm going to grab another beer – want me to get either of you a drink?'

'Another beer would be nice, thanks, Geoff,' Doyle said.

'No thanks,' Morgan said, and Doyle realised that she hadn't been drinking. He wondered whether that was because of a few days back, or something else. He was glad she had come, though; this was the first time he'd seen her out of work other than when he'd visited her in hospital. He knew that stemmed back to an incident with DS Felton, and Doyle hoped that his fall from grace might give Morgan some comfort.

'How are you feeling about things now?' Doyle asked when Hales was out of earshot.

'I don't know, really. Glad the case is over and I got through it. I'm glad we got the right person for Mia... I'm still not sure about myself. I was starting to fear that I wouldn't react if I needed to, but now I'm worried that I'll overreact.'

'But you didn't.'

'Only because Paige stopped me.'

'I should never have let things get to the point where you were in that situation on your own. You can't hold back when you're on your own with someone like that. Trust me, I know.'

'I guess you probably do. Have you decided what you're going to tell your therapist when you see her next?'

'Strange as this may sound, I was thinking of telling her the truth. If she decides from that I'm not fit to do the job, then so be it.' Doyle stopped talking abruptly as the French doors burst open behind him and Asif's twin boys came running out, hitting each other with plastic swords and charging around the muddy lawn. They were followed by Shaima's husband, Abbs, who stopped on the patio beside them.

'Sorry about those two. Honestly, they are a bloody nightmare. I don't know where they get their energy from.'

Doyle smiled. 'Not a problem, as long as they're having fun.' For all Harry's difficulties, he wasn't convinced that Shaima had it much easier. No wonder she always seemed so cheerful on Monday mornings. Work must be like a break for her after a weekend spent chasing after those two.

'Don't they make you want one, Anna?' the Pearl said, returning with two beers.

'Several,' Morgan said. Doyle noticed she was looking at the drinks, not at the kids.

'Boss?' Doyle turned to see Gadget coming out onto the patio. 'I've got something I need to ask you.'

'You don't have to call me boss, Gadget, we're not at work now. What's up?'

Gadget looked nervous. 'Well, you know the other night? What happened and that.'

'Yes, I had heard. What about it?'

'Well, I tried to stop him, but then I saw the knife too late and I couldn't get out of the way.'

'It's alright, Gadget, we know that. No one's blaming you for what happened. It's down to me. I should have had more officers there; you shouldn't have got hurt.'

'Everyone thinks you're a hero, lad, for taking him on,' Hales said.

'Thanks, but it's not that. It's just—'

'Spit it out, Gadget,' Morgan said.

'It's the jacket I was wearing. It's a North Face one, pretty new too. But it's got a cut in it from where he stabbed me. It cost me three hundred quid.'

'It's OK, Gadget,' Doyle said. 'I've got some good news for you.'

'Oh, does that mean—'

'It's Black Friday in a couple of weeks. You'll probably be able to get the same coat with forty per cent off.'

Despite his injuries and the swelling, the young detective's face fell in disappointment. Hales and Morgan tried to keep their faces straight.

'But I was hoping—'

Morgan couldn't contain her laughter. Gadget turned back to her, a pained look on his face.

Doyle decided to put him out of his misery. 'Of course we'll replace your coat.'

Epilogue

Five Days Later

Doyle stopped speaking and looked up, making eye contact with Dr Wade.

She smiled. 'So, there we have it. I'm glad that you finally felt able to share that with me. I think it says a lot about you that after weeks of holding back, it was your desire to get information about your case that convinced you to let go of this secret, having kept it so long.'

'What does it say? That I'm too absorbed in my work?'

'Maybe to a degree, but I wasn't meaning that. It's not about putting your career first – it's the outcome of the case that matters most to you. You made a personal sacrifice in order to help you reach the right conclusion.'

Sacrifice. What would that sacrifice end up being? 'And now you know, what are you going to do?'

'Do? Nothing.' Dr Wade frowned. 'Why would you think I would do anything now I know that?'

'Because I broke procedure,' Doyle said. 'I lied in my statement and then at the enquiry, and if I had missed I could've killed the girl.'

'But you didn't miss.' Wade lent forwards in her seat. 'This is another of those times when the outcome is what really matters.'

'I guess.' Doyle felt his shoulders start to loosen.

'What's the girl's name?'

'Tia.' Doyle had thought about her every day for a long time now and how close he had come to killing her, but it had been ages since he'd last said her name out loud.

'And how old will Tia be now?' Wade asked.

Doyle thought for a moment. 'I guess five, maybe six.'

'And do you know what happened to her after the incident?'

'She went to live with her mum's parents.' He'd learnt that at the inquest.

'And that poor child will have some awful trauma to come to terms with as she grows up.' Dr Wade caught Doyle's eye. 'What do you think she will think about you?'

'I don't know. I've never considered it.'

'What do you think she will think about the incident in the car park? Other than you, she is the only living person that was there.'

'I don't know... I guess I kind of hope that she doesn't remember it.' Doyle sensed his shoulders start to tighten back up.

'Whether she does or doesn't, I think it's likely that she will be told about it at some point.' Wade said. 'And what do you think she will think of the person who shot the man who was holding a knife to her throat? The man who had killed her mother?'

'I don't know.'

'I expect she will think you saved her life.'

'I'd never thought of it like that.' He'd not considered what the girl – Tia – might think of him. 'I was just relieved that I hit the right person.'

'Have you ever felt proud of what you did that day?'

'No.' Doyle almost laughed. 'Not once, not for one second.' There had never been a moment when he had felt anything good about what happened that day.

'And yet, when we strip everything away from the event and how it felt,' Dr Wade said, 'And focus on the outcome, the reality is you saved Tia's life. That's the bit that matters.'

Six months later

Will loved spring. Sitting here now, in the garden of the Pendle Heritage Centre, with the sun on his face and scent of the flowers filling his nostrils, felt good.

'Who's that with her?' Chattox said as he saw Dianne Berry enter the tea room followed by a familiar-looking elderly gentlemen. Dianne was talking to him, so the man must be real, Will thought.

'Hello, Will, it's been a while.' The man held out his hand.

'Professor Owen?' Will said, shaking his hand.

'Please call me Richard. I'm retired now.'

'I'll go and order some drinks,' Berry said.

'How have you been, Will?' Owen asked. 'I heard you had quite a rough time last year.'

'I'm still a bit bonkers,' Will said. 'But nowhere near as bad as I was when you last saw me.'

'Well, that sounds positive. I've got something for you,' the professor said. He fished around in the same battered old briefcase that Perkins remembered him having when he'd been his student. 'I kept hold of your dissertation. I guess I always hoped you might at some point want to take another look at it – change the conclusion and maybe resubmit it. That was all that stood in the way of you being awarded your degree.'

Will took the offered document and looked down at it. 'Thanks. I think maybe that ship has sailed.'

'I don't know, Will,' Berry said, sitting down next to him. 'It wouldn't hurt to take another look.'

'I thought you wanted me to stop thinking about witches and concentrate on what is real?'

'I did. I do. But the history part of it is real. Perhaps you could look again and focus on the history.'

'I could help you do that,' Owen said. 'I'm sure if you redid your dissertation I could approach the university and persuade them to look at awarding you your degree.'

'You really think that might be possible?' Perkins asked.

'I can't make any promises, but I think so.'

'And you wouldn't be against that?' Will asked, turning to Berry. 'You don't think it would mess with my head too much?'

'With you, Will, I'm starting to think if you can't beat them join them. So long as it's just the three of us I'm getting tea for, and not all the other voices you've got spinning round in your head.'

'She's got no manners, her,' Old Demdike said.

If You Enjoyed Witch Hunt...

Please consider leaving a rating or review on Amazon or Goodreads. It really helps other readers to discover the books and get to know Doyle and the team.
If you would like to be kept up to date first on further books in the series as well as exclusive bonus content, then sign up to the DCI Doyle Reader's Club using the link below:
https://www.bdspargo.com/readers-club

Thank you!

Author's Note

On 18-19 August 1612, ten people stood trial at Lancaster Assizes charged with offences related to witchcraft and using demonic magic to murder and cause harm to others and their livelihoods. Nine of those tried – Alizon Device, Elizabeth Device, James Device, Anne Whittle (known as Chattox), Anne Redferne, Alice Nutter, Katherine Hewitt, John Bulcock and Jane Bulcock were found guilty and hanged at Gallow Hill in Lancaster on 20 August 1612. Elizabeth Sowthernes, known as Old Demdike – mother of Elizabeth Device and grandmother of Alizon and James Device – died at Lancaster Castle while awaiting trial. Alice Grey was the only one of the group found not guilty. Jennet Preston was tried separately at the York Assizes on 27 July 1612 and found guilty and sentenced to death by hanging. She was executed on 29 July in Knavemire.

Pendle Hill and the towns and villages that surround it, is a lovely part of the world and I would encourage anybody who hasn't been before to visit (I'd also advise taking a raincoat). The legend of the Pendle witches is pretty prominent throughout the area and much of what is seen is of the mythical fantasy of witches, rather than the human tragedy that unfolded there. This doesn't bother me like it did Doyle and Perkins in the story, as it helps bring tourists and money into the region. It also helps to keep the Pendle witches names alive over 400 years later. For anyone visiting that wants to know the real story, there is plenty to find if you look for it.

Despite petitions requesting posthumous pardons for those wrongly executed for witchcraft between 1542 and 1735 when The Witchcraft Act was repealed, successive United Kingdom governments have failed to act. It may seem inconsequential now after many hundreds of years, but those innocent people were executed by the state and many of them would have gone to the gallows believing that they were witches facing an eternity in hell. Is it such an imposition now to finally give them justice?

Acknowledgements

I am very grateful to a great many people without whom this book would not have been published. In particular I would like to thank the following people who contributed their skills, knowledge and expertise alongside their unwavering encouragement. Rebecca Spargo, Hannah Chivers, Val Spargo, Christine Barnes, Jane Hammett and Ken Dawson. I would also like to thank my two children for keeping me grounded in reality throughout the whole process and in life in general.

I would also like to thank everyone who read Cut Short – the first book in the series, and sent me nice messages, left reviews or posted on blogs and social media about the book. I can't tell you how much your kind words warmed my heart and gave me the enthusiasm to keep on writing. In particular I would like to thank Liz Mistry, Maureen Webb, Caroline Maston and the admins at the UK Crime Book Club, Sean Campbell and the admins at Crime Fiction Addict and Rachel from Rachel's Random Resources. One of the very happy consequences of starting out as a crime author, is that I have met a lot of lovely people and discovered some incredibly talented authors. Thank you all!

About the Author

Fast approaching fifty; without enough money for a sports car, BD Spargo decided to express his mid-life crises by turning to crime ...

Thankfully for pretty much everyone this meant writing crime fiction rather than anything more nefarious. Originally from London, he spent his early career working in television and theatre including on the *Ruth Rendall Mysteries* broadcast on ITV.

A life changing accident necessitated retraining and a change of direction going on to work in mental health services. This culminated in ten years managing a groundbreaking forensic psychiatric service. He now lives in Lancashire with his family and is getting acclimatised to the rain.

Cut Short - Book 1

Detectives can't bury their mistakes, murderers can.

DCI Liam Doyle is haunted by the demons from his past and the challenges of the present: a broken marriage, a tarnished reputation, and a troubled young son. He's newly moved out of south London – and out of his comfort zone. When a murdered woman is found at a Lancashire beauty spot in his new patch, Doyle is tasked with finding her killer, along with his new detective sergeant, Anna Morgan. As the investigation progresses, it becomes clear that things are not as they seem. A clever killer has created a complex web of deceit and is always one step ahead of Doyle ... and the bodies are mounting up. When the stakes get higher, Doyle's need to find the killer becomes personal and the detective is plunged into a desperate race against time. Played out across the Lancashire landscape, Cut Short is a gripping crime thriller layered with plot twists and sprinkled with humour. This fast-paced novel, the first in a series featuring DCI Liam Doyle, will have readers on the edge of their seats.

Printed in Dunstable, United Kingdom